*Vineyards
and Wineries
of America*

Vineyards and Wineries of America

A TRAVELER'S GUIDE

Patrick W. Fegan

THE STEPHEN GREENE PRESS
BRATTLEBORO, VERMONT
LEXINGTON, MASSACHUSETTS

*To Steven and Monsieur Guy,
supporters in times
of need.*

This book is manufactured in the United States of America. It
is designed by Jeanne Ray Juster and published by The Stephen
Greene Press, Fessenden Road, Brattleboro, Vermont 05301.

Library of Congress Cataloging in Publication Data

Fegan, Patrick W., 1947-
  Vineyards and Wineries of America.

  Bibliography: p.
  1. Wine and winemaking – United States – Directories.
I. Title.
TP557.F43 1982   641.2′22′02573   82-15806
ISBN 0-8289-0489-8 (pbk.)

3572

Contents

Preface ix
Basic U.S. Statistics x
Introduction 1
General Tips on Touring the Wine Country 8
American Grapes 11
American Grapes: A Listing 20

California 47
The Northern Coastal Counties 61
Humboldt County 65
Solano County 66
Marin County 66
Napa County 68
Sonoma County 83
Mendocino and Lake Counties 96

The Central Coastal Counties 105
Alameda County 110
Contra Costa County 111
San Mateo County 112
Santa Clara and Santa Cruz Counties 113
Monterey and San Benito Counties 120
San Luis Obispo and Santa Barbara Counties 125

The Sacramento Valley and Sierra Foothills Counties 131
Amador County 136
Calaveras County 137
El Dorado County 138
Nevada County 138

Placer County 139
Sacramento County 139
Shasta County 139
Yolo County 139
Yuba County 140

Southern California Counties 142
Los Angeles County 143
Orange County 147
Riverside County 148
San Bernardino County 149
San Diego County 150
Ventura County 151

Central Valley Counties 153
Fresno County 159
Kern County 160
Madera County 161
Merced County 162
San Joaquin County 162
Stanislaus County 164
Tulare County 165
Tuolumne County 165
Leading California Grape Varieties 168

Introduction to the Other Wine States of the Country . 171

Northeastern/Midwestern Vineyard 175
Connecticut 182
Massachusetts 182
New Hampshire 182
New Jersey 183
Rhode Island 183
Illinois 184
Indiana 184
Iowa 185
Minnesota 186
Wisconsin 186

Michigan 189
Missouri 195
New York 201
Ohio .,.. 217
Pennsylvania 227

The Southeastern Vineyard 235
Alabama 241
Arkansas 241
Delaware 242
Florida 242
Georgia 242
Kentucky 243
Maryland 243
Mississippi 244
North Carolina 244
South Carolina 244
Tennessee 245
West Virginia 245
Virginia 247

The Southwestern Vineyard 255
Arizona 261
Colorado 261
Hawaii 261
New Mexico 261
Oklahoma 262
Texas 262
Utah 263

The Northwestern Vineyard 265
Idaho 269
Oregon 269
Washington 273

The Wine-Lover's Vocabulary 277

List of Place-Names Including Viticultural Areas 291

Opinions of a Single Wine-Lover 298

Bibliography 307

Acknowledgments 310

Maps

United States xii
California Grapeland 48
Northern Coastal Counties 60
Northern Coastal Counties (detailed) 62
Napa County 70
Sonoma County 84
Mendocino County 98
Lake County 99
Central Coastal Counties 106
Central Coastal Counties (detailed) 108
Monterey and San Benito Counties 122
Sacramento Valley and Sierra Foothills Region 132
Sacramento Valley and Environs 134
Southern California 144
Southern California (detailed) 145
The Central Valley 154
The Central Valley Counties 156
Northeastern/Midwestern States 176
Michigan 190
Missouri 196
New York 202
The Finger Lakes 208
Ohio 218
Lake Erie/Chautauqua 222
Pennsylvania 228
The Southeastern United States 236
Virginia 248
The Southwestern United States 256
Pacific Northwest 266

Preface

WE HAVE 220,000,000 PEOPLE IN THIS COUNTRY AND ABOUT 800,000 acres of vines. Let's imagine that we put all that acreage in one flat, dry spot (mountain growers, bear with me), and let all of us convene to that one huge vineyard and space ourselves out evenly, like vines in a well-tended vineyard. I calculate that we would be not much more than twelve feet from one another in any direction.

And let's all have some wine, a bit for each of us, though not too much.

With a little stretching and reaching out, we could all clink glasses of wine and drink to one another. We would drink and talk and laugh and be "right neighborly" for a time. The wine, as is usually the case, would help us to shed our fears, our inhibitions; and we would let our minds soar with one another, and our ideas flow back and forth, and our friendliness grow; and we would talk and laugh and ... well, just imagine *that* scene!

Soaring, with a glass of good California pot-still brandy,

Patrick W. Fegan
Chicago, August, 1981

State	Acreage	Wineries (mid 1982)	Per capita consumption (gallons
Alabama (SE)	100	1	1.12
Alaska (NW)	trace	0	3.27
Arizona (SW)	4,160	2	2.55
Arkansas (SE)	4,100	8	0.74
California	704,938	553	4.50
Colorado (SW)	25	1	2.65
Connecticut (NE)	100	5	2.78
Delaware (SE)	50	1	2.01
Florida (SE)	500	3	2.47
Georgia (SE)	800	2	1.23
Hawaii (SW)	20	1	2.68
Idaho (NW)	500	3	1.92
Illinois (NE/MW)	95	4	2.17
Indiana (NE/MW)	485	8	1.10
Iowa (NE/MW)	60	13	0.83
Kansas (SW)	60	0	0.76
Kentucky (SE)	200	3	0.64
Louisiana (SE)	trace	0	1.62
Maine (NE)	trace	0	1.88
Maryland (SE)	300	8	2.18
Massachusetts (NE)	125	3	3.10
Michigan (NE/MW)	13,640	18	1.77
Minnesota (NE/MW)	345	2	1.67
Mississippi (SE)	100	4	0.63
Missouri (NE/MW)	1,236	24	1.32
Montana (NW)	trace	0	1.98
Nebraska (NW)	trace	0	1.24
Nevada (NW)	25	0	4.98
New Hampshire (NE)	150	1	3.68

Statistics

State	Acreage	Wineries (mid 1982)	Per capita consumption (gallons)
New Jersey (NE)	450	9	3.17
New Mexico (SW)	65	5	1.87
New York (NE)	41,979	73	2.92
North Carolina (SE)	2,500	5	1.28
North Dakota (NW)	trace	0	1.08
Ohio (NE/MW)	4,000	44	1.34
Oklahoma (SW)	25	2	0.95
Oregon (NW)	2,100	39	3.09
Pennsylvania (NE)	14,275	30	1.43
Rhode Island (NE)	100	5	3.33
South Carolina (SE)	1,700	4	1.16
South Dakota (NW)	trace	0	1.15
Tennessee (SE)	200	4	0.79
Texas (SW)	900	11	1.45
Utah (SW)	200	1	0.78
Vermont (NE)	trace	0	3.06
Virginia (SE)	600	24	1.66
Washington (NW)	27,693	27	3.32
West Virginia (SE)	100	2	0.84
Wisconsin (NE/MW)	100	9	1.94
Wyoming (NW)	trace	0	1.41
Washing, D.C. (SE)	-----	0	6.94
United States	829,101	962	2.21

The *California Crop and Livestock Reporting Service* estimates there will be a total of about 697,500 acres bearing as of 1985; with a non-bearing total added to this, California's total grape acreage could be 800,000 by 1985.

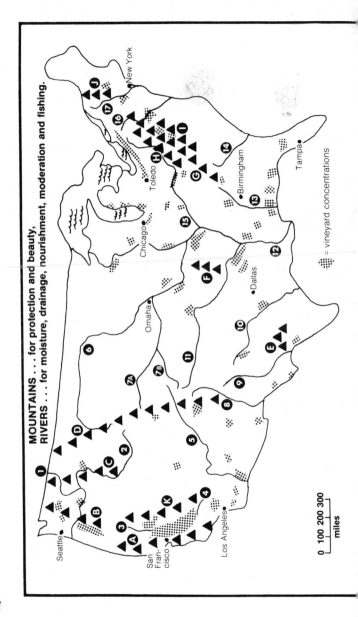

MOUNTAINS . . . for protection and beauty,
RIVERS . . . for moisture, drainage, nourishment, moderation and fishing.

Seattle

San Fran-cisco

Los Angeles

Omaha

Chicago

Toledo

New York

Dallas

Birmingham

Tampa

0 100 200 300
miles

⬟ = vineyard concentrations

River Key
1. Columbia
2. Snake
3. Sacramento
4. San Joaquin
5. Colorado
6. Missouri
7. Platte
8. (7A North, 7B South) Rio Grande
9. Pecos
10. Brazos
11. Arkansas
12. Mississippi
13. Tombigbee
14. Savannah
15. Ohio
16. Susquehanna
17. Hudson

Mountain Key
A. "Coast Ranges"
B. Cascades
C. Bitterroot
D. Rockies
E. Edwards Plateau
F. Ozarks
G. Appalachians
H. Allegheny
I. Blue Ridge
J. Green
K. Sierra Nevadas

Wine Production
425,000,000 gallons (90% from California)

Per Capita Consumption
2.11 gallons

Acreage of Vines
850,000 (85% in California)

Tons of Grape Produced
5,600,000 (60% crushed by wineries)

Bonded Wineries
900 plus (nearly 60% in California); at least 70% bonded since 1970.

Introduction

MY PURPOSE IN COMPILING THIS BOOK IS TO MAKE IT EASIER TO know about and to visit our vineyards and wineries. The book, therefore, tells, both generally and specifically, where the wineries are – via semi-detailed maps and complete name-and-address listings – and gives the reader a handle on the many and varied grape varieties planted in this country.

It is not a descriptive book, intending to provide historical overviews or cameos of winegrowers; nor is it a travelogue. I feel Leon D. Adams covered that ground in his excellent book *The Wines of America,* the third edition of which is due to be published soon. The more I read it, the more I am amazed at the physical and mental effort involved in compiling the book. It is a monument not only to American winegrowers, but to Adams himself.

Nor is this an opinion book, one which seeks to evaluate individual operations, personalities, or wines. These change so quickly that it would take yearly revisions to maintain accuracy. But let the reader beware. I do have some general opinions on the subject of wine and have included these in the back of the book where they will offer the least intrusion to those interested only in facts.

The nature of the book will be self-evident shortly. But an introductory paragraph or two on the specific chapters will be worthwhile.

ON VITICULTURAL AREAS:

This is a long term for an area or areas of vineyard land. A viticultural area, like *appellation d'origine, denominazione di origine, denominación de origen* in France, Italy, and Spain, respectively, indicates a vineyard or a group of vineyards that have something in common. The characteristics these vineyards have in common usually include climate, soil nature, hill protection, water moderation, and other particulars of a specific area. In the case of the European countries mentioned, viticultural areas also prohibit or allow only specific grape varieties for that area's wines. Europe has many such areas with names such as Bordeaux or Rheingau, Lugana or Rioja. The United States has several as well, though relatively few of them have had official sanction for more than a short time. Most of Europe's areas have long had offical boundaries.

Over the years, certain of these areas have developed greater (or lesser) reputations for yielding fine wine than others, and the winegrowers in these prized areas have sought to promote their areas. In addition, the winegrowers in these areas in European countries learned – through several centuries of experience – which grape varieties survived best and consistently yielded what the locals considered good to great wines. Hence, in Burgundy, Pinot noir and Chardonnay thrive to the exclusion of Cabernet-Sauvignon and Sémillon, while exactly the reverse is true in Bordeaux. With this experience in mind, the French and others developed laws defining not only the limits of their viticultural areas, but also stating which grape varieties could and could not be planted to make the "official" wines of the region. This type of legislation has worked quite successfully in Europe. However, advances in viticulture, made as winegrowers experiment further with traditional and hybrid varieties, may gradually bring changes in these laws.

While the Europeans have developed these areas and their attendant reputations for hundreds of years, we Americans are just getting our palates wet. We have been at this game only since Prohibition ended, about fifty years ago. Still, like the headstrong, do-it-quickly band of iconoclasts that we are, Americans are fast making headway with this business.

Just a few years ago, the Bureau of Alcohol, Tobacco and Firearms (BATF) held hearings which involved the wine industry, consumers, and other interested parties. As a result of the hearings, the BATF issued a notice that American wine-growers would have to submit data concerning their land if they wanted to use the name of the land on their wine labels. The BATF notice stated that information such as climatic reports, soil findings, geologic formation studies, and historic data would have to be submitted as proof that a particular winegrowing region was, in fact, distinct and worthy of being considered a viticultural area. For example, the winegrowers of the Napa Valley, in mid-northern California, had to prove that, because of natural and historic factors, their grapes, and hence, their wines, were different from those of the Sonoma Valley to the west. In addition, Napa Valley winegrowers had to draw boundaries to show where the Napa Valley began and ended. When the BATF approved these boundaries, in 1981, the Napa Valley became California's first official viticultural area (Augusta, Missouri, winegrowers, although only a handful in number, had been the first Americans to petition successfully for their viticultural area).

While Napa County was presenting its case to the BATF, about three dozen other areas – ranging from the multi-county Finger Lakes area of New York to the tiny Rocky Knob area of Virginia – requested viticultural area status. I have integrated most of these areas, whether or not they have as yet been approved by the BATF or its successors*, into the appropriate maps. So, the next time you pick up a bottle of "Rocky Knob Seyval Blanc," you will know where it comes from.

In terms of knowing which grape varieties best acclimate themselves to which viticultural areas, and which produce the most desired wines, we Americans are still relative toddlers compared to the Europeans. But we are learning quickly. For instance, we have learned with some certainty that the Cabernet-Sauvignon grape does well in the Rutherford area of the Napa Valley (and elsewhere) and not so well in the Chiles Valley area. And we are quickly beginning to realize that White Rieslings

---

* At this writing, questions involving the federal budget make it uncertain whether the BATF will continue to exist. No provisions have as yet been made for delegating the bureau's wine-related authority to another governmental office.

do better in the cooler climes of the Northwest than in most sections of California. But whether or not our government and our winegrowers will work together to make laws prohibiting the planting of some varieties and not others within a given viticultural area – *à la* many European countries – is another question. We may also have to consider limiting the yields of grapes within such a prized area, as is done in most areas in Europe, if only to protect producers of consistently fine wines in the area from the bad reputation which an overproducer can give to the entire area.

ON THE WINERY LISTINGS:

No flourishes here, only names, addresses, telephone numbers, and visiting/tasting information. This is an alphabetical list of all of the American wineries whose names were bonded as of mid 1982. For convenience, and to provide a better guide for the traveling wine-lover, the wineries are listed county-by-county or state-by-state. In a case where a county or a state is replete with wineries, I have added geographical pointers to make the planning of wine trips a bit easier. For instance, for New York state, I have indicated whether the given winery is in or near the Finger Lakes (FL), Chautauqua-Erie-Niagara (CH/ER), or general Eastern (E) region.

For the statisticians-cum-wine-lovers, I have included an indication of the general size of as many wineries (per their storage capacities) as possible. The number(s) listed at the bottom right of most listings is coded to the schedule below. In those few cases where there are two numbers, such as 4/3, it indicates that there is more than one winery (not always in the same county) owned and used by the company named. The first figure gives the size of the single winery listed; the second number indicates the combined size of all that company's outlets.

Lastly, while I have indicated whether or not appointments are necessary, I think it is a good idea to call ahead to make sure that someone can accommodate you. At a one-man operation, the winemaker may be out shagging deer from the Chardonnay; at a large place, especially during the harvest season, pressures and confusions may lead to problems, however rare.

Code	Gallonage	Description
10	under 25,000	Hobbyist-cum-toe-in-the-water
9	25,001-50,000	Smaller but serious
8	50,001-100,000	Small but serious
7	100,001-500,000	Little big gang
6	500,001-1,000,000	Big little gang
5	1,000,001-5,000,000	Young (and big) bucks in waiting
4	5,000,001-25,000,000	Central Valley Dukes
3	25,000,001-50,000,000	Barons of Burgundy
2	50,000,001-150,000,000	Vermillionaires
1	150,000,000 plus	Gallo

Code	Meaning
T	Tastings and/or tours during regular hours.
T*	Tastings and/or tours with irregular schedules or with stipulations about large groups.
T/A	Tastings and/or tours by appointment only.
P	Picnic facilities available.
NT	No tours or tastings

ON THE MAPS:

These are not meant to be detailed cartographical depictions of winery locations. Rather they are generalized guides for the label-curious or the traveler. While normal maps contain all or most of the towns and cities, highway systems and roads, rivers and streams, within a given state or area, these maps indicate only those locations and features of prime importance to the wine-lover.

I have included few mountain ranges in the maps. By their omission, however, I do not mean to overlook their importance in grape growing (or any form of agriculture). For without a water source, natural or in the form of irrigation, winemaking would be impossible. And without mountains, hills, and tree lines—to act as windbreaks, or to trap warmth or cold, or to promote good drainage or solar exposure – interesting wines would be rare. Keep that in mind as you trace the wine areas on these maps.

For further uses of the maps, see "General Tips on Touring the Wine Country" on page 8.

ON THE GRAPE LIST:

I do not mean to sound too basic or obvious, but without grapes you cannot make grape wine (well, you can, but if you are a licensed winemaker you will eventually be caught and stopped). I have noticed a great deal of confusion in the way we describe grape varieties and species, mixing names without regard for accuracy. In fact, even experts would be hard-pressed to name and describe more than twenty varieties, especially those used predominantly outside of California.

To that end, I have compiled a list of several hundred grape varieties that flourish, to a greater or lesser degree, in these United States. While many of them are usually considered table or juice grapes, all have been crushed for winemaking purposes at one time or another. I have listed, where possible, their species and, in cases of natural or artificial hybrids, their parentage. A brief introduction should help to clarify a subject that confused me for years.

ON THE VOCABULARY:

How we talk about wines is a never-ending source of amusement to many, including me. The lingo that is used by American experts – words learned primarily by reading and copying the British wine tomes – are relatively unsuited to helping people understand what it is wine folk are talking about. What, for instance, does "it has breed" mean? Or why is one wine "restrained" and another "austere?" Why start an argument with your friend because he or she objects to your use of the word "feminine" (or "masculine") to describe a wine?

"The Wine-Lover's Vocabulary" is intended to translate many of these words – and a few others – into a more understandable language. Words are good tools for someone who wants to bring people and ideas together; they can also be used to pull or keep people apart. Nothing more reinforces the image of the wine expert as a "snob" or an "elitist boob" than his continued use of ambiguous and relatively incomprehensible words and phrases to describe wines or wine flavors. This is one reason that I think. . . oops. . . sorry. I'll save the soapbox for the end of the book.

General Tips on Touring the Wine Country

IF YOU ARE THE TYPE OF WINE TOURIST WHO IS SIMPLY INTERested in having a fun-filled weekend in wine country—with no special desires to compare wines, wine styles, philosophies, etc.—skip this section and have a ball.

If you want to pursue your wine tour in a manner calculated to help you learn a lot in the shortest possible time, however, some tips follow. I have compiled these after long and arduous business journeys into vine land (and a few rosé-filled picnics with Bacchus-like wine folk).

1. Plan your moves; know what you want to experience and schedule your time accordingly. If you are visiting only the larger wineries that have guided tours all day and for which appointments are not necessary, your schedule can be flexible. However, if you need to make an appointment, make and keep it, or call and cancel within a reasonable time beforehand. Wine folk are usually generous and accommodating, but they are at the wineries to make wine and not to cater to tourists and other visitors. Some lay out a spread of foods and wines for an expected guest and then do a slow burn when the visitor does not show. I had to learn "wine country etiquette" (which is really simple courtesy but sometimes that is forgotten given the almost fantasyland atmosphere in these areas) the hard way: more than one fellow raked my ears for not showing up at a spot I had made an appointment to see.

2. Do not visit more than four wineries in one day, and put a meal in there between them if possible. Unless you have a photographic memory, and a very resilient palate, winery visits are a senseless exercise beyond that fourth stop. Visits to too many wineries can also lead to good old "precarious pathway movement due to an altered state of consciousness" (you will become so high that you cannot drive well).

3. Vary your visits not only on a geographical basis but on the basis of size or style as well. Visit one very large winery to experience how most wines are actually made, and then visit a smaller winery. You may be surprised by the differences in winemaking techniques. Or check out a small firm that has not changed very much (i.e., a "traditional" firm) versus a stainless steel factory of the same size. Or perhaps, based upon your personal tasting experiences, visit two wineries that make the same type of wine in different ways. For example, arrange to visit a winery noted for its very oaky interpretations of Chardonnay before or after having visited an establishment noted for its aversion to wood-aged Chardonnays.

   What? You do not like some tours or tour agents because they smell of too much self-promotion? Well, buy a bottle or two from several wineries using the above or similar rationales to make your choices. Then, pull into a camping area or a secluded spot in the woods nearby and, as long as it is legal, perform your own in-depth sensory analysis. If you have brought along a friend and some food, so much the better. And a little nap with the trees, sun, and light wind caressing you is a perfect way to start anew.

4. Use the maps and try to plan your winery visits to avoid wasting time and fuel and to prevent driving fatigue. If you have three days to do the Napa Valley, for instance, it would not make much sense to visit wineries in Calistoga and Yountville on the same day. Instead, visit three or four wineries in the southern section of the area on one day, do the same around St. Helena the next day, and concen-

trate on Schramsberg, Chateau Montelena and other northern valley spots the third day.

5. If you are offered a barrel-sample, take it. Then evaluate
   it and spit it out. Don't worry about normal, at-home etiquette. The winemakers expect spitting (even when the
   wine is good!), so do not be embarrassed. Besides, if you
   swallow much of this brand-new wine, your body will
   become a source of embarrassment later on. And do not
   worry that someone will be taking note of the accuracy of
   your shot, just make sure you don't hit anyone and that
   you don't dribble; wine stains on a nice, bright shirt are
   a pain to clean.

6. If you drink, don't drive, and *vice versa*. This holds true even
   for those sophisticated wine-lovers among us who feel that
   wine will not affect us. Baloney. Wine is wine, it contains
   alcohol, and sooner or later, the alcohol in a refined
   Cabernet-Sauvignon will have the same effect as the alcohol
   in wine that comes in jugs (or in brown bags). Obviously,
   it's difficult to visit most wineries without a car and to avoid
   driving in a slightly "altered" state once the visits are over.
   Just keep in mind that alcohol-related highway collisions
   account for many unnecessary deaths. Take a brisk walk
   after you have sampled your wines. Or stop drinking an
   hour or so before you move on to the next stop. Have fun,
   but use your head.

7. Keep a diary and, when possible, take photos of each
   winery or vineyard you visit. Believe me, when you return
   home, most of your wonderful recollections will have
   merged into one big vinous blur. No paper? If you can, soak
   the labels off the bottles and record your observations on
   the back: "12/5/81, picnic lunch and tasting and Elmo's
   winery in Pawtucket, the Late Harvest Norton Special
   Reserve' was exceptional with burnt chicken wings, James
   proposed to me but later said that I should not take wine-
   affected promises seriously." Or that sort of thing.

American Grapes

HEALTHY, RIPE, ACCESSIBLE GRAPES ARE ESSENTIAL TO THE WINE-maker, American or otherwise. While most grapes will make wines of some sort or other, we have learned that it is the juice of only a few hundred varieties, of the many thousands available, that make commercially acceptable wines. Of those few hundred, perhaps two dozen have etched their names into our minds by yielding truly praiseworthy beverages. Cabernet, Chardonnay, Nebbiolo, Sangiovese, Riesling, Pinot noir, Syrah, and Sauvignon blanc are a few of the varieties that have pleased wine-lovers for decades, even centuries. With more time to prove themselves, hybrids such as Seyval blanc, Baco noir, Maréchal Foch, Cayuga, Aurore, and others will follow suit.

Hybrids? The name connotes both impurity and a connivance, by scientists, with nature – something best left in the lab. Many hybrids, including those mentioned above, were developed by breeders for specific reasons and to be grown in particular geo-climatological regions. Others, such as many American varieties, came about as the result of natural, or chance, crossings in the vineyards of early America and the rest of the world. Strictly speaking, all of the varieties we know today are hybrids of one sort or another. Some are easily classified; others keep ampelographers, or scientists of the vine, up long nights trying to identify clues in a leaf, a shoot, or a bunch structure.

With the help of ampelographers, we can approach the many hundreds of varieties of grapes in this country with some sense of order.

All grapes belong to the group, or *genus*, called *vitis*. Within this *genus* there are many species. The best-known – to Europeans and Californians at least – is that species called *vitis vinifera*. **11**

All of the renowned vineyards of Europe are planted with varieties of grapes within this species. When Europeans colonized the Americas, they brought cuttings of *vinifera* with them. The Mission grape, which the Spanish missionaries brought from their country, was the most widely diffused *vinifera* variety, but other varieties, such as Cabernet, Chardonnay, and Pinot noir, dominate today. The missionaries and colonists planted *vinifera* from coast to coast. Those established in the hospitable climate of California flourished; others, planted in the cooler areas of the East where vines were more disease-ridden, did not. But *vinifera* in the East left its mark, as we will see.

The wine-loving colonists who settled in the East found many vines that were native to America growing wild all around. These are now called "native American species" and include *labrusca(na), riparia* (a.k.a. *vulpina), aestivalis,* and others. When *vinifera* failed to survive, wines made from these native species' varieties were the only alternatives. To most Europeans used to the flavor of *vinifera* wines, however, the flavor of the American species was a shock. But, they made do.

While the *vinifera* grapes were unsuccessful on their own, they did have the opportunity to affect the eastern vineyards in a very important way. Some *vinifera* varieties pollinated, or naturally crossed with, various of the native varieties to create natural hybrids. Most, if not all of the prominent varieties of grapes grown in the east and midwest today are the result of these natural crossings of *vinifera* varieties with one or more native American varieties. Examples are Concord, Catawba, Delaware, Dutchess, and Niagara.

The only native American species of any importance whose varieties persist in our vineyards are those within the species *vitis rotundifolia,* part of a sub-group of *vitis* generically referred to as the Muscadines. The most famous member of the group is the Scuppernong. It and its relatives flourish mainly in our southeast. But even Muscadines are being scientifically crossed to accommodate local conditions.

So, to this point, we have mentioned three large categories of vines found in our vineyards: *vinifera,* primarily in California; American varieties resulting from chance crosses with *vinifera* which were brought here by the colonizers; and native, "wild" species including Muscadines. But there is a fourth group, one which many see as eventually rivaling the *vinifera* in fame – the French-American hybrids.

These hybrids have been, and continue to be, the result of methodical, scientific breeding programs by scientists on both sides of the Atlantic. The reasons behind these attempts are many, but a major one is the reaction of the early colonists to the taste of the American varieties, such as Concord. Many colonists just didn't like what we would call their "Welch's Grape Juice" flavor. The colonists figured that if they could not drink pure *vinifera* wine, they would compromise, crossing varieties of *vinifera* with the American varieties. Their hope was to obtain a wine with a flavor close to that of wines made in Europe and with an American hardiness.

Their success in these endeavors continues to the present. Today we have many promising so-called French (*vinifera*)-American varieties, some whose often fanciful names (Captivator, Aurore, Cascade) proudly adorn American wine labels. Many more will undoubtedly be developed as the experimental stations in Europe and America – especially that in Geneva, New York – continue their research and breeding programs.

But grape breeding is not a monopoly of the Easterners, nor does it deal solely with crossing American varieties and their descendants with *viniferas*.

Dr. Harold Olmo, of the University of California at Davis, has worked for decades crossing *viniferas* with other *viniferas*. Such crosses of varieties within the same species are called *intra*specific crosses. Crosses of varieties of different species, such as *vinifera* with *labrusca* or *labrusca* with *riparia*, are referred to as *inter*specific crosses. Olmo concentrated on the former.

His goal was simple: combine the warm-weather sturdiness and high-bearing characteristics of more common varieties, such as Carignane, Grenache, and others, with the more interesting and complex qualities of "noble" varieties such as Cabernet-Sauvignon, Merlot, and Gamay. One widely planted variety, Ruby Cabernet, is the result of such a cross, a hybrid of Cabernet-Sauvignon and Carignane. Work of this type has resulted in a measurable upgrading of the quality of some of our basic jug wines (combined with huge increases in winemaking technology).

In another area of experimentation, many breeders, again primarily in the East and Midwest, are performing crosses with second, third, and fourth generation varieties. These are crosses of *vinifera* and an American variety *or* crosses of two American varieties *or* crosses of varieties that are themselves French-American hybrids. In the Southeast, growers and breeders of Muscadine grapes are performing crosses on Scuppernong and its relatives to arrive at improved varieties, varieties that will grow better and/or produce more interesting table or wine grapes.

Such inter- and intraspecific hybridization is continuing at a fast clip in all parts of the world, including France and Germany, countries where most interspecific hybrids are banned from commercial vineyard use. Indeed, the Germans are in the middle of a dilemma, according to Philip Wagner, long-time Eastern grower and a man who has studied the French-American hybrid scene for decades. Their government prohibits the use of interspecific hybrids, but the viticulturists who develop and work with such crosses maintain that such varieties are the future of Germany. The breeders in France are in the same predicament, and it will be interesting to see what develops in those two countries in the next ten years or so.

Appellation d'origine and the German wine laws might have to be changed to accommodate the realities of the latter years of the 20th century. Stay tuned.

GRAPES FOR WINE, FOR RAISINS, AND FOR FRESH EATING

This may sound confusing – it did to me when I first confronted it – but grapes are classified not only by species or variety but also by their ultimate use on the market. They can be used for wine (to make beverage wines or for use in distilled wine or brandy), for drying to make raisins, or as fresh grapes for eating, canning, or juice purposes.

In California, of the approximately 700,000 acres of grapes – the great majority being *vinifera* – about 50 percent are considered wine grapes; that is, they are grown and harvested for the express purpose of producing juice for some kind of wine, whether table (less than 14 percent alcohol), dessert/fortified (more than 14 percent), sparkling, or as wine for a brandy base. Zinfandel is one of many wine grape varieties, Pinot noir, Chardonnay, and White Riesling are others.

About 40 percent of the total vineyard area in California is planted to raisin grapes, predominately *vinifera*, of which Thompson seedless is the most widespread (with 260,000 acres, it is the most heavily planted grape in the country). Raisin varieties are usually picked early in the harvest season – July or August – and left out to dry, shrivel, and become raisins. California has a huge worldwide market for its raisin varieties.

The remaining 10 percent or so – about 73,000 acres – is planted to table grapes for eating, canning, or juicing purposes. Emperor and Flame Tokay are the leading varieties.

Most of the raisin and table varieties – 97 percent – are planted in what is called the Central Valley. And until rather recently, a healthy percentage – in 1965, it was 72 percent – of California wine was produced from these raisin and table varieties. Most of this wine was in the form of inexpensive jug wines. With the vast increase in wine grape acreage since the beginning of the 1970s, the amount of wine made from raisin and table grapes has shrunk to between 15 percent and 20 percent of the total. Those grapes which serve more than one purpose are referred to as "two-way" or "three-way" varieties, Thompson seedless being the classic.

Although few states outside California grow varieties for raisin purposes, many grow grapes – usually American and French-American varieties – for juice, canning, or eating. One example is the 20,000 acres of Concords in the state of Washington, at least 80 percent of which is used for purposes other than winemaking. Also, many of the approximately 43,000 acres in New York state – again, mostly Concords – are devoted to other-than-wine use.

THE LOUSE THAT WAS LOOSED

One final viticultural subject: the devastating louse, or *phylloxera vastatrix*, and its role in American – indeed, worldwide – viticulture.

There are many types of grapes pests, some visible, others invisible. Most can be "taken care of" with a little bug spray or some sulfur compound. Others just do not give up. *Phylloxera* is an example of the latter. This louse, actually one form of several of the insect, the rest being harmless, gnaws at the roots of a vine causing it to lose vigor and, ultimately, to die.

Some plants are partially or totally invulnerable to the louse and it does not cause them great problems. Most of the native American species and many of the naturally-crossed varieties have this invulnerability. *Vinifera* and many French-American hybrids do not.

For very many years, *phylloxera* resided primarily in North America. With transatlantic commerce and colonization, however, some of the cuttings of American vines were exported to Europe. Here is where science intervened for the worse.

According to George Ordish, in his book, *The Great Wine Blight, phylloxera* brought from America to Europe in sailing vessels died during the long trip. With the advent of the faster steamship, however, the trip to Europe became a pleasure cruise for the lice. And what a welcoming meal awaited them!

During the latter half of the 19th century, plant researchers began to notice the lice on their *vinifera* vines in England. From there, the lice spread east and southward, slowly infecting the vineyards of France, Italy, Spain, and the rest of Europe. It was not long before the European vineyards suffered declines in yields and in size as their vines died by the millions. Many remedies were tried – burning, spraying, even flooding – but none succeeded entirely. Many pragmatic Europeans decided they had better replant with invulnerable American varieties, vines whose grapes gave strong and un-*vinifera*-like flavors. A million acres of these so-called direct producers are still planted in France, although none are legally allowed for use in any of France's highly regarded *appellation d'origine* wines.

Other growers eventually hit upon the idea of actually grafting *viniferas* with American species rather than crossing the two sexually. They took the fruit-bearing upper part of the *vinifera* vine and grafted it onto the lower part, or rootstock, of an invulnerable American variety. *Voila!* The wine was *vinifera* in flavor* and the vine was protected from the ravages of *phylloxera*. Today almost every *vinifera* (and many non-*vinifera*) vineplant in the world is grafted onto either the rootstock of an American variety, or a rootstock with a good dose of the American varieties' invulnerability to *phylloxera*. Very few patches of ungrafted plants – or, to the French "vieilles vignes" (old vines) – exist, although many growers in Monterey County, California, and elsewhere grow them. It will be interesting to see what these brave growers do when *phylloxera* moves into the neighborhood.

I have listed as many grape varieties as I thought would make sense from either a commercial or educational viewpoint. I have included many table and raisin varieties as well for two reasons: 1) many wines on both coasts and in between are made from non-wine grapes; and 2) grapes are grapes, pure and simple, and this is a winery *and* vineyard guide (I wanted to attract the teetotaling grape muncher audience, if the truth be known). I have included, wherever possible, the parentage of specific varieties created through a cross of one sort or other, the ultimate use of the variety, (wine, fresh, or raisin) and in a few cases, the acreage of the variety planted in the United States. In the cases of the non-California varieties – largely French-American crosses – the acreage is relatively small when compared with acreage of California varieties. California accounts for 85 percent of our vineyard land, and fully three-fifths of all American grapes outside of California are Concords, Catawbas, Niagaras, Delawares, and other older American varieties make up another 12,000 to 15,000 acres, meaning that the remainder – 25,000 to 30,000 acres – is divided between many dozens of varieties in quantities of a few hundred acres each.

---

* Many old-timers argue that present-day, grafted *vinifera* varieties make wines less interesting than their pre-*phylloxera* kin. It's academic really. And how many customers return their wine to the retailer with the complaint that "it tastes grafted?"

Flow-chart for American Grape Varieties

	"European"	Euvitis	"American"	*Muscadiniae*
GENUS		VITIS		
SUB-GENERA		*Euvitis*		*Muscadiniae*
EXAMPLE SPECIES	*v. vinifera*		v. labrusca(na) v. Berlandieri v. aestivalis v. riparia (vulpina)* v. Bourguiniana v. candicans, etc.	v. rotundifolia
EXAMPLE VARIETIES	Chardonnay Pinot noir Cabernet-Sauvignon Carignane White Riesling Sauvignon blanc		few pure varieties: haphazard crosses of vinifera with one or more of the above resulted in the following varieties: Concord, Delaware, Niagara, Catawba, Isabella, etc. OR intentional crosses like Noah	Scuppernong
Intraspecific cross—*vinifera* hybrid	Ruby Cabernet			
Interspecific cross—French (*vinifera*-) American hybrid	Folle blanche Baco blanc			

Cabernet-Sauvignon + Carignane → Ruby Cabernet

Folle blanche + Noah → Baco blanc

*riparia and vulpina are the same species

Some crosses/hybrids were named after their breeders and/or popularizers, including the following:

Maurice Baco (Baco noir), Georges Couderc (Couderc), Eugene Kuhlman (K 188-2 "Maréchal Foch"), Pierre Landot (Landot noir), Thomas Volnay Munson (Munson red), Joseph Burdin (B 7705 "Florental"), Albert Seibel (S 5279 "Aurore"), George Remailly (Remailly seedless), Joannes Seyve (J-S 21,205 "Chambourcin"), Loren H. Stover (Stover), Elmer Swenson (ES 439 "Swenson red"), Andrew Jackson Caywood (Dutchess), J.L. Vidal (V 256 "Vidal blanc"), Victor Villard and Bertille Seyve, Jr., (who combined to develop S-V 5276, "Seyval blanc") and others including the Frenchman Francois Baco (father of Maurice), Ferdinand Gaillard, Bertille Seyve, Sr., Victor Ganzin and Antoine Gailbert as well as Americans such as Hermann Jaeger, D.C. Paschke and the legendary Dr. Harold Olmo, who, along with aide Al Koyama, gave us several *vinifera* hybrids, including Emerald Riesling, Ruby Cabernet, Carnelian, Centurion, and the latest, Symphony.

American Grapes: A Listing

Agawam a red American variety sparsely planted but offering Concord-like juice and wine.

Albemarle a recent Muscadine cross used for table purposes; red.

Alden a red table grape hybrid (Ontario X Gros Guillaume).

Aleatico a red *vinifera* wine grape of little importance in California with about 170 acres planted there; it is often used to produce white dessert wines.

Alicante Bouschet a red-juiced *vinifera* cross (Teinturier du Cher X Aramon) X Grenache which is used for color and rarely bottled as a varietal (Papagni, in Madera County, does so); 4,960 acres in California, one-third in Fresno County.

Alicante Ganzin see Grenache.

Aligoté a white *vinifera* wine grape of little importance in California and less importance outside the state. Preston Wine Cellars and Vinifera Wine Cellars bottle it as a varietal.

Almeria a.k.a. Ohanez (in Spain); a white *vinifera* table grape planted to about 700 acres in California, two-thirds in Tulare county.

Almission a little-planted red wine grape producing low quality wines; it is a *vinifera* cross of Mission X Carignane.

Alphonse Lavalée see Ribier.

Ambros a.k.a. S 10,713; a sparsely-planted white wine grape found in the Midwest and East.

America white *vinifera* planted to 112 acres in California, mostly in the Central Valley.

Aramon a.k.a. Ugni noir; a red *vinifera* wine grape of little importance with less than 100 acres planted in California, three-fourths in the Central Valley.

Aurelia a French-American white wine variety planted in north and south central Texas.

Aurore (Aurora) a.k.a. Seibel 5,279; a white French-American hybrid (S.788 X S.29) used for still and sparkling wine purposes; concentrated in the East, especially in New York.

Baco noir a.k.a. Baco No. 1; a French-American red hybrid wine grape (Folle blanche X *vitis riparia*).

Baco 22A a.k.a. Baco blanc; the only French-American hybrid allowed in France for an alcoholic beverage with an *appellation contrôlée* (Armagnac); it is a cross of the Folle blanche X Noah.

Barbera one of the most heavily planted red *vinifera* wine grapes in the state of California; of its 18,000 acres planted, fully 98 percent are in the Central Valley; makes fuller-bodied, "Italian style," dry red wines.

Barlinka a black *vinifera* table grape of low importance in the United States, but more important in South Africa.

Bath a red American cross (Fredonia X NY 10,805), introduced in 1952, used mainly for table purposes and less used for winemaking.

Beacon a native red variety used primarily for the table market; what little acreage there is can be found in the South in areas such as central Texas.

Beauty seedless another Olmo (1954) cross; this red *vinifera* table grape has some Muscat Reine des Vignes in its parentage.

Beclan a red *vinifera* wine variety; less than 100 acres exist in California, all in the Central Valley.

Bellandais a.k.a. Seibel 14,596; French-American hybrid used primarily for red wines; it is a cross of S.6,468 X S.5,455.

Berenda red a variety planted to less than 100 acres, all in Riverside County, California.

Beta a red, quite winter-hardy, American variety used often for dessert wines.

Black Corinth a.k.a. Zante Currant; a red *vinifera* raisin variety with about 1,600 acres planted in the Central Valley of California.

Black Hamburg a red *vinifera*, seeded table grape; sparsely planted.

Black Malvoisie a.k.a. Cinsau(l)t (in southern France), Blue Imperial (in Australia), and Hermitage (in South Africa); a red *vinifera* grape used largely for dessert wines in California; about 500 acres exist in California, most planted since 1972.

Black Monukka a seedless, red *vinifera* table grape with about 600 acres in California's Central Valley.

Black Morocco   a red *vinifera* table grape with about seventy acres planted in the Central Valley.

Black Prince   a seeded, red *vinifera* table grape; approximately eighty acres in California, two-thirds of which is in Southern California.

Blackrose   a.k.a. H3-47; red *vinifera*, seeded table grape of minor importance in California; it is a cross (released in 1951 of (Damas rose X Black Monukka) X Ribier.

Black Spanish   see Jacquez or Lenoir.

Blauburgunder   a.k.a. Pinot noir (in Austria and Germany); see Pinot noir.

Blauer Klevner   same as Blauburgunder.

Blauer Portugieser   see Early Burgundy.

Blauer Spätburgunder   see Pinot noir.

Blue Imperial   see Black Malvoisie.

Blue Lake   a dark purple table grape developed by Professor Loren Stover in 1950 and released in 1960; (Florida 43-47 X Caco); concentrated in the Southeast.

Brocton   a sparsely-planted, white hybrid introduced by the Geneva station in New York in 1919; a cross of Brighton X (Winchell X Diamond).

Brunello   a form of Sangiovese; see Sangiovese.

Buffalo   a black, seeded table grape originated in 1938, (Herbert X Watkins). It is sold on the roadsides of the Southeast.

Bunch   generic name for any non-Muscadine variety.

Burdin 4672   a French-American white wine grape (S.5-4554 X *vinifera*).

Burdin 7705   see Florental.

Burgaw   a red Muscadine variety used for both table and winemaking purposes.

Burger   a.k.a. Monbadon (in France); a white *vinifera* "filler" wine variety more often than not found in jug wines; there are about 1,800 acres in California, 60 percent in the Central Valley.

Cabernet franc   a.k.a Breton (Loire) and Gros Bouchet (Bordeaux); a red wine variety long-known in Bordeaux – and more recently in California – as a complementary grape for Cabernet-Sauvignon; there are about 200 acres in California, 99 percent in the Northern and Central Coastal counties. Vinified on its own, it is usually an expensive curiosity.

Cabernet-Sauvignon   a.k.a. Bouchet (in Bordeaux); a red *vinifera* wine variety planted to about 23,000 acres in the Golden State; a few hundred acres can be found outside of California, mainly in the Midwest and Northeast. Blended with Merlot, Cabernet franc, Malbec, and others in Bordeaux, it is used to make that area's famous clarets. The same blending practice is becoming common in the United States, though 100 percent varietals are still often found.

Caco   American red, seedless table grape said to have come from a cross of the Concord and Catawba grapes.

Calmeria   a.k.a. C:11:31.5; a white *vinifera* table grape developed in 1950 from the Almeria grape; there are about 4,000 acres in California, all in the Central Valley.

Calzin   a red *vinifera* wine variety very sparsely planted in California; a cross of Zinfandel X Refosco (Mondeuse).

Campbell's Early   sparsely-planted American (*Labrusca?*) red wine variety.

Canada Muscat   a 1961 cross of Muscat Hamburg X Hubbard.

Canadice   American red, seedless table variety; it is a cross of the Bath and Himrod vines. Demand usually exceeds supply of this popular, new (1977) variety.

Canner   a red *vinifera* wine variety with about sixty acres planted, all in the Central Valley.

Captivator   a highly regarded red, seeded table variety, grown on a very small basis in the East.

Cardinal   a.k.a G10-30; a red *vinifera* cross (Flame Tokay X Ribier) released in 1946; found mainly in the Imperial Valley of California and around Phoenix, Arizona.

Carignane   a widely planted (21,300 acres in California) red *vinifera* variety used mainly in jug wines, although some wineries bottle it as a varietal; the Midi region of France is home to many thousands of acres of the variety.

Carlos   a white (bronze) Muscadine wine variety grown mainly in the Southeast; it (and Magnolia and Dixie) are supplanting the traditional Scuppernong in the southeastern vineyards.

Carman   an American red wine and table variety found in eastern Texas and other southern and southeastern sections of the country.

Carmine   a red *vinifera* cross of (Carignane X Cabernet-Sauvignon) X Merlot released in 1975; not yet widely planted.

Carnelian   a.k.a. B12; released in 1973, this red *vinifera* wine variety is a cross of (Carignane X Cabernet-Sauvignon) X Grenache; planted to about 1,825 acres in California, 97 percent of which is in the Central Valley. Franciscan, and a few others, bottle it as a varietal.

Carolina Blackrose   a red French-American hybrid used for both table and wine purposes which flourishes in north central Texas.

Cascade   a.k.a. Seibel 13,053; a French-American hybrid red wine variety used as a varietal in the Piedmont section of the East. It is gaining in popularity.

Catawba   a natural hybrid of *labrusca* with either *vinifera* or *aestivalis* in its background; it is a light red wine grape used on its own or as the basis for much New York state sparkling wine; there are about 5,000 acres of the variety, concentrated in the Northeast.

Cayuga (white)   originally known as G(eneva) W(hite) 3; a recent (1972) cross now being used to make varietal wines by a growing number of Eastern wineries; it is interesting to note that Zinfandel is in the background of the variety; its parents are Seyval Blanc and Schuyler the latter of which is a cross of Ontario X ole Zin.

Centurion   a.k.a. B-5; this red wine *vinifera* variety is a new (1974) cross of (Carignane X Cabernet-Sauvignon) X Grenache; all but a few of its 1,000 acres lie inside the Central Valley.

Chambourcin   a.k.a. Joannes-Seyve 26,205; a red French-American hybrid used to make claret-style wines; plantings are found in the Midwest and East.

Champanel   a red American variety used for winemaking but also for table use; a few acres are planted in north central Texas.

Chancellor   a.k.a. Seibel 7,053; a red French-American hybrid of S.5,163 X S.800. It is gaining in popularity as it yields a good red wine.

Charbono   they say this red *vinifera* wine variety is widely planted in the Piedmont area of Italy; no ampelographer I spoke with was able to trace its origins to that country, however; not widely planted in California; less than 100 acres exist, most of it in the Napa Valley. Only two or three producers make a varietal wine out of it. It is usually a medium full-bodied dry red wine (Inglenook, Davis Bynum, Parducci).

Chardonnay   a.k.a. Weisser Klevner (?); the most famous white wine *vinifera* variety of California (20,000 acres, 94 percent of which is in the Central Coastal and North Coastal counties). It is also turning out delightful, lighter bodied dry whites from midwestern, eastern, and Pacific Northwest wineries. You may see wines labeled "Pinot Chardonnay" from California; although Chardonnay is not a member of the Pinot group of vines (noir, gris, blanc, etc.) the old, incorrect terminology persists.

Chasselas doré a.k.a. Fendant (Switzerland) and Gutedel (Germany).

Chaucé Gris see Grey Riesling.

Chelois a.k.a. Seibel 10,878; a red French-American hybrid wine variety found in the East and Midwest; its background is S.5,163 X S.5,593. Its plantings are few but growing. You say "shell oy" and I say "shell wah."

Chenin blanc a.k.a. Pineau de la Loire, Steen (South Africa), and White Pinot (California: archaic); after Thompson seedless and French Colombard, it is the most heavily planted variety in California (37,600 acres, 69 percent in the Central Valley); it is a white *vinifera* wine variety used primarily to make medium dry wines, although some bone-dry and/or oak aged versions are made. Informing vine of Vouvray, in the Loire region of France.

Chevrier a.k.a. Sémillon.

Chief a black Muscadine table variety which, on occasion, will be vinified.

Chowan a recent Muscadine cross.

Cinsau(l)t see Black Malvoisie.

Clairette blanche a white *vinifera* wine variety of low flavor.

Clinton a red wine variety of American descent; some contend it is a member of the *vitis vulpiana/riparia* species; planted in the Midwest and East.

Colobel a.k.a. Seibel 8,357; a *teinturier* French-American red wine hybrid (S.6,150 X S.5,455); most often used as a blending grape; see teinturier.

Colombard see French Colombard.

Concord a native American red wine and table variety that is the most widely cultivated grape outside California; although *labrusca* dominates its background, many consider it to be a natural cross of *labrusca* with another American species; there are nearly 80,000 acres of the variety planted in the United States, mainly in the East and Midwest, but with concentrations in Washington (about 20,000 acres); and even a tad (63 acres) in Butte County, California. A healthy dose of Washington state Concord is shipped south to California.

Cornichon   a red *vinifera* table grape of minor importance in California.

Cot   see Malbec.

Couderc noir   a.k.a. Couderc 7,120; a *rupestris* X *vinifera* hybrid red wine variety.

Cowart   a red Muscadine that flourishes in the Gulf and Southeast areas of the country; its main use is for juice and eating purposes, though it is rated "acceptable" as a wine grape.

Creek   another red Muscadine juice/table variety.

Cynthiana   see Norton.

Dearing   a white Muscadine variety used mainly for home juice and table purposes but also used in some wines of the South.

DeChaunac   a.k.a. Seibel 9,549; this red wine hybrid is the namesake of Adhemar de Chaunac, the winemaker for the Canadian firm called Brights Wines Ltd., of Ontario (it had originally been named "Cameo" until the Canadians objected to the nomenclature). It is one of the most popular varieties in the East, especially in the Finger Lakes district of New York.

Delaware   this pink variety is an American cross of *labrusca, aestivalis* with, according to Galet, *vinifera* in there somewhere; it is a table and wine grape, heavily used in the East and Midwest; there are just under 3,000 acres of the variety, mainly in the East and Midwest.

Delight   a little-seen *vinifera* cross released by Olmo in 1947; it is a white table variety.

Diamond   a white American species with *labrusca* and *vinifera* (Iona X Concord) in its background. It is widely used in the East as a varietal and as a base for bubbly.

Dixie   a southeastern American hybrid from the common Dog Ridge (rootstock for Central Valley *vinifera* vines) and *vitis candicans*; released in 1976 after experiments by Florida and North Carolina researchers. It is widely supplanting Scuppernong in the Southeast (along with Magnolia).

Dulcet   another red Muscadine serving many purposes, home use being the major one.

Dog Ridge   a *vitis candicans* rootstock variety widely used in the sandy soil of the Central Valley named for the Dog Ridge Mountains in Texas.

Durif considered by many the Petite Sirah of California; the variety flourishes in the Rhône Valley of southern France (it is not allowed for use in *appellation contrôlée* wines of the area). So far one California winery (Santa Cruz Mountain) uses the name Durif instead of Petite Sirah as a varietal.

Dutchess a white American variety developed after chance, natural crossings of the *labrusca* (and possibly *bourquiniana* and *aestivalis*) and *vinifera* species. It, like Delaware, Catawba, and Diamond is used both as a white wine varietal as well as a base for sparkling wine of the East.

Early Burgundy a.k.a Blauer Portugieser; a red *vinifera* wine variety used mainly in blends, but it has been bottled as a varietal; there are about 600 acres in California.

Early Muscat a white *vinifera* table variety of minor importance; released by Olmo in 1958.

Edelweiss a.k.a. E.S.40; a white hybrid wine variety grown mainly in the northern Midwest (Minnesota); developed by Elmer Swenson, long-time breeder in the northern Midwest.

Elbling see Kleinberger.

Ellen Scott an American red variety used for the table market; found in the South and Southwest.

Elvira *vitis riparia* variety grown to some extent (500 to 600 acres in New York) in the Northeast; its thin skin leads to easy cracking; used to produce white wine, mainly for blending.

Emerald Riesling there are now about 3,000 acres of this white *vinifera* cross, 78 percent of which is in the Central Valley; it was derived by Olmo (1936, released 1948) from the White Riesling and Muscadelle varieties. Usually this variety goes unnoticed into jug wines, but some wineries (Paul Masson and San Martin) bottle it as a varietal.

Emperor red *vinifera* table grape, widely hailed for its storing and shipping qualities; all 21,200 or so acres are planted in the Central Valley, 70 percent in Tulare County.

Exotic a.k.a. G8-30; another red *vinifera*, seeded table grape from Flame

Tokay X Ribier; there are about 1,300 acres in California, mostly in Kern County.

Favorite   this American hybrid (Black Spanish X Herbemont) is a red table grape found largely in Texas; it was released by the USDA in 1973.

Feher Szagos   a white *vinifera* wine variety, little-planted (300 acres in California, half in Fresno County) and less well known.

Fendant   see Chasselas.

Fiesta   a.k.a. F18-94; a white, seedless raisin grape cross released by the USDA in 1965; there are about 500 acres in California, all in the Central Valley.

Flame seedless   red *vinifera* table grape cross planted to 7,000 acres; a cross of (Cardinal X Thompson seedless) X (Red Malaga X Tifafihi Ahmer) X (Muscat of Alexandria X Thompson seedless); USDA by Harmon and Weinberger, 1961. Talk about mutts.

Flame Tokay   white *vinifera* table grape more and more in use as a wine grape for brandies of California; there are 18,200 acres of this variety in California, 99 percent of which is in San Joaquin County.

Flora   another Olmo (1938; released 1958) cross (Gewürztraminer X Sémillon); it is used largely for blending into jug wines though Parducci and others have bottled it as a varietal; there are about 400 acres in California, 50 percent in the Central Valley.

Florental   a.k.a. Burdin 7,705; a French-American hybrid (Gamay noir à jus blanc X S.8,365) used to make light- to medium-bodied red wines in the Midwest and East.

Foch   see Maréchal Foch.

Folle blanche   a.k.a. Gros Plant & Picpoul (in France); a sparsely-planted white *vinifera* wine variety of California (360 acres). One winery, Louis Martini, makes an interesting, tart and dry, light white wine from it.

Fox   generic name for "foxy" American species.

Frandsdruift   see Palomino.

Franken Riesling   see Sylvaner.

Fredonia   a blue-black table grape grown to a limited degree in the Northeast; it is recommended for use in jams and juices; an American variety.

French Colombard a.k.a Colombard; this white, fairly neutral *vinifera* wine variety is the most widely planted wine variety in California (with 56,600 acres, 90 percent in the Central Valley). It is used in jug wines, but occasionally turns up "on its own" (Parducci, Chalone and others).

Fry a bronze-white Muscadine variety used mainly in the home (southeastern homes, that is).

Fumé blanc alternate name for the Sauvignon blanc variety; usually, but, frustratingly, not always, "Fumé Blancs" are drier than "Sauvignon Blancs."

Gamay Beaujolais variety planted to approximately 4,000 acres, 95 percent in the Northern and Central coastal counties of California. One of these days, someone will drop the other shoe and call this variety for what many think it is: a clone of the Pinot noir of Burgundy.

Gamay (Napa) see Gamay noir à jus blanc; some, however, consider it to be the French variety call Valdiguié.

Gamay noir à jus blanc technical name for the famous red *vinifera* grape from which true Beaujolais of France is made; in California, the variety travels under the name of Napa Gamay, although some doubt the relationship; there are about 4,400 acres of the variety in California with traces outside the state (Washington, Oregon, Idaho).

Garonnet (formerly known as Seyve-Villard 18,283) this red French-American hybrid is sparsely planted; it serves as a blending wine grape (cross of S.7053 X S.6905).

Gewürztraminer a white *vinifera* wine grape which flourishes in Alsace, France, parts of Germany and Eastern Europe, and California, where there are about 4,700 acres planted. When fermented bone-dry in the Golden State, it has a spicy character with an attractive lightly bitter finish. Recent examples from the Northwest have been gaining attention, perhaps because the climate there is more similar to northern Europe, "Gerwitz" 's home.

Gionina a table grape grown on a small scale in the Midwest (Indiana).

Glenora seedless (NY 35,814) a black table grape of good quality; it is a cross of Ontario X Russian seedless. Makes for good eating.

Gold a minor *vinifera* hybrid (from Davis) with a noticeable Muscat flavor. East Side makes a varietal of the variety.

Golden Muscat a white hybrid cross (Muscat Hamburg X Diamond); less than 100 acres exists in California, three-quarters in the Central Valley. Peter Kerensky, of the St. Hilary's Vineyard in New Hampshire, has a small plot going, to most easterners' surprise.

Goldriesling a very sparsely planted *vinifera* cross of White Riesling and Courtiller musqué; found in the west.

Grand noir (de la Calmette) a red *vinifera* wine variety with a name more interesting than winegrowers' use for it; most of its ninety or so acres are planted in the Northern and Central coastal counties.

Green Hungarian a white, fairly neutral *vinifera* wine variety with about 400 acres planted in California's coastal counties. A handful of wineries (Weibel, Sebastiani) release it as a varietal, perhaps in search of the huge Magyar-Gaelic market.

Grenache a.k.a. Garnacho nero and Alicante Ganzin; a light red *vinifera* variety widely planted in France's southern regions and in California's Central Valley (about 90 percent of the 17,000 acres). It is used in many a California rosé blend but occasionally winds up varietally labeled (David Bruce [winery] sometimes makes an atypically dark interpretation).

Grey Riesling a.k.a. Chaucé gris; another rather neutral white *vinifera* wine variety which usually goes into blended jug "Chablis" or "Rhine" wines, though a few wineries release it as a varietal. Eighty percent of California's approximately 2,400 acres is planted in the coastal counties.

Grignolino a light red *vinifera* wine variety; only about fifty acres planted in California (Napa and Santa Clara counties). Heitz makes it into both a rosé and red table wine. There are also Italian versions from Piedmont.

Grillo a black *vinifera* variety very sparsely planted in California (only four acres in Stanislaus County).

Gutedel see Chasselas.

GW/GR code names for Geneva White and Geneva Red, respectively. Experimental varieties being tested by the Geneva station in the Finger Lakes region of New York are given such code names, followed by a numeral. Some, such as Cayuga White (GW3) have made it big and have been given their own names. Others await their turn.

Herbemont a *vinifera* and *aestivalis* (?) cross; it is a red wine variety, little used now.

Hermitage a.k.a. Shiraz in Australia and Cinsault in South Africa; see Black Malvoisie.

Higgins a bronze Muscadine variety used for the table or for light wine use; it is planted in the Southeast (Florida) and Southwest (East Texas).

Himrod this 1952 seedless, yellow table grape is a cross of Ontario X Sultanina; it is widely popular with the eastern home grape grower.

Hunt a red Muscadine table variety which grows in the Carolinas, Georgia, and eastern Texas.

Interlaken seedless a moderately recommended golden table grape grown in the Northeast; developed in 1947, it is another Ontario X Sultanina cross.

Isabella a very old, red American variety; named after Mrs. Isabella Gibbs of Brooklyn, it was once widely planted in the East but is now declining with the introduction of other varieties.

Italia a white *vinifera* table grape with about 1,000 acres planted in California, 99 percent in the Central Valley.

Ives noir an older, blue-black American variety; its use in the Northeast is declining because—many contend—of its vulnerability to modern pollutants; there are about 1,000 acres planted.

Jacquez a.k.a. Black Spanish and Lenoir; an older American hybrid (*aestivalis* and *vinifera* in there somewhere) now more widely planted in Europe than in America. Being a "direct producer," it is banned for use in *appellation contrôlée* French wines.

Johannisberg Riesling colloquial and common name for the White Riesling of Germany; there are about 11,100 acres in California with another several hundred scattered throughout the Northeast and Northwest. Americans appropriated the Johannisberg part of the name supposedly because "Schloss Johannisberg," a wine estate of some renown in Germany, was catchy and marketable. Its wines are usually fermented to retain a bit of residual sugar (*à la* German style) but can be found bone-dry in the Alsace tradition. New York, Washington, Oregon, and Pennsylvania seem to have more success with the drier versions, while sunny California excels in the sweeter interpretations.

Jumbo   a red Muscadine variety used mainly for table purposes.

Kay gray   a white hybrid developed by Elmer Swenson for use as either a table or wine variety; rather newly introduced. You might find some in Minnesota.

King Ruby   a red table grape with 125 acres planted in Fresno and Tulare counties, California.

Kleinberger   a.k.a. Elhling; a white *vinifera* wine grape of little importance in this country and slightly greater importance in Germany.

Kuhlmann 194.2   see Léon Millot.

Lake Emerald   a 1945 cross (Pixiola X Golden Muscat) by Professor Loren Stover; this bronze hybrid variety is used for the table and for wine purposes; sparsely planted in the Southeast (Florida).

Lakemont seedless   this yellow hybrid variety is considered a superior table grape with moderate plantings in the East and Midwest.

Landal   a.k.a. Landot 244; a red French-American hybrid variety (S.5,455 X S.2,816) used primarily for wines.

Landot 2281   a pink-colored French-American variety (S.V.5,276 X S.5,455) used primarily in the Midwest and Northeast for blending purposes.

Landot 4511   a.k.a. Landot noir (L.244 X S.V.12,375); a blue-red wine variety producing quite coarse wines used for blending purposes.

Lenoir   a red hybrid (*aestivalis* and *vinifera*, perhaps *cinerea*) used widely in France after the *phylloxera* and *oidium* crises as a substitute for the diseased *vinifera* varieties; now, it is disallowed for use in producing *appellation contrôlée* wines, but is still planted in France, and, to a very small degree, in this country.

Léon Millot   (a.k.a. Kuhlmann 194.2) a black *riparia* X *rupestris* hybrid similar in character to Maréchal Foch; very sparsely planted at present (50 or so acres in New York).

Madeleinangevine   a white *vinifera* table variety used more as a parent in the production of hybrids than on its own.

Magoon   a red Muscadine table grape also used for wines.

Magnolia a white Muscadine wine variety which is, with Carlos and Dixie, supplanting Scuppernong in the southeastern vineyard.

Malaga blanc a.k.a. white Malaga, Dabouki; this white *vinifera* table grape is often used to produce low-end wine for distilling purposes; 99 percent of the 3,100 or so acres are planted in the Central Valley.

Malbec a.k.a. Cot; a red *vinifera* wine variety, one of several (Merlot, Petit Verdot, Carmanère, Cabernet franc) that is blended with Cabernet Sauvignon in Bordeaux to produce many of the fine clarets of France; there is less than 100 acres in California, some in Napa County and some in quite warm Stanislaus County, which does not portend similar blending possibilities in the Golden State. It is considered a coarse cousin in Bordeaux.

Malvasia bianca a Muscat-flavored white *vinifera* wine variety with about 850 acres planted in California (over 60 percent in the Central Valley); it is often made into a sweet fortified dessert wine.

Maréchal Foch a.k.a. (Kuhlmann 188.2) a French-American hybrid (with *vinifera, riparia* and *rupestris* in its background) that has received rave comments on the quality of its Burgundy-style red wines. The acreage in the East and Midwest is steadily growing. Sometimes it is referred to as Foch.

Mataro a.k.a. Mourvedre; widely planted in southern France to produce the vinous red jug wines for the average Jacques; it does similar duty in California though it is planted to only about 900 acres, mostly in Riverside County.

Melon a.k.a. the Muscadet white *vinifera* variety of the Loire Valley in France, but often misidentified as Pinot blanc.

Merlot a red *vinifera* wine variety unknown in California only a few years ago, now planted to about 2,300 acres, primarily in the Northern and Central coastal counties. In Bordeaux, and more and more in California, it is used to "soften" the more bitter wine of the Cabernet-Sauvignon grape and to enable the latter's wines to develop more quickly. Many wineries, some outside the Golden State, are bottling it as a varietal.

Meunier see Pinot Meunier.

Meynieu 6 a French-American white wine hybrid planted to a small degree in the upper Midwest.

Mission once the most widely planted *vinifera* variety in California; now relegated to 3,300 acres, mostly in the Central Valley and in its "original home" of Southern California. The Spanish Missionaries reportedly propagated it from cuttings brought from Europe in the 1500's. In South America, the same thing happened, only there they called it "Criolla." Harbor Winery of West Sacramento releases a "Mission del Sol" dessert varietal as do a few others, but it is largely used now as a blending grape.

Missouri Riesling   not a true (White) Riesling but a French-American hybrid; it is a white wine variety that is both prolific and hardy.

Mondeuse   see Refosco.

Monterey Riesling   euphemism for Sylvaner.

Monticello   a seeded, red hybrid (mainly Fredonia in the background) similar to Steuben.

Montonico   a red *vinifera* variety of Italian background. San Martin winery develops the state's only 8.5 acres for its varietal wine of the same name.

Moored   a Fredonia X Athens hybrid red table grape rated high for that purpose.

Mourvedre   see Mataro.

Müller-Thurgau   a white wine *vinifera* cross of White Riesling and Sylvaner (though some ampelographers contend it is a cross of two strains of the White Riesling alone). It is produced as a medium dry varietal, more often from the Northwest than from anywhere else in the United States. Sokol Blosser, Chateau Benoit, and Eyrie from Oregon and Manfred Vierthaler from Washington are producers.

Münch   a red hybrid wine variety developed by breeder Thomas Volnay Munson in the late 1800's. Mount Pleasant Vineyards, of August, Missouri, produces it as a varietal.

Munson red   generic name for a group of red hybrids developed by the Texan Thomas Volnay Munson in the late 19th century.

Muscadelle   a so-far unidentified white *vinifera* variety more famous as one of the parents of Emerald Riesling (other parent: White Riesling); sparsely planted. The variety we know of in California is not the same as that grown in France (see next entry).

Muscadelle de Bordelais   the "true" Muscadelle of the Sauternes region of Bordeaux, France, which forms a very small part of the blend in Sauternes with Sémillon and Sauvignon blanc. Not widely planted in California though Hanns Kornell once made some tasty sparkling wine from it.

Muscat of Alexandria a white *vinifera* table grape often used to produce some lightly sweet varietal table wines and the bulk of California's cheap "Muscatels." Ninety-nine percent of the 9,900 or so acres are in the Central Valley. When made into a medium dry varietal, its flavor is usually coarser than Muscat blanc's.

Muscat blanc a.k.a. Muscat á gros grains, Muscat Cannelli, Muscat Frontignan, and others; this white *vinifera* is most famous as the base variety for Italy's Asti Spumanti wines; considered a wine variety. the 1,400 or so acres in California are used in meduim sweet table wines and sweet white sparkling wines often called "Spumante."

Muscat Hamburg a.k.a. Black of Alexandria; a red *vinifera* wine variety very sparsely planted (less than 100 acres in California, all in the Central Valley); sometimes produced as a varietal dessert wine (Novitiate, Weibel).

Muscat Ottonel a white *vinifera* wine variety widely planted in central and eastern Europe with only traces in our Northeast and Northwest areas.

Muscat Reine des Vignes see Queen of the Vineyards.

Muscat Sylvaner a.k.a. Sauvignon blanc.

Musqué some strains of many wine varieties display varying degrees of Muscat-like flavor, an apricot/peach-like character, that tends to separate them from the main strain; for example, Chardonnay musqué is a strain of Chardonnay that displays Muscat character while Sauvignon musqué does so within its Sauvignon milieu.

Mustang Indian term for the *vitis candicans* species.

Mzwani a white Russian variety grown, to my knowledge, only at Dr. Konstantin Frank's vineyard (Vinifera Wine Cellars) in New York's Finger Lakes area and at Chicama Vineyards in Massachusetts; considered a *vinifera* variety.

Nagyburgundi a.k.a. Pinot noir, in Hungary.

Napa Gamay see Gamay.

Nebbiolo a.k.a. Spanna, Picoutener, and Chiavennasca (in northwest Italy where it is used to produce big-bodied red wines such as Barolo, Barbaresco, and Valtellina Superiore); (red *vinifera* wine variety) it is not widely planted in California. Cary Gott, of Monteviña in Amador County, grows an acre or so, but the rest is in Fresno, Stanislaus, and Tulare counties. Gott abandoned his attempts at producing it as a varietal. Donn Caparone, of Paso Robles, is about to release a varietal under his label.

New York Muscat   a red-black table variety also used to produce many of the Eastern wineries' "Muscatel" wines; a cross of Muscat Hamburg X Ontario; sparsely planted, at present.

Niagara   an American variety with *vinifera* and *labrusca* in its background; it is the most widely planted white American variety in the country (more than 4,000 acres in Michigan, New York, and Pennsylvania alone). It is used for wine, juice, and table purposes and is considered quite reliable. Many wineries bottle it as a varietal.

Niobell (Niabell)   a cross of Niagara X Early Campbell; this red wine hybrid is only planted to about eighty acres, all in Tulare County.

Noah   one of the early hybrids (*vinifera, labrusca,* and *riparia*) and one widely planted in Europe after *phylloxera* struck; considered a white wine variety, but sparsely planted for such use in this country.

Noble   a red-black Muscadine table variety grown in Florida and other parts of our Southeast. It is sometimes used for winemaking.

Norton   a.k.a. Cynthiana, Virginia seedling; it is, for better or worse, one of the few American varieties (*labrusca, aestivalis,* and possibly *vinifera*) that displays very little of the Concordy "grape juice" flavor so apparent in most American varieties; it is a red variety used for wine.

Oberlin noir   (a.k.a. Oberlin 595) an old Gamay X *riparia* hybrid used to produce common red wine.

Olivette blanche   often referred to as "Lady Fingers" on the fresh market, it is a seeded, white *vinifera* variety with small acreage in California.

Ontario   an early (1908) cross of Winchell X Diamond; this white table grape is now in decline.

Orange Muscat   a white *vinifera* wine variety; very few acres exist, but Andrew Quady of Madera County, California, does produce a sweet, white fortified dessert varietal from the variety.

Othello   an old hybrid (Clinton X Black Hamburg); it is used to produce lesser quality red wines in the East and Midwest.

Palomino a.k.a. Frandsdruift (South Africa); used to produce the famous Sherries of southern Spain; the white *vinifera* wine variety is planted to about 3,800 acres in California, two-thirds in the Central Valley.

Pamlico a recent Muscadine cross (Lucida X Burgaw); this light green grape is most often found in the Southeast where it is used for the home table.

Pedro Ximenes white wine *vinifera*, often referred to as "PX"; it is used, with Palomino, in the wines of Sherry; little planted (200 acres) in California, all in the Central Valley and in Southern California.

Perelli 101 high-colored red wine variety; the late Antonio Perelli-Minetti introduced it in the mid-1960s; all 130 or so acres of the variety are in Kern County, California.

Perlette another Olmo (1946) cross; this white, seedless table grape is widely planted in Riverside County, California, with a total of 6,300 or so acres in all of that state.

Petit(e) Sirah see Durif and Syrah. The red, *vinifera*, wine variety is likely the same variety grown in the Rhône area of France, but disallowed for use in *appellation contrôlée* wines of the region. There are about 8,500 acres of "Pet," as the winegrowers refer to it, in California, half in the coastal counties and half in the Central Valley. When vinified traditionally, and not aged in wood too long, its wines often do resemble the famous Rhône red of Côte-Rôtie and Hermitage.

Petit Verdot a red *vinifera* wine variety cultivated in Bordeaux, France, to blend with Cabernets and Merlot. It is not at all widely planted in California or the United States, except for test plots.

Peverella a white *vinifera* wine variety sparsely planted in California (about 425 acres).

Picpoul see Folle blanche.

Pinot Beurot see Pinot gris.

Pineau de la Loire see Chenin blanc.

Pinot blanc a.k.a. Weissburgunder, in Germany; this white *vinifera* wine variety is planted in California to the tune of about 1,930 acres, 50 percent of which is in Monterey County alone. Pinot blanc wines are often confused with those of Chardonnay (to which, it is not related). Strangely, Burgundy, France, which once had thousands of acres of the variety planted now has less than 25 acres. Both the French and the Californians recognize Pinot blanc wines' proneness to easy oxidation.

Pinot gris   a.k.a. Pinot Beurot, Malvoisie, Tokay d'Alsace, Ruländer, and others; in the United States, this gray-pink-white *vinifera* variety is planted on a very small basis, mostly outside of California.

Pinot Meunier   a.k.a. Wrotham Pinot (England) and Müllerebe (Germany); the variety is widely planted throughout France's Champagne region and only experimentally in California. Eyrie in Oregon makes it as a varietal.

Pinot noir   a.k.a. Pinot nero (Italy), Blauerklevner and Schwarzeklevner (Germany) Blauburgunder and Spätburgunder are also accepted synonyms in German-speaking countries; this red *vinifera* wine variety is fairly widely planted in California's coastal/ mountainous regions, to the tune of about 9,000 acres; outside California the variety is planted on a very small basis: New York, Oregon, Washington, and few others. It is used mainly for producing dry red table wines though some sparkling wine producers use it, blended with Pinot blanc, Chardonnay, and other varieties, in their cuvées. It is probably the least successful of the Big Four varieties – with Cabernet-Sauvignon, White Riesling, and Chardonnay – in yielding European-style wines. Some examples, however, have been stunning.

Pinot St. George   a red wine *vinifera* variety not widely planted in California (about 475 acres, mostly in Monterey County); formerly also called "Red Pinot." It produces wines that approach the Pinot noir's in style. Not to be confused with Rupestris St. George, a widely used rootstock.

Portuguese blue   see Blauer Portugieser and Early Burgundy.

Price   a blue-red French-American table variety similar in flavor to Concord. Pennsylvania has some plantings where it is an early ripener.

Queen   a red, seedless table grape crossed by Professor Olmo from Muscat Hamburg and Thompson Seedless; there are about 800 acres of the variety in California, more than 99 percent in the Central Valley.

Queen of the Vineyards   a.k.a. (Muscat) Reine des Vignes; a white *vinifera* table variety used as a breeding parent in this and other countries and rarely planted in the United States for commercial purposes.

Ravat blanc   (Ravat 6) a cross of Chardonnay and S.5,474; it is a white wine variety planted to a small degree in the East and Midwest.

Ravat 51   a.k.a. Vignoles; a French-American hybrid cross of a strain of Pinot noir and S.6,905. It is somewhat popular in Michigan and Illinois where it is used to make a dry, light-bodied white wine.

Ravat noir   (Ravat 262) another Pinot cross with a Seibel (S.8,365); this red wine variety is less widely used than its white cousin.

Rayon d'Or   (S.4,986) a white French-American wine variety moderately planted in the East and Midwest. (S.405 X S.2,007).

Red Malaga   a.k.a. Molinera; more than 99 percent of the 500 acres of this red *vinifera* table variety is planted in the Central Valley of California.

Red Veltliner   a *vinifera* wine variety nearly gone from the California vineyards where it is planted to about sixty-five acres, all in Napa, Monterey, and San Benito counties.

Refosco   a.k.a. Mondeuse; probably most widely known as one of the ingredients in Beaulieu's "Burgundy"; 100 acres or so are planted in a few coastal counties; more widely distributed in southern France and Italy.

Regale   a black Muscadine variety used for wine and table purposes.

Rhine Riesling   in Switzerland, the Sylvaner; elsewhere, the White Riesling.

Ribier   a.k.a. Alphonse Lavallée, this red-black *vinifera* table variety is widely planted – 5,500 acres – in the Central Valley.

Richard's Black   a red table variety found mainly in Kern County and, less so, in Riverside County, California.

Riesling   see Monterey Riesling, Sonoma Riesling.

Riesling Renano   see White Riesling.

Rivaner   see Müller-Thurgau.

Rkatsiteli   a white *vinifera* Russian wine variety; a few acres exist in Livermore County, California. Rkatsiteli was made into a light and dry wine by Concannon of Livermore County.

Roanoke   a recent Muscadine variety; this white-yellow variety is used mainly in the home.

Robin Cardinal see Thornsburg Robin.

Romulus a seedless, yellow table variety; it is meeting with mixed reviews in the field (Ontario X Thompson seedless).

Rose-Ito a table variety; eighty-eight acres exist in California, most in Fresno County.

Rosette (S.1,000) an early French-American cross which is being replaced by others. Because of its low color, it is used to make rosés.

Rossola bianca a.k.a. Trebbiano, Saint Émilion; see Ugni blanc.

Roucaneuf (Seyve-Villard 12,309) a pink-red hybrid of low flavor and little planting, mainly in the Southeast.

Rougeon (S.5,898) red hybrids. Rougeon's high color makes it an excellent blending grape for eastern wines.

Royalty a early *vinifera* cross (Alicante Ganzin X Trousseau) made by Professor Olmo in 1938; there are about 1,875 acres of it in California, all in the Central Valley. It is a high-color *teinturier* used for blending and for port-style wines (Weibel made a varietal of it).

Rubired another 1938 *vinifera* cross by Olmo (Alicante Ganzin X Mourisco preto); this *teinturier* wine variety is planted to 9,700 acres in the Central Valley. Like its cousin, Royalty, it is used for blending and port-style wines.

Ruby Cabernet Professor Olmo likes R's, apparently; this *vinifera* hybrid (Cabernet Sauvignon X Carignane) was a successful attempt to combine the attractive flavor of the Cabernet with the sturdiness of the Carignane; it is widely planted in California with 14,500 acres, 96 percent of which is in the Central Valley.

Ruby seedless Olmo strikes again; this Emperor X Pirovano red table grape is planted to about 2,300 acres in the Golden State, all in the Central Valley (half in Fresno County alone).

Ruländer see Pinot gris.

Rupestris St. George a common and widely used rootstock in the California coastal counties.

Saint Croix another Elmer Swenson hybrid; this red variety is used both for wine and table purposes.

Saint-Émilion see Ugni blanc.

Saint Macaire a little-planted (150 acres) red *vinifera* wine variety, 95 percent of which is found in the Central Valley.

Salt Creek   along with Dog Ridge, a widely-used rootstock in the Central Valley.

Salvador   a high-color red wine grape used primarily for blending into jug wines; there are 1,700 acres of this *rupestris/vinifera* cross, all in the Central Valley of California.

Sangiovese   the famous red *vinifera* variety used to produce Chiantis (Italy); it is sparsely planted in California, most in Sonoma County.

Saperavi   a red *vinifera* wine variety from Russia; Dr. Konstantin Frank, of Vinifera Wine Cellars, in Hammondsport, New York, grows the variety.

Sauvignon blanc   the famous white *vinifera* variety used to produce the bone-dry Loire wines called Pouilly-Fumé and Sancerre as well as dry white Bordeaux wines (along with Sémillon); there are about 9,560 acres in California, mostly in the coastal counties, and a few hundred acres in Washington and Oregon. The wine from this grape is often called "Fumé Blanc" or, sometimes, simply "Fumé" prefixed by a county appellation; for example, "Sonoma Fumé" (Foppiano Winery). It is a very credible substitute for high-priced Chardonnays.

Sauvignon vert   a white *vinifera* wine variety, usually blended with other low-interest grapes to yield jug whites; there are about 525 acres in California, mostly in the coastal areas.

Scheurebe   German *vinifera* cross of White Riesling and Sylvaner. Scheurebe is making a tiny entrance into California via varietals by Joseph Phelps and Balverne wineries. It produces a light, Riesling-style wine.

Schuyler   a black table grape hybrid (Zinfandel X Ontario) famous as being one of the parents of Cayuga; see Cayuga.

Schwarzeklevner   see Pinot noir.

Schwarzriesling   a.k.a. Pinot Meunier.

Scuppernong   the original and most famous of the Muscadines, widely planted throughout the southeast; recently, however, it is being replaced by other Muscadines, notably Carlos, Dixie, and Magnolia. Vinified as a varietal, it is usually semi-sweet.

Sémillon   Groensdruift (South Africa) and Chevrier (under the Vichon Winery of Napa County label); in California, the variety is planted to just under 2,900 acres and is not so highly regarded by most winegrowers. Myron Nightingale, then of Cresta Blanca did turn out a marvelous, Sauternes-like wine called "Premier Semillon" which is still talked about in wine circles. This white *vinifera* variety is the main squeeze in Bordeaux where it is used to produce their sweet Sauternes.

Senoia a red Muscadine variety (a cross of Carlos and Higgins) recently developed by Georgia grape breeder B. O. Fry. It is said to produce light but excellent red wines.

Seyval blanc the hottest of the white wine French-American hybrids; it is planted relatively widely throughout the Northeast and Midwest. Its wines are considered quite fine and its future quite rosy. It is called Seyve-Villard 5,276 on many crop reports and is a cross of S.5,656 X S.4,986.

Sheridan a blue-black table grape now little seen or planted.

Shiraz Australian and South African name for the Syrah.

Sonoma Riesling euphemism for Sylvaner.

Souzão one of several grapes used to produce authentic Porto wines of Portugal; it is little-planted (c. 200 acres) in California, Paul Masson and Cresta Blanca have produced varietal port-style wines from it.

Spanna Piemontese (Italy) nickname for the Nebbiolo.

Steen (pronounced "steern") see Chenin blanc.

Steuben a blue-black Muscadine table grape not widely-planted, but considered "promising" by ampelographers. When it is used for winemaking, it is often made into a rosé.

Stover a white hybrid wine grape introduced by Floridian Professor Loren Stover; a cross of Mantey X Roucaneuf.

Suffolk red a seedless, red hybrid (Fredonia X Russian seedless) table grape recently introduced into the Eastern and Midwestern vineyards. It is considered by some to be the best eating variety in the country.

Sultana in California, also called Round seedless; confusingly, in Australia, Sultana is the name for Thompson seedless; there are only about 660 acres of this white *vinifera* raisin variety in the Golden State.

Sultanina a.k.a. Thompson seedless.

Superior Seedless a sparsely-planted seedless, white *vinifera* table grape.

Swenson red (E.S.439) another of Minnesota breeder, Elmer Swenson's hybrids; this one is a red table variety.

Symphony a recent *vinifera* cross (Muscat Alexandria X Grenache); another in the long list of Professor Olmo's successes. It was developed for use in the production of "Light Wines," but Olmo also discovered that it lacks the tell-tale Muscat bitterness when fermented dry. Just being planted in 1982.

Sylvaner a.k.a. Franken Riesling in Germany and Rhine Riesling in Switzerland; it is also masked in California under various Riesling misnomers, such as Sonoma Riesling and Monterey Riesling; this white *vinifera* wine variety is declining in its Motherland of Germany and planted to about 1,400 acres in California where it is released under its own name as a varietal only rarely.

Syrah a.k.a. Shiraz and Hermitage in Australia; widely planted in the Rhône Valley to yield the perfumed reds called Côte-Rôtie, St.-Joseph, Cornas, Crozes-Hermitage, and Hermitage. In California, only Joseph Phelps of Napa County produces it as a varietal, although Estrella River Winery in San Luis Obispo County has a relatively large planting of it and will, reportedly, produce it on its own label. In the Rhône, it is also called Serene.

Szúrkebarát Magyar name for Pinot gris.

T-Budding process of changing one variety of vineplant to another by means of selective grafting.

Teinturier generic name for any variety with red juice.

Thomas a red Muscadine table variety found mainly in the Carolinas.

Thompson seedless the most heavily cultivated variety in the country, with about 270,500 acres planted in California, 10 percent not yet bearing; 60 percent of the total is planted in Fresno County alone (where it is semi-jokingly referred to as "Fresno Chardonnay" or "Thompson tasteless"), with the great majority of the rest elsewhere in the Central Valley or in Southern California; there are also about 2,000 acres in Arizona. As recently as 10 years ago nearly two-thirds of the acreage of the variety was used to blend into jug wines or as fillers in white varietals even though it is primarily considered a raisin variety. With the increased plantings of the so-called noble wine varieties in the state, its use in winemaking has dropped to about 20 percent. On its own, the wine prduced from this grape is rather neutral; though Thomas Kruse Winery of Santa Clara county had fun with a varietal wine from it.

Thornsburg Robin   a.k.a. Robin Cardinal; this red *vinifera* table grape is sparsely planted in California (all 70 acres in Riverside County), with traces found in Arizona.

Tinta caõ   a.k.a. Mourisco preto; one of a number of generically-named "Tinta" varieties used to produce port-style wines.

Tinta Madeira   a *vinifera* wine variety planted to 400 acres in California; with Tinta Caõ, it is usually found in blends and port-style wines.

Tokay d'Alsace   see Pinot gris.

Topsail   a white-green Muscadine table variety.

Touriga   another red *vinifera* wine variety found in port-style wines of California.

Traminer   a white *vinifera* wine variety with origins in the vineyards of Alsace and Germany. A spicy, more interesting strain of the Traminer – called "Gewürz", or spicy, Traminer – is more widely known. It is on the decline in California.

Trebbiano   a.k.a. Ugni blanc, in Italy.

Ugni blanc   (pronounced oó nyee blahn) a.k.a. Trebbiano, Saint-Émilion, and Rossola bianca; this white *vinifera* wine variety is more often used as a blender for jug wines.

Urbana   older hybrid red table variety whose prime virtues are good keeping qualities.

Valdepeñas   a red *vinifera* wine variety planted to 1,500 acres in California, all in the Central Valley. It is usually blended into jug reds.

Valdiguié   a red *vinifera* variety found in southern France. Some researchers feel that it is the same as what is billed as "Gamay Beaujolais" or "Napa Gamay" in California. More research will tell.

Van Buren   an older cross (Fredonia X Worden); a red-black table variety.

Veeblanc   a recent cross of Cascade and Seyve-Villard 14-287; there is little experience with this white wine variety; a Canadian development.

Ventura   another new cross (Chelois X Elvira) that is proving to be winter-hardy, a fact which is more impressive when one considers that it was introduced by Canadians.

Verdelet (S.9,110) a white French-American wine variety (S.5,455 X S.4,938) sometimes used for table fruit as well.

Vergennes a red hybrid sometimes varietally labeled in the East.

Vidal blanc (a.k.a. Vidal 256); it is a cross of Ugni blanc and S.4,986; it is considered a good to very good and hardy producer of dry white wines in the East and Midwest. More and more wineries are making it as a varietal.

Vignoles see Ravat 51.

Villard blanc (a.k.a. Seyve-Villard 12,375); though sometimes used as a table grape, this French-American hybrid (S.6,468 X S.6,905) is more often used to produce eastern dessert wines.

Villard noir (a.k.a. Seyve-Villard 18,315); this red-black hybrid (S.7,053 X S.6,905) usually produces a neutral red wine for blending.

Vincent a dark, blue-red hybrid of Canadian origin which yields dark red wines for blending; some patches are found in Minnesota where it is also used for eating purposes.

Virginia seedling see Norton.

Weissburgunder a.k.a. Pinot blanc, though some maintain it is actually the Chardonnay.

White Hannepoot a.k.a. Muscat of Alexandria, in South Africa.

White Riesling a.k.a. Johannisberg Riesling, Rhine Riesling, Riesling Renano, and others; a white *vinifera* wine grape relatively widely planted in the East, Midwest, and Northwest (perhaps 2,000 acres all told), and with about 11,000 acres in California's coastal counties. It is usually vinified to retain a slight amount of natural grape sugar, though sometimes it is fermented *à la* the great sweet Riesling of Germany and held for many years to develop. Understandably, the cooler areas of New York, Oregon, and Washington seem to be more hospitable than the relatively warm California climes; at least, that's what the experts on Northwest Rieslings maintain.

Wilder a bronze Muscadine table and wine variety.

Worden a blue-black American table variety little used now.

Wrotham Pinot see Pinot Meunier.

Yates a seeded, red, hybrid (Mills X Ontario) table variety.

Yuga   a red-bronze Muscadine table variety without back problems.

Zante Currant   see Black Corinth.

Zibibbo   a.k.a. Muscat of Alexandria, in southern Italy.

Zinfandel   the most widely planted red variety in California and the second-most widely cultivated – after Concord – in the country; a red *vinifera* wine variety whose origins are masked by "the mists of time," as they say; nearly 40 percent of the variety is planted in San Joaquin County alone, with the rest scattered in the Central Valley and the coastal counties; almost 2,000 acres in the Sacramento Valley/Sierra Foothills area; there are small plantings of the variety in both Australia and South Africa. Many say that it came from Agoston Haraszthy's native Hungary while others maintain it came from Toscana, Chiantiland. Recent laboratory analysis indicates that it is closely related to, or may well be the same variety as, the "Primitivo" which flourishes in southern Italy and which produces "Late Harvest Zinfandel" sweet red wines on occasion. When vinified traditionally, Zinfandel wines can be quite tasty, medium full-bodied, claret-style wines.

CALIFORNIA

California Grapeland

❶ North Coastal Counties

T—	27 acres
R—	12
W—	70,411

     70,450 (10% of the state total)

❷ Central Coastal

T—	63
R—	6
W—	55,368

     55,437 (7.9%)

❸ Sacramento Valley/ Sierra Foothills

T—	215
R—	18
W—	9,422

     9,655 (1.4%)

❹ Central Valley

T—	69,898
R—	279,568
W—	198,554

     548,020 (77.7%)

❺ Southern California

T—	8,547
R—	3,806
W—	9,023

     21,376 (3.0%)

Table grapes   78,750 a. (80.6% bearing*), 11.2% of state
Raisin grapes 283,410 a. (88.1% bearing), 40.2% of the state
Wine grapes 342,778 a. (81.4% bearing), 48.6% of the state

    704,938 acres total of which 84.0% are bearing.

*for purposes of classification, "bearing" vines are those that have been in the ground for more than three years, after which they begin to "bear" or produce fruit normally (i.e., yield an average amount of fruit).

There are approximately 550 bonded wineries in the state; at least two thirds of these were bonded, or legally established, since 1970; one half were bonded since 1975, and less than 10% were bonded before 1900.

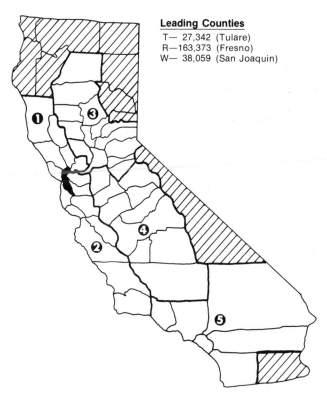

Leading Counties

T— 27,342 (Tulare)
R—163,373 (Fresno)
W— 38,059 (San Joaquin)

Map and statistics from the *California Crop and Livestock Reporting Service.*

BY ITSELF, CALIFORNIA IS THE SEVENTH LARGEST WINE-PRODUCING entity in the world. It annually turns out several hundred million gallons of basic, no-frills table wine as well as a few million of so-called fine wine, wine that can command the respect of any honest and competent winemaker in Europe or elsewhere. California boasts 700,000 acres of grape land, more than 500 wineries, and enough technical expertise to give any wine country a run for the money, whatever the wine style. And that's just the beginning: scientists and statisticians maintain that, to keep up with the expected American (and, perhaps, foreign) demand of the coming decades, another 200,000 acres of vines will have to be planted soon. This from a state which did not really establish itself as a winegrowing area until Repeal in 1933, only half a century ago. Fifty years is a siesta by comparison with most winegrowing nations' experiences.

GEOGRAPHY:

The state is divided into two basic sections: the Central Valley and its offshoots, and the coastal/inland semi-periphery which comprises areas north, northeast, and south of the San Francisco Bay. Usually but not always, the wines from these areas are different from one another.

The Central Valley is a 220 by 50 mile multi-county area between the Sierra Nevadas in the east and the so-called coastal ranges in the west. It is not completely homogeneous in climate or soil, as will be illustrated in the Central Valley introduction, but essentially, the valley's sub-areas can be described either as hot and flat or hotter and flatter.

This is the region of five- and ten-ton-an-acre yields, of consecutive 100 degree Fahrenheit days, lower interest grape varieties (a good percentage of which are not even classified as wine grape varieties – see "Grapes"), and grand scale irrigation. Its wineries handle grapes, and ultimately wines, in much the same way as other foods are handled by huge food processors – in million-unit batches. The result is the same as it would be in any similar region of the world: serviceable jug or basic table wines, dessert wines, and sparkling wines which can be made slightly more interesting if the right winemaking techniques are applied. Nevertheless, just about every glass of California wine the average American has ever drunk has come from this largely unheralded area.

The more "high profile" wine regions, those either a few hours south and north of San Francisco or a short drive from Sacramento, draw much more interest and much more press, and their wines cost, usually with justification, more money.

The most acclaimed wines of these areas come from "pedigreed" varieties, shy-bearing grapes whose growers often thank the Lord after getting a four-ton-per-acre yield. The climate, by no means as cold as that of the fine wine areas of Europe, is still relatively free of the scorching temperatures of Modesto, Fresno, and Bakersfield. Here the scale of winemaking is generally much smaller than in the Central Valley. For instance, the rather large winemaking company called The Christian Brothers, located in the Napa Valley, operates several wineries whose combined storage capacity is less than one-sixth that of the Central Valley's E & J Gallo. Many small lots in these acclaimed areas are treated almost as if they were the winemaker's children, and the results are, like children, often extremely different from one another. In addition, wines from these areas may vary in taste from one year to the next. Add to these factors the use of small (sixty-gallon) oak barrels for the aging of a large proportion of these wines and you can begin to understand some of the disparity in the prices, quality, and press reviews between these and Central Valley wines.

CLIMATE:

Much of the information about California's climate has been mentioned above or will be illustrated in the individual sections. However, a note about how California's wine regions have been divided climatically – primarily by heat measurements – will help you to understand some of the wine lingo used by California wine-lovers.

Since California's general climate, at least in the wine regions mentioned in this book, is rather steady, warm, and predictable, climatologists have been able to classify the state's many sub-regions in neat little groups based largely upon the units of heat surrounding a grapevine over a period of time.

Several decades ago, Professors Maynard Amerine and A. J. Winkler perfected a system of categorizing California's wine regions by measuring the temperature of an area during the growing season of grapes, April through October. Their theory was that vines will flourish only as long as a certain minimum temperature—many say this minimum is fifty degrees Fahrenheit—is attained. If the temperature drops below fifty degrees, the plant will not grow. Once the temperature climbs beyond this magic mark, the plant will grow. (The plant will also "shut down" or stop metabolizing if the air becomes too warm.) Amerine and Winkler maintained that by adding the number of degrees above fifty on each day that the temperature reached on each day in the 214-day growing season, they would arrive at a figure which could help growers to decide which areas were best suited for which grape varieties.

Using this "degree-day" system, Amerine and Winkler divided California into five regions as follows: those spots with degree-day readings of less than 2,500 units were classified into Region I (coastal or mountainous locations, mainly); areas that accumulated between 2,501 and 3,000 units fit into Region II (most of the North and Central coast counties); Region III included those areas between 3,001 and 3,500 degree-days; Region IV areas fell within the 3,501 and 4,000 unit range; and Region V, the warmest, included locations over the 4,001 mark, most of which are in the Central Valley.

Region I areas were considered especially suited for cool-climate, northern European varieties such as White Riesling and, sometimes, Pinot noir. Chardonnay and Gewürztraminer were thought to thrive best in Region II, Cabernet and Sauvignon blanc in Region III, etc. (with many exceptions). With this information in mind, a grower could feel secure planting his cool-climate variety in Carneros or not even thinking of setting up a Gewürztraminer vineyard in Modesto.

The system of classification by temperature measurement remains fairly valid today, if only in the specific case of California vineyards. However, for a variety of reasons, the system will no doubt be revised (and expanded to perhaps ten regions) in the future to accommodate new findings.

NOMENCLATURE:

Americans, – and that includes Californians, – use three types of labeling: generic, proprietary, and varietal.

Generic wines are those labeled with the name of a famous European wine area: Chablis, Burgundy, Champagne (France), Rhine, Moselle (Germany), Chianti (Italy), Port (Portugal), Sherry (Spain), and others. In the beginning, such labeling was used to signify a style of wine reminiscent of the original product; that is, "California Chablis" was supposed to remind people of that crisp, dry, white wine made from Chardonnay grapes that came from Chablis, France. Most generic wines, however, bear only the slightest organoleptic resemblance to the original article. "California Chablis" is usually made from very inexpensive grapes (often even the Thompson seedless, a raisin variety), as opposed to the quite costly Chardonnay of the authentic Chablis. The grapes for California's Chablis are grown in a hot climate on alluvial or sandy soil, as opposed to the grapes for real Chablis which are grown on chalk-rich soils in a cold region of northern France. "California Chablis" is often red or pink; French law states that any French wine labeled "Chablis" must be white. Most of the other American generic wines likewise fit the authentic original's taste-nature much the way a size twelve shoe would fit Minnie Mouse, and many have complained that Americans should discontinue using such foreign names because they give no real indication of style or taste, or because it is outright fraud to imply that California Burgundy will taste anything like Gevrey-Chambertin, the real thing. But Americans have been using generic names for so long that the practice seems likely to stay with us at least for the foreseeable future.

Some wineries utilize fantasy names for their wines and give them patented or trademarked "proprietary" appellations, such as E & J Gallo's "Rhinegarten." In this case the name does give an indication of the style of the wine: light, medium dry, and white, in the German sense. Some names, such as Trefethen's "Eschol Red" and "Eschol White," do not indicate style, except for color. Some wineries such as Robert Mondavi, simply use the designation "Red (or White) Table Wine." More and more American wine producers are implementing similar nomenclature.

Usually, the finest wines of any particular variety will be named after the grape variety which was used to make them. Hence, these are called "varietal wines" or simply "varietals." By present United States law (as of January, 1983) a wine labeled with the name of a variety (with the exception, inexplicably, of some American varieties such as Concord) must derive at least 75 percent of its volume from that variety. It is thought that if a winery uses this minimum amount, the wine will usually taste varietally true. Some have argued that if a wine label simply gives the name of the grape variety, then 100 percent of the wine in the bottle – not just a portion of it – should come from that variety. While logic and honesty are on the side of these people, it seems unlikely that the 75 percent rule will be changed. (In France, the varietal minimum is 100 percent, while that of the Common Market is 85 percent unless a member country's own laws are stricter.) As of this writing, these is a suit before a federal judge to decide this issue.

Other laws involving how Americans name their wines include restrictions on geographic terminology. If a wine's name refers to a specific geographic area – for example, "Sonoma County Chardonnay" – most of the wine in the bottle must have come from the named geographic entity. (California state law mandates that 100 percent of the grapes used in any wine labeled "California" must be grown within California.) "American Chardonnay" can, by law, be a blend of Chardonnay grapes from two or more states whose names might or might not be mentioned on the label. The minimum percentages of wine from the given area change, as the given area is more or less precisely defined as the legal origin of the grapes. With the advent of viticultural areas, United States laws will most likely become more complex. Currently, the law states that if a wine is labeled with an officially approved viticultural area as its indication of origin, at least 85 percent of the wine in the bottle must have come from the viticultural area named. Whether or not this minimum will be increased as a result of court action similar to that referred to above as a matter of speculation.

As of January 1, 1983, the term "Estate Bottled" on a label can be used only if the label also lists a viticultural area as its indication of origin (states and counties cannot be considered viticultural areas) and if the bottling winery:

1. is located within the viticultural area;
2. grew all the grapes used to make the wine on land owned or controlled by the winery within the boundaries of that area; and
3. crushed the grapes, fermented the resulting must, and finished, aged, and bottled the wine in a continuous process (the wine at no time having left the premises of the bottling winery). (27 CFR Part 4—Labeling and Advertising of Wine.)

Lastly, if a wine label lists a vintage year, at least 95 percent of the wine in the bottle must come from grapes grown and picked within that year.

Since the above represent federal, and not state, laws (with the one exception I mentioned), they apply to all states. See "Opinions" for further discussion on American wine laws.

GRAPE VARIETIES:

As opposed to the non-California wine areas of the country, most of whose grapes are either native to America (the Muscadines) or are descendants of native American varieties which were haphazardly hybridized with vines brought from Europe (mainly Concords), California is *vitis vinifera* country. From the very beginning, when Spanish settlers, conquerors, and missionaries first came to the Pacific, European grape varieties were used for winemaking purposes. The first widely-known variety was one called the Mission grape, which, for quite a spell, was the only cultivar of any consequence in California. It is still to be found in California vineyards, mainly in the Central Valley and in the Southern California counties. Nowadays there are about 3,300 acres of these grapes, a mere drop in the tank.

As the state became more civilized, other European varieties were imported, propagated, and planted the length of California. Although the story is not quite clear even today, it is said that Agoston Haraszthy, a Hungarian gentleman of many interests and occupations, was responsible for the greatest dissemination of European varieties in the history of the state. He had traveled to many countries in Europe, collected cuttings of different varieties, and he expected to be paid by the California legislature for helping to develop the wine industry of that state. The politicians reneged, so the story goes, and Haraszthy, in order to recoup his losses, was forced to sell his cuttings piecemeal up and down the state to whoever would buy them. In the process, some of the cuttings were confused and mixed with others, creating some interesting situations in the vineyards. Even as late as a decade ago Australian wine growers who had purchased California cuttings labeled "Pinot blanc" were complaining that they received Chenin blanc instead. Next time you want to see a wine grower squirm, ask him what is in his "Gamay Beaujolais:" Napa Gamay, Gamay Beaujolais, or Pinot noir (see "Grapes" section).

The building of California's grape and wine industry continued, after a fashion, until the beginning of the second decade of this century when temperance forces struck a blow for their version of saintliness and had the production of alcoholic beverages branded illegal. Overnight the livelihood of many families was taken away from them as winegrowers, save those few who could survive either by selling grapes or grape concentrate to home winemakers or by making sacramental wines, and had to find other work. Those grapes that did survive the Prohibition period had to be fairly firm varieties, grapes that could stand the rigors of cross-country shipment to eastern markets. More robust varieties, such as Alicante Bouschet, edged out the finer, more delicate varieties such as Pinot noir. After the government had the sense to repeal Prohibition, the situation in the field was slow to come around. Even as late as 1959 there were only a little over 5,000 acres of what we would consider the noble varieties – Cabernet-Sauvignon, Pinot noir, the Gamays, Merlot, White Riesling, Chardonnay, Chenin blanc, Gewürztraminer, Pinot and Sauvignon blanc, Sémillon and Sylvaner* – planted in California. This constituted about six-and-a-half per cent of the total for wine grapes.

In the 1970s, things began to move: 200,000 new acres of wine varieties were planted in a wild, decade-long fit of enthusiasm. There were some minor problems – such as the fact that Americans today are drinking twice as much white wine as red, and red varieties were planted on a two-to-one ratio over white during the decade – but the path was clear: California was back on the winemaking track and all was right with the wine world. As of 1981, those thirteen varieties mentioned above accounted for 130,000 acres of grapes, or over a third of the total for wine varieties.

As you will note as you turn the pages, not all *vinifera* varieties did equally well throughout California. Some, more suited to warmer temperatures, produced more desirable results in a Region III, IV, and V area, whereas cool-climate grapes, such as Gewürztraminer adapted better to a Region I or II spot. This presented something of an obstacle to California winegrowers in the Central Valley who would have loved to have 500,000 acres of great-tasting Cabernet or Chardonnay in their vineyards instead of some other, less interesting, less marketable cultivars. But those two varieties and their noble cousins produce lackluster wines in the Central Valley's climate. Scientists from the University of California, primarily Professor Harold Olmo and his staff, began to develop hybrids of *viniferas*, grapes that would adapt well to the heat of the valley and have many of the interesting taste characteristics common to the noble varieties. Ruby Cabernet, Emerald Riesling Flora, and others – including Symphony, Olmo's most recent hybrid – are examples of such *vinifera* crosses. An elaboration of this development, as well as of the development of American grape varieties in general, is found in the "American Grapes" section.

All this winey fury must be put into perspective, for California's grape acreage is not primarily used for beverage wines. Like the grapes of eastern vineyards, where Concords dominate, most California grapes are used for juice or for eating as fresh fruit, or, as raisins. Of the approximately five million tons of grapes picked in 1980, for example, less than 40 percent were wine types. And even home grown Californians, steeped in wine culture and living in close proximity to vineyards, drink only four-and-a-half gallons of wine *per capita* annually, which is less than a fifth (pardon) of the average French, Italian, or Spanish rate. So while California's industry produces 90 percent of all United States wine, it still is tiny in comparison to Europe's and California's market is still in its infancy.

I have listed as many wineries as I possibly could given the dictates of having a manuscript on the publisher's desk nine months to a year before its publication and dissemination. If you want to be as up-to-date as possible, I suggest you contact The Wine Institute, 165 Post Street, San Francisco, California 94108, for news on new openings (100 wineries were bonded in the time it took to compile this book). They are also the source of much information – statistical, economic, educational, and the like – about California wines in general. Or contact The Hiaring Corporation, 1800 Lincoln Avenue, San Rafael, California 94901, which publishes the industry periodical "Wines & Vines" as well as the yearly *Directory*, which includes a list of all the wineries that exist or that have been bonded (in the United States) in the past year.

I have grouped the winegrowing counties of California into five sections: North Coastal, Central Coastal, Sacramento Valley/Foothills area, Southern California, and the Central Valley counties. These are somewhat arbitrary divisions, I realize, and might conflict with some experts' notions of California's acreage breakdowns. But they provide a framework for attacking the subject and are consistent with most of the realities of a technical-viticultural delimitation.

Within each section I have provided a brief commentary meant to give the reader an idea of what is happening with existing grape varieties, the location of many of these relative to viticultural areas, developments in winegrowing, and the like. Obviously, those counties with heavy concentrations of wineries are treated on a grander scale. Some, such as Monterey, which has fewer than a score of wineries, are specially dealt with because of the great number of wine grape varieties planted therein. Others, such as Amador and Sacramento, receive special attention because they are the scene of intense activity and/or growth.

Lastly, I have provided the names and addresses of some agencies or associations of winegrowers in many counties. Most of these organizations are meant to deal with the problems of the local members and do not provide economic or statistical information; what many do provide is free literature, including maps, concerning the wine region in question. They do not usually offer touring service though many will refer you to these operations.

Have a good trip!

Northern Coastal Counties

	County	# wineries (mid-1982)	Planted acreage	% of total	Leading Variety
❶	Humboldt	4	—	—	—
❷	Mendocino	22	10,605	15.1	Carignane
❸	Lake	5	2,884	4.1	Cabernet-Sauvignon
❹	Sonoma	107	28,755	40.8	Chardonnay
❺	Napa	123	26,982	38.3	Cabernet-Sauvignon
❻	Solano	5	1,212	1.7	Cabernet-Sauvignon
❼	Marin	5	12	neg.	Cabernet-Sauvignon
	TOTALS	271*	70,450**	100.0	Cabernet-Sauvignon & Chardonnay

* which equals 10% of California's total planted acreage and 20.6% of its wine grape planting. 99.9% of these are wine grapes.
** of which over 80% were bonded since 1970

The
Northern Coastal
Counties

THIS SEVEN-COUNTY REGION BOASTS THE LONGEST CONTINUOUS HIS-
tory of fine wine growing in the state. Its approximately 70,000
acres of grapes represent only 10 percent of the state's total, yet
50 per cent of California's wineries are located in this prime vineyard land.

The region's vineyards, often referred to as part of the "cooler
coastal" county vineyards, are really neither. Most of the acreage
is at least forty miles from the Pacific, and 100 degree Fahrenheit
days during the growing season are common. But for the sake
of comparison to the rest of California's wine growing regions,
the description is apt.

Most of the area's grapes, like any others in the wine world,
are planted on flatlands or slightly rolling hills. This makes both
cultivation and picking fairly easy. Very few acres are planted
in the mountains, although many contend that the most interesting wines come from these higher (c. 2,000 feet) elevations,
especially from spots in the Mayacamas range.

The two most planted varieties, Cabernet-Sauvignon and Zinfandel, together account for nearly 30 percent of the acreage.

Northern Coastal Counties

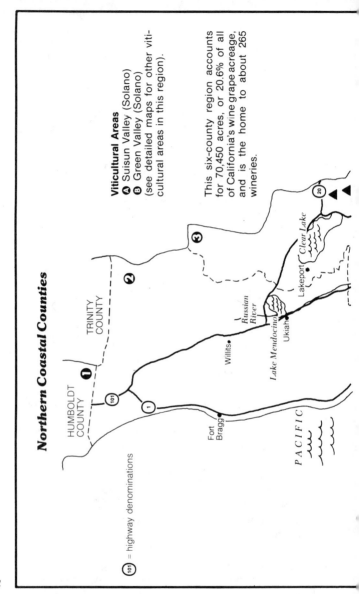

Viticultural Areas

A Suisun Valley (Solano)
B Green Valley (Solano)
(see detailed maps for other viticultural areas in this region).

This six-county region accounts for 70,450 acres, or 20.6% of all of California's wine grape acreage, and is the home to about 265 wineries.

(101) = highway denominations

HUMBOLDT COUNTY

TRINITY COUNTY

101

1

Fort Bragg

Willits

Ukiah

Lakeport

Russian River

Lake Mendocino

Clear Lake

20

PACIFIC

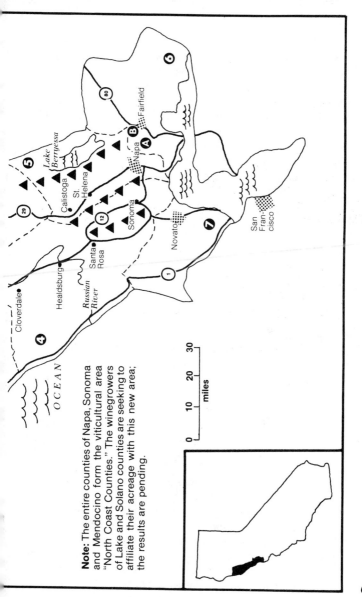

Note: The entire counties of Napa, Sonoma and Mendocino form the viticultural area "North Coast Counties." The winegrowers of Lake and Solano counties are seeking to affiliate their acreage with this new area; the results are pending.

Pinot noir, Petite Sirah, and the Gamays are other well-represented reds. Chardonnay and White Riesling plantings account for about 20 percent of the acreage. Other whites, such as Chenin and Sauvignon blanc, and French Colombard, are being more and more widely exploited. At present, six of the so-called noble varieties—Cabernet, Zinfandel, Pinot noir, Chardonnay, White Riesling, and Sauvignon blanc—account for two-thirds of all the grapes in the area, although this may change as growers obtain more information on where to plant what varieties.

If you can visit during the "crush" (at harvest season), you will see trucks and trailers, laden with grapes, traveling the highways, bound for the bigger wineries such as Christian Brothers, Krug, Martini, and Mondavi. These firms greatly depend upon independent growers, with whom they have short-term or long-term contracts, for their grapes. The larger firms, with few exceptions anywhere in California, own few vineyards outright. These larger firms usually can be depended upon to turn out consistently good quality, and often quite fine, products on a grand scale.

The several dozen smaller wineries—and by "small" I mean less than 25,000 gallon capacity—often use only their own grapes to produce the equivalent of the European *domaine* or *château* wines. Usually these wines will be more distinctive—and more expensive—interpretations of a particular variety, and are worth their prices as often as not.

Unlike some other California regions, the North Coast is a relatively cramped area. The true coastal strip is unsuited to successful grape growing, as are the slough sections in the south near the San Francisco Bay. Great amounts of acreage, especially in northern Lake and Mendocino counties, are occupied by forests or by bodies of water, Lake Berryessa, Clear Lake, and Lake Mendocino being the largest of these. Add to this the growing impingement of urban sprawl and you have a compact region, limited for the planting of most agricultural goods.

The increasing influx of people into the North Coast may prove even more problematic to both the nascent and the established winegrower. Until recently the county boards have been dominated by people who had agricultural leanings, if not outright sympathies and interests. They enacted various laws that would prevent "settlers" from occupying much vital vineyard space. Recently, however, the boards have been increasingly moved to allow manufacturers and other industries, as well as housing developers, into the area.

The need for human beings to live in homes on land currently devoted to vineyards or wineries may well shrink even further the available space for grape growing. Doubters simply need look at San Jose where vineyards once thrived and where two-legged critters are now more often seen. This is a major problem of winegrowers in the North Coast.

Nevertheless, the beat goes on in northern grape land and no growers seem to be getting ready to take condominium management courses.

As far as viticultural areas are concerned, there are many proposals and already several officially defined boundaries. Most will be described in the individual county introductions, and a glimpse at the accompanying maps will help. There is one multi-county area that should be mentioned here: the "North Coast Counties" area. So far, the growers in Napa, Mendocino, and Sonoma counties have persuaded the BATF to consider parts of their land for inclusion in this viticultural area. Growers in Lake and Solano counties, however, feel that certain sections of their counties should have the same designation. The issue remains unresolved as of this writing.

Names in parentheses indicate other corporate names or second- or third-label names.

HUMBOLDT COUNTY

Fieldbrook Valley Winery
Fieldbrook Road
Fieldbrook, 95521
(707) 839-4140
T/A   10

Kirkpatrick Cellar Winery
3801 H. Street
Eureka, 95501
(707) 443-4474
(only Fruit wine)
T/A   10

Willow Creek Vineyards
1904 Pickett Road
McKinleyville, 95521
(707) 839-3373
(Dean Williams Winery)
T/A 10

Wittwer Winery
2440 Frank Avenue
Eureka, 95501
(707) 443-8852
T/A 10

SOLANO COUNTY

Cadenasso Winery
Box 22 (1955 Texas Street)
Fairfield, 94533
(707) 425-5845
(Solano)
T 7

Chateau de Leu Winery
205 West Mason Road
Suisun, 94585
(707) 864-1517/1107
T/* 10

Diablo Vista Winery
674 East H Street
Benicia, 94510
(707) 837-1801
T/A 10

Susiné Cellars
301 Spring Street
Suisun, 94585
(707) 425-0833
T/A 10

Wooden Valley Winery
Route 1, P.O. Box 124
Suisun, 94585
(707) 864-0730
(Mario Lanza)
T* 7

MARIN COUNTY

Endgate Vineyards
310 Capetown Street
Novato, 94947
(415)
(Mont D'Ede L'Escuate)
T/A

Grand Pacific Vineyard
  Company
134 Paul Drive, #9
San Rafael, 94901
(415) 479-9463
(Alta Vista)
T 10

Kalin Cellars
61 Galli Drive Stations B,F,G
Novato, 94947
(415) 883-3543
(Kendall Cellars)
T/A 10

Pacheco Ranch Winery
5495 Redwood Highway
Ignacio, 94947
(415) 456-4099/883-5583
(Howland Ranch)
T/A 10

Sonoma Vineyards (Tiburon)
72 Main Street
Tiburon, 94901
(415) 435-3113
(see also Sonoma County listing)
(Tasting Room only)
T/P

Woodbury Winery
32 Woodland Avenue
San Rafael, 94901
(415) 454-2355
("Coast Range")
T/A   **10**

NAPA COUNTY

THE NAME NAPA, ACCORDING TO LEON ADAMS, WAS GIVEN TO THE county (and the city and the river) by the Indians, members of the Wappo and Coastal Miwok tribes that inhabited the county before the advent of Chardonnay. After the BATF defined the viticultural area known as "Napa Valley," its boundaries became nearly the same as those of Napa County itself. "Napa Valley" on a wine label now legally means "Napa County," with the exception of the county's extreme northern and northeastern parts.

I will leave commentary on the wisdom of this interpretation to other forums; but the wine drinker should not be left with the impression that the county's growing conditions are homogeneous, for they are not. The government is currently listening to several proposals to define smaller viticultural areas within this half million acre tract of land.

In the southwest, for instance, is the well-known Carneros/ Huichica area. This sub-region of the Napa Valley actually extends into Sonoma County and was officially delimited as a viticultural area in its own right as of late December, 1981. This area is colder than the more northerly reaches of the valley because of its proximity to San Pablo Bay and the bay's cooling winds which sweep up the valley. For this reason, most growers argue that it is an optimum growing area for cool-climate varieties such as White Riesling, Gewürztraminer, Chardonnay, and Pinot noir. Many wineries, including Martini, Beaulieu and Domaine Chandon, own or contract for acreage there. One high profile grower, Rene di Rosa, has a good-sized chunk of grape land which he calls Winery Lake and whose name appears on ten or so wineries' labels to indicate the special origin of those wineries' grapes.

From the city of Napa, north along Highway 29, there are dozens more sub-regions suitable for viticultural area status and where some varieties do much better than others. On the flats around Rutherford, for instance, Cabernet-Sauvignon has yielded extremely interesting wine for decades. Men such as the octogenarian "little giant," André Tchelistcheff, have produced wines that rival the great clarets of France in finesse and character while displaying their own stylistic peculiarities, one of which is described as "Rutherford dust."

Other areas, notably some in the vicinity of Calistoga and the Atlas Peak, are touted as Zinfandel territory. Indeed, as you travel north from Carneros and its wind influence, the climate becomes warmer and warmer (and the soils differ slightly as well), making for diverse growing conditions. Warmer pockets, such as the Foss and Wooden valleys, may well be suited only to such varieties as Chenin blanc, Zinfandel, Gamay, and French Colombard. The mountainous areas to the east and west of the main road, Highway 29, seem very well suited to yielding interesting Cabernets and Merlots.

Experimentation in the area is intense and ongoing as winegrowers slowly discover which microclimates and which soil structures are hospitable to some, and inhospitable to other, varieties. Still, the area is relatively young by comparison with most of the world's winegrowing regions, so it will most likely be several more decades before even this fine wine county is varietally defined.

Despite all this experimentation, energy, and interest, Napa County has grown less in terms of plantings of wine grapes than the North Coast in general and substantially less than California. Add to this the dangers of urban sprawl and you can foresee the potential for an ominous future in Napa County. The Napa Valley Foundation, 21 Oak Grove Way, Napa, 94558, was established in 1981 to study these matters and to recommend courses of action to solve the problems. The foundation's hopes are high.

Good sources of information (other than statistical or eco-

Napa County

The county size is approximately 485,000 acres; approximately 27,000 are currently planted to grapes.

Note: A 1/28/1981 decision of the BATF defined the so-called "Napa Valley" as all of the county save for Land northeast of Putah Creek and Lake Berryessa. Over the next few years a number of Napa County sub-regions will be "defined" for BATF purposes. Most likely viticultural areas will be "Carneros," / Huichica," "Pope Valley" and others (in italics on map).

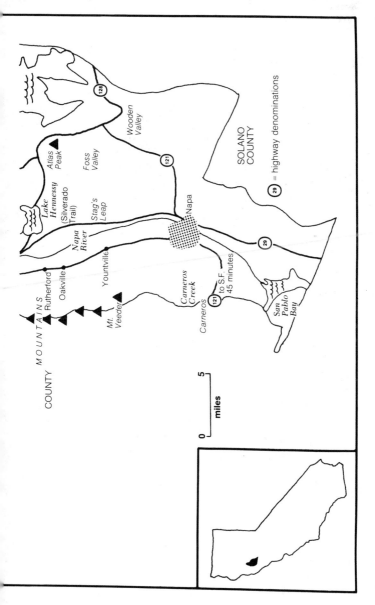

nomic) about Napa County's wines and vines include the Napa Valley Grape Growers' Association, 4075 Solano Avenue, Napa, 94558, and the Napa Valley Vintners, P.O. Box 141, St. Helena, 94574.

The winery listings include a letter reference to indicate whether the winery in question lies in or south (S) of the city of Yountville, in the central (C) area of the valley, between Yountville and St. Helena or in the north (N) part of the valley, beyond St. Helena. This should help with your touring plans.

NAPA COUNTY

Acacia Winery
2636 Las Amigas Road
Napa, 94558
(707) 226-9991
T/A   9   S

Alatera Vineyards
5225 St. Helena Highway
Napa, 94558
(707) 944-2914
T/A   10   S

Alta Vineyard Cellar
1311 Schramsberg Road
Calistoga, 94515
(707) 942-6708
T/A   10   N

Altamura Winery
4250 Silverado Trail
Napa, 94558
(707) 255-1000
T   8   S

S. Anderson Vineyard
1473 Yountville Crossroad
 (Box 3046)
Napa, 94558
(707) 944-8642
T/A   10   S

Louis Bartolucci
(see Mount St. John Cellars)

Beaulieu Vineyard
1960 St. Helena Highway
Rutherford, 94573
(707) 963-3671
T   5   C

Beringer Vineyards/
 Los Hermanos
2000 Main Street (Box 111)
St. Helena, 94574
(707) 963-7115
T   5   C

Bouchane Vineyards
1075 Buchli Station Road
Napa, 94558
(707) 252-9065
(Old Garetto Winery)
T/A   9   S

Buehler Vineyards
820 Greenfield Road
St. Helena, 94574
(707) 963-2115
T/A   10   C

Burgess Cellars
1108 Deer Park Road (Box 282)
St. Helena, 94574
(707) 963-4766
(Bell Canyon)
T/A   7   C

Cakebread Cellars
8300 St. Helena Highway
  (Box 216)
Rutherford, 94573
(707) 963-9182
T/A   9   C

Calafia Wines
6150 Silverado Trail
Napa, 94558
(707) 944-2666
T/A   10   S

Carneros Creek Winery
1285 Dealy Lane
Napa, 94558
(707) 226-3279
T/A   8   S

Casa Nuestra
3473 Silverado Trail North
St. Helena, 94574
(707) 963-4684
(Kirkham Winery)
T/A   10   C

Cassayre-Forni Cellars
1271 Manley Lane
Rutherford, 94573
(707) 255-0909
T/A   10   C

Caymus Vineyards, Inc.
8700 Conn Creek Road (Box 268)
Rutherford, 94573
(707) 963-4204
(Liberty School)
T/A   9   C

Domaine Chandon
California Drive (P.O. Box 2470)
Yountville, 94599
(707) 944-8844
(Fred's Friends, Panache)
T*   6   S

Chappellet Winery
1581 Sage Canyon Road
St. Helena, 94574
(707) 963-7136
(Pritchard Hill)
T/A   7   C

Chateau Boswell
3468 Silverado Trail
St. Helena, 94574
(707) 963-5472
T/A   10   C

Chateau Chevalier Winery
3101 Spring Mountain Road
St. Helena, 94574
(707) 963-2342
(Mountainside Vineyards)
T/A   9   C

Chateau Chevre Winery
2040 Hoffman Lane
Yountville, 94599
(707) 944-2184
T/A   10   S

Chateau Montelena Winery
1429 Tubbs Lane
Calistoga, 94515
(707) 942-5105
T/A   7   N

The Christian Brothers/
  Mont LaSalle Vineyards
4411 Redwood Road (Box 420)
Napa, 94558
(707) 226-5566
(see Mont LaSalle)
T   10/3   S

The Clos du Val Wine
  Company, Ltd.
5330 Silverado Trail
Napa, 94558
(707) 252-6711
(Granval)
T/A   8   S

Conn Creek Winery
8711 Silverado Trail
St. Helena, 94574
(707) 963-9100/963-3945
T/A   8   C

Cuvaison, Inc.
4550 Silverado Trail
Calistoga, 94515
(707) 942-6266
(Calistoga Vineyards)
T*/P   7   N

Deer Park Winery
1000 Deer Park Road
Deer Park, 94576
(707) 963-5411
T/A   10   N

Diamond Creek Vineyards
1500 Diamond Mountain Road
Calistoga, 94515
(707) 942-6926
T/A   10   N

Duckhorn Vineyards/
  St. Helena Wine Company
3027 Silverado Trail
St. Helena, 94574
(707) 963-7108
T/A   10   C

B. Ehlers Winery
(see VWB Winery Co.)

Evensen Vineyards
8254 St. Helena Highway
  (Box 127)
Oakville, 94562
(707) 944-2396
T/A   10   C

Evilsizer Cellar
1760 Partridge Road
Napa, 94558
(707) 944-8568
T/A   10   S

Far Niente Winery
1150 Darms Lane
Napa, 94558
(707) 226-6238/
  (415) 332-0662
T/A   10   S

Flora Springs Wine Company
1978 West Zinfandel Lane
St. Helena, 94574
(707) 963-5711
T/A   10   C

Folie à Deux Winery
3070 St. Helena Hwy.
St. Helena, 94574
(707) 963-1160
T/A   10   C

Forman Winery
2555 Madrona Avenue
St. Helena, 94574
(707) 963-4613
T/A   10   C

Franciscan Vineyards
1178 Galleron Road (Box 407)
Rutherford, 94573
(707) 963-7111
T   6   C

Freemark Abbey
3022 St. Helena Highway
  (Box 410)
St. Helena, 94574
(707) 963-9694
T*   7   C

Frog's Leap Winery
3358 St. Helena Highway
St. Helena, 94574
(707) 963-4704
T/A   10   C

Girard Winery
7717 Silverado Trail (Box 372)
Oakville, 94562
(707) 944-8577
(Stephens)
T/A   8   C

Green and Red Vineyards
3208 Chiles Pope Valley Road
St. Helena, 94574
(707) 965-2346
(Jay Hemingway Vineyards)
T/A   10   C

Grgich Hills Cellar
1829 St. Helena Highway
  (Box 450)
Rutherford, 94573
(707) 963-2784
T/A   9   C

Hagafen Cellars
P.O. Box 3035
Napa, 94558
(707) 252-0781
NT   10   S

Heitz Wine Cellars
500 Taplin Road
St. Helena, 94574
(707) 963-3542
T   7   C

Heitz Wine Cellars
436 St. Helena Highway South
St. Helena, 94574
(707) 963-4309
(Tasting Room only)
T   C

William Hill Winery
P.O. Box 3989
Napa, 94558
(707) 224-6565/226-8800
T/A   8   S

Hopper Creek Winery
2209 Jefferson St.
Napa, 94558
(707) 252-8444
T/A   10   S

Inglenook Vineyards
1991 St. Helena Highway
Rutherford, 94573
(707) 963-7184
T   5   C

Johnson Turnbull Vineyards
8210 St. Helena Highway
Oakville, 94562
(707) 963-5839
T/A   10   C

Karakasevic Winery
3220 North St. Helena Highway
St. Helena, 94574
(707) 963-9327
T/A   10   C

Robert Keenan Winery
3660 Spring Mountain Road
St. Helena, 94574
(707) 963-9177
T/A   9   C

Kirkham Winery
(see Casa Nuestra)

Hanns Kornell Champagne
   Cellars
1901 Larkmead Lane (Box 249)
St. Helena, 94574
(707) 963-2334
T   7   C

Charles Krug Winery
2800 Main Street (Box 191)
St. Helena, 94574
(707) 963-2761
(C. Mondavi, C-K Mondavi)
T   4   C

Lakespring Winery
2055 Hoffman Lane
Napa, 94558
(707) 944-2475
T/A   9   S

Long Vineyards
P.O. Box 50
St. Helena, 94574
(707) 963-2496
T/A   10   C

Manzanita Cellars
P.O. Box 1014
St. Helena, 94574
(707) 253-8698
NT   10   C

Markham Winery
2812 St. Helena Highway, North
St. Helena, 94574
(707) 963-5292
(Vinmark)
T* 5 C

Louis Martini Winery
St. Helena Highway (Box 112)
St. Helena, 94574
(707) 963-2736
T 5 C

J. Mathews Napa Valley Winery
1711 Main Street
Napa, 94558
(714) 642-1234
(in Newport Beach)
(Napa Deluxe)
NT 9 S

Mayacamas Vineyards
1155 Lokoya Road
Napa, 94558
(707) 224-4030
T/A 9 S

F. J. Miller & Company
8329 St. Helena Highway
Napa, 94558
(707) 963-4252
(premises in Rutherford)
T/A 10 S

Richard P. Minor Winery
(see Ritchie Creek)

Robert Mondavi Winery
7801 St. Helena Highway
  (Box 106)
Oakville, 94562
(707) 963-9611
T* 5/4 C

Monticello Cellars
4242 Big Ranch Road
Napa, 94558
(707) 944-8863
T/A 9 S

Mont La Salle Vineyards
2555 Main Street
St. Helena, 94574
(707) 963-2719
(Christian Brothers
  Champagne facility)
T 5/3 C

Mount Saint John Cellars
5400 Old Sonoma Road
Napa, 94558
(707) 255-8864
(Louis Bartolucci)
T 9 S

Mount Veeder Winery
1999 Mount Veeder Road
Napa, 94558
(707) 224-4039
T/A 10 S

Napa Creek Winery
1001 Silverado Trail
St. Helena, 94574
(707) 963-9456
T/A 10 C

Napa Valley Cooperative Winery
St. Helena Highway (Box 272)
St. Helena, 94574
(707) 963-2335
(Vin Mont)
NT   5   C

Napa Wine Cellars
7481 St. Helena Highway
Oakville, 94562
(707) 944-2665
T   8   C

Nash Creek Vineyards
3520 Silverado Trail, North
St. Helena, 94574
T/A   C

Newlan Vineyards & Winery
5225 St. Helena Highway
Napa, 94558
(707) 944-2914
T/A   10   S

Neyers Winery
P.O. Box 1028
St. Helena, 94574
(707) 963-2654
T/A   10   C

Nichelini Vineyards
2349 Lower Chiles Road
St. Helena, 94574
(707) 963-3357
T/A/P   9   C

Niebaum-Coppola Estate
1460 Niebaum Lane (Box 208)
Rutherford, 94573
(707) 963-9435
T/A   10   C

Charles Ortman
(see St. Andrew's Winery)

Pannonia Winery, Inc.
3103 Silverado Trail
Napa, 94558
(707) 253-1821
T/A   9   S

Robert Pecota Winery
3299 Bennett Lane
Calistoga, 94515
(707) 942-6625
T/A   10   N

Robert Pepi Winery
7585 St. Helena Highway
  (P.O. Box 421)
Oakville, 94562
(707) 944-2807
T/A   10   C

Joseph Phelps Vineyards
200 Taplin Road (Box 1031)
St. Helena, 94574
(707) 963-2745
(Le Fleuron Insignia,
  Stone Bridge)
T/A   7   C

Pina Wine Cellars
8050 Silverado Trail
Napa, 94558
(707) 944-2229
T/A   10   C

Pine Ridge
5901 Silverado Trail
Napa, 94558
(707) 253-7500
T*/P   9   S

L. Pocai & Sons
Highway 29, Route 1 (Box 231)
Calistoga, 94515
(707) 942-4572
T/A   8   N

Pope Valley Winery
6613 Pope Valley Road (Box 108)
Pope Valley, 94567
(707) 965-2192
T*   8   N

Prager Winery & Port Works
1281 Lewelling Lane
St. Helena, 94574
(707) 963-3720
T*   10   C

Quail Ridge
1055 Atlas Peak Road
Napa, 94558
(707) 224-2022/944-8128
T/A   10   S

Raymond Vineyard & Cellar
849 Zinfandel Lane
St. Helena, 94574
(707) 963-3141
T/A   8   C

Ritchie Creek (Richard Minor)
4024 Spring Mountain Road
St. Helena, 94574
(707) 963-4661
T/A   10   C

Riverbend Winery
(See Shown & Sons)

Roddis Cellar
1510 Diamond Mountain Road
Calistoga, 94515
(707) 942-5868
T/A   10   N

D. C. Ross Winery
1721 C Action Avenue
  (Box 2502)
Napa, 94558
(707) 255-9463
(Napa Valley Wines,
  Napa Vintners)
T/A   10   S

Round Hill Cellars
1097 Lodi Lane
St. Helena, 94574
(707) 963-5251
(Rutherford Ranch Cellars)
T/A   8   C

Rutherford Hill Winery
3022 St. Helena Highway
(Box 410)
St. Helena, 94574
(707) 963-9694
T   7   C

Rutherford Vintners
1673 St. Helena Highway
(Box 238)
Rutherford, 94573
(707) 963-4117
(Rutherford Cellars/Vineyards)
T*   8   C

St. Andrew's Winery, Inc.
2921 Silverado Trail
Napa, 94558
(707) 252-6748
(Charles Ortman)
T/A   10   S

St. Clement Vineyards
2867 St. Helena Highway, North
St. Helena, 94574
(707) 963-7221
NT   10   C

St. Helena Wine Company
(See Duckhorn Vineyards)

V. Sattui Winery
St. Helena Highway and
   White Lane
St. Helena, 94574
(707) 963-7774
(Hibbard-Braden Estate)
T/P   9   C

Schramsberg Vineyards
   Company
Schramsberg Road
Calistoga, 94515
(707) 942-4558
T/A   8   N

Schug Cellars
3835 Highway 128
Calistoga, 94515
(707) 942-5950
NT   10   N

Sequoia Grove Vineyards
8338 St. Helena Highway
Napa, 94558
(707) 944-2945
T/P   10   S

Shafer Vineyards
6154 Silverado Trail
Napa, 94558
(707) 944-2877
T/A   9   S

Charles F. Shaw Vineyard
   & Winery
1010 Big Tree Road
St. Helena, 94574
(707) 963-5459
T/A   9   C

Shown & Sons Vineyards
8643 Silverado Trail
Rutherford, 94573
(707) 963-9004
(Riverbend Winery)
T*   8   C

The Silverado Vineyard
6121 Silverado Trail
Napa, 94558
(707) 257-1770
T/A   8   S

Silver Oak Cellars
6525 Washington Street
Oakville, 94562
(707) 944-8866
T/A   10   S

Sky Vineyards
1500 Lokoya Road
Napa, 94558
(707) 226-5670
T/A   10   S

Smith-Madrone Vineyards
4022 Spring Mountain Road
   (P.O. Box 451)
St. Helena, 94574
(707) 963-2283/963-4470
T/A   10   C

Spring Mountain Vineyards
2805 Spring Mountain Road
St. Helena, 94574
(707) 963-5233
T/A   7   C

Stag's Leap Wine Cellars
5766 Silverado Trail
Napa, 94558
(707) 944-2020
(Hawkcrest)
T/A   8   S

Stags' Leap Winery, Inc.
6150 Silverado Trail
Napa, 94558
(707) 253-1545
(Pedregal)
T/A   9   S

Sterling Vineyards
1111 Dunaweal Lane
Calistoga, 94515
(707) 942-5151
T*   6   N

Stonegate, Inc.
1183 Dunaweal Lane
Calistoga, 94515
(707) 942-6500/942-6365
T/A   9   N

Stony Hill Vineyard
P.O. Box 308
St. Helena, 94574
(707) 963-2636
T/A   10   C

Storybook Mountain Vineyards
3835 Highway 128
Calistoga, 94515
(707) 942-5950
T/A   10   N

Sullivan Vineyards Winery
1090 Galleron Road (Box G)
Rutherford, 94573
(707) 963-9644
T/A   10   C

Sutter Home Winery, Inc.
277 South St. Helena Highway
St. Helena, 94574
(707) 963-3104
T   6   C

Traulsen Vineyards
2250 Lake County Highway
Calistoga, 94515
(707) 942-0283
T/A   10   N

Trefethen Vineyards
1160 Oak Knoll Avenue
Napa, 94558
(707) 255-7700
T/A   7   S

Tudal Winery
1015 Big Tree Road
St. Helena, 94574
(707) 963-3947
T/A   10   C

Tulocay Winery
1426 Coombsville Road
Napa, 94558
(707) 255-4699
T/A   10   S

Turkey Wine Cellars
3358 St. Helena Highway
St. Helena, 94574
(707) 963-4704
T/A   10   C

Vichon Winery
1595 Oakville Grade (Box 363)
Oakville, 94562
(707) 944-2811
T/A   9   C

Villa Mount Eden Winery
600 Oakville Crossroad
  (Box 147)
Oakville, 94562
(707) 944-2414
T/A   8   C

Vose Vineyards
4035 Mount Veeder Road
Napa, 94558
(707) 944-2254
T/A   10   S

VWB Winery Company
3222 Ehlers Lane
St. Helena, 94574
(707) 963-7697
(B. Ehlers Winery)
T/A   8   C

Whitehall Lane Winery
1563 St. Helena Highway
St. Helena, 94574
(707) 963-9454
T/A/P   10   C

Yverdon Vineyards
3787 Spring Mountain Road
St. Helena, 94574
(707) 963-4270
T/A   9   C

ZD Wines
8383 Silverado Trail
Napa, 94558
(707) 963-5188/938-0750
T/A   9   S

SONOMA COUNTY

SONOMA COUNTY WINEGROWERS HAVE USUALLY PLAYED SECOND fiddle to their more illustrious counterparts across the Mayacamas Mountains in Napa. Coming from Chicago, I can understand this "second county" syndrome which has many locals in its grip. Yet, from a purely factual viewpoint, Sonoma is the superior county. It has a longer grape growing history and more grapes to boot. It also has more room in which to grow grapes than does Napa, and is doing so at a greater rate, a fact which might prove telling in the next decade.

Like Napa and most other wine counties in the state, Sonoma is divided into many sub-regions. The far southeastern tip comprises the Sonoma part of the Carneros/Huichica sub-region, as well as the distinctive growing area around the town of Schell-ville from which some interesting Pinot noirs have come.

The Sonoma Valley, another sub-region, lies between the Mayacamas and Sonoma mountains. The stretch of land runs from just south of the city of Sonoma almost to Santa Rosa, the county capital. It was officially designated a viticultural area in late 1981. The area includes several divisions along its twenty-five mile length, the most prominent of which is probably the Bennett Valley, of late the source of some fine Chardonnays. But each little town along Highway 12 has vineyard sections that display their own little peculiarities of climate and soil. In that way, the area is much like the Côte d'Or of Burgundy, France.

Sonoma County

MENDOCINO COUNTY

Cloverdale
Russian River
Dry Creek
Asti

1

MENDOCINO HIGHLANDS

Cazadero

E

Rio Nido

Guerneville
Russian River

PACIFIC

OCEAN

Occidental

```
0        5
   miles
```

Bodega Bay

Viticultural Areas
A Dry Creek
B Alexander Valley
C Knight's Valley
D Sonoma Valley/Valley of the Moon
E Russian River/Santa Rosa Plain
F Chalk Hill
⬚ Umbrella area tentatively called
"Sonoma Russian River Valley"

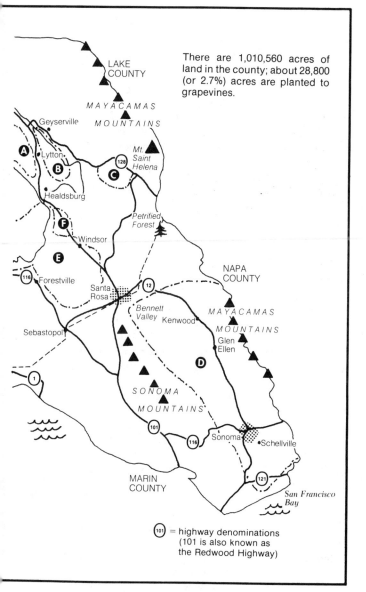

There are 1,010,560 acres of land in the county; about 28,800 (or 2.7%) acres are planted to grapevines.

LAKE COUNTY

MAYACAMAS MOUNTAINS

Geyserville

A

Lytton

B

Mt. Saint Helena

(128)

C

Healdsburg

Petrified Forest

F

Windsor

E

NAPA COUNTY

(116)

Forestville

Santa Rosa

(12)

Bennett Valley

Kenwood

MAYACAMAS MOUNTAINS

Glen Ellen

Sebastopol

D

(1)

SONOMA MOUNTAINS

(101)

(116)

Sonoma

Schellville

MARIN COUNTY

(121)

San Francisco Bay

(101) = highway denominations (101 is also known as the Redwood Highway)

The winding Russian River, which flows from Cloverdale, in the north, to the mouth on the Pacific, passes through or near several other distinct sub-regions. The major regions include the Alexander Valley and the Dry Creek areas between Geyserville and Healdsburg on the river's eastern and western banks, respectively. A mix of varieties has been successful here: Chardonnay and Cabernet, Gewürztraminer and Sauvignon blanc – juxtapositions of supposedly incompatible varieties that would make a Carneros grower wonder.

A few miles to the east, along Highway 128, lies the tiny Knight's Valley, from which area Beringer Vineyards has taken well-received Cabernets and Rieslings.

A triangular patch of land called the Santa Rosa Plain is still another distinct area of the county. This, in turn, is enveloped by the much larger Sonoma Russian River Valley area which includes just about all of the county's vineyards north of Santa Rosa.

Cabernet, Chardonnay, and Zinfandel make up half the county's acreage planted to grapes. Carignane, French Colombard, Gewürztraminer, Petite Sirah, and White Riesling are represented with 1,000 to 1,500 acres each. And Sonoma is home to more Pinot noir than any other county in the state, although, according to one Sonoma Valley grower, "most of it is planted in the wrong places."

With 100 wineries and many more growers in the county, the idea market and the energy level are unlikely to stagnate. One significant factor should not be overlooked: the E & J Gallo Winery in the Central Valley vinifies anywhere from 25 percent to 40 percent of Sonoma County's grapes in its Frei Brothers outlet in Healdsburg, which says something for both that large firm and Sonoma grapes.

Each year at harvest time the county stages a fair at which Sonoma wines are judged and given awards by panels of American experts. The contest is considered one of the best run in the state.

Good sources of non-statistical or non-economic information include the Sonoma County Winegrowers Association, c/o Millie Howie, P.O. Box 198, Geyserville, 95441, and the Sonoma Valley Vintners Association, P.O. Box 238, Sonoma, 95476.

The winery listings include a letter reference to indicate whether the winery in question lies in the southern (S) section of the county, from the Bennett Valley south, in the central (C) section from Santa Rosa to near Healdsburg, or in the northern (N) section from Healdsburg to the Mendocino border. This should aid you in your tour planning.

SONOMA COUNTY

Adler-Fels
5325 Corrick Road
Santa Rosa, 95404
(707) 539-3123
T/A   10   C

Alderbrook Vineyards
Magnolia Street
Healdsburg, 95448
(707) 433-9154
T/A   10   N

Alexander Valley Vineyards
8644 Highway 128
Healdsburg, 95448
(707) 433-7209
T   8   N

Arroyo Sonoma Winery
155 Cherry Creek Road
Cloverdale, 95425
(Bandiera,
   The California Wine Co.)
(707) 894-4295
T/A   7   N

Balverne Wine Cellars
10810 Hill View Road
Healdsburg, 95448
(P.O. Box 70 in Windsor, 95492)
(707) 433-6913
T/A   10   N

Bandiera
(See Arroyo Sonoma)

Bellerose Vineyard
435 West Dry Creek Road
Healdsburg, 95448
(707) 433-1120
T/A   10   N

Belvedere Wine Company
4035 Westside Road
Healdsburg, 95448
(707) 433-8113
NT   9   N

Benziger Family
   Vineyard & Winery
(See Glen Ellen Winery)

C. Bilbro Cellars
2062 Mill Creek Road
Healdsburg, 95448
T/A   10   N

Blue Heron Wine Cellar
P.O. Box 1053 (71 W. North)
Healdsburg, 95448
(707) 433-8164
T/A   10   N

Brenner Cellars
(see Lytton Springs)

Buena Vista Winery & Vineyards
27000 Ramal Road
Sonoma, 95476
(707) 938-8504
(938-1266 is tasting room phone)
T/P   6   S

Davis Bynum Winery
8075 Westside Road
Healdsburg, 95448
(707) 433-5852
(Riverbend Cellars)
T/A   8   N

Cambiaso Winery & Vineyards
1141 Grant Avenue (Box 548)
Healdsburg, 95448
(707) 433-5508
T   6   N

Chateau St. Jean, Inc.
8555 Sonoma Highway (Box 293)
Kenwood, 95452
(707) 833-4134
T   7   S

Chateau St. Jean
3000 Bowen Avenue
Graton, 95444
(707) 823-9989/544-1863
(facilities for the production
   of sparkling wine)
T/A   9   C

Clos du Bois
5 Fitch Street
Healdsburg, 95448
(707) 433-5576/433-8266
T/A   7   N

Cordtz Brothers
28237 River Road
Cloverdale, 95425
(707) 894-5245
T*/P   8   N

H. Coturri & Sons, Ltd.
6725 Enterprise Road
Glen Ellen, 95442
(707) 996-6247
T   10   S

Dehlinger Winery
6300 Guerneville Road
Sebastopol, 95472
(707) 823-2378
T/A   9   S

DeLoach Vineyards
1791 Olivet Road
Santa Rosa, 95401
(707) 526-9111
T   9   C

Diamond Oaks Vineyard
26900 Dutcher Creek Road
Cloverdale, 95425
(P.O. Box 2703,
   South S.F. 94080)
(707) 224-2022
T   9   N

Domaine Laurier
(see Shilo Vineyards)

Donna Maria Vineyards
10286 Chalk Hill Road
Healdsburg, 95448
(707) 838-2807
T/A   8   N

Dry Creek Vineyard, Inc.
3770 Lambert Bridge Road
  (Box T)
Healdsburg, 95448
(707) 433-1000
T/P   7   N

Fenton Acres Winery
6192 Westside Road
Healdsburg, 95448
(707) 433-2305
T/A   10   N

Fieldstone Winery
10075 Highway 128
Healdsburg, 95448
(707) 433-7266
(Redwood Ranch & Vineyards)
T*   9   N

Fisher Vineyards
6200 St. Helena Road
Santa Rosa, 95404
(707) 539-7511
T/A   9   C

L. Foppiano Wine Company
12707 Highway 101 (Old
  Redwood Highway, Box 606)
Healdsburg, 95448
(707) 433-1937/433-7272
(Riverside Farm)
T*/P   6   N

Chris A. Fredson Winery
1960 Dry Creek Road
Healdsburg, 95448
(707) 433-3913
NT   7   N

Frei Brothers Winery
(see E & J Gallo Winery)

Fritz Cellars
24691 Dutcher Creek Road
Cloverdale, 95425
(707) 894-2561
T/A   9   N

E & J Gallo Winery
3387 Dry Creek Road
Healdsburg, 95448
(707) 433-4849/542-7363
(Frei Brothers Winery)
T/A   5/1   N

Geyser Peak Winery
22280 Geyserville Road (Box 25)
Geyserville, 95441
(707) 433-6585
(Summit)
T*/P   5   N

Glen Ellen Vineyards
1700 Moon Mountain Drive
Sonoma, 95476
(707) 996-5870
T/A   10   S

Glen Ellen Winery
1883 London Ranch Road
Glen Ellen, 95442
(707) 996-1066
(Benziger Family
  Vineyard and Winery)
T/A   10   S

Grand Cru Vineyards
1 Vintage Lane (Drawer B)
Glen Ellen, 95442
(707) 996-8100
T*/P 8 S

Gundlach-Bundschu Winery
3775 Thornsberry Road (Box 1)
Vineburg, 95487
(707) 938-5277
T/P 7 S

Hacienda Wine Cellars, Inc.
1000 Vineyard Lane (Box 416)
Sonoma, 95476
(707) 938-3220
(Estancia)
T/A/P 9 S

Hanzell Vineyards
18596 Lomita Avenue
Sonoma, 95476
(707) 996-3860
T/A 10 S

J. J. Haraszthy & Son
14301 Arnold Drive
Glen Ellen, 95442
(707) 996-3040
T/A 10 S

Haywood Winery
18701 Gehrick Road
Sonoma, 95476
(707) 996-4298
T/A 9 S

Healdsburg Wine Company
130 Plaza Street
Healdsburg, 95448
(707) 433-8164
(William Wheeler Winery)
T/A 10 N

Healdsburg Winegrowers, Inc.
4151 Westside Road (storage)
Healdsburg, 95448
(415) 435-2272
(Bacigalupi Vineyards)
NT 10 N

Herrera Cellars
(see Toyon Vineyards)

Hop Kiln Winery
6050 Westside Road
Healdsburg, 95448
(707) 433-6491
(Sweetwater Springs, Griffin)
T 10 N

Horizon Winery
2594 Athens Court (Box 191)
Santa Rosa, 95401
(707) 544-2961
T/A 10 C

Hultgren & Samperton
2201 Westside Road
Healdsburg, 95448
(707) 433-5102
T/A 10 N

Iron Horse Vineyards
9786 Ross Station Road
Sebastopol, 95472
(707) 887-1909
T/A 9 S

Italian Swiss Colony
P.O. Box 1
Asti, 95413
(707) 894-2541
(many alternate labels bottled)
T*/P 4 N

Jade Mountain Winery
1335 Hiatt Road
Cloverdale, 95425
(707) 894-5579
T/A 10 N

Johnson's Alexander
  Valley Wines
8333 Highway 128
Healdsburg, 95448
(707) 433-2319
T/P 10 N

Jordan Vineyard & Winery
1474 Alexander Valley Road
  (Box 878)
Healdsburg, 95448
(707) 433-6955
T/A 7 N

Kenwood Vineyards
9592 Sonoma Highway (Box 447)
Kenwood, 95452
(707) 833-5891
T* 7 S

Kistler Vineyards
997 Madrone Road
Glen Ellen, 95442
(707) 833-4662
T/A 10 S

F. Korbel & Brothers
13250 River Road
Guerneville, 95446
(707) 887-2294
T*/P 4 C

La Crema Vinera
1314 D Ross Street (Box 976)
Petaluma, 94953
(707) 762-0393
(Petaluma Vineyards)
T/A 10 S

Lambert Bridge
4085 West Dry Creek Road
Healdsburg, 95448
(707) 433-5855
T/A 9 N

Landmark Vineyards
9150 Los Amigos Road
Windsor, 95492
(707) 838-9466
T*/P 8 C

Laurel Glen Vineyard
6611 Sonoma Mountain Road
Santa Rosa, 95404
(707) 546-2875
NT 10 C

Lyeth Winery
P.O. Box 558
Geyserville, 95441
(707) 857-3761
T/A   10   **N**

Lytton Springs Winery, Inc.
650 Lytton Springs Road
Healdsburg, 95448
(707) 433-7721
(Brenner Cellars)
T/A   9   **N**

Mark West Vineyards
7000 Trenton-Healdsburg Road
Forestville, 95436
(707) 544-4813
(Russian River Valley Vineyards)
T   9   **C**

Martini & Prati Wines, Inc.
2191 Laguna Road
Santa Rosa, 95401
(707) 823-2404
(Fountain Grove, M & R)
T   5   **C**

Matanzas Creek Winery
6097 Bennett Valley Road
Santa Rosa, 95404
(707) 542-8242
T/A   10   **C**

Mill Creek Vineyards
1401 Westside Road (Box 331-E)
Healdsburg, 95448
(707) 433-5098
(Felta Springs, Claus Vineyards)
T   8   **N**

Mountain House Winery
(see listing in Mendocino
    County)

Nervo Winery   (Box 25)
19550 Geyserville Avenue (101)
Geyserville, 95441
(707) 857-3417
(owned by Geyser Peak)
T/P   9   **N**

North Coast Cellars
(see Souverain Cellars)

Pastori Winery
23189 Geyserville Avenue
Cloverdale, 95425
(707) 857-3418
T   8   **N**

Pat Paulsen Vineyards
25510 River Road
Cloverdale, 95425
(707) 894-3197
T/A   9   **N**

Pedroncelli Winery
1220 Canyon Road
Geyserville, 95441
(707) 857-3619
T*   6   **N**

Piper Sonoma
11455 Old Sonoma Road
Healdsburg, 95448
(707) 433-3090
T   7/8   **C**

Pommeraie Vineyards
10541 Cherry Ridge Road
Sebastopol, 95472
(707) 823-9463
NT 10 S

Preston Vineyards
9282 West Dry Creek Road
Healdsburg, 95448
(707) 433-4748/433-3977
T/A 10 N

A. Rafanelli Winery
4685 West Dry Creek Road
Healdsburg, 95448
(707) 433-1385
T/A 10 N

Ravenswood Winery
5700 Gravenstein Highway
Forestville, 96436
(707) 996-4226
T/A 10 S

Richardson Vineyards
2711 Knob Hill Road
Sonoma, 94576
T/A 10 S

River Road Vineyards
7145 River Road
Forestville, 95436
(707) 887-7890
T/A 10 C

River Oaks Vineyards
(see Clos du Bois)

Russian River Vineyards
(see Topolos)

Saint Francis Winery
8450 Sonoma Highway
Kenwood, 95452
(707) 833-4666
T/A 8 S

Sausal Winery
7370 Highway 128
Healdsburg, 95448
(707) 433-2285/433-2893
T/A 7 N

Sea Ridge Vineyards & Winery
Box 433
Cazadero, 95421
(707) 874-3234/847-3469
T/A 10 C

Sebastiani Vineyards
389 Fourth Street, East
Sonoma, 95476
(707) 938-5532
T 5 S

Seghesio Winery, Inc.
24035 Chianti Road
(Box 24035)
Cloverdale, 95425
(707) 857-3581
NT 7/6 N

Seghesio Winery, Inc.
14730 Grove Street
Healdsburg, 95448
(707) 433-3579
NT 6/5 N

Thomas Sellards Winery
6400 Sequoia Circle
Sebastopol, 95472
(707) 823-4107
T/A 10 S

Shilo Vineyards & Company
(Domaine Laurier)
8075 Martinelli Road (Box 836)
Forestville, 95436
(707) 963-9004

| T/A | 10 | C |

Simi Winery
16275 Healdsburg Avenue
(Box 946)
Healdsburg, 95448
(707) 433-6981

| T | 6 | N |

Soda Rock Winery
8015 Highway 128
Healdsburg, 95448
(707) 433-1830

| T/P | 7 | N |

Sonoma County Cellars
Box 925
Healdsburg, 95448
(707) 433-4366

| T/A | 7 | N |

Sonoma County
  Cooperative Winery
Box 36
Windsor, 95492
(707) 838-6649
(mainly for E & J Gallo storage)

| NT | 6 | C |

Sonoma-Cutrer Vineyards
4401 Slusser Road
Windsor, 95492
(707) 528-1177

| T/A | 10 | C |

Sonoma Vineyards
(Rodney Strong Winery)
11455 Old Redwood
  Highway (101)
Windsor, 95492
(707) 433-6511
(Windsor Vineyards,
  Tiburon Vineyards)

| T | 5 | C |

Sotoyome Winery
641 Limerick Lane
Healdsburg, 95448
(707) 433-2001

| T/A | 9 | N |

Souverain Cellars
400 Souverain Road (Box 528)
Geyserville, 95441
(707) 433-6918

| T | 5 | N |

(North Coast Cellars is second
label; plus various other jobbed-
out brands for negociants or
other wineries).

Robert Stemmler Winery
3805 Lambert Bridge Road
Healdsburg, 95448
(707) 433-6334

| T/A | 10 | N |

Rodney Strong Winery
(new name for Sonoma
  Vineyards)

Joseph Swan Vineyards
2916 Laguna Road
Forestville, 95436
(707) 546-7711
(Trenton Cellars)

| NT | 10 | C |

Topolos at Russian River
5700 Gravenstein Highway
(Box 358)
Forestville, 95436
(707) 887-2956
T* 10 C

Toyon Winery & Vineyards
427 Allan Court
Healdsburg, 95448
(707) 433-6847
(Herrera, Bodega)
T/A 10 N

Trentadue Winery
19170 Redwood Highway (101)
Geyserville, 95441
(707) 433-3104
T 8 N

Valley of the Moon Winery
777 Madrone Road
Glen Ellen, 95442
(707) 996-6941
T 7 S

View's Land Company
18901 Gehricke Road
Sonoma, 95476
(707) 938-3768
T/A 10 S

Vina Vista Vineyard
24401 Old Redwood Highway
(Box 47)
Geyserville, 95411
(707) 857-3722
T/A 10 N

Vineburg Wine Company
(see Gundlach-Bundschu)

William Wheeler Winery
(see Healdsburg Wine Co.)

White Oak Vineyards
208 Haydon Street
Healdsburg, 95448
(707) 433-8429
(Fitch Mountain Cellars)
T/A 10 N

Willowside Vineyards
3349 Industrial Drive
Santa Rosa, 95401
(707) 528-1599/544-7504
T/A 10 S

Stephen Zellerback Vineyards
14350 Chalk Hill Road
Healdsburg, 95448
(707) 433-6142
T/A 10 N

MENDOCINO
AND
LAKE COUNTIES

IF ANY COUNTIES OF THE NORTHERN COASTAL COUNTIES REGION
are at all vinously underdeveloped and waiting, these two fit
the bill. Perhaps the reason for this is their distance from San
Francisco and the attendant tourist traffic that would help to
support the wine industry. But things are changing.

Together, Lake and Mendocino counties account for about 18
percent of the region's grape acreage and almost 10 percent of
the wineries. Cabernet-Sauvignon accounts for nearly half of
Lake's varieties, and winemakers in both areas have used this
cultivar to make lighter bodied interpretations for easy and current drinking.

Lake County growers have, for a while, felt that many varieties
grown around the towns of Kelseyville and Lower Lake yield
the most interesting fruit in the county. Perhaps that is why the
county's largest grower, Turner Winery, has about 600 acres just
north of Kelseyville, also the site of another large plot, the 120
acres of Cabernet-Sauvignon, White Riesling, and Zinfandel of
Myron Holdenreid. Napa Gamay and Sauvignon blanc are also
relatively well-represented with a few hundred acres each, and
Chenin blanc accounts for a little over 100 acres. The two dozen

member cooperative known as the Lake County Vintners bottles much of the county's wine under its Konocti label. The cool nights and hot days make the vineyards of Lake County's southern and central sections especially appealing to grape growers, and there seems to be much more land available for such purposes.

Carignane is the most widely planted variety in Mendocino County, accounting for almost 2,000 acres, or 20 percent of the county's total acreage. It is used largely for blending into generic wines but a few wineries bottle it as a light- to medium-bodied varietal. French Colombard and Zinfandel add about 1,000 acres each to the total, while Chardonnay and Cabernet are each just under that mark. John Parducci is a pioneer in identifying specific microclimates within the county, especially those best for growing the Cabernet grapes. After he began listing the names of these spots on his labels and spreading the idea, other wineries in and outside of the county saw the wisdom—and market value—of this and did the same.

Both counties' winegrowers seem to be the least urbanized of the North Coast. Here even the growers you see at press tastings have the weather-worn look of farmers and ranchers. Perhaps it is their low profile that has kept these men and women relatively free of winegrowing neighbors. In any case, contrary to what their appearance might suggest, the growers follow the most modern winemaking and grape growing practices.

In Mendocino, along Highway 101—the Redwood Highway—there are several distinct viticultural areas. One of these, the McDowell Valley near Hopland, has already been officially defined. Good, dry Chenin blanc and Cabernet-Sauvignon wines have been produced from grapes grown there. The most northerly of these sub-regions, the Potter Valley, looks like White Riesling country, judging from early returns.

To the west, beginning at Navarro near the Pacific and following the river of the same name southeasterly to Boonville, lies the Anderson Valley, home of some excellent Chardonnays and Gewürztraminers. But good Cabernets and White Rieslings have been produced in this area as well.

The most recently established viticultural area is the Guenoc

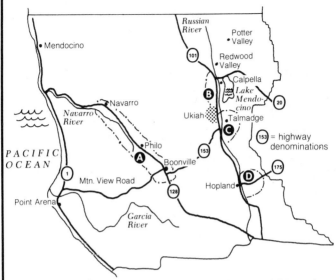

Mendocino County Viticultural Areas

153 = highway denominations

PACIFIC OCEAN

In addition, the areas around the towns of Potter Valley and Redwood Valley are considered distinct viticultural areas.

The county, one of California's largest wine-producing political divisions, is planted to about 10,600 acres of grapes out of a total land mass of 2,247,040 acres.

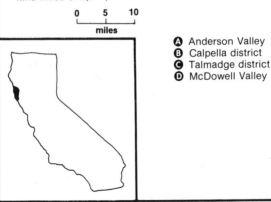

0   5   10
miles

A Anderson Valley
B Calpella district
C Talmadge district
D McDowell Valley

Lake County Viticultural Areas

NATIONAL FOREST

Clear Lake

Lakeport

Kelseyville

Mt. Konocti

Lower Lake

(175) = highway denominations

Middletown

E

In addition, the areas around the towns of Kelseyville and Lower Lake are considered distinct viticultural areas.

The county has about 2,900 acres of land devoted to grape growing out of a total land mass of 807,040 acres.

0   6
miles

E Guenoc Valley

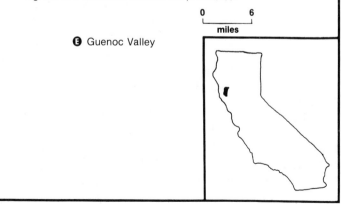

Valley, once home to Lily Langtry and now the site of about 250 acres of grapes. It lies right on the southern border with Napa County, just southeast of Middletown. Bordeaux-like Cabernets are one of the promises of the area's only winery, Chateau Magoon-Lambert.

Those with further interest should contact The Mendocino County Vintners' Association, c/o Jim Milone, Milano Winery, 14594 South Highway 101, Hopland, 95449, or the Lake Wine Producers, c/o Carol Carter, P.O. Box 925, Kelseyville, 95441.

MENDOCINO COUNTY

Braren & Pauli Winery
12507 Hawn Creek Road
Potter Valley, 95469
(707) 743-1173
(B & P)
T/A   10

Cresta Blanca Winery
2399 North State (Box 455)
Ukiah, 95482
(707) 462-2987
T   5/2
(part of Guild Wineries
 and Distilleries)

Dach Vineyards
9200 Highway 128 (P.O. Box 86)
Philo, 95466
(707) 895-3245/895-3173
T/A   10

Dolan Vineyards
1482 Inez Way
Redwood Valley, 95470
(707) 485-7250
T/A   10

Edmeades, Inc.
5500 Highway 128
Philo, 95466
(707) 895-3232
T*   9

Fetzer Vineyards
1150 Bel Arbres Road (Box 227)
Redwood Valley, 95470
(707) 485-8802/485-7634
(Bel Arbres)
T/A   5

Fetzer Vineyards (tasting room)
13500 South Redwood Highway
Hopland, 95449
(707) 744-1737

Frey Vineyards
14000 Tomki Road
Redwood Valley, 95470
(707) 485-5177
T/A   10

Greenwood Ridge Vineyards
1090 Star Route
Philo, 95466
(707) 877-3262
T/A   10

Hidden Cellars
Box 1
Talmadge, 95481
(707) 462-0301
T/A   10

Husch Vineyards
4900 Star Route
Philo, 95466
(707) 895-3216
T/P   10

Lazy Creek Vineyard
4610 Highway 128 (Box 176)
Philo, 95466
(707) 895-3623
T/A   10

McDowell Cellars, Inc.
3811 Highway 175
Hopland, 95449
(707) 744-1774
(McDowell Valley Vineyards)
T/A   9

Milano Winery
14594 South Highway 101
Hopland, 95449
(707) 744-1396
T*   10

Mountain House Winery
38999 Highway 128
Cloverdale, 95425
(707) 894-3074
(winery has a Sonoma County
mailing address but is actually
located two miles north of
Mendocino County line)
T/A   10

Navarro Vineyards
5601 Highway 128
  (P.O. Box 47)
Philo, 95466
(707) 895-3686
(Indian Creek)
T/A/P   10

Parducci Winery, Ltd.
501 Parducci Road
Ukiah, 95482
(707) 462-3828
T*/P   5

Parson's Creek Winery
3001 South State Street, #4
Ukiah, 95482
(707) 462-8900
T/A   10

Scharffenberger Cellars
3001 South State Street, #23
Ukiah, 94582
(707) 462-8996
T/A   9

Tyland Vineyards
2200 McNab Ranch Road
Ukiah, 95482
(Tjsseling)
(707) 462-1810
T/A   8

Villa Baccala
10400 S. Highway 101 (winery)
185 E. Church (office)
Ukiah, 95482
(707) 468-8936 (office)
(Graziano)
T   9

Weibel Champagne Vineyards
7051 North State
Redwood Valley, 95470
(707) 485-0321
(Redwood Valley Cellars)
T*/P   **6/5**

Whaler Vineyard
6200 Eastside Road
Ukiah, 95482
(707) 462-6355
T/A   **10**

LAKE COUNTY

Chateau du Lac
700 Mathews Road
Lakeport, 95453
(707) 263-9333
T/A   **10**

Guenoc Vineyards
Butts Canyon Road
Middletown, 95461
(707) 987-2385
(Chateau Magoon-Lambert)
T/A

Konocti Winery (Lake County
    Vintners cooperative)
4350 Thomas Drive (Box 925)
Kelseyville, 95451
(707) 279-8861/9475
T*/P   **7**

Lower Lake Winery
Highway 29 (P.O. Box 950)
Lower Lake, 95457
(707) 994-4069
T/A   **10**

Quercus Vineyards
4150 Soda Bay Road
Kelseyville, 95451
(707) 279-4317
(private label of Quercus Ranch)
T/A

Variety (in acres)	Lake	Marin	Mendocino	Napa	Solano	Sonoma	Total North Coast	% of state
Cabernet-Sauvignon	1,103	12	928	5,463	234	4,551	12,291	54.6
Carignane	1	-	1,865	165	33	994	3,058	14.3
Chardonnay	123	-	986	4,827	11	5,220	11,167	56.5
Chenin blanc	159	-	552	2,295	198	1,017	4,221	11.2
French Colombard	5	-	1,156	408	81	1,293	2,943	5.2
Gamay Beaujolais	13	-	688	431	14	505	1,651	44.0
Gewürztraminer	17	-	270	526	4	1,275	2,092	44.4
Gray Riesling	6	-	197	306	46	98	653	26.9
Merlot	67	-	62	733	-	566	1,428	63.1
Napa Gamay	295	-	108	1,025	210	407	2,045	46.7
Petite Sirah	50	-	529	836	148	811	2,374	27.9
Pinot blanc	5	-	32	221	-	175	433	21.9
Pinot noir	7	-	322	2,289	22	2,719	5,359	59.6
Sauvignon blanc	478	-	509	2,150	26	1,300	4,463	46.7
Sémillon	6	-	23	196	-	199	424	14.6
White Riesling	150	-	382	1,430	7	1,534	3,503	31.5
Zinfandel	321	-	1,341	2,135	26	4,682	8,505	30.0
Other wine varieties	77	-	653	1,535	152	1,384	3,801	-
TOTALS	2,883	12	10,603	26,971	1,212	28,730	70,411	20.6*

*Percent of wine varieties in state

The
Central
Coastal Counties

GROWTH IN THIS SPRAWLING NINE-COUNTY REGION HAS BEEN ENORmous. Its rate of grape planting has more than doubled that of Napa and others. In 1965, when urban development around the Bay Area was threatening vineyard areas, and some University of California professors saw the possibilities of "going south" with plantings, the total acreage was less than 10,000. Today the region boasts over 50,000 acres of wine grapes, more than half of which is devoted to the six noble varieties: Cabernet-Sauvignon, Pinot noir, Zinfandel, Chardonnay, Sauvignon blanc, and White Riesling. Monterey County alone has 60 percent of the region's total.

In the late 1950s and early 1960s, many winegrowers—both those with establishments in the Bay area and those who were thinking of setting up wineries—realized that the population trends would obviate further plantings in the area. Neither did the North Coast counties offer much in the way of grape development. The only solution for those who did not want to make jug wines in the Central Valley was to explore the land to the south. Viticulturists, using the Amerine-Winkler degree-day sys-

Central Coastal Counties

County	# of wineries (mid-1982)	Planted acreage	% of total	Leading variety
❶ Contra Costa	3	867	1.6	Zinfandel
❷ Alameda	18	1,724	3.7	Gray Riesling
❸ San Mateo	8	9	neg.	Cabernet-Sauvignon/ Chardonnay
❹ Santa Clara	40	1,586	2.9	Cabernet-Sauvignon
❺ Santa Cruz	19	92	0.1	Pinot noir
❻ Monterey	11	31,953[1]	57.6	Cabernet-Sauvignon[2]
❼ San Benito	8	4,474	8.1	Chardonnay
❽ San Luis Obispo	17	4,882	8.8	Zinfandel
❾ Santa Barbara	15	9,850	17.8	White Riesling/ Chardonnay
TOTALS	139	55,437[3]	100.0	Chardonnay

[1] this figure is at variance—to the tune of about 2,000 acres—with the one provided by the Monterey County Crop Service. For the sake of consistency I have used the California Crop and Livestock Reporting Service's figure.

[2] Cabernet-Sauvignon and other red varieties are being T-budded in large quantities with the result that Chardonnay and White Riesling will soon overtake it in dominance.

[3] equals 7.9% of the state's planted acreage and 16.2% of the wine grape acreage.

99.9% of these are wine grapes.

tem, and soil experts forecasted that a great many varieties could be planted south of the Bay, especially in the rich valley in Monterey. Thousands of acres were planted in what many would later call haphazard fashion. Today, while Cabernet and other reds account for half the acreage, it is becoming clear that much of the Central Coast is white wine territory. With that in mind, many winegrowers are converting their Cabernet *et al.* – by means of T-budding or the like – into Chardonnay, White Riesling, and other white-bearing plants. The fact that the current generation of winegrowers prefers to drink white wine may also have something to do with the conversions.

While many locals are loath to admit it, wines from this part of California seem to taste "vegetal," no matter the grape variety used. Some varieties, such as Cabernet and Sauvignon blanc, do indeed contain a distinctive acid component which researchers have discovered is responsible for the flavor of green bell peppers. But other varieties do not contain the acid, and still taste like perfect matches for salads.

Some have concluded that this flavor results from the youth of the vines, many of which are less than a decade old. Others say that the flavor of plants such as lettuce and other greens that previously existed in the area and are still widely dispersed have steeped the soil. Still others maintain that because many of the area's vines are on their own rootstocks and have not been grafted onto root systems invulnerable to *phylloxera vastatrix,* their wines resemble those of the pre-*phylloxera* period of Europe. These wines were said to be more vegetal than their present-day counterparts.

In any event, many winegrowers have modified this vegetal character so that it does not dominate in the blend. Other winegrowers, who either have not succeeded in toning down the flavor or who desire not to do so, continue to produce wines with this character. Judging from general sales figures, it does not matter much – at least to the average consumer who seems to be developing a taste for these wines.

The most recent development in this region has occurred in the two southernmost counties, San Luis Obispo and Santa Barbara. Wines from these areas, especially those from the Edna,

Central Coastal Counties

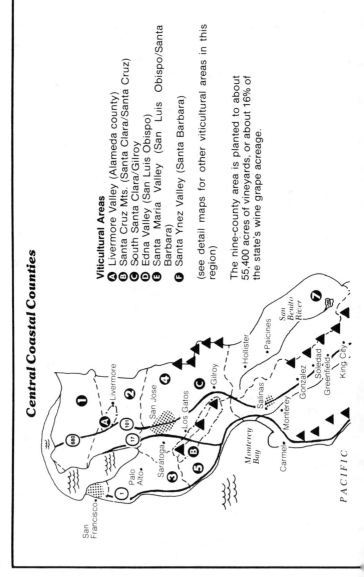

Viticultural Areas

A Livermore Valley (Alameda county)
B Santa Cruz Mts. (Santa Clara/Santa Cruz)
C South Santa Clara/Gilroy
D Edna Valley (San Luis Obispo)
E Santa Maria Valley (San Luis Obispo/Santa Barbara)
F Santa Ynez Valley (Santa Barbara)

(see detail maps for other viticultural areas in this region)

The nine-county area is planted to about 55,400 acres of vineyards, or about 16% of the state's wine grape acreage.

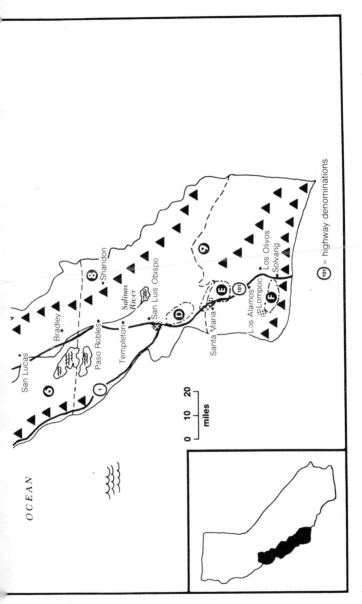

OCEAN

San Lucas

Bradley

Paso Robles

Templeton

Salinas River

San Luis Obispo

Shandon

Santa Maria

Los Alamos

Lompoc

Los Olivos

Solvang

⑥

①

⑧

⑦

Ⓓ

Ⓔ

⑩①

Ⓕ

0   10   20
miles

⑩ = highway denominations

Santa Maria, and Santa Ynez valleys, have been exceptional. Still, there are too few returns in at this time to make conclusive statements about this or any new winegrowing region.

Further information can be obtained by writing the California Central Coast Wine Growers Association, 1000 E. Betteravia Road, Santa Maria, California 93454; phone (805) 922-8394.

A L A M E D A C O U N T Y

Brookside Winery
6839 Foothill Boul
Oakland, 94612
(415) 568-9223
(tasting/retail outlet only)

R. Carey Winery
1695 Martinez Street
San Leandro, 94577
(415) 352-5425
(Torosa Vineyards)
T* 10
(tastings available also at Pier 39 in San Francisco)

Channing Rudd Cellars
2157 Clinton Avenue
Alameda, 94501
(415) 523-1544
T/A 10

Concannon Vineyard
4590 Tesla Road
Livermore, 94550
(415) 447-3760
T 7

Fenestra
83 East Vallecitos Road
Livermore, 94550
(408) 258-1092
T/A 10

Fretter Wine Cellars, Inc.
805 Camelia Street
Berkeley, 94710
(415) 525-1762
T/A 10

Livermore Valley Cellars
1508 Wetmore Road
Livermore, 94550
(415) 447-1751
T/A/P 10

Llords & Elwood Winery
P.O. Box 3397
Fremont, 94539
(408) 286-3124
T/A 9/7

R. Montali Winery
4th and Allston
Berkeley, 94710
(415) 834-9531
T 9
(Sonoma Mission, Lombard Hill, Jonathan)

Montclair Winery
180 Maxwelton Road
Piedmont, 94618
(415) 658-1014
T/A   **10**

Oak Barrel Winery
1201 University Avenue
Berkeley, 94702
(415) 849-0400
T   **9**

Piedmont Cellars
429 Linda Avenue
Piedmont, 94611
(415) 654-3617
T/A   **10**

Rosenblum Cellars
1775 16th Street
Oakland, 94612
(415) 834-6067
T/A   **10**

Schenley Distillers, Inc.
5050 Arroyo Road
Livermore, 94550
(415) 447-3023
NT   **10/5**

Stony Ridge Winery
1188 Vineyard Avenue
Pleasanton, 94566
(415) 846-2133
T/A   **8**

Villa Armando Winery
553 St. John Street
Pleasanton, 94566
(415) 846-5488
T/A   **5**

Weibel Champagne Vineyards
1250 Sanford Avenue
Mission San Jose, 94539
(415) 656-2340
(see also Mendocino County
   listing)
T/P   **5/5**

Wente Brothers
5565 Tesla Road
Livermore, 94550
(415) 447-3603
T   **5**

Wine and the People, Inc.
   (Berkeley Wine Company)
907 University Avenue
Berkeley, 94710
(415) 549-1266
T   **10**

CONTRA COSTA COUNTY

J. E. Digardi Winery
3785 Pacheco Boulevard
Martinez, 94553
(415) 228-2638
T*   **8**

Conrad Viano Winery
150 Morello Avenue
Martinez, 94553
(415) 228-6465
T   **10**

J. W. Morris Wineries
4060 Pike Lane
Concord, 94520
(415) 680-1122
T/A   **9**

SAN MATEO COUNTY

Brookside Winery
1645 El Camino Real
Belmont, 94002
(415) 592-9894
(tasting/retail outlet only)

Cronin Vineyards
11 Old Honda Road
Woodside, 94062
(415) 851-1452
T/A   10

Eagle Vineyards
3147 Sunset Terrace
San Mateo, 94403
(415) 345-9033
T/A   10

J. H. Gentili Wines
60 Lowell Street
Redwood City, 94062
(415) 368-4740
NT   10

Thomas Fogarty Winery
5937 Alpine Road
Portola Valley, 94025
(415) 851-1946
T/A   10

E. Martinoni Company
543 Forbes Boulevard
South San Francisco, 94080
(415) 873-3000
T/A   10

Obester Winery
12341 San Mateo Road (#92)
Half Moon Bay, 94019
(415) 726-WINE
T/A   10

Sherrill Cellars
1185 Skyline Boulevard
Palo Alto, 94062
(415) 941-6023
(Village Hill, Skyline)
T/A   10

Woodside Vineyards (La Questa)
340 Kings Mountain Road
Woodside, 94062
(415) 851-7475
T/A   10

SANTA CLARA AND SANTA CRUZ COUNTIES

POPULATION GROWTH IN THE BAY AREA HAS FORCED MANY WINE-growers farther and farther south as well as into the mountains separating these two counties. These Santa Cruz mountains, in fact, were granted official viticultural area status as of late 1981.

Although these Silicon Valley counties have only 3 percent of the Central Coast's acreage, nearly half the region's wineries are located here. Most of the wineries are in the southern Santa Clara Valley area, between Los Gatos and Gilroy, which many consider a distinct winegrowing area. This valley's wineries, for one reason or another and with a few exceptions such as Alma-dén, Mirassou, Paul Masson and San Martín, display a relatively low profile in comparison to those in other growing areas. But some of their Cabernets, Zinfandels, and Petite Sirahs – grapes which account for a healthy percentage of the valley's total – have been widely acclaimed.

Still, much of the drama, along with many finer wines, comes from the mountain wineries. Some outstanding Chardonnays and Cabernets have been produced by tiny estates, and even Pinot noir grapes, long the prodigal son of California cultivars, have yielded exceedingly fine wines in the last decade. Perhaps it is because of the tiny yields common to mountain vineyards that *113* concentrate character and interest; or perhaps it is the maverick mentality of the winemakers themselves – or maybe it is a combination of the two. But many foresee the super-premium wines of the future coming from the Santa Cruz and Gabilan (in Monterey County) ranges.

The climate of these two counties is diverse. The Santa Clara Valley can get extremely warm in the summer while certain sections of western Santa Cruz County are among the coldest wine-growing regions in the state, according to the Amerine-Winkler degree-day system.

The wineries and/or grape growers of the region include the Santa Clara Valley Winegrowers Association, P.O. Box 1192, Morgan Hill, 95037, and the Santa Cruz Mountain Vintners, c/o Ahlgren Vineyards, P.O. Box 931, Boulder Creek, 95006.

SANTA CLARA COUNTY

Almaden Vineyards
1530 Blossom Hill Road
San Jose, 95118
(408) 269-1312
(Charles Lefranc, Le Domaine)
T*   3/3

B & R Vineyards, Inc.
4350 North Monterey Highway
Gilroy, 95020
(408) 842-5649
(Rapazzini, Los Altos, San Juan)
T   8

Bertero Winery
3920 Hecker Pass Highway
Gilroy, 95020
(408) 842-3032
(Italian California
    Wine Company)
T   7

Brookside Winery
200 El Camino Real
Mountain View, 94940
(415) 967-9865
(tasting/retail outlet only)

Cloudstone Vineyards
27345 Deer Springs Way
Los Altos Hills, 94022
(415) 948-8621
T/A/*

Congress Springs Vineyards
23600 Congress Springs Road
Saratoga, 95070
(408) 867-1409
T/A   10

Conrotto Winery
1690 Hecker Pass Highway
Gilroy, 95020
(408) 842-3053
T/A   7

De Santis Vineyard
2825 Day Road
Gilroy, 95020
(408) 847-2060
T/A   10

Fortino Winery
4525 Hecker Pass Highway
Gilroy, 95020
(408) 842-3305
T*/P   7

Gemello Winery Corp.
  (Mountain View)
2003 El Camino Real
Mountainview, 94040
(415) 948-7723
T*   8

Peter & Harry Giretti
791 5th Street
Gilroy, 95020
(408) 842-3857
T/A   10

A. Giurlani & Brothers, Inc.
1266 Kifer Road
Sunnyvale, 94086
(408) 738-0220
(Star)
T/A   10

Emilio Guglielmo Winery
1480 East Main Avenue
Gilroy, 95037
(408) 779-2145
(Emile's Cavalcade,
  Mount Madonna)
T/A   7

Hecker Pass Winery
4605 Hecker Pass Highway
Gilroy, 95020
(408) 842-8755
T   9

Kathryn Kennedy
13180 Pierce Road
Saratoga, 95070
(408) 867-4170
T/A   10

Kirigin Cellars
11550 Watsonville Road
Gilroy, 95020
(408) 847-8827
(Uvas)
T*/P   7

Thomas Kruse Winery
4390 Hecker Pass Road
Gilroy, 95020
(408) 842-7016
T*/P   10

Ronald T. Lamb Winery
17785 Casa Lane
Morgan Hill, 95037
(408) 779-4268
T/A   10

Live Oaks Winery
3875 Hecker Pass Highway
Gilroy, 95020
(408) 842-2401
T   7

Llords & Elwood Winery
12 North 25th Street
San Jose, 95113
(408) 286-3124
(see also Alameda County listing)
T/A 7

Paul Masson Vineyards
"The Mountain Winery"
Saratoga, 95070
T/A 8

Paul Masson Vineyards
13150 Saratoga Avenue
Saratoga, 95070
(408) 257-7800
T 4

Mirassou Vineyards
3000 Aborn Road
San Jose, 95121
(408) 274-3000
T 5

The Mountainview Winery
2406 Thaddeus Drive
Mountainview, 94040
(408) 964-5398
T/A 10

Mount Eden Vineyards (MEV)
22020 Mount Eden Road
Saratoga, 95070
(408) 867-5783
T/A 10

Novitiate Wines
College Avenue (P.O. Box 128)
Los Gatos, 95030
(408) 354-6471
T 6

Page Mill Winery
13686 Page Mill Road
Los Altos Hills, 94022
(415) 948-0958
T/A 10

Pedrizzetti Winery
1645 San Pedro Avenue
Morgan Hill, 95037
(408) 779-7380
T* 7

Pendleton Winery
2156 O'Toole
San Jose, 95131
(408) 946-1303
(Arroyo)
T/A 10

La Purissima Winery
970 B O'Brien Drive
Menlo Park, 94025
(408) 738-1011
T* 10

Rapazzini Winery
(see B & R Vineyards)

Martin Ray Vineyards, Inc.
(La Montana)
22000 Mount Eden Road
Saratoga, 95070
(408) 867-9450/(415) 321-6489
T/A 10

Ridge Vineyards, Inc.
17100 Montebello Road
(Box A-1)
Cupertino, 95014
(408) 867-3233
T/A 7

San Martin Winery
12900 Monterey Road
(P.O. Box 53)
San Martin, 95046
(408) 683-2672/683-4000
T*   5

Sarah's Vineyard
4005 Hecker Pass Highway
Gilroy, 95020
(408) 842-4278
T/A   10

Silver Mountain Vineyards
P.O. Box 1695
Los Gatos, 95030
(408) 353-2278
T/A   10

Sommelier Winery
2560 Wyandotte Street, "C"
Mountainview, 94043
(415) 969-2442
T/A   10

Sonoma Vineyards
19664 Stevens Creek Boulevard
Cupertino, 95014
(Tasting Room only)

Summer Hill Vineyards
3920 Hecker Pass Highway
Gilroy, 95020
(408) 842-3032
T/A/P   7

Sycamore Creek Vineyards
12775 Uvas Road
Morgan Hill, 95037
(408) 779-4738
T/A   10

Turgeon-Lohr Winery
1000 Lenzen Avenue
San Jose, 95126
(408) 288-5057
(J. Lohr)
T*   6

Villa Paradiso
1840 West Edmundson
Morgan Park, 95037
(408) 778-1555
T/P   10

Walker Wines
25935 Estacada Drive
Los Altos Hills, 94022
(415) 948-6368
T/A   10

SANTA CRUZ COUNTY

Ahlgren Vineyard
20320 Highway 9
Boulder Creek, 95006
(408) 338-6071
T/A   10

Bargetto's Winery
  (Santa Cruz Cellars)
3535 North Main Street
Soquel, 95073
(408) 475-2258
T   7

Bonny Doon Vineyard
6617 Bonny Doon Road
Santa Cruz, 95060
(408) 423-8789
T/A   10

David Bruce Winery, Inc.
21439 Bear Creek Road
Los Gatos, 95030
(408) 354-4214
T*   9

Cook-Ellis Winery
2900 Buzzard Lagoon Road
Corralitos, 95076
(408) 688-7208
(Buzzard Lagoon Vineyards)
T/A   10

Crescini Winery
P.O. Box 216
Soquel, 95073
(408) 462-1466
T/A   10

Devlin Wine Cellars
P.O. Box 723
Soquel, 95073
(408) 476-7288
T/A   10

Felton-Empire Vineyards, Inc.
379 Felton Empire Road
Felton, 95018
(408) 335-3939
T*   9

Frick Winery
303 Potrero Street #39
Santa Cruz, 95060
(408) 426-8623
T/A   10

Grover Gulch Winery
7880 Glen Haven Road
Soquel, 95073
(408) 475-0568
T/A   10

McHenry Vineyards
Bonny Doon Road
Santa Cruz, 95060
(408) 426-4665/(916) 756-3202
   (in Davis)
T/A   10

McKenzie Creek Winery
(see Roudon-Smith)

Nicasio Vineyards (Wheeler)
14300 Nicasio Way
Soquel, 95073
(408) 423-1073
T/A   10

Michael T. Parsons Winery
170 Hidden Valley Road
Soquel, 95073
(408) 867-6070
T/A   10

River Run Vintners
65 Rogge Lane
Watsonville, 95076
(408) 722-7520
T/A   10

Roudon-Smith Vineyards
513 Mount View Road
Santa Cruz, 95065
(408) 427-3492
(McKenzie Creek Winery)
T*/A   9

Santa Cruz Mountain Vineyard
2300 Jarvis Road
Santa Cruz, 95065
(408) 426-6209
T*   **10**

Smothers Wines
2317 Vine Hill Road
Santa Cruz, 95060
(408) 438-1260
T/A   **10**
(Moving to Sonoma Co. in 1983)

P and M Staiger
1300 Hopkins Gulch Road
Boulder Creek, 95006
(408) 338-4346
T/A   **10**

Sunrise Winery
16001 Empire Grade Road
Santa Cruz, 95060
(408) 423-8226
T/A   **10**

Vine Hill Wines, Inc.
(see Smothers Wines)

MONTEREY
AND SAN BENITO
COUNTIES

THIS TWO-COUNTY REGION IS THE REVERSE OF SANTA CLARA/SANTA Cruz in one sense: although the region accounts for about 70 percent of the grapes in the Central Coast, only 15 percent of the wineries are located here.

Monterey alone accounts for over 60 percent of the Central Coasts' grape area. White varieties, such as Chardonnay, Chenin blanc, and White Riesling, are well represented with over 3,000 acres each, but such reds as Cabernet, Petite Sirah, and Zinfandel make up nearly half the acreage.

Bounded on the east side by the Gabilan and Mustang ranges and on the west by the Pacific, the county is home to a wide variety of *vinifera*, most of which were planted less than two decades ago. Population growth around San Jose, Livermore, and the south bay in general forced firms like Mirassou and Wente to look for elbow room in Steinbeck country, the Salinas Valley.

This growing area, stretching some sixty miles from the town of Salinas to San Lucas, represents a curious anomaly to most students of geography and climate. For one would expect that as one drives south from the San Francisco Bay, it would become warmer; but it does not, at least not in the northern part of the valley. Like the climate of the Carneros/Huichica sub-region of Napa County, the climate in the northern Salinas Valley is influenced by the cooling winds that come in off Monterey Bay. Hence, cool-climate varieties such as Pinot noir and Chardonnay seem both to ripen well and to produce good wines. As one travels further south and the Bay's winds have less effect, the valley becomes better suited to Cabernet, Zinfandel, and Petite Sirah. At least that is the current wisdom in this very young winegrowing area. With more harvest experience from which to draw, different conclusions may appear.

To the west of the Salinas Valley there is a much smaller sub-region called Carmel Valley. Not a valley in the same sense as the San Joaquin, it is more elevated, more like a rutted plateau at 1,200 to 1,600 feet. So far, some well-balanced Cabernets and Chenin blancs have been produced from Carmel Valley grapes.

For further information about the growers of the county, contact Monterey Winegrowers Council, c/o Marjorie Lumm, 60 George Lane, Sausalito, 94965.

In San Benito county, near Hollister, the earthquake capital of the state, there are several small wineries such as Calera and Enz. They "compete" with the monster *Almaden Vineyards* which owns over 90 percent of the county's 4,600 acres.

Many San Benito wines share the vegetal quality of Monterey wines and for probably the same reasons mentioned in the "Central Coast" section. But, like other distinctive wines, they need getting used to.

Look for greater numbers of wineries to be bonded in this two-county region over the next decade or so. Failing this, Napans and Sonomans, who have been using the area's grapes for their own wines, will have easy pickings in the region.

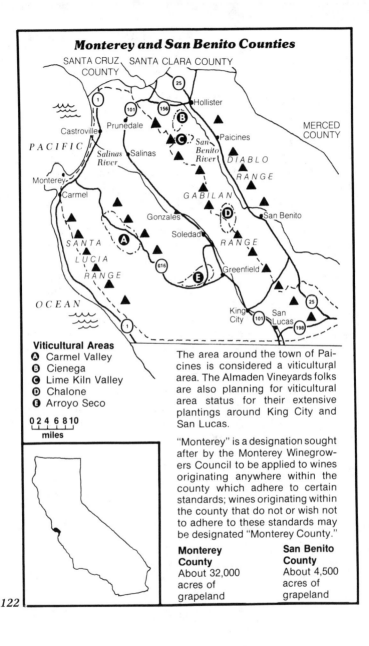

Monterey and San Benito Counties

SANTA CRUZ COUNTY
SANTA CLARA COUNTY
Hollister
MERCED COUNTY
Castroville
Prunedale
PACIFIC
Salinas River
Salinas
Paicines
San Benito River
DIABLO RANGE
Monterey
Carmel
GABILAN
Gonzales
Soledad
RANGE
San Benito
SANTA LUCIA RANGE
OCEAN
Greenfield
King City
San Lucas

Viticultural Areas
Ⓐ Carmel Valley
Ⓑ Cienega
Ⓒ Lime Kiln Valley
Ⓓ Chalone
Ⓔ Arroyo Seco

0 2 4 6 8 10
miles

The area around the town of Paicines is considered a viticultural area. The Almaden Vineyards folks are also planning for viticultural area status for their extensive plantings around King City and San Lucas.

"Monterey" is a designation sought after by the Monterey Winegrowers Council to be applied to wines originating anywhere within the county which adhere to certain standards; wines originating within the county that do not or wish not to adhere to these standards may be designated "Monterey County."

Monterey County
About 32,000 acres of grapeland

San Benito County
About 4,500 acres of grapeland

122

MONTEREY COUNTY

Carmel Bay Winery
P.O. Box 2496
Carmel, 93921
(408) 624-4154
T/A   10

Chalone Vineyard
  (Gavilan/Chaparral)
P.O. Box 855
Soledad, 93960
(415) 441-8975
  (S.F. office number)
T*/A   8

Durney Vineyard
Cachagu Road (P.O. Box 1146)
Carmel Valley, 93924
(408) 659-2690/625-1561
T/A   9

Fairview Farm Vineyard
Route 2, Box 40
Templeton, 93465
(805) 434-1247
T/A   10

Jekel Vineyard
40155 Walnut Avenue
Greenfield, 93927
(408) 674-5522
T   7

Paul Masson Vineyards
1777 Metz Road
Soledad, 93960
(408) 678-3991
T/A   4/3

Monterey Peninsula Winery
2999 Monterey-Salinas Highway
Monterey, 93940
(408) 372-4949
(Monterey Cellars, Big Sur)
T*   8

The Monterey Vineyard
800 South Alta Street
Gonzales, 93926
(Taylor California Cellars)
(408) 675-2481
T*   4

Smith & Hook Winery
37700 Foothill Road (Box 1010)
Gonzales, 93926
(408) 678 2132
T/A   7

Taylor California Cellars
(see The Monterey Vineyard)

Ventana Vineyards Winery, Inc.
Los Coches Road (P.O. Box G)
Soledad, 93960
(408) 678-2306
(Los Coches Cellars)
T/A   9

Zampatti's Cellar
25445 Telarana Way
Carmel, 93923
(408) 624-2491
T/A   10

SAN BENITO COUNTY

Almaden Vineyards
(tasting room)
8090 Pacheco Pass Highway
Hollister, 95023
(408) 637-7554
T   0/3

Almaden Vineyards
9970 Cienega Road
Hollister, 95023
(408) 637-1631
NT   4/3

Almaden Vineyards (Paicines)
385 Panoche Road
Paicines, 95043
(408) 628-3502
NT   4/3

Calera Wine Company
11300 Cienega Road
Hollister, 95023
(408) 637-9170
T/A   9

Casa de Fruta
6680 Pacheco Pass Road
Hollister, 95023
(408) 637-7775
T/P   10

Cygnet Cellars
11736 Cienega Road
Hollister, 95023
(408) 733-4276
T/A   10

Enz Vineyards
1781 Limekiln Road
Hollister, 95023
(408) 637-3956
T/A   10

Ozecki-San Benito
249 Hillcrest
Hollister, 95023
(408) 637-9217
T/A   7
(for tastings, visit their outlet
on Pier 39, San Francisco)

San Benito Vineyards
251 Hillcrest
Hollister, 95023
(408) 637-4447
T/A   10
(for tastings, visit their outlet
on Pier 39, San Francisco)

SAN LUIS OBISPO AND SANTA BARBARA COUNTIES

ALTHOUGH GRAPES HAVE BEEN GROWN IN THESE TWO COUNTIES for over 150 years, it has been only in the last ten that real interest has developed. Yet already some extremely fine wines have come from certain vineyards, both mountain and flatland, just a three or four hour drive from Los Angeles.

Together, San Luis Obispo and Santa Barbara counties account for almost 22 percent of the Central Coast's wine grape acreage. Red varieties account for slightly more than half of the former's acreage while whites dominate in the latter with nearly two-thirds of the total. There are currently about two and a half dozen bonded wineries in the counties, but that figure is sure to grow in the next decade as more and more winegrowers test the area.

In San Luis Obispo, the Bordelais-type grapes—Cabernet-Sauvignon and Sauvignon blanc—are relatively widely planted, along with California's own Claret grape, the Zinfandel. These seem to do best in the northern section of the county in a roughly triangular area bounded by Paso Robles, Templeton, and Shandon. Pinot noir and Chardonnay wines from vineyards in the 1,600-foot-high mountains to the west of the triangle have also proven impressive.

South of the city of San Luis Obispo lies all of Edna Valley and a small portion of the Santa Maria Valley. Burgundian varieties such as Chardonnay and Pinot noir seem well-suited to these areas, as does White Riesling. Growth in this county has been staggering: in but twenty years the number of acres planted to grapes has increased over 1,110 percent.

The climate of Santa Barbara is like that of its immediate northern neighbor in its diversity. In the cooler spots, especially around Lompoc and Los Olivos, Chardonnays and Pinots grow to be extremely varietally true wines in the hands of competent winemakers. Elsewhere, Cabernet and Sauvignon blanc yield good results. Together with White Riesling, these five highly-regarded varieties account for over half of the county's acreage.

Many tons of grapes from both counties were, and still are, shipped to Monterey and even to Napa and Sonoma county winemakers for blending into their own products. At the deflated prices of late, the getting was good. Now, however, more and more local wineries that will utilize their own grapes adorned with San Luis Obispo and Santa Barbara place names are being established.

SANTA BARBARA COUNTY

Alamo Pintado Vineyards
  & Winery (Carey Cellars)
1711 Alamo Pintado Road
Solvang, 93463
(805) 688-8554
T   10

Ballard Canyon Corporation
  Winery
1825 Ballard Canyon Road
Solvang, 93463
(805) 688-7585
T/A   10

Brander Winery
2620 W. Highway 154 (Box 92)
Los Olivos, 93441
(805) 688-2455
T/A   10

Copenhagen Cellars/Vikings 4
448 Alisal Road (Box 558)
Solvang, 93463
(805) 688-4218
T

The Firestone Vineyard
P.O. Box 244
(Zaca Station Road)
Los Olivos, 93441
(805) 688-3940
T   7

Hale Cellars
  (Los Alamos Winery)
P.O. Box 5
Los Alamos, 95476
(805) 344-2390
T*   10

Los Vineros Winery, Inc.
618 Hanson Way (P.O. Box 334)
Santa Maria, 93456
(805) 928-5917
T   10

Rancho Sisquoc Winery
Route 1, Box 147
Santa Maria, 93454
(805) 937-3616
T   10

Ross-Kellerei (Buellton)
900 McMurray Road (Box 1753)
Buellton, 93427
(805) 733-4324
(Jonata, Zaca Creek)
T   10

Sanford & Benedict Vineyards
Santa Rosa Road
Lompoc, 93436
(805) 688-8314
T/A   9

Santa Barbara Winery
  (Solvang Fruit Wines)
202 Anacapa Street
Santa Barbara, 93101
(805) 962-3812
T   9

Santa Ynez Valley Winery
365 North Refugio Road
Santa Ynez, 93460
(805) 688-8381
T/A   9

Vega Vineyards Winery
9496 Santa Rosa Road
Buellton, 93427
(805) 688-2415
T/A/P   10

La Zaca Vineyard Company
P.O. Box 68
Los Olivos, 93441
(805) 688-4632
T/A   10

Zaca Mesa Winery
Foxen Canyon Road
Los Olivos, 93441
(805) 688-3310
T/P   7

SAN LUIS OBISPO COUNTY

California Cellar Masters/
  Coloma Cellars
80 North Ocean Boulevard
Cayucos, 93430
(Tasting Room Only)

Caparone Winery
Route 1 (Box 176 G)
Paso Robles, 93446
(805) 467-3827
T/A 10

Chamisal Vineyards
Orcutt Road (Box 264-N)
San Luis Obispo, 93401
(805) 544-3001
(Corral de Piedra)
T/A 10

Edna Valley Vineyard
Route 3, P.O. Box 255
San Luis Obispo, 93401
(805) 544-9594
T/A 9

El Paso de Robles
  Winery & Vineyards
Willow Creek Road
  (Rt. 1, Box 101)
Paso Robles, 93446
(805) 238-6986
T/A 10

Estrella River Winery
Highway 46 (P.O. Box 96)
Paso Robles, 93446
(805) 238-6300
T/P 7

Hoffman Mountain Ranch
  Vineyards
Adelaide Road, Star Route
Paso Robles, 93446
(805) 238-4945
T/A 10

Las Tablas Winery (Rotta)
P.O. Box 697
Templeton, 93465
(805) 434-1389
T 8

Lawrence Winery
P.O. Box 698 (off Highway 227)
San Luis Obispo, 93406
(805) 544-5828
T 6

Martin & MacFarlane, Inc.
Buena Vista Road
  (off Highway 46)
Paso Robles, 93446
(805) 239-1640/238-2520
T/A 10

Mastantuono
101 3/4 Willow Creek Road
Paso Robles, 93446
(805) 238-1078
T/A 10

Old Casteel Vineyards
Route 1, Vineyard Drive
  (Box 93)
Paso Robles, 93446
(805) 238-7776
T/A 10

Paso Robles Vineyards
Highway 46
Paso Robles, 93446
(805) 238-0751
T/A 10

Pesenti Winery
2900 Vineyard Drive
Templeton, 93465
(805) 434-1030
T   7

Ranchita Oaks Winery, Inc.
Estrella Route
San Miguel, 93451
(213) 993-9695
T/A/P   10

Tobias Vineyards
2001 Kiler Canyon Road
Paso Robles, 93446
(805) 238-6380
T/A   10

Watson Vineyards
Adelaide Road
Paso Robles, 93446
(805) 238-6091
T/A   10

York Mountain Winery
P.O. Box 191, Route 2
Templeton, 93465
(805) 238-3925
T   8

Variety (in acres)	Alameda	Contra Costa	Monterey	San Benito	San Luis Obispo	San Mateo	Santa Barbara	Santa Clara	Santa Cruz	Totals Central Coast	% of state
Cabernet-Sauvignon	39	-	4,212	509	942	4	1,029	203	12	6,950	30.9
Carignane	23	260	-	7	3	-	-	116	-	409	1.9
Chardonnay	115	-	3,491	979	573	4	2,266	96	19	7,543	38.2
Chenin blanc	171	-	3,917	96	567	-	950	47	1	5,749	15.3
French Colombard	40	-	1,174	-	70	-	-	80	-	1,364	2.9
Gamay Beaujolais	36	-	969	416	38	-	355	93	1	1,908	50.8
Gewürztraminer	-	-	996	262	93	-	1,202	10	5	2,568	54.5
Gray Riesling	444	-	678	85	90	-	-	10	-	1,307	53.9
Merlot	2	-	359	-	58	-	184	2	-	605	26.7
Napa Gamay	65	-	885	-	91	-	-	1	-	1,042	23.8
Petite Sirah	91	-	1,577	-	112	-	63	79	-	1,922	22.6
Pinot blanc	44	-	1,106	172	-	-	56	69	1	1,448	73.2
Pinot noir	76	-	1,856	764	96	1	652	84	25	3,554	39.5
Sauvignon blanc	116	-	1,337	15	633	-	313	37	-	2,451	25.6
Sémillon	188	3	624	22	24	-	12	68	-	941	32.5
White Riesling	17	-	3,563	327	187	-	2,458	48	18	6,618	59.5
Zinfandel	35	361	2,343	204	1,018	-	64	137	7	4,169	14.7
Other wine grapes	222	217	2,866	616	286	-	205	405	3	4,820	-
Totals	1,724	841	31,953	4,474	4,881	9	9,809	1,585	92	55,368	16.2*

*(percent of wine varieties)

THE SACRAMENTO VALLEY AND SIERRA FOOT-HILLS COUNTIES

THIS SCATTERED FOURTEEN-COUNTY REGION ACCOUNTS FOR VERY little of the state's wine grape acreage (c. 2 percent) and only three dozen of its wineries. It has also bucked the trend towards white grape planting with reds accounting for seventy percent of the total, making the winemakers of the area seem a little staid. But the action is relatively fast-paced, especially in Sacramento and Amador counties, the first having achieved a seventy-fold increase in grape acreage in the last fifteen years. For purposes of clarification, I will deal with the eight-county region of the Sacramento Valley and the Sierra Foothills counties separately.

The county of Sacramento, with 3,500 acres of grapes, today boasts over 50 percent of the total acreage planted in the Sacramento Valley. Fifteen years ago it had fewer than 500 acres. Since then, varieties such as Cabernet-Sauvignon, Chenin blanc, Napa Gamay, Petite Sirah, Ruby Cabernet, Zinfandel, and even Merlot and White Riesling, have made stunning inroads in a county once famous only for being host to the state capital. Most *131*

Sacramento Valley/Sierra Foothills Region

	County	# of wineries (mid-1982)	Planted acreage	% of total	Leading variety
❶	Shasta	1	24	0.2	Sauvignon blanc
❷	Tehama	—	216	2.2	Chardonnay
❸	Glenn	—	1,572	16.3	Grenache/French Colombard
❹	Butte	—	812	8.4	Cabernet-Sauvignon
❺	Colusa	—	128	1.3	Chenin blanc
❻	Sutter	—	—	—	—
❼	Yuba	1	391	4.0	Cabernet-Sauvignon
❽	Nevada	1	26	0.3	Chardonnay
❾	Placer	1	111	1.1	Zinfandel
❿	Yolo	7	738	7.6	Chenin blanc
⓫	Sacramento	3	3,540	36.7	Chenin blanc/ Cabernet Sauvignon
⓬	El Dorado	8	365	3.8	Zinfandel
⓭	Amador	15	1,611	16.7	Zinfandel
⓮	Calaveras	2	121	1.3	Zinfandel
	TOTALS	39	9,655*	100.0	Zinfandel

*97.6% of which are wine grapes.

of the acreage is planted in the Delta Region, a relatively cool area at the southern tip of the county which extends into Yolo and San Joaquin counties. Most of the grapes are bought and used by out-of-county wineries, as Sacramento itself has only three.

Most of the remaining acreage is in the counties of Butte and Yolo. Butte concentrates on middling varieties such as Napa Gamay, Petite Sirah, French Colombard, and Barbera, and half of Yolo is planted to Chenin blanc. There are also comparatively large amounts of Cabernet and Zinfandel planted in Glenn.

Much of the Sacramento Valley that is suitable for growing grapes has not yet been exploited. Whether the expected return of profits would be worth the investment in setting up more vineyards and wineries will be the determinant in the next decade.

More than three-quarters of the Sierra foothills lie in an eighteen mile long isosceles triangle formed by the towns of Placerville (El Dorado County), Plymouth, and Fiddletown (both Amador County). Of that, the bulk lies in the so-called Shenandoah Valley* on the border between the two counties. Zinfandel is the predominant variety – in fact, almost the sole variety – planted.

This variety has evidently adapted itself quite well to the schizoid environment of the low Sierras. Daytime winds bring wilting heat from the San Joaquin Valley to the south which raise grape sugars to absurd levels. At night, the winds come down from the cold mountains and cool off the area before much raisining sets in. The result is a foothills specialty: late harvest (dry or sweet) Zinfandels with alcohols running past 17 percent and residual sugars often keeping pace. And the 1,000 or so acres of the variety already planted in this triangle are being augmented yearly as hundreds more acres are planned. Ironically, while Amador County grapes first drew attention to these "Amazon Zins", many predict that, in time, El Dorado County fruit will far outshine that of its southern neighbor.

Other varieties have been successful as well, notably Sauvignon blanc, Barbera, and Cabernet-Sauvignon. Monteviña wine-

---

*Not to be confused with the valley of the same name in Virginia, whose growers – like those in Amador – have proposed their area for viticultural area status.

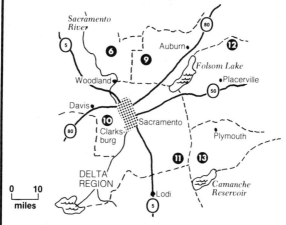

Sacramento County and Environs

The acreage devoted to grapeland in this region is concentrated in the areas depicted in the surrounding maps: Sacramento County, Amador County, and Yolo County.

In terms of huge expanses of vineyard land, the region is small grapes. However, one of the world's most respected wine education and research centers, the University of California at Davis, is right in the middle of this particular region.

The fourteen-county region is planted to about 9,450 acres of grapes, 20% of which are Zinfandels.

(50) = highway denominations

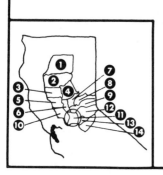

134

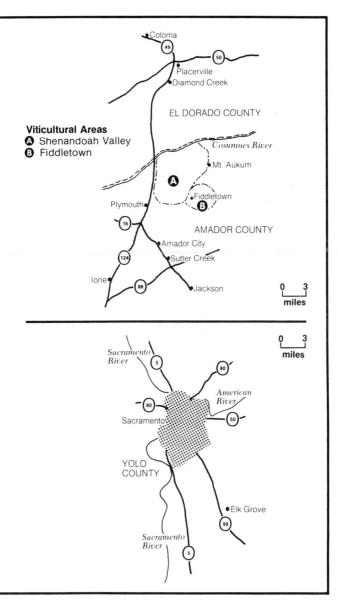

Viticultural Areas
Ⓐ Shenandoah Valley
Ⓑ Fiddletown

maker Cary Gott tried several times to grow one of the only patch of Nebbiolo outside the Central Valley, but as of this writing, he has discontinued using this prime Italian wine variety.

There are a few hundred acres—one-third Zinfandel—and a handful of wineries in Calaveras, Nevada, and Placer counties. Whether or not these counties, like some in the Sacramento Valley area, will see much development is unknown as of this writing.

While you are waiting for things to develop in and around Sacramento, you might want to visit the University of California at Davis campus, a half-hour drive west of the capital. It is from here and from Fresno State that America recruits most of its young winemakers. The campus is expansive and tranquil—no car traffic allowed, only people and bikes—so you just might want to check out the library or the bookstore for reading on California's scientifically vinous past. Sit down with a text and learn about the giants who have helped California and the rest of the world along the grapey path: Amerine, Berg, Bioletti, Cruess, Fessler, Guymon, Joslyn, Kliewer, Kunkee, Nightingale, Olmo, Ough, Roessler, Singleton, Webb, Winkler. . . .

AMADOR COUNTY

Amador City Winery
Highway 49 (P.O. Box 166)
Amador City, 95601
(209) 267-5320
T   **10**

Amador Foothills Winery
Steiner Road
Plymouth, 95669
(209) 245-6307
T/A   **10**

Argonaut Winery
13675 Mt. Echo Road (Box 612)
Ione, 95640
(209) 274-2882/4106
T/A   **10**

Baldinelli Shenandoah Valley
  Vineyards
E 16 (Box 223)
Plymouth, 95669
(209) 245-3398
T/A   **10**

Beau Val Wines, Inc.
Star Route 2 (P.O. Box 8D)
Plymouth, 95669
(209) 245-3281
T/A 10

D'Agostini Winery
Shenandoah Road (Route 2,
  Box 19)
Plymouth, 95669
(209) 245-6612
T* 7

Greenstone Winery
Highway 88 and Jackson
  Valley Road
P.O. Box 1146
Ione, 95640
(209) 274-2238/4182
T/A/P 10

Karly Wines
10651 Valley Drive
Plymouth, 95669
(209) 245-3922
T/A 10

Kenworthy Vineyards
Shenandoah Road (Route 2,
  Box 2)
Plymouth, 95669
(209) 245-3198
T/A 10

Montevina
Shenandoah School Road
  (Box 30A)
Plymouth, 95669
(209) 245-3412/6942
T/A 7

Santino Wines
21 A Steiner Road (Route 2)
Plymouth, 95669
(209) 245-3555
T/A 9

Shenandoah Vineyards
Steiner Road (Route 2, Box 23)
Plymouth, 95669
(209) 245-3698
T/A 10

Stoneridge
Ridge Road (Route 1, Box 36B)
Sutter Creek, 95685
(209) 223-1761
T/A 10

Story Vineyards
Willets Road (Bell Road)
Plymouth, 95669
(209) 245-6208/(916) 446-7788
(Cosumnes River Vineyard)
T/A 10

TKC Vineyards
Route 2, Valley Drive
Plymouth, 95669
(714) 446-3166
T/A 10

CALAVERAS COUNTY

Chispa Cellars
425 Main Street (Box 255)
Murphys, 95247
(209) 728-3492
T/A 10

Stevenot Winery
San Domingo Road (Box 548)
Murphys, 95247
(209) 728-3793
T/A   9

EL DORADO COUNTY

Boeger Winery
1709 Carson Road
Placerville, 95667
(916) 622-9084
(Hangtown)
T/P   9

Carson Ridge Vineyards
Gatlin Road (P.O. Box 454)
Camino, 95709
(916) 644-1154
(Madrona Vineyards)
          10

El Dorado Vineyards
3551 Carson Road
Camino, 95709
(916) 644-3773
T*/P

FBF Winery
Fairplay Road
Somerset, 95684
(916) 626-7348
(209) 245-3240
(Fitzpatrick)
T/A   10

Gerwer Foothill Wines
(see Stoney Creek)

Granite Springs Winery
6060 Granite Springs Road
Somerset, 95684
(209) 245-6395
T/A/P   10

Herbert Vineyards
Grizzly Flat Road
Somerset, 95684
(916) 626-0548
T/A   10

Madrona Vineyards
(see Carson Ridge)

Sierra Vista Winery
4560 Cabernet Way
Pleasant Valley (Placerville)
  95667
(916) 622-7221
T/A   10

Stoney Creek Vineyards
8221 Stoney Creek Road
Somerset, 95684
(209) 245-3467
(Gerwer and Gerwer
  Foothill Wines)
T/A/P   10

NEVADA COUNTY

Snow Mountain Winery
P.O. Box 832
Nevada City, 95959
(916) 265-3314
(Nevada City Cellars)
T/A   9

PLACER COUNTY

Ferreira Wines, Inc.
5990 Wine Road
Newcastle, 95658
(916) 663-1550
T/A 10

SACRAMENTO COUNTY

Brookside Winery (Mills W.)
9910 Folsom Blvd.
Sacramento, 95827
(916) 363-6416
T 8/4

Brookside Winery
6449 65th Street
Sacramento, 95827
(916) 366-9959
(tasting/retail outlet only)

Brookside Winery
2734 Auburn Boulevard
Sacramento, 95821
(916) 484-9556
(tasting/retail outlet only)

James Frasinetti & Sons
7395 Frasinetti Road (Box 28213)
Sacramento, 95828
(916) 383-2444
T* 7

Gibson Wine Company
9750 Kent Street
(at Grantline Rd & Hwy 99
P.O. "E")
Elk Grove, 95624
(916) 685-9594
T/A/P 5

SHASTA COUNTY

Palo Cedro Cellars
10222 Deschutes Road
Palo Cedro, 96073
(916) 574-4389
T/A 10

YOLO COUNTY

Bogle Vineyards, Inc.
Route 144
Clarksburg, 95612
(916) 744-1669
T/A

Caché Cellars
Pedrich Road
Davis, 95616
(916) 756-6068
T/A 10

R & J Cook
Netherlands Road (P.O. Box 227)
Cortland (Clarksburg), 95613
(916) 775-1234/665-1205
9

Harbor Winery
610 Harbor Boulevard
West Sacramento, 96991
(916) 371-6676/392-7954
T/A   10

McHenry Vineyards
330 11th Street
Davis, 95616
(916) 756-3202
(winery in Santa Cruz Co.)

Orleans Hill Vinicultural Assn.
811 Second Street
Woodland, 95695
(916) 662-1928
(winery at 1111 Pendegast Street)
T*   10

Sequoia Cellars
1101 Lincoln Avenue
Woodland, 95695
(916) 756-3081/487-3210
(Davis office numbers)
T/A   10

Winters Wine Company
15 Main Street
Winters, 95694
(916) 795-3201
T/A   10

Y U B A   C O U N T Y

Renaissance Vineyard & Winery
Box 602
Oregon House, 95962
(916) 692-1331/1653
T/A   10

Variety (in acres)	Amador	Butte	Calaveras	Colusa	El Dorado	Glenn	Nevada	Placer	Sacramento	Shasta	Tehama	Yolo	Yuba	Totals	% of state
Barbera	10	22	-	-	20	203	-	5	40	-	-	-	38	338	1.9
Cabernet-Sauvignon	62	337	9	-	32	-	3	5	520	5	27	41	130	1,171	5.2
Carignane	23	-	-	49	-	12	-	16	16	-	-	-	-	116	0.6
Chardonnay	36	30	10	-	27	-	5	1	32	-	54	6	13	214	1.0
Chenin blanc	33	10	24	79	26	-	-	-	535	-	11	359	42	1,119	3.0
French Colombard	10	-	21	-	-	410	-	-	243	-	24	15	-	723	1.3
Gray Riesling	-	10	-	-	1	7	-	-	49	-	-	93	-	160	6.6
Grenache	-	-	-	-	-	416	-	2	-	-	-	-	-	418	2.4
Merlot	6	2	1	-	6	-	-	-	98	-	-	-	-	113	5.0
Napa Gamay	-	53	2	-	10	251	-	-	280	-	40	20	-	646	14.7
Petite Sirah	2	71	-	-	4	264	-	-	351	-	20	63	12	815	9.6
Ruby Cabernet	5	-	-	-	-	-	1	1	211	-	15	15	-	248	1.7
Sauvignon blanc	258	50	10	-	92	-	4	5	231	19	59	26	-	754	7.9
White Riesling	-	-	-	-	8	-	2	-	221	-	-	54	-	285	2.6
Zinfandel	1,097	85	38	-	128	9	4	24	432	-	47	-	12	1,876	6.6
Other wine grapes	64	94	6	0	10	0	6	49	122	0	9	35	21	426	
Totals	1,606	764	121	128	364	1,572	26	108	3,381	24	210	738	380	9,422	2.8*

*(percent of wine varieties)

SOUTHERN CALIFORNIA COUNTIES

IN TERMS OF SHEER LAND MASS, THIS SIX-COUNTY REGION RANKS number one. But in terms of grapes, the area is miniscule in both number of wineries (two dozen) and grape acreage. And while small parts of the region are considered, by some, to be fine wine land, less than half of the grape acreage is devoted to wine varieties.

Huge San Bernardino and Riverside counties account for all but a few hundred of the 22,000 acres, the former planted mainly to wine grapes while the latter is largely table grape country. San Bernardino's main growing area, the Cucamonga Valley, located just south of the city of the same name, once had 50,000 acres of grapes and a thriving industry. Today, however, the vineyards are compacted by urbanization in the area, and some are left untended. A chat with the growers does not bring much talk of revival as spirits are low.

The two most widely planted varieties in this very hot climate are Zinfandel and Mission, the latter of which was once California's dominant grape. Together with Grenache and Palomino, they make up the less-than-noble varietal mix. As land costs spiral, you can expect another once-famous wine region to bite 142 the dust.

Riverside County is table and raisin grape country with only 20 percent of the acreage given to wine varieties. The Cucamonga Valley extends into northwestern Riverside forming the major growing area. Another area is the Coachella Valley, east of Palm Springs, between the San Bernardino and the San Jacinto mountains. Dependable older varieties such as Thompson seedless, Perlette, and Cardinal abound, but a new variety called the Red Flame Seedless – a very tasty hybrid grape with a complex parentage – is catching on here and in the Central Valley. The area is the first in the country each year to pick and ship grapes, starting as early as May.

Temecula provides the only real wine grape interest in the region, and it is simply too early to determine whether Temecula is an area truly suited to fine wine varieties, an expensive experiment, or windy hype.

In San Diego County, there is hope of establishing a fine wine region in the San Pasqual Valley as well as proposals for defining it as a viticultural area. But there is little in the way of substantial evidence so far. Some have suggested that the county's climate is similar to that of the Napa Valley and will, therefore, support the same kind of grape varieties. Time will tell.

LOS ANGELES COUNTY

Ahern Winery
715 Arroyo Avenue
San Fernando, 91340
(213) 989-3898
T/A   **10**

Brookside Wineries in Los Angeles County include facilities in Torrance, San Pedro, Pasadena, Van Nuys, Agoura, Glendale, Long Beach, Marina Del Rey, Northridge, and Chatsworth. These are tasting and retail sales outlets only.

Donatoni Winery
10620 South La Cienega
  Boulevard
Inglewood, 90304
(213) 645-5445
T/A   **10**

J. Filippi Vintage Company
9613 Valley Boulevard
El Monte, 91734
(213) 442-8955
(tasting/retail outlet only)

Southern California

County	# of wineries (mid-1982)	Planted acreage	% of regional total	Leading variety
❶ San Bernardino	10	6,170	28.9	Zinfandel
❷ Ventura	3	8	neg.	Chenin blanc
❸ Los Angeles	7	—	—	—
❹ Orange	2	41	0.2	Chenin blanc
❺ Riverside	11	14,956	70.0	Perlette
❻ San Diego	5	201	0.9	Chenin blanc
TOTALS	38	21,376*	100.0	Perlette

*equals 3.0% of the state's total planted grape acreage. 42.2% of these are wine grapes.

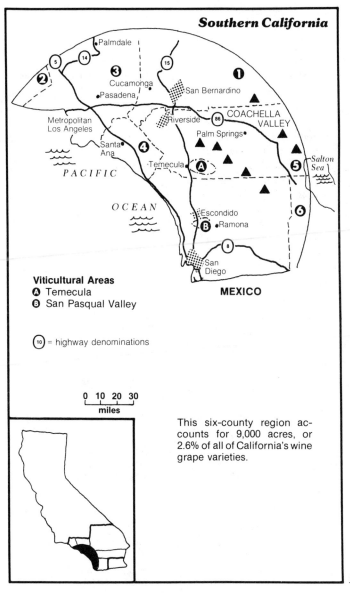

Southern California

Palmdale

❸

Cucamonga
Pasadena

San Bernardino

Metropolitan
Los Angeles

Riverside

**COACHELLA
VALLEY**

Santa
Ana

❹

Palm Springs

Temecula **ⓐ**

*Salton
Sea*

❺

P A C I F I C

❻

O C E A N

Escondido
ⓑ Ramona

San
Diego

MEXICO

Viticultural Areas
ⓐ Temecula
ⓑ San Pasqual Valley

(10) = highway denominations

0 10 20 30
miles

This six-county region accounts for 9,000 acres, or
2.6% of all of California's wine
grape varieties.

J. Filippi Vintage Company
8255 Sunland Boulevard
Sun Valley, 91352
(213) 767-3646
(tasting/retail outlet only)

J. Filippi Vintage Company
5107 El Segundo Boulevard
Hawthorne, 90250
(213) 644-4297
(tasting/retail outlet only)

J. Filippi Vintage Company
8447 Rosemead Boulevard
Pico Rivera, 90660
(213) 869-9672
(tasting/retail outlet only)

Martin Winery, Inc.
  (Chateau St. Martin)
11800 West Jefferson Boulevard
Culver City, 90230
(213) 390-5736
T   10

McLester Winery
10670 South LaCienega
  Boulevard
Lennox/Inglewood, 90304
(213) 641-9686
T/A   10

San Antonio Winery (main)
737 Lamar Street
Los Angeles, 90031
(213) 223-1401
T   5

San Antonio Winery
  (tasting room)
90 West Colorado Boulevard
Pasadena, 91101
(213) 449-2648

San Antonio Winery
  (tasting room)
12221 Santa Monica Boulevard
West Los Angeles, 90025
(213) 820-1212

San Antonio Winery
  (tasting room)
8764 Corbin
Northridge, 91324
(213) 701-0556

San Antonio Winery
  (tasting room)
1418 South Pacific Coast
  Highway
Redondo Beach, 90277
(213) 375-8585

San Antonio Winery
  (tasting room)
2221 Lincoln Boulevard
Venice/Marina Del Rey, 90291
(213) 822-1423

San Antonio Winery
  (tasting room)
22323-1 Sherman Way
Canoga Park, 91304
(213) 883-2380

South Coast Cellar
12901 B. South Budlong Avenue
Gardena, 90247
(213) 324-8006
T/A 10

Trader Joe Winery (Market)
538 Mission Street
South Pasadena, 91030
(213) 441-1177
T/A 10

ORANGE COUNTY

Brookside Winery
711 South Brookhurst Street
Anaheim, 92804
(714) 778-9933
(tasting/retail outlet only)

Brookside Winery
2050 West Lambert Road
La Habra, 90631
(213) 697-9054
(tasting/retail outlet only)

Brookside Winery
24292 Del Prado
Dana Point, 92629
(714) 496-9025
(tasting/retail outlet only)

Brookside Winery
2925 Bristol Street
Costa Mesa, 92626
(714) 754-9270
NT 10/4

Brookside Winery
5565 East Santa Ana
   Canyon Road
Anaheim Hills, 92807
(714) 998-9813
(tasting/retail outlet only)

Brookside Winery
24012 Alicia Parkway
Mission Viejo, 92675
(714) 951-9920
(tasting/retail outlet only)

Brookside Winery
1525 A. Placentia Avenue
Placentia, 92670
(714) 528-9048
(tasting/retail outlet only)

J. Filippi Vintage Company
12872 South Harbor Boulevard
Garden Grove, 92642
(714) 534-7990
(tasting/retail outlet only)

J. Mathews Napa Valley Winery
P.O. Box 1042
Newport Beach, 92663
(714) 642-1234
(see also Napa County listing)
T/A 9

San Antonio Winery
2122 North Tustin Avenue
Santa Ana, 92706
(714) 547-8792
(tasting/retail outlet only)

San Antonio Winery
1500 Newport Boulevard
Newport/Costa Mesa, 92626
(714) 645-8940
(tasting/retail outlet only)

R I V E R S I D E
C O U N T Y

Callaway Vineyard and Winery
32720 Rancho California Road
Temecula, 92390
(714) 676-4001
T/A   7

Cilurzo Winery
41220 Calle Contento
Temecula, 92390
(714) 676-5250
T/A   10

J. Filippi Vintage Company
10082 County Line (Box 2)
Mira Loma, 91752
(714) 984-4514
(Chateau Filippi,
   Thomas Vineyards)
T/A   6

Filsinger Vineyards & Winery
39050 Di Portola Road
Rancho, California, 92390
(714) 676-4594
T*   10

Galleano Winery, Inc.
4231 Wineville Avenue
Mira Loma, 91752
(714) 685-5376
T   7

Hart Winery
41300 Avenida Biana (Box 956)
Temecula/Rancho California,
   92390
(714) 676-6300
T/A   10

Hugo's Cellar (Glenoak
   Hills Winery)
40607 Los Ranchos Circle
Temecula, 92390
(714) 676-5831
T/A   10

Chateau D'Ivresse, Inc.
33685 Pathfinder Road
Mountain Center, 92361
(213) 394-6342
   (in Los Angeles Co.)
T/A   10

Mesa Verde Vineyards & Winery
34565 Ranch California Drive
Temecula/Rancho California,
   92390
(714) 676-2370
T   10

Mount Palomar Winery
33820 Rancho California Road
Temecula, 92390
(714) 676-5047
T/P   8

Piconi Winery
33410 Rancho California Road
Temecula, 92390
(714) 728-5774
T/A   10

SAN BERNARDINO COUNTY

Brookside Enterprises, Inc.
9900 Guasti Road
Guasti, 91743
(714) 983-2787
(Assumption Abbey, Vache,
  Guasti Cucamonga Vintners)
T/P   5/4

Brookside Winery (Archibald)
13105 Archibald Avenue
Ontario, 91761
NT   7/4

Brookside Winery
22900 Washington Avenue
Colton, 92324
(714) 825-9265
(tasting/retail outlet only)

Brookside Winery (Arrow Plant)
12281 Arrow Highway
Cucamonga, 91730
(714) 987-3116/983-2787
NT   5/4

Brookside Winery
14820 7th Street
Victorville, 92392
(714) 243-9941
(tasting/retail outlet only)

Cucamonga Vineyard Company
10013 8th Street (Box 607)
Cucamonga, 91730
(714) 980-9040
(Pierre Biane, Michele Margot)
T   5

J. Filippi Vintage Company
Etiwonda and Juropa Streets
Fontana, 92335
(714) 984-4514
T/P   6

J. Filippi Vintage Company/
  Thomas Vineyards
8916 Foothill Boulevard
Cucamonga, 91730
(714) 987-1612
T   8

Heublein, Inc.
12467 Baseline Boulevard
Etiwanda, 91739
(714) 987-1751
NT

Oak Glen Winery
34970 Yucaipa Boulevard
  (Box 381)
Yucaipa, 92399
(Fruit wine)
(714) 797-5862
T   10

Opici Winery, Inc.
Hermosa and Highland (Box 56)
Alto Loma, 91701
(714) 987-2710
T   10

Rancho de Philo
10050 Wilson Avenue
Alta Loma, 91701
(714) 987-4208
T/A   10

San Antonio Winery
2802 South Milliken Avenue
Ontario, 91761
(714) 947-3995
Tasting Only

SAN DIEGO COUNTY

Bernardo Winery
13330 Paseo del Verano Norte
San Diego, 92128
(714) 487-1866
T/P   7

Brookside Winery
2402 South Escondido Boul.
Escondido, 92025
(714) 743-9875
(tasting/retail outlet only)

Brookside Winery
4730 Mission Bay Drive
Pacific Beach, 92109
(714) 273-9512
(tasting/retail outlet only)

Brookside Winery
3901 Bonita Road
Bonita, 92002
(714) 422-9984
(tasting/retail outlet only)

Brookside Winery
707 Arnele Street
El Cajon, 92020
(714) 440-9480
(tasting/retail outlet only)

Brookside Winery
3776 Mission Avenue
Oceanside, 92054
(714) 439-9483
(tasting/retail outlet only)

John Culbertson Winery
2608 Via Rancheros
Fallbrook, 92028
(714) 728-0156
T/A   10

Ferrara Winery
1120 West 15th Avenue
Escondido, 92025
(714) 745-7632
T   9

J. Filippi Vintage Company
840 East Vista Way
Vista, 92083
(714) 724-0225
(tasting/retail outlet only)

Point Loma Winery
3655 Poe Street
San Diego, 92106
(714) 224-1674
T/A   10

San Pasqual Vineyards
13455 San Pasqual Road
San Diego, 92025
(714) 741-0855
T/A   7

VENTURA COUNTY

Brookside Winery
6580 Leland Street
Ventura, 93001
(805) 642-9867
(tasting/retail outlet only)

Leeward Winery
2511 Victoria Avenue
Channel Islands Harbor, 93030
(805) 985-1233
T/A   10

The Old Creek Ranch Winery
10024 Old Creek Road
Oakview, 93022
(805) 649-4132
T/A   10

Rolling Hills Vineyards
167 "L" Avidor
Camarillo, 93010
(805) 495-7275
NT   10

Variety	Orange	Riverside	San Bernardino	San Diego	Ventura	Totals	% of state
Cabernet-Sauvignon	-	211	-	-	1	212	0.9
Cardinal (t)	-	549	-	-	-	549	27.5
Chardonnay	-	315	-	-	1	316	1.6
Chenin blanc	26	267	11	34	2	340	0.9
Flame seedless (t)	-	1,747	-	-	-	1,747	25.0
Grenache	-	119	632	8	-	759	4.4
Mission	-	206	1,124	14	-	1,344	40.9
Palomino	-	87	648	-	-	735	19.8
Perlette (t)	-	5,009	-	-	-	5,009	79.2
Superior seedless (t)	-	592	-	-	-	592	30.4
Thompson seedless (r)	-	3,743	8	-	-	3,751	1.4
White Riesling	15	590	-	-	-	605	5.4
Zinfandel	-	131	1,979	20	-	2,130	7.5
Other varieties (all)	0	1,390	1,768	125	4	3,868	-
Totals	41	14,956	6,170	201	8	21,376	3.0*

t = table variety

r = raisin variety

* Percent of all grape varieties in the state

THE
CENTRAL VALLEY

EVERYTHING ABOUT THIS MULTI-COUNTY REGION IS ENORMOUS: ITS 548,000 acres planted to grapes make it the thirteenth largest "country" in the world for that category; several of its wineries have yearly outputs equal to that of certain countries; single "farms" consist of 10,000 or more acres of vines where laser beams must be used to perfectly align the rows; the soil, from the mountains on either side, washed down into the valley over centuries, is among the richest in the world; experimentation with viticultural and enological techniques is continuing on a massive scale; and it satisfies the wine (and olive and cotton and other fruit) needs of the great majority of Americans. So why is this area not usually discussed when the subject of California wines comes up? Why are the winemakers of the seventy or so wineries in the region – whose talents are equal or superior to those of most of their counterparts in Napa, Monterey, or Amador – not touted in the same glowing terms as winemakers of those counties? Why do birds fly and fish swim? Could it be just the nature of things?

Sure, few Frenchmen will praise the Midi (their Central Valley) as their most famous wine growing region, even though just about every one of them drinks Midi wines every day. Nor does the average Italian talk with great pride about Puglian, Sicilian, **153**

The Central Valley

County	# of wineries (mid-1982)	Planted acreage	% of total	Leading variety
❶ San Joaquin	18	56,496	10.3	Flame Tokay/Zinfandel
❷ Stanislaus	4	22,005	4.0	French Colombard
❸ Tuolumne	2	—	—	—
❹ Merced	2	17,096	3.1	French Colombard
❺ Mariposa	0	—	—	—
❻ Madera	7	74,469	13.6	Thompson seedless/French Colombard
❼ Fresno	19	208,538	38.1	Thompson seedless/French Colombard
❽ Kings	0	3,602	0.7	Thompson seedless/Muscat Alexandria
❾ Tulare	4	81,833	14.9	Thompson seedless/Emperor
❿ Kern	10	83,981	15.3	Thompson seedless/French Colombard
TOTALS	66	548,020*	100.0	Thompson seedless/French Colombard

*equals 78% of the state's total grape acreage and 58% of the wine grape acreage. 36.2% of these are wine grapes.

or Emilian wines, even though they make up the great majority of his *vino*. I suppose it is human nature to overlook the substantial, the dependable, the ongoing, and the everyday and prick up the ears, instead, to the dramatic, the different, and, often, the public relations machinery.

This huge region probably deserves a book of its own, but the following few paragraphs will serve this particular tome's needs.

From Lodi in the north to Bakersfield in the south, the crow flies about 225 miles. If the crow were interested, he would notice on his overflight a broad, flat, fairly homogeneous and very warm valley bounded on either side by moderate-sized mountain ranges. Were Monsieur Crow a viticulturist, and not flying too high, he would straight-away see that, though they may be grapes down there, they be grapes used mainly for the purpose of making raisins or for human eating pleasure. For only a little more than a third of all the crow saw would be wine grapes. If our crow knew the reputation of the area for turning out a lot of wine, he might find that curious indeed.

The answer lies in the fact that some of the many table and raisin grapes in the valley are also crushed for wine and brandy making purposes. As recently as 1974, 50 percent or more of California's wine came from such varieties, largely the ubiquitous Thompson seedless. This wine, to be sure, was sold mainly as bulk generic wine and the taste confirmed this. At the time there was not really much of a choice since relatively few wine varieties were available for wine use.

Now, however, the great plantings of the 1970s have resulted in substantial increases in the proportions of wine-grape varieties, although most of the increases were made outside this great valley. So today it is estimated that about 20 percent of all California wine is the result of the crushing and vinifying of raisin and table grapes. And with superior winemaking techniques, even Thompson seedless "Chablis" does not taste too bad.

If the crow concentrated on four, large, adjacent counties—Madera, Fresno, Tulare, and Kern—he would see over 80 percent of the region's acreage (three fifths of it old Thompson seedless) and 60 percent of the bonded wineries. At picking time—as early as June and through August—millions of bunches of

The Central Valley Counties

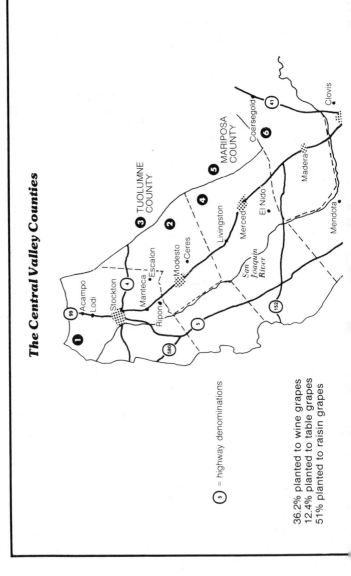

⑤ = highway denominations

36.2% planted to wine grapes
12.4% planted to table grapes
51% planted to raisin grapes

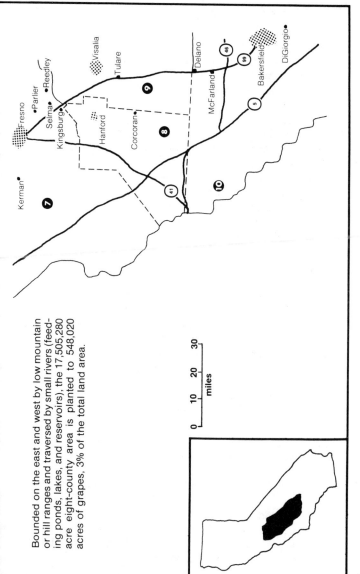

Bounded on the east and west by low mountain or hill ranges and traversed by small rivers (feeding ponds, lakes, and reservoirs), the 17,505,280 acre eight-county area is planted to 548,020 acres of grapes, 3% of the total land area.

Kerman

Fresno
Parlier
Selma • Reedley
Kingsburg
Hanford
Corcoran
Visalia
Tulare
Delano
McFarland
Bakersfield
DiGiorgio

7
8
9
10

41
5
99
46

| 0 | 10 | 20 | 30 |

miles

grapes are picked and laid out to dry. They will shrink to perhaps one-fourth their original weight and be sprayed, packed, and shipped to all parts of the world as raisins.

Others will be picked, packed, and, with luck, rushed off as fresh table grapes to an eager American marketplace whose customers usually call them simply "green," "blue," or "black" grapes. And, though Thompson seedless is considered a raisin variety, it is used for fresh grapes purposes as well, rounding out its three-way duties.

But other varieties, for both table and raisin use, are being developed and tested every year by scientists and breeders at the various nurseries and universities in California. So, while Thompson dominates, grapes such as Calmeria and Flame, Ruby and other seedless grapes are playing increasingly stronger roles. In addition to these, old stand-bys such as Emperor, Muscat of Alexandria, Cardinal, Malaga, and Ribier account for small but significant percentages of the acreage.

The wine varieties that do thrive in these areas must be able to survive the heat and to give more than lackluster grapes. Warm climate varieties that grow in the area include French Colombard, Barbera, Carignane, Chenin blanc, and Grenache. Also, in experiments to further adapt wine varieties to the stern conditions and to obtain better-than-blah results from them, growers have planted *vinifera* crosses including Emerald Riesling, Ruby Cabernet, Carnelian and the like. Now, nearly 20 percent of all the wine varieties in the valley are such crosses. Similar experimentation is ongoing.

In the northern part of the valley, in San Joaquin County, the situation is slightly different. For one thing, much of this county is cooler than the bulk of the southern valley; hence, the grapes are different. Over 90 percent of the central valley's 11,200 acres of Zinfandel is in San Joaquin alone, most of it around Lodi and Stockton. A raisin variety, the Flame Tokay, which is used primarily to produce "Lodi Scotch," or brandy, is planted to about 18,000 acres. Carignane, Chenin blanc, French Colombard, Grenache, and Petite Sirah round out the acreage with a few thousand acres each.

As would be expected, few acres of the "premium" varieties

are planted in the hot valley. Most wines produced from these tempermental cultivars grown in the valley have been what kind people call "interesting," although there are always exceptions.

FRESNO COUNTY

Almaden Vineyards (Kingsburg)
965 Sierra
Kingsburg, 93631
(209) 897-2984
NT   4/3

Bianchi Vineyard
5806 North Modoc Avenue
Kerman, 93630
(Villa Sorrento)
(209) 846-7356
T   6

JFJ Bronco Winery
7409 West Central Avenue
Fresno, 93745
(209) 264-3036
T/A   4/3

Farnesi Winery
2426 Almond Avenue
Sanger, 93657
(209) 875-3004
T   10

E & J Gallo Winery
5610 East Olive Avenue
Fresno, 93727
(209) 255-3093
NT   2/1

Gibson Wine Company
1720 Academy Avenue
Sanger, 93657
(209) 875-2505
T   4

Guild Wineries & Distilleries
  (Cribari Winery)
3223 East Church Street
Fresno, 93714
(209) 485-3080
T   4/2

Guild Wineries & Distilleries
  (Fresno Winery)
1545 North Clovis Avenue
Fresno, 93727
(209) 255-0451
NT   5/2

Guild Wineries & Distilleries
  (McCall Winery)
1042 South McCall Avenue
Sanger, 93657
(209) 255-0475
NT   5/2

Mont LaSalle Vineyards
2202 South Cedar Avenue
Fresno, 93725
(209) 264-3570
NT   4/3

Mont LaSalle Vineyards
8418 Lac Jac Avenue (Box 589)
Reedley, 93654
(209) 638-3544
NT   5/3

Noble Vineyards, Inc.
18559 West Lincoln Ave.
  (Box 31)
Kerman, 93630
(209) 846-7361
(Pacific Land & Viticulture, Inc.)
NT   5

A. Nonini Winery
2640 North Dickenson Avenue
Fresno, 93711
(209) 264-7857
T   8

Nordman of California
4836 East Olive Avenue
Fresno, 93727
(209) 638-9923
T/A   7

United Vintners, Inc.
  (Fresno Winery)
398 North Clovis Avenue
Fresno (Clovis), 93727
(209) 291-3555
NT   4/2

United Vintners, Inc.
  (Sanger Winery)
2916 South Reed Avenue
Sanger, 93657
(209) 638-3511
NT   4/2

Nicholas G. Verry, Inc.
400 First Street (Box 248)
Parlier, 93648
(209) 646-2782
T*   7

Vie-Del Winery
Plant No. 1 (Box 2896)
11903 South Chestnut Avenue
Fresno, 93745
(209) 834-2525
NT   4/3

Vie-Del Winery
Plant No. 2
S. Indianola and E. Mountainside
Kingsburg, 93631
(209) 896-3065
NT   4/3

George Zaninovich, Inc.
700 Center (P.O. Box 398)
Orange Cove, 93646
(209) 626-7337
T/A   7

KERN COUNTY

Almaden Vineyards
  (Cal Mission)
Whistler Road and Highway 99
McFarland, 93250
(805) 792-3071
NT   4/3

ASV Wines
Box 910, Route 1
Delano, 93215
(805) 725-3445
T/A   10

Blackwell Wine Company
Star Route (P.O. Box 337)
Lost Hills, 93249
(805) 465-5611
(a vineyard company)
NT

Delano Growers' Cooperative
  Winery
Route 1, Bassett Avenue
  (Box 283)
Delano, 93215
(805) 725-3255
T/A   5

Giumarra Vineyards
  Corporation
Edison Highway (P.O. Box 1969)
Bakersfield, 93393
(805) 366-5511
(Breckenridge Cellars)
T*   4

Guild Wineries & Distilleries
Road 188 and Avenue 4
  (Box 280)
Delano, 93215
(805) 725-9546
(L. K. Marshall Winery)
NT   4/2

M. Lamont Winery, Inc.
DiGiorgio Road (P.O. Box 428)
DiGiorgio, 93217
(805) 327-2200
T*   3

Sierra Wine Corp.
Highway 99 and Pond Road
  (Box 818)
Delano, 93216
(805) 792-3164
(formerly Perelli-Minetti
  Winery)
T   4/2

Sierra Wine Corporation
Route 2 (P.O. Box 374)
Delano, 93215
(805) 725-9533
(Philip Posson)
NT   4/2

Tejon Agricultural Corporation
500 Laval Road
Arvin, 93203
(805) 858-2291
(principally vineyardists)
NT   10

MADERA COUNTY

Bisceglia Brothers Wine Co.
25427 Avenue 13 (Box 1149)
Madera, 93637
(209) 673-3594 (La Croix,
  Canterbury, Old Rose,
  Paradise)
Owned by Canandaigua Wine
  Company, Inc., of New York
        4

Coarsegold Wine Cellar
Highway 41
Coarsegold, 93614
(209) 683-4850
T

Ficklin Vineyards
30246 Avenue 7½
Madera, 93637
(209) 674-4598
T/A   8

Paul Masson Vineyards
22004 Road 24
Madera, 93637
(209) 673-5961
T   4

Papagni Vineyards
31754 Avenue 9
Madera, 93637
(209) 674-5652
(Rancho Yerba Buena)
T/A   5

Quady Winery
13181 Road 24
Madera, 93637
(209) 674-8606
T/A   9

United Vintners, Inc.
12667 Road 24
Madera, 93637
(209) 673-7071
NT   /2

MERCED COUNTY

E & J Gallo Winery & Ranch
5953 North Weir Road
Livingston, 95334
(209) 394-6271
NT   2/1

E & J Gallo Winery (Leraxa)
18000 West River Road
Livingston, 95334
(209) 394-6219
NT   2/1

SAN JOAQUIN COUNTY

Barengo Vineyards
(see Verdugo)

Bella Napoli Winery
J 21128 South Austin Road
Manteca, 95336
(209) 599-3885
(Vine Flow, Ala Sante,
    Family Vineyard)
T/A   9

Borra's Cellar
1301 East Armstrong Road
Lodi, 95240
(209) 368-5082
T/A   10

Cadlolo Winery
P.O. Box 188
Escalon, 95320
(209) 838-2457
T   7

California Cellar Masters/
    Coloma Cellars
18678 North Highway 99
Acampo, 95220
(209) 368-7822
Tasting Only **0**

California Cellar Masters/
  Coloma Cellars
1203 First Street #51
Escalon, 95320
(209) 838-7060
Tasting Only **0**

California Cellar Masters/
  Coloma Cellars
2459 East Highway 132 #2
Vernalis, 95376
(209) 836-0273
Tasting Only **0**

Ciriaco Borelli Winery
5471 North Jack Tone Road
Stockton, 95205
(209) 931-2447
(Borelli & Ciriaco)
T/A   **9**

Delicato Vineyards
12001 South Highway 99
Manteca, 95336
(209) 982-0679/239-1215
T   **4**

East Side Winery
6100 East Highway 12 (Box 440)
Lodi, 95240
(209) 369-4768
(Royal Host, Gold Bell,
  Conti Royale)
T/P   **4**

Franzia Brothers Winery
P.O. Box 697
Ripon, 95366
(209) 599-4111
T   **3**

Guild Wineries & Distilleries
  (Bear Creek Winery)
1199 North Furry Road
Lodi, 95240
(209) 368-5151
NT   **4/2**

Guild Wineries & Distilleries
  (Central Cellars)
Myrtle & Filbert Streets
Lodi, 95240
(209) 368-5151
T   **4/2**

Guild Wineries & Distilleries
  (Del Rio Winery)
555 East Woodbridge Road
  (Box 30)
Lodi/Woodbridge, 95258
(209) 368-5151
NT   **4/2**

Liberty Winery, Inc. (Gallo)
6055 East Acampo Road (Box 66)
Acampo, 95220
(209) 368-6646
NT   **5/1**

Lucas Home Wine
18196 North Davis
Lodi, 95240
(209) 368-2006
T/A   **10**

Robert Mondavi Winery
  (Woodbridge)
5950 East Woodbridge Road
Acampo, 95220
(209) 369-5861
T/A   **4/4**

Turner Winery
3750 East Woodbridge Road
Acampo, 95220
(209) 486-7330
T/A   5

United Vintners, Inc.
  (Community Winery)
1 West Turner (Box 730)
Lodi, 95240
(209) 368-2431
NT   5/2

United Vintners, Inc.
  (Petri Winery)
21801 East Highway 120
  (Box 368)
Escalon, 95320
(209) 838-3575
NT   2

Verdugo Vineyards
3125 East Orange Street
Acampo, 95220
(209) 369-2746
(formerly Barengo Vineyards)
T   5

Woodbridge Vineyard
  Association
4614 West Turner Road
Lodi, 95240
(209) 369-2614
(a growers' cooperative)
T/A   4

STANISLAUS COUNTY

JFJ Bronco Winery
6342 Bystrum Road
  (P.O. Box 789)
Ceres, 95307
(209) 538-3131
(CC Vineyard)
NT   4/3

E & J Gallo Winery (Main)
600 Yosemite Road (Box 1130)
Modesto, 95353
(209) 521-3111
(Paisano, The Wine Cellars of
  Ernest & Julio Gallo, Carlo
  Rossi, Thunderbird, Ripple,
  Boone's Farm, Madria Madria,
  Andre, Tyrolia, Spanada,
  Night Train).
NT   2/1

Oak Valley Winery
1390 West H (Box 399)
Oakdale, 95361
(209) 847-5907
T/A   10

Pirrone Wine Cellars
5258 Pirrone Road (Box 15)
Salida, 95368
(209) 545-0704
T   10

TULARE COUNTY

Anderson Wine Cellars
20147 Avenue 306
Exeter, 93201
(209) 592-4682
T/A 10

California Growers Winery
38558 Road 128 (P.O. Box 21)
Yettem, 93670
(209) 528-3033
(Growers, Setrakian, Bounty)
T/A 4

Robert Setrakian Vineyards
P.O. Box 21
Yettem, 93670
(209) 398-1122
(see California Growers Winery)
T/A

Sierra Wine Corporation
1887 North Mooney Boulevard
Tulare, 93724
(209) 686-2807
(Ambassador, Greystone, Guasti,
Perelli-Minetti, Aristocrat A. R.
Morrow and California Wine
Association)
NT 4/2

TUOLUMNE COUNTY

California Cellar Masters/
Gold Mine Winery
22265 Parrotts Ferry Road
Columbia, 95310
(209) 532-3089
T 10

Yankee Hill Winery
Coarsegold Lane (P.O. Box 163)
Columbia, 95310
(209) 532-3015
(Columbia Cellars,
Golden Bonanza)
T/P 10

Variety (in acres)	Fresno	Kern	Kings	Madera	Merced	San Joaquin	Stanislaus	Tulare	Totals	% of state
Alicante Bouschet	1,411	460	99	235	18	570	3	895	3,691	89.1
Barbera	5,112	3,336	9	3,783	1,169	1,056	1,669	1,385	17,519	97.2
Calmeria (t)	352	1,191	-	47	-	-	-	2,739	4,329	100.0
Carignane	1,775	1,444	268	4,270	858	6,326	1,656	1,036	17,633	82.3
Carnelian	712	485	5	250	-	152	10	-	1,614	88.4
Chenin blanc	4,482	5,423	119	4,878	2,643	4,274	2,528	1,791	26,138	69.6
Emerald Riesling	315	1,739	-	219	42	39	-	42	2,396	78.0
French Colombard	10,145	9,655	84	12,753	3,728	5,982	4,216	5,025	51,588	91.1
Emperor (t)	1,601	4,703	-	60	-	16	-	15,642	22,022	100.0
Flame Tokay (r)	94	79	-	-	9	17,815	-	56	18,053	99.0
Grenache	2,800	2,458	190	4,228	1,239	1,898	1,864	473	15,150	88.6
Mission	442	198	61	5	104	527	333	158	1,828	55.6
Muscat Alexandria (r)	3,817	1,723	1,055	548	-	10	-	2,669	9,822	99.3
Palomino	831	99	-	397	44	339	429	243	2,382	64.3
Petite Sirah	538	492	-	185	268	1,472	193	152	3,300	38.7
Royalty	497	352	-	633	16	84	68	223	1,873	100.0
Rubired	2,654	2,919	237	1,736	196	688	125	1,087	9,642	99.4
Ruby Cabernet	3,288	4,085	-	1,537	1,747	573	1,910	738	13,878	95.7
Thompson seedless (r)	157,251	28,888	1,297	36,383	3,223	10,744	3,453	35,810	266,749	98.6
Zinfandel	182	66	-	76	102	433	518	-	11,688	41.2
Other grapes (all)	10,239	14,186	178	2,246	1,690	3,498	3,030	11,669	46,725	-
Totals	208,538	83,981	3,602	74,469	17,096	56,496	22,005	81,883	548,020	77.7*

t = table variety   r = raisin variety   * Percent of all varieties in state

Leading California Grape Varieties (over 2,000 acres)

Variety	North Co.	Central Co.	Sac/Sierras	So. Calif.	Central V.	Total
Thompson seedless (r)	-	1	10	3,751	266,749	270,500
French Colombard (w)	2,943	1,364	723	21	51,588	56,639
Chenin blanc (w)	4,221	5,749	1,119	340	26,138	37,421
Zinfandel (w)	8,505	4,169	1,876	2,130	11,688	28,368
Cabernet-Sauvignon (w)	12,291	6,950	1,171	212	1,872	22,496
Emperor (t)	-	-			22,022	22,022
Carignane (w)	3,058	409	116	214	17,633	21,430
Chardonnay (w)	11,167	7,543	214	316	526	19,766
Flame Tokay (t)	2	14	159	10	18,053	18,238
Barbera (w)	104	61	338	0	17,519	18,022
Grenache (w)	140	634	418	759	15,150	17,101
Ruby Cabernet (w)	85	248	248	42	13,878	14,501
White Riesling (w)	3,503	6,618	285	605	107	11,118
Muscat of Alexandria (r)	12	5	8	44	9,822	9,891
Rubired (w)	0	0	0	55	9,642	9,697
Sauvignon blanc (w)	4,463	2,451	754	290	1,600	9,558
Pinot noir (w)	5,359	3,554	35	5	40	8,993

Petite Sirah (w)	2,374	1,922	815	112	3,300	8,523
Flame seedless (t)	0	37	0	1,747	5,204	6,988
Perlette (t)	0	0	0	5,009	1,311	6,320
Ribier (t)	0	0	0	9	5,404	5,413
Gewürztraminer (w)	2,092	2,568	7	16	26	4,709
Napa Gamay (w)	2,045	1,042	646	22	627	4,382
Calmeria (t)	0	0	0	0	4,329	4,329
Alicante Bouschet (w)	124	27	6	294	3,691	4,142
Gamay Beaujolais (w)	1,651	1,908	29	46	120	3,754
Palomino (w)	496	84	7	735	2,382	3,704
Mission (w)	11	28	74	1,344	1,828	3,285
Emerald Riesling (w)	2	548	47	78	2,396	3,071
Malaga (t)	0	0	0	18	3,002	3,020
Sémillon (w)	424	941	139	2	1,389	2,895
Merlot (w)	1,428	605	113	5	113	2,264
Others (t/r/w)	3,950	5,957	298	3,145	28,871	42,339
Totals	70,450	55,437	9,655	21,376	548,020	704,938

t = viewed as primarily a grape for table (eating) purposes; r = raisins; w = wine purposes.

INTRODUCTION
TO THE OTHER
WINE STATES
OF THE COUNTRY

OBSERVERS OF THE NON-CALIFORNIA WINERY AND VINEYARD SCENE might get the sense that they have moved to San Francisco and turned back the clock ten years or so. And perhaps the newest saying among non-California winegrowers (you remember one of the earliest ones: "see, we searched all over the state to find just the right patch of land for our Ruby Cabernets.") is "we're where California was ten years ago, son; we're just starting out, but watch us go." For any number of reasons, the fires of enthusiasm range from kindling temperatures to a blazing fury, depending upon the region of this wine-crazy country. Some reasons are obvious, others are not.

For one thing, a growing number of Americans no longer think of wine as a drink for sissies or eggheads only. Our "beer and booze" image, though still kicking, is fast on the decline. And at the beginning of this decade, for the first time in history, our consumption of wines equaled our consumption of spirits. Just a glance at the *per capita* consumption figures shows that the inhabitants of every state, not just those of California, have more or less accepted the idea of wine and its pleasures.

Advances in viticultural and enological techniques have spread across the wine world and have spurred growth. New grape varieties, improved by painstaking hybridization, are better able to handle the humid conditions and furious winters of many of our "other wine states." Rootstocks are being developed which can help the pure-blooded but tender *vinifera* varieties to weather this weather. And once the grapes are in the winery, the producer has new opportunities to handle grapes that he or she did not have as recently as five years ago.

The loosening of many of the states' once puritanical grips on wine legislation is another reason for the growth. More and more states are passing Farm Winery laws or planning the groundwork to establish them. Such laws make it easier to open a winery and to sell its products. Spearheaded by wine-loving activists from Alabama to Arizona, such legislation can only increase awareness of the positive aspects of moderately alcoholic beverages.

For whatever reasons, growth in most of the "other 49" has been unprecedented since the New England wine scene commenced three centuries ago. One stark statistic will highlight the surge: of the nearly 400 wineries outside of California, 73 percent were bonded since 1970, half in the last five years alone.

I have divided the forty-nine other wine growing states of the country fairly arbitrarily into four large regions of roughly equal land mass, if not grape acreage: Northeastern/Midwestern, Southeastern, Southwestern, and Northwestern. Within each of these region's sections I have placed each pertinent state and its winery listings. To those states with appreciable amount of acreage and/or at least twenty wineries I have devoted separate, albeit brief, commentary and semi-detailed maps.

The reader will form an idea of the nature of each region's activity on a state-by-state basis from reading the commentary but a quick look at the statistics below will put the non-California grape scene into perspective.

Percentages of the Four Major Types of Grapes in the Other 49

	American*	French-American	Vinifera	Muscadines
NORTHEAST/ MIDWEST	87.1%	11.8	1.0	0.1
SOUTHEAST	35.2	17.4	5.3	42.1
SOUTHWEST	0.9	7.3	90.0	1.8
NORTHWEST	73.5	0.9	25.6	-
TOTALS (of c. 125,000 acres)	73 %	9 %	10 %	8 %

*All native American species (aside from *vitis rotundifolia*) including natural—i.e., not intentional—hybrids therefrom.

There are some parallels to be drawn with the California scene. One is that a simple grape variety, the Concord, is dominant in most of the regions with about 76,000 acres, or 60 percent, of the grand total, in much the same way Thompson seedless holds precedence in the Golden State. Another is the fact that not all of the grapes picked are utilized for winemaking purposes. Indeed, outside of California, the proportions are strikingly tilted against winemaking usage: less than 25 percent of all the grapes picked are eventually used for wines. Combine these figures with the surge of enthusiasm over the past decade or so and you have a scene made for conflict and change. Perhaps it will be in parts of our country outside of California that the most vital, most interesting winemaking activity will be taking place in the next century.

NORTH-EASTERN/MID-WESTERN VINEYARD

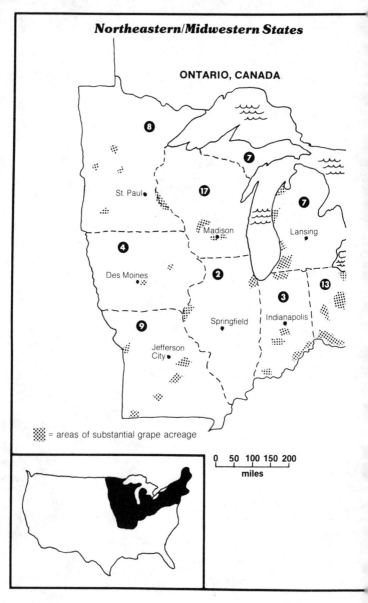

Northeastern/Midwestern States

ONTARIO, CANADA

8

7

17

St. Paul

Madison

7

Lansing

4

Des Moines

2

13

Springfield

Indianapolis

3

9

Jefferson
City

▦ = areas of substantial grape acreage

0 50 100 150 200
miles

176

The seventeen-state region has about 250 wineries and about 77,150 acres of grapeland on a total land mass of 392,693,120 acres.

Viticultural Areas

Ⓐ New Hampshire Lakes
Ⓑ Martha's Vineyard (Massachusetts)
Ⓒ Newport (Rhode Island)
Ⓓ Central Delaware Valley (partially in New Jersey)

(for other viticultural areas, see individual maps for specific states)

THIS SEVENTEEN-STATE REGION IS A SCHIZOPHRENIC WINE AREA IF ever there was one. While there has been frenetic progress in developing new wine hybrid varieties and considerable success with older ones (such as Seyval blanc and Maréchal Foch), the region's grapefolk are largely content to grow fruit for jam, jelly, juice, or table purposes. And while such thoroughbred *vinifera* varieties as Chardonnay, White Riesling and Gewürztraminer are decking the labels of more and more bottles, the lowly but dependable Concord still accounts for over 80 percent of the region's acreage.

If you look at it another way, however, isn't it the same situation in California where over half the grapes are grown for non-wine purposes and less than 20 percent of the state's acreage is planted to the so-called noble varieties?

Actually, from any number of points of view, this region of our country resembles the Golden State as it was a short time ago. There is a great deal of boasting about the future. There is feverish experimentation with both vineyard and winery techniques. And there is justifiable pride in the newly discovered (or perhaps re-discovered) high quality of many different wines, including the abundant but often scorned wines based on American varieties. (Despite all the hubbub, it seems as if *vinifera* supporters in the cold, inhospitable northeast, after three centuries of high hopes and deep frustrations, are still looking to a future of only limited success.)

But there are exceptions to every rule or saying, so a little glimpse into the situation on a state-by-state basis will prove useful. You will note that I have grouped together the "small-action" states of each area. Those states with large grape plantings and/or more than twenty wineries within their boundaries I have dealt with separately.

Viniculturally smaller Northeastern states: (Connecticut, Maine, Massachusetts, New Hampshire, New Jersey, Rhode Island, and Vermont)

The acreage of grapes in these seven smaller states could easily fit into the dot over the "i" of a decent-sized map of California; but don't sell the area short yet.

In proportion to its acreage, there are twenty times more

vinifera plantings in these states, especially in Massachusetts and Rhode Island and even New Jersey, than in the entire northeastern vineyard. The severity of the region's winters obviates the use of warm climate varieties, other than experimentally. Hence, as in the Northwest, white varieties such as Chardonnay, Gewürztraminer, Chenin blanc, Müller-Thurgau, and White Riesling are considered likely fine wine producers. For the reds, Pinot noir and Gamay seem likely candidates, but Merlot, Cabernet, and even Zinfandel and Ruby Cabernet are planted with expectations of success.

Nearly 50 percent of this small area's acreage is planted to French-American hybrid varieties. For the whites, Aurore is widely planted, and both Seyval and Vidal blanc (as well as the relatively new hybrid, Cayuga) have taken awards at the recently organized New England Wine Competition. Reds such a Maréchal Foch, and, to a lesser degree Chelois, de Chaunac, and Rougeon have been successful as varietals, while Baco noir and Chancellor seem better used as blending varieties. It would seem probable that French-American hybrids, especially the whites, will continue to experience the most growth of any group.

American varieties account for a little over one-third of the acreage of these smaller states in which, surprisingly or not, Concord plays a limited role. Delaware and (Pink) Catawba wines have been successful and should continue to be so considering their proven winter hardiness and good yields.

Land prices and climatic difficulties seem to pose the greatest problems for these winegrowers, and they will be the first to admit that things vinous are really just beginning. But Yankee enthusiasm and tenacity combined with sensible farm winery legislation may win the harvest season. Look at it this way: if New Jersey can have its own viticultural area (Hunterdon County's Central Delaware Valley, which is shared with Pennsylvania) there must be some cause for optimism.

A good source to contact for further information on most of the states in this area is Wine Institute of New England, 25 Huntington Avenue, Suite 208, Boston, Massachusetts 02116.

Viniculturally smaller midwestern states: (Illinois, Indiana, Iowa, Minnesota, and Wisconsin).

These five states, areas more commonly associated with grains than grapes, share about forty wineries and 1,000 acres of vineyards. They also share equal parts of misery and joy and the possibility for either a vineyard/winery resurgence or a gloomy future.

My native Illinois' wine industry shares with that of neighboring Iowa the dubious distinction of having been laid low by a bug spray: 2-4-D. Nearly 30,000 acres of grapes covered these two states until grain growers began using the herbicide. The affects linger and leave a pitiful site. Hybrids suffered more than the less vulnerable American varieties. There are now fewer than 200 acres in the two states whose governments do not seem likely to provide the few remaining growers with any legal protection against such withering sprays.

From the point of view of image, Illinois has plummeted in the ranks of leading wine producers in the country owing to the loss of its Mogen David operations in Chicago and that company's large output of wines of Lake Erie origin. In Iowa, even the Amish and other winemakers now depend upon out-of-state grapes when they are not making Piestengel, or rhubarb wine.

There are, however, some positive developments. In a small vine nursery in Iowa City, vineyardist Ed Schmidt cultivates hybrid varieties and sells them to vine-minded positive thinkers, however few in number. Schmidt's Vitis Vineyard and Nursery is an advice center for this viticultural band, who live mostly along the border area between the two states. The Mississippi Valley Wine Society and its foremost members, Willy and Linda Enders, also provide winemaking advice. (The Enders' Terra Vineyards in Port Byron should be bonded by 1983.) If winery bills now being considered in Illinois and Iowa can be turned into law by the efforts of these stubborn few, there may be renewed and strong wine activity along the mighty Mississippi.

There are two organizations that will provide pertinent information: Mississippi Valley Wine Society, c/o Irene Huffman, 1225 W. 5th Street, Milan, Illinois 61264, and The Upper Mississippi Valley Grape Growers Association, 1907 D Street, Iowa City, Iowa 52240, or 27927 108th Avenue, North, Port Byron, Illinois 61275.

My notes for Indiana simply state "resurgence," a succinct but accurate description of winegrowing activity in the Hoosier State. The accent is on French-American hybrids to the tune of about 350 acres. Most of this is concentrated in the middle, southeastern, and southwestern sections of the state, with the latter being part of the Ohio River Valley viticultural area which extends into Ohio and Kentucky. Varieties such as Seyval blanc, Aurore, Vidal blanc, Baco noir, Foch, Chelois and de Chaunac are planted on a decent-sized scale.

Most of the state's American variety acreage is of the Concord sort and is located in the two northern counties of LaPorte and Saint Joseph. It is used mainly for juice purposes. There is currently very little interest in producing *vinifera* wines although one winery did contract to make such wine from West Virginia grapes.

A good information source is the Indiana Wine Growers Guild which publishes a small brochure on the wineries of the state. Write for it in care of the guild at Ben Spark's Possum Trot Vineyard, 8310 North Possum Trot Road, Unionville, Indiana 47468.

The northern states of Wisconsin and Minnesota seem to display a greater, if quite cautious, optimism about their vinous future than either Illinois or Iowa.

While Wisconsin produces excellent wines from cherries and other fruits, the grape action is limited. Wollersheim Winery in Prairie du Sac boasts a third of the state's acreage of about 100. Bob Wollersheim concentrates on French-American hybrids, although the American varieties dominate in the state. There is very little *vinifera* action in Wisconsin, but one source maintains that Chardonnay and White Riesling batches have brought $1,200 a ton. Minnesotans are not very well known for their wines (snow and cold, perhaps) but two wineries (with three more on the way) and about 350 acres doth an industry make.

Fully 90 percent of the state's fairly well scattered acreage is in French-American hybrids with traces of American and *vinifera* varieties to be seen. Traditional hybrids, including Foch, de Chaunac, and Seyval are interspersed with some of the cultivars of local breeder Elmer Swenson. Chardonnay, Riesling,

Gewürztraminer, and Cabernet are *vinifera* involved in current experimentation.

The Minnesota Grape Growers Association seems to be an extremely competent organization. Write them at 6133 Oaklawn Avenue, Edina, Minnesota 55424.

CONNECTICUT

Haight Vineyards
Chestnut Hill
Litchfield, Connecticut 06759
(203) 567-4045
T*   10

Hamlet Hill Vineyards
Quasset Road
Pomfret, Connecticut 06258
(203) 928-5550
T/A   10

Hopkins Vineyard
Hopkins Road
New Preston, Connecticut 06777
(203) 868-7954
T*   10

St. Hilary's Vineyards
Route 12, RFD 1
North Grosvenordale,
   Connecticut 06255
(203) 935-5377
T/A   10

Stonecrop Vineyards
Box 151 A, Rural Delivery #2
Stonington, Connecticut 06378
(203) 535-2497
T   10

MASSACHUSETTS

Chicama Vineyards
Stoney Hill Road
West Tisbury, Massachusetts
   02575
(617) 693-0309
(Sea Mist)
T*   10

Commonwealth Winery
Court Street, Cordage Park
  (Building #44)
Plymouth, Massachusetts 02360
(617) 746-4138
T*   10

Nashoba Valley Winery
Damonmill Square
Concord, Massachusetts 01742
(617) 369-0885
Fruit wine
T*   10

NEW HAMPSHIRE

White Mountain Vineyards
RFD 2, Box 218
  (Province Road & Belmont)
Laconia, New Hampshire 03246
(603) 524-0174
(Lakes Region)
T*   8

NEW JERSEY

Antuzzi's Winery
Bridgeboro-Moorestown Road
Delran, New Jersey 08075
(609) 764-1075
T*/P   10

Balic Winery
Route 40, Route 2, Box 25
Mays Landing, New Jersey
   08330
(609) 625-2166
T*   9

Del Vista Vineyards
R.D. 1, Box 84
Frenchtown Everittstown Road
Frenchtown, New Jersey 08825
(201) 996-2849
T   10

Gross' Highland Winery
306 E. Jim Leeds Road
Absecon, New Jersey 08201
(609) 652-1187
(Bernard D'Arcy,
   Country Vineyards)
T*   7

Gross' Highland Winery
2516 Route 35
Manasquan, New Jersey 08736
(201) 528-6888
(tasting/retail outlet only)

Jacob Lee Winery
RFD 1, Route 130
Bordentown, New Jersey 08505
(609) 298-4860
T/A   9

Regina Wine Company
828 Raymond Boulevard
Newark, New Jersey 07105
(201) 589-6911
T/A   7

Renault Winery, Inc.
Bremen Avenue, R.D. 3, Box 21B
Egg Harbor City, New Jersey
   08215
(609) 965-2111
(Dumont)
T   7

Tewksbury Wine Cellars
Burrell Road, R.D. 2
Lebanon, New Jersey 08833
(201) 832-2400
T/A   10

Tomasello Winery
225 North White Horse Pike
Hammonton, New Jersey 08037
(609) 561-0567
(Chateau Ranier)
T   8

RHODE ISLAND

Philip R. DeSano Vineyards
Stony Lane
Exeter, Rhode Island 02822
(401) 272-2900
T/A   10

Diamond Hill Vineyard
3145 Diamond Hill Road
Cumberland, Rhode Island
   02864
(401) 333-5642
T/A   10

Prudence Island Vineyards
Prudence Island, Rhode Island
  02872
(401) 683-2452
T/A   10

Sakonnet Vineyards
West Main Road
Little Compton, Rhode Island
  02837
(401) 635-4356
T*   9

South County Vineyards
Brow Lane (P.O. Box 2)
Slocum, Rhode Island 02877
(401) 294-3100
NT   10

I L L I N O I S

Brookside Winery
1000 Dundee Avenue
East Dundee, Illinois 60118
(312) 888-9504
(tasting/retail outlet only)

Brookside Winery
1013 South Arlington Heights
Road
Arlington Heights, Illinois 60005
(312) 640-0808
(tasting/retail outlet only)

Fenn Valley Wine Cellars
9801 West 191st Street
Mokena, Illinois 60448
(312) 479-9473
(tasting/retail outlet only)

Gem City Vineland Company
South Parley Street
Nauvoo, Illinois 62354
(217) 453-2218
(Old Nauvoo)
T*   9

Lynfred Winery
15 South Roselle Road
Roselle, Illinois 60172
(312) 529-1000
T   10

Terra Vineyards
27927 108th Avenue, North
Port Byron, Illinois 61275
(309) 523-2670
T/A   10

Thompson Winery
Pauling Road (P.O. Box 127)
Monee, Illinois 60449
(312) 534-8050
(Calumet and Peres Marquette
  & Hennepin)
T/A   10

I N D I A N A

Banholzer Wine Cellars, Inc.
Route 1000 North
Hesston, Indiana
(219) 778-2448
(mailing: RD 1, Three Oaks,
  Michigan 49128)
T*   9

Boulder Hill Vineyard
3366 West County Road 400-N
LaPorte, Indiana 46350
(219) 326-7341
T*   10

Easley Enterprises, Inc.
205 North College Avenue
Indianapolis, Indiana 46202
(317) 636-4516
T/A   10

Golden Raintree Winery, Inc.
Rural Route 2
Wadesville, Indiana 47638
(812) 963-6441
T*   9

Huber Orchard Winery
Route 1 (Box 202)
Borden, Indiana 47106
(812) 923-9463
(Flavor Country)
T*   9

Oliver Wine Company, Inc.
8024 North Highway 27
Bloomington, Indiana 47401
(812) 876-5800
(Camelot)
T   9

Possum Trot Vineyards
8310 North Possum Trot Road
Unionville, Indiana 47468
(812) 988-2694
(Uncle Ben, Benora)
T*   10

Swiss Valley Vineyards
101 Ferry South
Vevay, Indiana 47043
(513) 521-5096
T*   10

I O W A

Ackerman Winery, Inc.
South Amana, Iowa 52334
(319) 622-3379
(South Amana Wines)
T*   10

Christina Wine Cellars
123 A Street
McGregor, Iowa 52157
(319) 873-3321
T   10

Colony Village Winery
Interstate 80, Exit 55 (Box 108)
Williamsburg, Iowa 52334
(319) 622-3379
T   10

Colony Wines, Inc.
Amana, Iowa 52203
(319) 668-2712
(Old Wine Cellar)
T*   9

Der Weinkeller
(see Little Amana Winery)

Ehrle Brothers Winery, Inc.
Homestead, Iowa 52236
(319) 622-3241
(Homestead)
T*   10

Little Amana Winery, Inc.
Box 172 A
Amana, Iowa 52172
(319) 668-1011
(Der Weinkeller)
T*   10

Okoboji Winery, Inc.
Highway 71 (Box 449)
Arnolds Park, Iowa 51355
(319) 332-2674
T   10

Old Style Colony Winery, Inc.
Third Street
Middle Amana, Iowa 52037
(319) 622-3451
T*   10

Old Wine Cellar Winery
Amana, Iowa 52203
(319) 622-3116
T*   10

Old Wine Cellar Winery
Interstate 80 at Exit 225
Williamsburg, Iowa 52361
(319) 668-2712
T   10

Private Stock Winery, Inc.
926 Eighth Street
Boone, Iowa 50036
(319) 432-8348
T   10

Sandstone Winery, Inc.
Box 7
Amana, Iowa 52203
(319) 622-3081
T*   10

Village Winery
Amana, Iowa 52203
(319) 622-3448
T*   10

M I N N E S O T A

Alexis Bailly Vineyard, Inc.
18200 Kirby Avenue
Hastings, Minnesota 55033
(612) 437-1413
T*   10

Lake Sylvia Vineyard
Route 1, Box 149
South Haven, Minnesota 55382
(612) 236-7743
T/A   10

W I S C O N S I N

Christina Wine Cellars
109 Vine Street
LaCrosse, Wisconsin 54601
(608) 785-2210
(The Lawlor Family Winery)
T/A   9

Door-Peninsula Wine Company
Route 1
Sturgeon Bay, Wisconsin 54235
(414) 743-7431
T*/P   10

Fruit of the Woods Wine Cellar
1113 Wall Street
Eagle River, Wisconsin 54521
(715) 479-4800
T   10

The Lawlor Family Winery
(see Christina Wine Cellars)

Old Style Colony Winery
608A Verona Avenue
Verona, Wisconsin 53593
T/A   **10**

Renick Winery
5600 Gordon Road
Sturgeon Bay, Wisconsin 54235
(414) 743-7329
T/A   **10**

Stone Mill Winery, Inc.
North 70, West 6340,
  Bridge Road
Cedarburg, Wisconsin 53012
(414) 377-8020
(Newberry)
T/*/P

Von Stiehl Wine, Inc.
115 Navarino Street (Box 45)
Algoma, Wisconsin 54201
(414) 487-5208
T*   **8**

Wisconsin Winery
529 Main Street
Lake Geneva, Wisconsin 53147
(414) 248-3245
T/A   **10**

The Wollersheim Winery
Highway 188
Prairie du Sac, Wisconsin 53578
(608) 643-6515
T*/P   **9**

MICHIGAN

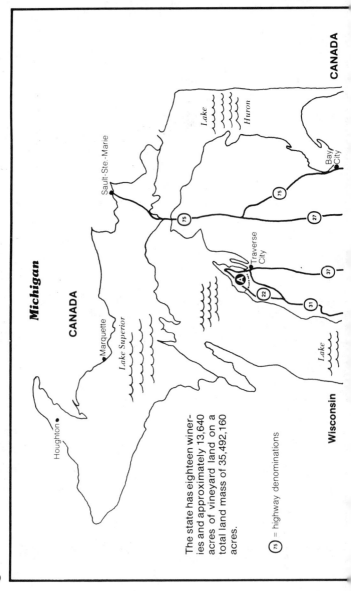

Michigan

CANADA

CANADA

CANADA

Houghton

Marquette

Lake Superior

Sault-Ste.-Marie

Lake Huron

Bay City

Traverse City

Lake

Wisconsin

The state has eighteen winer- ies and approximately 13,640 acres of vineyard land on a total land mass of 35,492,160 acres.

⑦⑤ = highway denominations

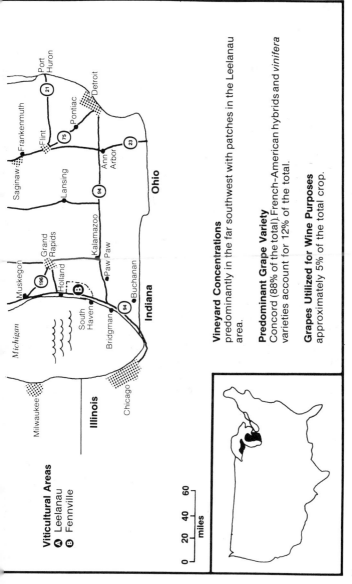

Viticultural Areas
Ⓐ Leelanau
Ⓑ Fennville

Vineyard Concentrations
predominantly in the far southwest with patches in the Leelanau area.

Predominant Grape Variety
Concord (88% of the total). French-American hybrids and *vinifera* varieties account for 12% of the total.

Grapes Utilized for Wine Purposes
approximately 5% of the total crop.

My beer-drinking comrades in the Upper Peninsula will bear with me when I say that all the action in Michigan is south of Sault Saint Marie. In fact, except for a hundred or so acres in the Traverse city zone in the Leelanau viticultural area, and sixty or seventy more acres just north of Muskegon, all of the state's grapes are tucked into four counties near Lake Michigan in the extreme southwest of the state.

It may be getting boring to repeat this, I realize, but nearly 90 percent of the acreage in Michigan — as in most of the Northeast and Midwest — is in American varieties, with Concords dominant. The vast majority of these grapes are used for other-than-wine purposes with only about 5 percent of the tonnage actually used to make wine. The climate is the main problem in the state.

Still, French-American hybrids are increasing from their relatively small base of about 1,500 acres. A modest 100 acres of *vinifera* varieties are used to make wines which are sometimes blended with the same varieties from the northwest or further east.

Of the French-American varieties, winegrowers are most enthusiastic about Vidal blanc, Vignoles, Seyval blanc, Baco noir, Foch and Chancellor. They have mixed feelings about Aurore and de Chaunac. Tabor Hill, Boskydel, and Fenn Valley Vineyards have put great energies into these varieties which many feel will dominate the state's fine wine trade.

Of the *vinifera* planted, White Riesling, Chardonnay, and Gewürztraminer can be successful but need a lot of attention, as does Pinot noir. Of the wines so far produced from the varieties, the results have been fair.

For more information and for a brochure on the state's wineries, contact The Michigan Wine Institute, 322 West Ottawa, Lansing, Michigan 48933.

M I C H I G A N

Boskydel Vineyard
Route 1, Box 522
Lake Leelanau, Michigan 49563
(616) 256-7272
T* 10

Bronte Champagne & Wines
  Co., Inc.
Route 2 (Keeler Center)
Hartford, Michigan 49057
(616) 621-3419
(Jean Doreau, Sister
  Lakes District)
T 6

Chateau Grand Travers, Ltd.
12239 Center Road
Traverse City, Michigan 49684
(616) 223-7355
T 9

Chi Company
(see Tabor Hill)

Fenn Valley Vineyards
6130 122nd Avenue (Route 4)
Fennville, Michigan 49408
(616) 561-2396
T* 8/8

Fenn Valley Vineyards
41 Courtland Street
Rockford, Michigan 49341
(616) 866-1630
T 10/8

Fink Winery
208 Main Street
Dundee, Michigan 48131
(313) 529-3296
(Crest brands)
T/A 10

Frontenac Vineyards, Inc.
3418 W. Michigan Ave. (Box 215)
Paw Paw, Michigan 49079
(616) 657-5531
(Chateau Club, Chantilly)
T* 7

Good Harbor Vineyards
Route 1, Box 891
Lake Leelanau, Michigan 49653
(616) 256-9165
T 10

Lakeside Vineyard, Inc.
13581 Red Arrow Highway
Harbert, Michigan 49115
(616) 469-0700
(Molly Pitcher)
T 7

Leelanau Wine Cellars, Ltd.
12683 County Road, 626 (Box 13)
Omena, Michigan 49624
(616) 386-5201/946-1653
T 8

Leelanau Wine Cellars
726 North Memorial Highway
Traverse City, Michigan 49684
(616) 946-1653
(tasting/retail outlet only)
T 0

Leelanau Wine Cellar
975 South Main Street
Frankenmuth, Michigan 48734
(517) 652-3171
(tasting/retail outlet only)
T   **0**

L. Mawby Vineyards Winery
4519 Elm Valley Road (Box 237)
Suttons Bay, Michigan 49682
(616) 271-3522
T/A   **10**

Milan Wineries, Inc.
4109 Joe Street at 6000 Michigan
Detroit, Michigan 48210
(313) 894-6464
(Cadillac Club, Nature Bay)
T/A   **7**

St. Julian Wine Company
716 South Kalamazoo Street
Paw Paw, Michigan 49079
(616) 657-5568
(Windsor Club, Sholom Kosher)
T   **5**

St. Julian Wine Co.
127 South Main Street
Frankenmuth, Michigan 48734
(517) 652-3281
T   **9**

Tabor Hill/Chi Company
Route 2, Box 720
Buchanan, Michigan 49107
(616) 422-1161
T*   **8**

Tabor Hill Champagne Cellar
10243 Red Arrow Highway
Bridgman, Michigan 49106
(616) 465-6566
T*   **0**

Vendramino Vineyards Co.
Route 1, Box 257
Paw Paw, Michigan 49079
(616) 657-5890
(Cask, Pol Pereaux)
T*   **10**

Warner Vineyards, Inc.
706 South Kalamazoo Street
Paw Paw, Michigan 49079
(616) 657-3165
T   **5**

Warner Vineyards
North Main Street
Lawton, Michigan 49065
(616) 624-4381
NT   **6**

Warner Vineyards
5450 West Jefferson
Detroit, Michigan 48214
(313) 849-0220
(distribution center only)
NT   **0**

MISSOURI

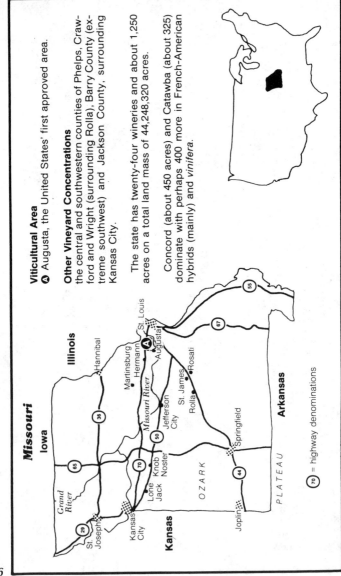

Viticultural Area

Ⓐ Augusta, the United States' first approved area.

Other Vineyard Concentrations

the central and southwestern counties of Phelps, Crawford and Wright (surrounding Rolla), Barry County (extreme southwest) and Jackson County, surrounding Kansas City.

The state has twenty-four wineries and about 1,250 acres on a total land mass of 44,248,320 acres.

Concord (about 450 acres) and Catawba (about 325) dominate with perhaps 400 more in French-American hybrids (mainly) and *vinifera*.

Missouri

Iowa

Illinois

Grand River

St. Joseph

29

Kansas City

Hannibal

36

65

Martinsburg

Hermann

Augusta

St. Louis

Lone Jack

Knob Noster

50

70

Missouri River

Jefferson City

St. James

Rolla

Rosati

67

55

Springfield

OZARK

44

Joplin

P L A T E A U

Kansas

Arkansas

70 = highway denominations

"Explosive development" were the words used to describe this state's wine industry in the 1980s by Bruce Zoecklein, Missouri's extension enologist. The fact that the Show Me State even hired an official enologist is indicative of some expectation. Indeed, my notes for Missouri were the most often amended throughout the compilation of this book.

Missouri was once the nation's second largest wine producer (after Ohio), but disease, climate, prohibition, and competition helped to set the state back many years until the last decade or so. Leftover Concords, Catawbas, and Niagaras still dominate in the fields, and half of them go towards jellies and juice.

But renewed interest, combined with advances in viticultural and enological techniques, are radically changing the state from a grapey backwater into an area that, if not a powerhouse among winegrowing states, is at least worth watching. Even Zoecklein was willing to admit that a lot of what is "happening" in Missouri is still actually in the "talking" stage, so don't pack any bags yet.

Only one winery, Carver Wine Cellars, near Rolla, is showing real interest in *vinifera*. The majority of the effort to grow non-American varieties is aimed at growing French-American hybrids and producing good wines from them. Currently (although I have not checked the statistics in the last hour), hybrids account for an astounding thirty percent of all the acreage. Varieties such Seyval, Vidal and Villard blanc, and, of course, Missouri Riesling look quite promising, and whites, in general, seem to have a – 'scuse me – rosy future. Red hybrids such as Baco, Chelois, and Chancellor have already yielded decent beverages.

The American variety, Norton, is making a comeback in the eyes of several, though its detractors consider its wines too heavy.

An incredibly hard and deep topsoil, and the resulting drainage and other moisture problems, seems to pose the largest obstacle to more widespread plantings. Drip irrigation is being studied as a counter to that problem.

I will most likely have to revise the Missouri chapter first.

For a pamphlet on Missouri's wineries, along with a fairly detailed tour map, write the Missouri Winegrowers Association, Route 2, Box 139, Saint James, Missouri 65559, (Heinrichshaus Vineyard & Winery).

MISSOURI

The Abbey
(see Winery of the Abbey)

Ashby Vineyards
Route 1, Box 55
St. James, Missouri 65559
(314) 265-8629
T*   8

Axel Arneson Winery
(see Peaceful Bend Vineyard)

Bardenheier's Wine Cellars
1019 Skinker Parkway
St. Louis, Missouri 63102
(314) 862-1400
(Caladina, Frisco, Del Rio, Reception,
Ozark Mountain, Old Fashion, Rosie
O'Grady, Missouri Tradition,
Barcelona)
T*   6

Bias Vineyards & Winery
Route 1
Berger, Missouri 63014
(314) 834-5475
T   10

Bowman Wine Cellars
500 Welt Street
Weston, Missouri 64098
(816) 386-5588/5235
(Weston Winery)
T   10

Bristleridge Winery
Route 1, Box 95
Knob Noster, Missouri 65336
(816) 747-5713
T/A   10

Carver Wine Cellars
P.O. Box 1316
Rolla (Vida), Missouri 65401
(314) 364-4335
T*   10

James F. Dierberg
(see Hermannhof Winery)

Eckert Winery
(see Sunnyslope Winery)

Edelweiss Winery & Stone
   Church Vineyards
Highway E & Stone Church
   Road, Rt. 7
New Haven, Missouri 63068
(314) 237-2841
T/A   10

Ferrigno Vineyards & Winery
Highway B, Route 1, Box 227
St. James, Missouri 65559
(314) 265-7742
T/A   10

Green Valley Vineyards
Highway D, Rural Route
Portland, Missouri 65067
(314) 676-5771
T/P   10

Heinrichshaus Vineyard
& Winery
Route 2, Box 139
St. James, Missouri 65559
(314) 265-5000
T   10

Hermannhof Winery
330 East First Street
Hermann, Missouri 65041
(314) 486-5959
T/P   9

Kruger Winery & Vineyard
Route 1
Nelson, Missouri 65347
(816) 837-3217/761-4311/
784-2325
T/A   10

Midi Vineyards, Ltd.
Route 1
Lone Jack, Missouri 64070
(816) 566-2119/524-7760
T   10

Montelle Vineyards, Inc.
Route 1, Box 94
Augusta, Missouri 63332
(314) 228-4464
(River Country, Miraclair)
T*   10

Mount Pleasant Vineyards
101 Webster Street
Augusta, Missouri 63332
(314) 228-4419
T   8

Ozark Vineyard Winery, Inc.
Highway 65, west at
Highway 176
Chestnut Ridge, Missouri 65630
(417) 587-3555
T*   10

Peaceful Bend Vineyard
Route 2, Box 131
Steeleville, Missouri 65565
(314) 775-2578
T   10

Reis Winery
Route 4, Box 133
Licking, Missouri 65542
(314) 674-3763
T*/P   10

Rosati Winery
(see Ashby Vineyards)

St. Clair Vineyards & Winery
Route 4
Sullivan, Missouri 63080
(314) 862-8742/741-3057
T/A   10

St. James Winery
Route 2, Box 98A
St. James, Missouri 65559
(314) 265-7912
T/P   8

Stone Hill Wine Company
Route 1, Box 26
Hermann, Missouri 65041
(314) 486-2221
T   7

Sunnyslope Winery & Vineyard
1721 Horseshoe Ridge
Chesterfield, Missouri 63017
(314) 532-3680
(Eckert Winery)
T/A   **10**

Weston Winery
(see Bowman Wine Cellars)

The Winery of the Abbey
Route 3, Box 199
Cuba, Missouri 65453
(314) 885-2168
T   **10**

Ziegler Winery
1419 Sequoia, I.H.
Cuba, Missouri 65453
(314) 885-7496
T*   **10**

NEW YORK

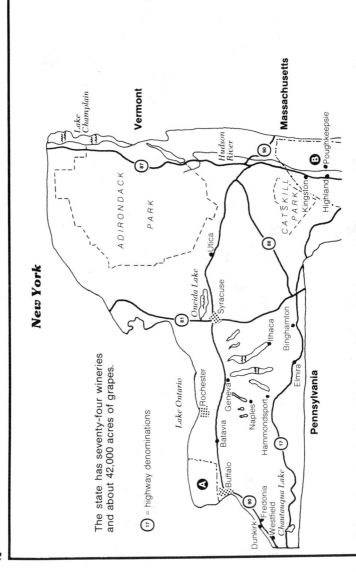

New York

The state has seventy-four wineries
and about 42,000 acres of grapes.

(17) = highway denominations

Vermont

Massachusetts

Pennsylvania

Lake Champlain

ADIRONDACK

PARK

Hudson River

CATSKILL
PARK

Utica

Oneida Lake

Syracuse

Ithaca

Binghamton

Elmira

Kingston
Highland
Poughkeepsie

Lake Ontario

Rochester

Batavia
Geneva
Naples
Hammondsport

Buffalo

Dunkirk
Fredonia
Westfield
Chautauqua Lake

A

B

202

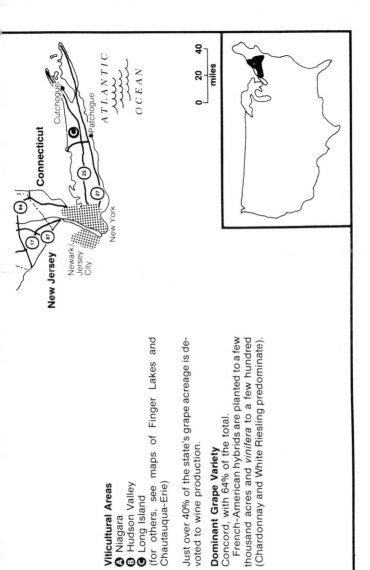

Viticultural Areas

Ⓐ Niagara
Ⓑ Hudson Valley
Ⓒ Long Island
(for others, see maps of Finger Lakes and Chautauqua-Erie)

Just over 40% of the state's grape acreage is devoted to wine production.

Dominant Grape Variety

Concord, with 64% of the total.

French-American hybrids are planted to a few thousand acres and *vinifera* to a few hundred (Chardonnay and White Riesling predominate).

WITH ABOUT 42,000 ACRES OF GRAPES AND NEARLY SEVENTY WINE-
ries, New York is far and away the leading wine state other than
California. However, one half of the state's grapes are used for
non-wine purposes, while the ubiquitous Concord accounts for
two-thirds of the plantings. But New York, like the Golden State,
is diverse in its grape endeavors and each of its areas has goals
of its own.

The state can be divided into four main wine sub-regions: the
Chautauqua-Erie-Niagara area in the extreme west, the Finger
Lakes district in the west-center, and two small areas in the east
known as the Hudson River Valley and Long Island regions. Of
the four, the first dominates in acreage with 60 percent of the
total, while the Finger Lakes is home to the largest portion of
the wineries.

The Chautauqua-Erie-Niagara region lies roughly between Buffalo and Westfield, along Lake Erie, which the largest winery,
Mogen David, calls home. Its approximately 23,000 acres of
grapes − 85 percent Concord − form part of the Chautauqua-
Lake Erie grape belt that stretches into Ohio and Pennsylvania.
Although there are a dozen large and small wineries in the New
York state section, only about 25 percent of the grapes grown
along this belt are actually used for winemaking. However, current research indicates that a far greater number of wine varieties
could and should be planted in the area. Good drainage, sufficient sunshine, and very good yields for most varieties are pre-
dicted. Currently, several wineries produce wines from French-
American hybrids and American varieties and a very few play
around with *viniferas:* White Riesling, Chardonnay, and Gewürztraminer.

The Finger Lakes district is home to thirty wineries which
make everything from ersatz Sherry to white and red *vinifera*
wines in the European style, to what Dr. Konstantin Frank calls
"Château Mystery" wines, or those from French-American hybrids.

Frank, president of Vinifera Wine Cellars in Hammondsport,
was one of a very few people who knew that the *vinifera* species
could grow in the hard northeastern climate. He had worked
with such varieties all his life in such areas as the frigid Ukraine,

which does not exactly remind people of Miami Beach. With the support of Charles Fournier, then president of Gold Seal Vineyards, Frank proved his point and, since the 1950s, has been growing dozens of such European plants in the Finger Lakes district. Though some still maintain that Frank is just an exceptional, persistent, and lucky man, others have followed his advice and produced successful *vinifera*-based wines.

While Frank has no use for the French-American hybrids, whose wines contain substances called "diglucosides" which Frank maintains causes genetic damage, many winegrowers in the area do grow the hybrids. The approximately 4,000 acres of hybrids in the area amounts to double the proportion planted in the Northeast as a whole. Aurore dominates with about 1,500 acres, Baco noir and de Chaunac account for about 600 and 860 acres, respectively, Seyval blanc, Rougeon, Maréchal Foch, and the recently developed Cayuga are represented, though on a smaller scale.

Researchers at the New York State Agricultural Experimental Station at Geneva, like those at the University of California at Davis, are constantly testing for adaptable new hybrids. The station, under the new direction of grape breeder Dr. Bruce Reisch, has released several certified varieties in the last year alone. Ex-director Robert M. Pool, states: "I am very confident that the vineyard and winemaking qualities of the vines in the grape breeding programs at Geneva and Vineland, Ontario are such that they should form the fundamental base on which the eastern wine industry will grow." Still, American varieties at present account for three-quarters of the plantings and provide the backbone of the wine and grape economy of the district.

A new organization was developed recently which offers information and maps of the district: Finger Lakes Winegrowers Association, 116 Buffalo (Canandaigua Winery), Canandaigua, New York 14424.

Most of the grape growing of the Hudson River area is concentrated in two counties, Ulster and Columbia, with a few patches in Dutchess County. But from Albany to Westchester, 1,000 acres of grape plants thrive. Three-quarters of these are American varieties and the remaining acreage is equally divided between *vinifera* and French-American hybrids. The latter two are slowly but surely gaining in both reputation and plantings.

Long Island, currently two wineries and a handful of acreage strong, may well surprise everyone (save the locals) with its *vinifera* wines. Pinot noir, White Riesling, Chardonnay, Cabernet-Sauvignon, and Sauvignon blanc are grown on a very limited basis between the "chogue" twins, "Pat" and "Cut." Some examples of *vinifera* wines from Long Island have been exceptional.

For "A Guide to New York State Wineries," send your request to the State of New York, Department of Agriculture and Markets, Albany, New York 12235.

The recent loosening of restrictive legislation in the state can only spur consumer awareness of New York's and other regions' wines. Look for increased income for the state's wine industry and subsequent, if cautious, expansion.

The winery listings include an abbreviated indication of the general location of each operation, which should help make touring easier. "FL" next to a winery's name and address will tell you that the winery is in or near the Finger Lakes district. "CH/ER" indicates that the winery is in the Chautauqua-Erie district and includes those wineries in or near the sub-district of Niagara. "E" tells you that the winery is in the eastern regions which includes the Hudson River area as well as the areas in or near the city of New York and Long Island.

N E W   Y O R K

Americana Vineyards
4367 East Covert Road
R.D. 1, Box 58A
Interlaken, New York 14847
(607) 387-6901

T*/P   10   FL

The Barry Wine Company, Inc.
7107 Vineyard Road
Conesus, New York 14435
(716) 346-2321
(O-Neh-Da)

T*   7   FL

Benmarl Wine Company
Highland Avenue
Marlboro, New York 12542
(914) 236-7271
(Cuvee du Vigneron)

T/A   9   E

Bluff Point Winery
R.D. 5, Vine Road
Penn Yan, New York 14527
(315) 536-2682

T/A   10   FL

Brimstone Hill Vineyard
Box 142, R.D. 2 Brimstone
  Hill Road
Pine Bush, New York 12566
(914) 744-2231

| T | 10 | | E |

Brotherhood Corporation
35 North Street
Washingtonville, New York
10992
(914) 496-3661

| T* | 7 | | E |

Bully Hill Vineyards, Inc.
Greyton H. Taylor
  Memorial Drive
Hammondsport, New York
14840
(607) 868-3610/4825
(Walter St. Bully)

| T | 8 | | FL |

Frank & Hale Burch Farms, Inc.
1593 Hamlin Parma Town
  Line Road
527 North Avenue
Hilton, New York 14468
(716) 392-3140

| T* | 10 | | FL |

Cagnasso Winery
Route 9W
Marlboro, New York 12542
(914) 236-4630

| T* | 9 | | E |

Canandaigua Wine Company,
  Inc.
116 Buffalo
Canandaigua, New York 14424
(716) 394-3630
(Richard's, Virginia Dare, Vino
Casata, J. Roget, Bisceglia, in
California)

| T*/P | 4/4 | | FL |

Casa Larga Vineyards
2287 Turk Hill Road
Fairport, New York 14450
(716) 223-4210

| T* | 10 | | FL |

Cascade Mountain Vineyards
Flint Hill Road
Amenia, New York 12501
(914) 373-9021

| T* | 10 | | E |

Chadwick Bay Wine Company
10001 Route 60
Fredonia, New York 14063
(716) 672-5000

| T/A | 10 | | CH/ER |

Chateau Esperanza
Route 54A, Box 76A
Bluff Point, New York 14417
(315) 536-7481

| T* | 10 | | FL |

Chateau Valois
Route 414
Valois, New York 14888
(607) 546-5235

| T/P | 10 | | FL |

The Finger Lakes

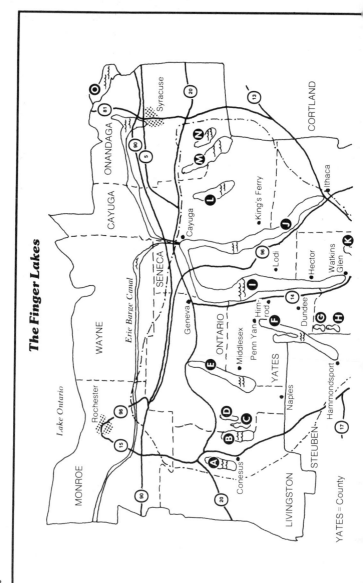

YATES = County

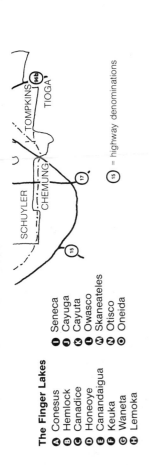

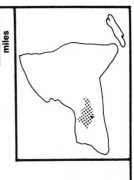

The Finger Lakes

- **Ⓐ** Conesus
- **Ⓑ** Hemlock
- **Ⓒ** Canadice
- **Ⓓ** Honeoye
- **Ⓔ** Canandaigua
- **Ⓕ** Keuka
- **Ⓖ** Waneta
- **Ⓗ** Lemoka
- **Ⓘ** Seneca
- **Ⓙ** Cayuga
- **Ⓚ** Cayuta
- **Ⓛ** Owasco
- **Ⓜ** Skaneateles
- **Ⓝ** Otisco
- **Ⓞ** Oneida

⑮ = highway denominations

The viticultural area is made up of twelve contiguous counties, they include Steuben and Cortland, which are not given full representation on the map.

The Concord variety, with about 6,000 acres planted, dominates the total with almost 40%. Catawba, Aurore, Delaware, and Niagara combine for another 6,000 or so, with others such as de Chaunac, Baco noir, Seyval and others planted to another 2,000 or so. Vinifera, mainly Chardonnay and White Riesling, are planted to only a few hundred acres.

The Finger Lakes account for about 38% of the New York state total for grape acreage.

Chimney's Farm
(see Four Chimneys)

Clinton Vineyards
Schultzville Road
Clinton Corners, New York
   12514
(914) 266-5372/(212) 582-5816
T/A   **10**   **E**

Cottage Vineyards
Old Post Road (Box 608)
Marlboro, New York 12542
(914) 236-4870
T/A   **10**   **E**

Crown Royal Wine Cellars
657 Montgomery Street
Brooklyn, New York 11225
(212) 467-6218
T/A   **9**

Delmonico's
182 15th Street
Brooklyn, New York 11215
(212) 768-7020
NT   **7**   **E**

De May Wine Cellars
Route 88
Hammondsport, New York
   14840
(607) 569-2040
T   **10**   **FL**

East Branch Winery
R.D. 1, 5503 Dutch Street
Dundee, New York 14837
(607) 292-3999
(McGregor Vineyards)
T/A/P   **10**   **FL**

Eaton Vineyards, Inc.
P.O. Box 284
Pine Plains, New York 12567
(518) 398-7791
T/A   **10**   **E**

El Paso Winery
R.D. 1, Box 170
Ulster Park, New York 12847
(914) 331-8642
(Publio Felipe Beltra)
T/A   **10**   **E**

Finger Lakes Wine Cellars
R.D. 1, Hall Road
Branchport, New York 14418
(315) 595-2812
T/A   **10**   **FL**

Four Chimneys Farm Winery
R.D. 1, Hall Road
Himrod, New York 14852
(607) 243-7502
T   **10**   **FL**

Dr. Konstantin D. Frank & Sons
R.D. 2
Hammondsport, New York
   14840
(607) 868-4884
(Vinifera Wine Cellars)
T/A   **10**   **FL**

Fredonia Products Co., Inc.
Cliffstar Avenue (123 E. 3rd)
Dunkirk, New York 14048
(716) 366-6100
(Old Waldorf, Old Pioneer,
Star Brothers, Star Wine,
Maccabee)
T/A   **5**   **CH/ER**

Galante's Farm Winery
9813 Erie Road
Angola, New York 14006
(716) 549-0634
T/A   10   **CH/ER**

Giasi Vineyard
Box 72B, Route 414
Burdett, New York 14818
(607) 546-4601
T/A   10   **FL**

Glenora Wine Cellars, Inc.
Highway 14
Dundee, New York, 14837
(607) 243-7600
T*   9   **FL**

Gold Seal Vineyards, Inc.
Route 54A (Pultenny Road)
Hammondsport, New York
14840
(607) 868-3232
(Henri Marchant)
T   5   **FL**

Great River Winery & Marlboro
  Champagne Cellars
104 Western Avenue
Marlboro, New York 12542
(914) 236-4440
(Chaumont)
T*   8   **E**

Great Western Winery
(see Pleasant Valley Wine Co.)

Hammondsport Wine Company,
  Inc.
89 Lake Street
Hammondsport, New York
  14840
(607) 569-2255
(owned by Canandaigua, *q.v.*)
T/A   7   **FL**

Hargrave Vineyard
Alvah's Lane, Box 927 (Route 27)
Cutchogue, Long Island,
  New York 11935
(516) 734-5158
(Long Island Vineyards, Inc.)
T/A   9   **E**

Heron Hill Vineyards, Inc.
Middle Road (Routes 2 and 76)
Hammondsport, New York
  14840
(607) 868-4241
T/A   10   **FL**

Hi Tor Vineyards
Hi Tor Road
New City, New York 10956
(914) 634-7960
T*   10   **E**

Hudson Valley Winery, Inc.
Blue Point Road
Highland, New York 12528
(914) 691-7296
T/*/P   8   **E**

Frederick S. Johnson Vineyards
West Main Road, Box 52
Westfield, New York 14787
(716) 326-2191
T   8   CH/ER

The Vineyards of Patricia and
   Peter Lenz
Box 28, Main Road
Peconic, New York 11958
(516) 734-7499
T/A   10   E

Long Island Vineyards, Inc.
(See Hargrave)

Loukas Wines
910 Gerard Avenue
Bronx, New York 10452
(212) 992-1024
T/A   10   E

Lucas Winery
R.D. 2, County Road 150
Interlaken, New York 14847
(607) 532-4825
T/A   10   FL

McGregor Winery & Vineyards
(see East Branch Winery)

Merritt Estate Winery, Inc.
2264 King Road
Forestville, New York 14062
(716) 965-4800
(Sheridan Wine Cellars)
T   9   CH/ER

Mogen David Wine Corporation
85 Bourne Street (Box 1)
Westfield, New York 14797
(716) 326-3151
T/A   4   CH/ER

Monarch Wine Company
4500 Second Avenue
Brooklyn, New York 11232
(212) 965-8800
(Manischewitz, Pol d'Argent,
   Chateau Laurent)
NT   5   E

Niagara Wine Cellars
4100 Ridge Road (Route 104)
Cambria, New York 14094
(716) 433-0856
(Lilliput)
T/A   9   CH/ER

Northeast Vineyard
Silver Mountain Road
Millerton, New York 12546
(518) 789-3645
T/A   10   E

North Lake Vineyards
R.D. 2, Route 89 (Box 271)
Romulus, New York 14541
(607) 273-6804
(Fred O. Williams, Jr.)
T/A   10   FL

North Salem Vineyard, Inc.
Hardscrabble and Delancey
   Roads
North Salem, New York 10560
(914) 669-5518/(212) 534-7222
T/A   10   E

The Parson's Cellar
R.D. 1, Bath Road
Dundee, New York 14837
(607) 292-3842
T/A 10 **FL**

Peconic Bay Vineyards
P.O. Box 709
Cutchogue, New York 11935
(516) 567-7922/698-2741
T/A 10 **E**

Penn Yan Wine Cellars, Inc.
150 Water Street
Penn Yan, New York 14527
(315) 536-2361
(Yates County)
T/A 7 **FL**

Plane's Cayuga Vineyard
6799 Cayuga Lake Road (89)
Ovid, New York 14521
(607) 869-5158
T/A 10 **FL**

Pleasant Valley Wine Company
Old Bath Road
Hammondsport, New York
 14840
(607) 569-2121
(Great Western)
T* 5 **FL**

Poplar Ridge Vineyards
R.D. 1, Route 414
Valois, New York 14888
(607) 582-6421
T/A 10 **FL**

Robin Fils & Company
School Street and Hewitt Place
Batavia, New York 14020
(716) 344-1111
(Capri, Imperator)
T/A 5 **W**

Rolling Vineyards Farm Winery
P.O. Box 37, 5055 Route 414
Hector, New York 14841
(607) 546-9302
T* 10 **FL**

Royal Wine Corporation
Dock Road
Milton, New York 12547
(914) 795-2240
(Kedem)
T*/P 5/5 **E**

Royal Wine Corporation
418-430 Kent Avenue
Brooklyn, New York 11211
(212) 384-2400
NT 7/5 **E**

Royal Wine Corporation
107 Norfolk Street
New York, New York 10002
(212) 673-2780
T/A 8/5 **E**

Rotolo & Romeo Wines
234 Rochester Street
Avon, New York 14414
(716) 226-2620/461-2905
T/A 10 **FL**

Schapiro's Wine Company, Ltd.
126 Rivington Street
New York, New York 10002
(212) 674-4404
T* 7 E

Schloss Doepken Winery
East Main Road, R.D. 2
Ripley, New York 14775
(716) 326-3636
T* 10 **CH/ER**

Solano Winery, Inc.
6115 15th Avenue
Brooklyn, New York 11219
(212) 259-1188
(Jean Darney, St. Denis)
T/A 8 E

The Taylor Wine Company, Inc.
Old Bath Road
Hammondsport, New York
   14840
(607) 569-2111
(Great Western)
T*/P 3 FL

Transamerica Wine Corporation
Brooklyn Navy Yards
Building 120
Brooklyn, New York 10012
(212) 625-0990
(Villa Pinza, Melisande,
Miramar, Fucini, Merano)
NT 9 E

Valley Vineyards
Box 24, Oregon Trail Road
Walker Valley, New York 12588
(914) 744-3912/5287
T*/P 10 E

Villa D'Ingianni Winery, Inc.
1183 E. Keuka Lake Road,
   Route 54
Dundee, New York 14837
(607) 292-3914/(315) 536-3025
(Vintage Villa, Sunshine,
Foxlane, Golden Valley, Autumn
Harvest)
T 7 FL

Vinifera Wine Cellars
(see Dr. Konstantin Frank)

Wagner Vineyards
Route 414
Lodi, New York 14860
(607) 582-6450
T/P 7 FL

Walker Valley Vineyards
(see Valley Vineyards)

Wickham Vineyards
P.O. Box 62
Hector, New York 14841
(607) 546-2164
T/A 9 FL

Widmer's Wine Cellars, Inc.
West Avenue and Tobey Street
Naples, New York 14512
(716) 374-6311
(Lake Niagara, Lake Rosello,
Naples Valley)
T* 5 FL

Herman J. Wiemer Vineyard
Route 13, Box 4
Dundee, New York 14837
(607) 243-7971
T/A 10 FL

Windmill Farms
193 County Line Road
Ontario, New York 14519
(315) 265-0658
T/A   **10**   **FL**

Windsor Vineyards, Inc.
(see Great River Winery)

Woodbury Vineyards
South Roberts Road, Route 1
Dunkirk, New York 14048
(716) 679-1708
T   **9**   **CH/ER**

OHIO

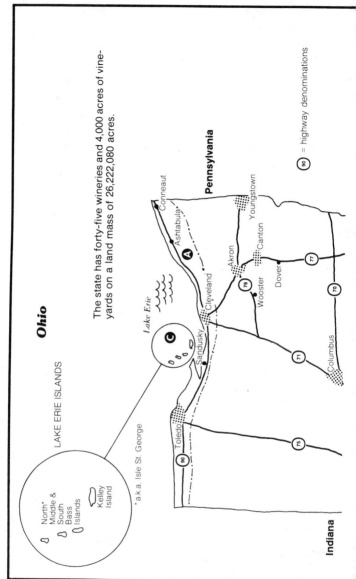

Ohio

LAKE ERIE ISLANDS

The state has forty-five wineries and 4,000 acres of vine-yards on a land mass of 26,222,080 acres.

North* / Middle & / South / Bass / Islands

Kelley Island

*a.k.a. Isle St. George

Lake Erie

Conneaut

Ashtabula

Pennsylvania

A

Cleveland

Sandusky

C

Akron

76

Youngstown

Wooster

Canton

Dover

77

Toledo

90

75

71

70

Columbus

Indiana

90 = highway denominations

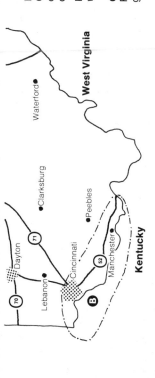

Predominant Grape Variety

Concord (2,600 acres) and other American grapes account for 83% of the total;

French/American (15%) and vinifera (2%) account for rest.

Grapes for Wine

From 33% to 50% of all Ohio grapes go for wine use.

Viticultural Areas

Ⓐ Lake Erie/Chautauqua (with New York and Pennsylvania)
Ⓑ Ohio River Valley (with Indiana and Kentucky)
Ⓒ Lake Erie Islands (see inset)

Other Vineyard Concentrations

small plantings in southwest and, especially, western counties (Miami and Warren).

West Virginia

Waterford●

●Clarksburg

Dayton

Lebanon●

Cincinnati

●Peebles

Manchester●

Kentucky

Ⓑ

(70) (71) (52)

0 25 50
miles

MUCH OF THE HESITANCY FOR PROGNOSTICATION I ENCOUNTERED with Pennsylvania winefolk was duplicated by Ohioans. Yet I sensed a greater, if restrained, enthusiasm from these winegrowers, especially – but not exclusively – from those in the center and south of the state.

Although Ohio's grape acreage is one-fourth that of Pennsylvania, proportionately twice as many of Ohio's grapes are devoted to wine use. The majority of the state's vineyards – about 85 percent – is located along the Lake Erie shores, and even offshore on the Lake Erie Islands. Over half of this acreage, of which 90 percent is Concord, is in the Ashtabula area near the Pennsylvania border. The rest, from Toledo to Cleveland, is split almost evenly between Concords and Catawbas with a few Niagaras in for laughs. As is the case in the rest of this grape belt in the other states, the climate here is dependable.

Ohio's percentage of French-American hybrid acreage is the highest in the seventeen-state region, next to Missouri's. In the south-central part of the state, particularly in the southeast along the Ohio River, such varieties account for three-quarters of the plantings. These areas are also home to half the state's wineries, primarily small operations.

Vinifera accounts for, at most, 100 acres throughout the state; but there are indications that the amount could rise if test plots – some funded by the state and located at several of its fifteen research stations throughout Ohio – prove positive. The largest plot of *vinifera* in the state lies on the Isle St. George and is owned by the Meier's Wine Cellars.

Write the Ohio Wine Producers Association, 3379 Cold Springs Road, Austinburg, Ohio 44010, for a pamphlet on the wineries of the state and for information about grape happenings in general.

The winery listings are divided into four categories. "ERIE" wineries are within or near the Lake Erie area of the north. "SE" indicates a winery in a small patch to the southeast of Canton. "WC" identifies all areas fairly immediately west and north of the city of Columbus. And a "SW" winery is one within a rather large area stretching from Cincinnati in the extreme southwest to the area near Waterford, following a parallel course along the Ohio River.

O H I O

Breitenbach Wine Cellars, Inc.
R.R. 1
Dover, Ohio 44622
(216) 343-3603
T/A   10   SE

Leslie J. Bretz
P.O. Box 17
Middle Bass, Ohio 43446
(419) 285-2323
T/A   10   ERIE

Granville Vineyards
1037 Newark Road
Granville, Ohio 43023
(614) 587-0312
NT   10   WC

Brushcreek Vineyards
12351 Newkirk Lane, R.R. 4
Peebles, Ohio 45660
(513) 558-2618
T   10   SW

Buccia Vineyards
518 Gore Road
Conneaut, Ohio 44030
(216) 593-5976
T*   10   ERIE

Cedar Hill Wine Company
2195 Lee Road
Cleveland Heights, Ohio 44118
(216) 321-9511
(Chateau Lagniappe)
T*   10   ERIE

Chalet Debonné Vineyards, Inc.
7743 Doty Road
Madison, Ohio 44057
(216) 466-3485
T*   8   ERIE

Chateau Lagniappe
(see Cedar Hill Wine Company)

John Christ Winery
32421 Walker Road
Avon Lake, Ohio 44012
(216) 933-9672
T/A   10   ERIE

Colonial Vineyards
6222 North State Route 48
Lebanon, Ohio 45036
(513) 932-3842
(CVI)
T*   10   SW

Daughters Wine Cellar
5573 Ridge Road
Madison, Ohio 44057
(216) 428-5138
T/A   10   ERIE

Dover Vineyards, Inc.
24945 Detroit Road
Westlake, Ohio 44145
(216) 871-0700
T*/P   7   ERIE

E & K Wine Company
220 East Water Street
Sandusky, Ohio 44870
(419) 627-9622
(Mellow Monk)
T*   9   ERIE

Lake Erie/Chautauqua Viticultural Area

Flint

Port Huron

Lake Huron

CANADA

London

Lake St. Clair

Detroit

Windsor

Lake

Michigan

(23)

(80) (90)

Toledo

Lake Erie Islands
(see Ohio)

Sandusky

Conneaut

Ashtabula

(90)

Cleveland

(80)

Akron

Kent

Ohio

(76)

0   35   70
miles

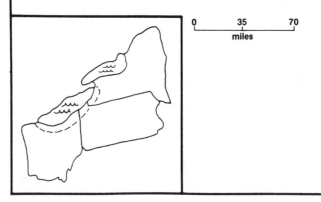

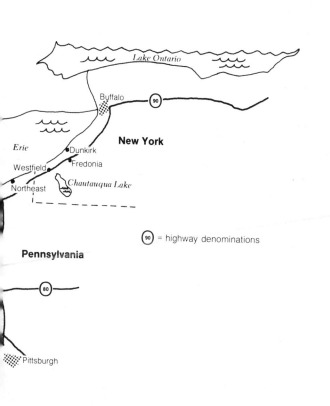

= highway denominations

This tri-state area is planted to about 40,000 acres of grapes:

85% of all varieties are Concords.

60% to 70% of all grapes harvested are used for jams, jellies, and/or juice.

20% to 30% are used for wine-making.

The remainder go to the fresh market.

Ferrante Wine Farm
5585 Route 307, W. Harpersfield
Geneva, Ohio 44041
(216) 466-6046
T/A   **10**   **ERIE**

Grand River Wine Company
5750 Madison Road
Madison, Ohio 44057
(216) 298-9838
T*   **10**   **ERIE**

Hafle Vineyards
2369 Upper Valley Pike
Springfield, Ohio 45502
(513) 399-2334/5742
T*/P   **10**   **SW**

Heineman Winery
Catawba and Cherry Avenue
Put in Bay, Ohio 43456
(419) 285-2811
(Lake Erie Islands)
T*   **9**   **ERIE**

Heritage Vineyards
6020 South Wheelock Road
West Milton, Ohio 45382
(513) 698-5369
T*   **10**   **WC**

Hilltop Winery
7337 Circle Road
West Farmington, Ohio 44491
(216) 921-3123
T/A   **10**   **ERIE**

Louis Jindra Winery
Box 186A, Route 1
    (Jackson City Road)
Jackson, Ohio 45656
(614) 286-6578
T/A   **10**   **SW**

Johlin Century Winery
3935 Corduroy Road
Oregon, Ohio 43616
(419) 693-6288
T/A   **10**   **ERIE**

Klingshirn Winery
33050 Webber Road
Avon Lake, Ohio 44012
(216) 933-6666
T*   **9**   **ERIE**

Le Boudin Vineyard & Winery
6045 County Road 25
Cardington, Ohio 43315
(419) 768-2091
(Le Boudin & Straits)
T*   **9**   **WC**

Carl M. Limpert
28083 Detroit Road
Westlake, Ohio 44145
(216) 871-0035
T/A   **10**   **ERIE**

Lonz Cellars
(see Meier's/Middle Bass)

Lukens Vineyard, Inc.
10104 State Route 73
Harveysburg, Ohio 45032
(513) 897-1776
(Lakeside, Blanc du Lac)
T   10   **SW**

Mantey Vineyards, Inc.
917 Bardshar Road
Sandusky, Ohio 44870
(216) 625-5474
NT   7   **ERIE**

Markko Vineyard
South Ridge Road, R.D. 2
Conneaut, Ohio 44030
(216) 593-3197
(Underridge)
T/A   10   **ERIE**

Marlo Winery
3660 State Route 47
Fort Laramie, Ohio 45845
(513) 295-3232
T/A   10   **SW**

McIntosh's Ohio Valley Wines
2033 Bethel New Hope Road
  (Box 190)
Bethel, Ohio 45106
(513) 379-1159
T*/P   10   **SW**

Meier's Wine Cellars, Inc.
6955 Plainfield Pike
Silverton, Ohio 45236
(513) 891-2900
(Mantey, Mon Ami, Lonz,
  Chateau Reim)
T*   5   **SW**

Meier's Wine Cellars, Inc.
Sandusky, Ohio 44870
(see Mantey Vineyards)

Meier's Wine Cellars, Inc.
Middle Bass Island, Ohio 43446
(419) 285-5411
(Lonz Cellars)
T   8   **ERIE**

Mon Ami Champagne Co., Inc.
326 West Catawba Road (3845 E.
  Wine Cellars Road)
Catawba Island, Port Clinton,
  Ohio 43452
(419) 797-4445
NT   8   **ERIE**

Moyer Vineyards
U.S. Highway 52 (R.D. 1)
Manchester, Ohio 45144
(513) 549-2957
(River Valley)
T*   10   **SW**

Pompei Winery, Inc.
3994 East 89th Street
Cleveland, Ohio 44105
(216) 883-9370
(P.W.)
T/A   7   **ERIE**

Shawnee Vineyards
Route 4, Route 56 East, R.R. 1
Circleville, Ohio 43113
(614) 474-8918
T/A   10   **SW**

Steuk Wine Company
1001 Fremont Avenue
Sandusky, Ohio 44871
(419) 625-0803
T/A   10   ERIE

Stillwater Winery, Inc.
2311 State Route 55 West
Troy, Ohio 45373
(513) 339-8346
T*   8   SW

Stone Quarry Vineyards Winery
Box 142
Waterford, Ohio 45786
(614) 984-4423
T   10   SE

Warren J. Sublette Winery
2260 Central Parkway
Cincinnati, Ohio 45214
(513) 651-4570
T*   10   SW

Tarula Farms
1786 Creek Road
Clarksville, Ohio 45113
(513) 289-2181
T*/P   9   SW

Valley Vineyards Farm, Inc.
2041 East U.S. 22-3
Morrow, Ohio 45152
(513) 899-2485
T*   8   SW

Vinterra Farm & Winery
6505 Stoker Road
Houston, Ohio 45333
(513) 492-2071
T*   10   SW

Wickliffe Winery
29555 (Rear) Euclid Road
Wickliffe, Ohio 44092
(216) 943-1030
T/A   10   ERIE

Willoughby Winery
30829 Euclid Avenue
Willowick, Ohio 44094
(216) 943-5405
T*   10   ERIE

Wyandotte Wine Cellars, Inc.
4640 Wyandotte Drive
Gahanna, Ohio 43230
(614) 476-3624
T   10   WC

PENNSYLVAN

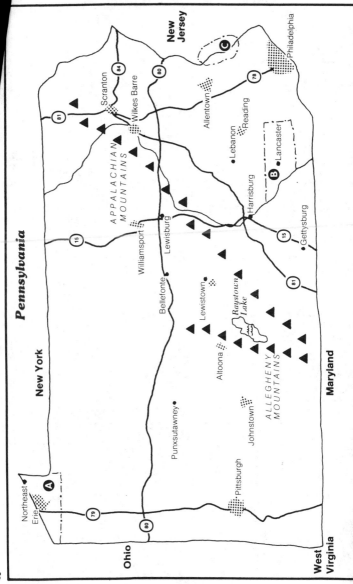

The state has thirty-one wineries and about 14,300 acres of grapeland.

(80) = highway denominations

Viticultural Areas

Ⓐ Erie (see Chautauqua/Erie map)
Ⓑ Lancaster Valley
Ⓒ Central Delaware Valley (mostly in New Jersey)

Other vineyard concentrations:
Blair County, in the Allegheny Mountains, and Mercer County, just below Erie, both have small vineyard acreages of little importance in the overall picture.

Dominant Grape Varieties:
Concord, with 82% of the total; French-American hybrids with 4.0% and less than 1% *vinifera.*

Between 18% and 25% of all the state's grapes go for winemaking.

0   20   40   60
miles

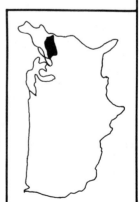

JUST ABOUT EVERYONE FROM THIS STATE I SPOKE WITH HEDGED in answering my questions. Q: Do you think that your industry in general will expand? A: Well ... maybe. Q: Do you think that other-than-American varieties can succeed in Pennsylvania's climate? A: Well ... can't really say.

Good thing I knew when the sun set.

Despite these hesitant responses, it does seem that Pennsylvania is moving forward in many areas. Their grape acreage, for example, has increased by 50 percent in the last decade. Grape prices have not been fantastic, but some predict steady increases. The legislative climate is much more favorable towards the small winegrower than previously. And the number of wineries, expecially smaller ones, has nearly tripled in the last eight years.

Like most of the other northeastern states, however, Pennsylvania is largely a grape juice, jam, and jelly state with less than one-quarter of its acreage devoted to winemaking purposes. More than 95 percent of the grapes are in one county, Erie, which helps to form the three-state Lake Erie grape belt. Ninety-six percent of Pennsylvania's grapes are American and most of that is good-old dependable Concord, though Catawba and Delaware made significant planting increases in the last decade. If this is saddening to most "classic" wine enthusiasts, it isn't to most winegrowers in the state. They realize that such American variety based, semi-sweet wines are what the local customer wants. That may change, but not quickly.

The state's other vineyards – 4 percent of the total – are scattered along the Allegheny Mountains, in the center of the state, and in the southeast, from Gettysburg to Philadelphia. It is in this area, and in Lancaster Valley, expecially, that scientists feel the highest quality wines, from both hybrids and *viniferas,* can be made. If the typical problems of disease and winter injury can be met and overcome, the southeast may surprise the doubters. Aurore, Seyval, Vidal, Foch, Chelois, Landot, Chancellor, Baco, Cascade, and Chambourcin are successful French-American hybrids, while northern European *vinifera* have also met with good, though limited, success.

Hudson Cattell and H. Lee Stauffer wrote "Presenting Pennsylvania's Wines," a little pamphlet on that state's pertinent activity. I am told a revised edition is in the works. Contact L & H Photojournalism, 620 North Pine Street, Lancaster, Pennsylvania 17603.

The winery listings are divided into four categories. "ERIE" indicates the winery is within or near the extreme northwestern portion of the state, along Lake Erie. "E," "W," or "C," for Eastern, Western (other than those near Lake Erie), and Central are self-explanatory.

PENNSYLVANIA

Adams County Winery
Peach Tree Road, R.D. 1
Ortanna, Pennsylvania 17353
(717) 334-4631
T*/P   10   E

Allegro Vineyards
R.D. 2, Box 64 (Chanceford
    Township)
Brogue, Pennsylvania 17309
(717) 927-9148
T/A   10   E

Stephen Bahn Winery
R.D. 1, Box 758, Goram Road
Brogue, Pennsylvania 17309
(717) 927-9051
T*   10   E

Buckingham Valley Vineyards
Route 413, Box 371
Buckingham, Pennsylvania
    18912
(215) 794-7188
T*   10   E

Bucks Country Vineyards, Inc.
R.D. 1, Route 202
New Hope, Pennsylvania 18938
(215) 794-7449
T*   8   E

Buffalo Valley Winery
Buffalo Road, R.D. 2
Lewisburg, Pennsylvania 17837
(717) 524-4850/2143/2279
T*   10   E

Calvaresi Winery
832 Thorn Street
Reading, Pennsylvania 19601
(215) 373-7821
T/A   10   E

Conestoga Vineyards, Inc.
415 South Queen Street
Lancaster, Pennsylvania 19421
(717) 393-0141
T*   9   E

Conneaut Cellars Winery
R.D. 1
Conneaut Lake, Pennsylvania
  16316
(814) 382-8621

T   10   ERIE

County Creek Winery
133 Cressman Road
Telford, Pennsylvania 18969
(215) 723-6516

T/A   10   E

Doerflinger Wine Cellars, Inc.
3248 Old Berwick Road
Bloomsburg, Pennsylvania 17815
(717) 784-2112/3138

T/A   10   E

Dutch Country Wine Cellar
R.D. 1, Route 143, North
Lenhartsville, Pennsylvania
  19534
(215) 756-6061

T/A   10   E

Heritage Wine Cellars
12162 Buffalo Road, Box 47
North East, Pennsylvania 16428
(814) 725-8015/8653

T/A   6   ERIE

Kolln Vineyards & Winery
State Road 550, R.D. 1, Box 146
Bellefonte, Pennsylvania 16823
(814) 355-4666

T*/P   10   C

La Fayette Vintners, Ltd.
251 West Pike Street
Philadelphia, Pennsylvania
  19140
(215) 223-7595

T/A   8   E

Lancaster County Winery
R.D. 1, Box 329
Willow Street, Pennsylvania
  17584
(717) 464-3555

T   9   E

Lapic Winery
682 Tulip Drive
New Brighton, Pennsylvania
  15066
(412) 846-2031
(La Pic)

T   10   W

Lembo's Vineyards
34 Valley Street
Lewiston, Pennsylvania 17044
(717) 248-4078

T   10   E

Mazza Vineyards, Inc.
11815 East Lake Road
North East, Pennsylvania 16428
(814) 725-8695

T*/P   9   ERIE

Mount Hope Vineyards &
  Winery
P.O. Box 685
Cornwall, Pennsylvania 17016
(717) 665-7021

T/A   9   E

Naylor Wine Cellars, Inc.
R.D. 3
Stewartstown, Pennsylvania
  17403
(717) 741-1236
(Grenadier)

| T | 10 | | E |

Neri's Winery
373 Bridgetown Pike
Langhorne, Pennsylvania 19047
(215) 355-9952

| T/A | 10 | | E |

Nissley Vineyards
Route 1
Bainbridge, Pennsylvania 17502
(717) 426-3514

| T*/P | 9 | | E |

Nittany Valley Winery
724 South Atherton
State College, Pennsylvania
  16801
(814) 238-7562

| T/A | 10 | | C |

Penn-Shore Vineyards, Inc.
10225 East Lake Road
North East, Pennsylvania 16428
(814) 725-8688

| T | 7 | | ERIE |

Presque Isle Wine Cellars
9440 Buffalo Road
Northeast, Pennsylvania 16428
(814) 725-1314

| T*/P | 10 | | ERIE |

Quarry Hill Winery
R.D. 2, Box 168
Shippensburg, Pennsylvania
  17257
(717) 776-3411

| T/A | 10 | | E |

Tucquan Vineyard & Winery
R.D. 2 Box 20
Holtwood, Pennsylvania 17532
(717) 284-2221

| T*/A | 10 | | E |

Wilmont Wines, Inc.
200 Mill Road
Schwenksville, Pennsylvania
  19473
(215) 287-6342

| T* | 10 | | E |

York Springs Winery
Route 1, Box 194
York Springs, Pennsylvania
17372
(717) 528-8490

| T* | 10 | | E |

Northeastern/Midwestern State	# of wineries (mid-1982)	grape acreage (mid-1982)	Vinifera	French-American (Percent of total acreage)	American	Muscadine
1. CONNECTICUT	5	100	10.0	65.0	25.0	-
2. ILLINOIS	4	95	5.3	31.6	63.1	-
3. INDIANA	8	485	2.1	72.2	25.7	-
4. IOWA	13	60*	NA	NA	NA	NA
5. MAINE	0	trace	NA	NA	NA	NA
6. MASSACHUSETTS	3	125	40.0	60.0	-	-
7. MICHIGAN	18	13,640#	0.9	11.1	88.0	-
8. MINNESOTA	2	345	1.0	90.0	9.0	-
9. MISSOURI	24	1,236	1.7	29.5	68.8	-
10. NEW HAMPSHIRE	1	150	-	80.0	20.0	-
11. NEW JERSEY	9	450	10.0	21.1	68.9	-
12. NEW YORK	73	41,979	0.78	11.9	87.2	0.1
13. OHIO	44	4,000	2.0	15.0	83.0	-
14. PENNSYLVANIA	30	14,275#	0.4	3.5	96.1	-
15. RHODE ISLAND	5	100	49.0	49.0	2.0	-
16. VERMONT	0	trace	NA	NA	NA	NA
17. WISCONSIN	9	100*	10.0	60.0	30.0	-
Totals	248+	77,140	1.0	11.8	87.1	0.1

*guesstimates   # from older-than-1981 data (oldest 1978)   +69% bonded since 1970

THE
SOUTHEASTERN
VINEYARD

The Southeastern United States

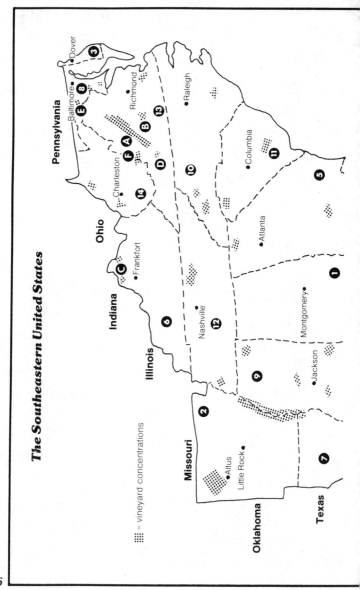

::: = vineyard concentrations

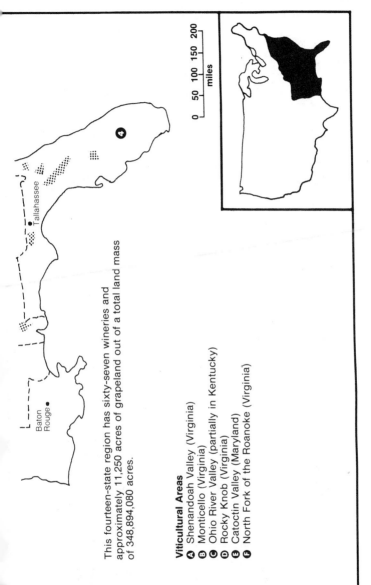

This fourteen-state region has sixty-seven wineries and approximately 11,250 acres of grapeland out of a total land mass of 348,894,080 acres.

Viticultural Areas
- **A** Shenandoah Valley (Virginia)
- **B** Monticello (Virginia)
- **C** Ohio River Valley (partially in Kentucky)
- **D** Rocky Knob (Virginia)
- **E** Catoctin Valley (Maryland)
- **F** North Fork of the Roanoke (Virginia)

It would not be hard to prove the "American-ness" of this fourteen state region: While there exists growing interest in the European *vinifera* and the French-American hybrids, almost 80 percent of the grapes grown are tried and true-blue (and greenish white and bronze) American varieties. Concords, Catawbas, and Delawares dominate in those states where Muscadines do not. Only Virginia (which is dealt with apart), Maryland, West Virginia, and, surprisingly, Tennessee have made modestly successful inroads into the European species and the hybrids.

Alabama, Florida, Georgia, North Carolina, and, to an extent, South Carolina are Muscadine states, and proud of it. The 6,000 or so acres in these states yield grapes for jams, jellies, and table fruit as well as a good deal of fruit that is turned into wine by two score establishments.

"Grapes in Florida are receiving much greater attention than current acreage and economic activity would suggest. Reasons for this are several: a four-decade breeding effort which is overcoming very serious disease problems and producing higher quality, more versatile cultivars with improved fresh, processed juice and wine characteristics; progressive enthusiastic grape growers; a sympathetic state legislature; and a long-term commitment by the Florida Grape Growers Association and the state, regional, and national agricultural establishment."

So says "Florida Grapes: The Next Decade" by Bates, Mortensen and Crocker. The enthusiasm and scientific progress, mentioned in this quote could apply to all the Muscadine states. Yet it is in Florida — astonishingly, to most classic wine lovers — that it is especially true. The first reference to grapes in the New World — discounting Leif Ericson's "Vineland" ad lib — was in Florida over four centuries ago. Since that time all kinds of obstacles have been faced and, eventually, surmounted by the state's grape growers — disease, prohibition, and a dead economy were three of the biggest. As it turned out, however, the ability of the native Muscadines to thrive in the climate spurred interest in the crossbreeding of its varieties as well as those of some non-*rotundifolians* to arrive at more disease-resistant varieties. The three gentlemen quoted above, as well as Professor Loren Stover, have been especially important in these endeavors which have resulted in the development of both wine and table grapes. Nowadays, the Scuppernong, the traditional Muscadine, is being replaced throughout the southeast by the more adaptable Carlos, Noble, Dixie, and Magnolia varieties.

Perdido Vineyards is Alabama's only winery and Muscadine names proudly adorn the labels. James Eddins, its president, has about fifty acres planted. He was also instrumental in getting the state's Farm Winery Bill drawn up and passed. He says that some *vinifera* and French-American hybrids are planted and could thrive in the hilly sections of the north.

Of Georgia's two wineries, one makes tomato wine and the other, Monarch Wine Company, concentrates on grapes, mainly Muscadines. As is the case in Alabama, some *vinifera* and hybrids grow in the northern hill country, though it may be rough going. Time will tell; Georgia is still a vinous toddler.

Three miles east of Highway 61, between the "Mighty Mississip" and the humble Sunflower rivers, lies The Winery Rushing, Mississippi's first modern winery ("the state boasted thirty at the turn of the century," declares owner Sam Rushing). Grapes? All Muscadines, naturally; Carlos, Noble, and Magnolia dominate. "We're trying to make southeastern wines from southeastern grapes," Rushing says. Although the state is in the midst of its own wine "boom" — four new wineries have licenses pending and/or approved — keeping things in perspective is necessary: there are currently fewer than 100 acres in grapes.

The Carolinas account for more grapes than any other states in the region. Nearly all of North Carolina, and the coastal areas of South Carolina, are planted to Muscadines which are used for both jelly and wine. Like Rushing and Duplin Wine Cellars in the North and Tenner Brothers in the South are leading Muscadine enthusiasts.

But don't count the non-Muscadines out, for outside the Deep South — and even in spots within — there is free experimentation. The Biltmore Estate of North Carolina has about 110 acres of grapes planted, nearly all *vinifera*. And, while disease and nematode problems still trouble the growers in Mississippi, the Thousand Oaks Vineyard and Winery in Starkville has some *vinifera* — good old Chardonnay and Cabernet Sauvignon — as well as some French-Americans planted. One organization to contact for more information is The Piedmont Grape Growers Association, Route 10, Box 345, Winston-Salem, North Carolina 27107.

Arkansas has about 4,000 acres of grapeland, most planted to American varieties, and even a dozen percent to Muscadines. In the northwest, 2,000 acres of Concords grow up to become largely non-alcoholic juice in the vats of the Welch's Grape Juice plant in Springdale. Still, there are nine wineries in the state so far, some of which make a little *vinifera* and hybrid wine as well. Most of the action − about 1,600 acres of largely French-American varieties − is in the Ozark foothills, near Altus, near the Arkansas River. One local winery, Wiederkehr, the state's largest, astounded a few experts with its Cabernet-Sauvignon.

Many critics contend that this area, along with sections of neighboring Missouri (see Northeast section), could prove the most successful *vinifera* regions outside California and the Northwest.

Kentucky and Tennessee share a few things in common: each has a like number of wineries and a similar amount of grape acreage, very little of which is either Muscadine or *vinifera;* and each is looking towards vineyards to support the flagging tobacco crop. Kentucky, however, has stuck with American varieties for the most part, while Tennessee is experimenting more with French-American hybrids. Both states are in the infant stage as far as winegrowing is concerned, and many winegrowers may "up and change their minds" if conditions merit it.

After two centuries of hibernation, the Kentucky Vineyard Society was reborn in 1981 with hopes for furthering vine and winery knowledge dissemination. Interested persons should write the Society care of Dr. Robert Miller, Route 10, 103 Lakeshore Drive, Richmond, Kentucky 40475.

Maryland and Delaware account for nine wineries and perhaps 350 acres of grapes, most of which are French-American hybrids. Montbray Wine Cellars, near the Pennsylvania border in Westminster, and Byrd Vineyards, in Myersville (in the Catoctin Valley viticultural area), grow some *vinifera* including some impressive Chardonnay. With the formation of the *Maryland*

Grape Growers' Association, the already heady optimism of winegrowers will be channeled into greater cooperation and movements for more rational state wine legislation. Contact Roger Wolf, Maryland Grape Growers' Association, Valley Road, Box 230, Knoxville, Maryland 21758.

More optimism, this time in West Virginia. With only 100 acres of commercial vineyard land under its belt, the state has defined four geographic wine regions with many sub-regions. These are the northern and eastern panhandles, the Parkersburg area in the west, and the southern section around Charleston. "This . . . makes grape growing thrilling and somewhat hazardous," says Robert F. Pliska, Executive Secretary of the West Virginia Grape Growers Association (write them at Piterra, Purgitsville, West Virginia 26852). One hazard has been the state's governor, who had vetoed farm winery legislation three times until the last was overruled by the state legislature in 1981. Another is a short growing season and damaging frosts, especially in the Charleston area. With a slogan like the WVGGA's, "Almost Heaven is Wine Country," things will probably work themselves out. And as the coal reserves dwindle and more people turn to farming, vineyards look like a natural.

A L A B A M A

Perdido Vineyards, Inc.
Route 1, Box 20-A
Perdido, Alabama
(205) 937-9463
T   8

A R K A N S A S

Cowie Wine Cellars
Route 2 (Box 284)
Paris, Arkansas 72855
(501) 963-3990
(Arkansas Grape & Ives)
T   10

William D. Freyaldenhoven
Highway 64 West
Morrilton, Arkansas 72110
(501) 354-4241
NT   10

Heckmann's Winery
Route 1 (Box 148)
Harrisburg, Arkansas 72432
(501) 578-5541
(Holiday, White Gold,
Little Giant)
T*   10

Mount Bethel Winery
U.S. 64 (Box 137)
Altus, Arkansas 72821
(501) 468-2444
T*   9

Neil's Winery
Route 1 (Main Highway)
Springdale, Arkansas 72764
(501) 361-2954
(Hillbilly Red, Neil's Native)
T*   10

Post Winery, Inc.
Route 1 (Box 1)
Altus, Arkansas 72821
(501) 468-2741
(Post Familie, Altus)
T*   7

Henry J. Sax
Route 1
Altus, Arkansas 72821
(501) 468-2332
T*   10

Wiederkehr Wine Cellars, Inc.
Route 1 (Box 9)
Altus, Arkansas 72821
(501) 468-2611/468-3611
(Granata, Chateau de Monte)
T   5

DELAWARE

Northminster Winery
215 Stone Crop Road
Wilmington, Delaware 19810
(302) 774-1801
T/A   10

FLORIDA

Alaqua Vineyard, Inc.
Route 1, Box 97 C4
Freeport, Florida 32439
(904) 835-2644
T*   10

Florida Heritage Winery
Box 116 (Highway 301)
Anthony, Florida 32617
(904) 732-3427
T/A   10

Fruit Wines of Florida, Inc.
513 South Florida Avenue
Tampa, Florida 33602
(813) 223-1222/226-3221
(Floriana, Palmetto Country)
T/A   7

GEORGIA

Happy "B" Farm Winery
Route 4, Bunn Road (Box 447)
Forsyth, Georgia 31029
(912) 994-6549
T/A   10

Monarch Wine Company
   of Georgia
451 Sawtell Avenue, S.E.
Atlanta, Georgia 30315
(404) 622-4496
(Bojangles, King Cotton, Red
Rooster, Roho Sangria, Deuce
Juice, Square Johnson, Granny's
Smoky Mtn., Heritage House,
Mother Goldstein, Embros,
Candelabra, Ace High, Schapiro's
Rocket)
T/A   5

KENTUCKY

Andrew Berg Cellars
P.O. Box 7891
Louisville, Kentucky 40207
(502) 897-1911
(Martin D. Berg)
T/A   10

Colcord Winery, Inc.
3rd and Pleasant Streets (Box K)
Paris, Kentucky 40361
(606) 987-7440
(Cane Ridge Estate)
T/A   10

Laine Vineyards & Winery
Route 5 (P.O. Box 247)
Fulton, Kentucky 42041
(502) 472-3345
T   9

MARYLAND

Berrywine Plantations Winery
13601 Glisans Mill Road
  (Box 247)
Mount Airy, Maryland 21771
(301) 662-8687
(Plantations)
T*   9

Bon Spuronza, Inc.
1522 Stone Road
Westminster, Maryland 21157
(301) 876-1100
T*/P   10

Boordy Vineyards
12820 Long Green Pike
Hydes, Maryland 21082
(301) 592-5015
T/A   10

Byrd Vineyards
Church Hill Road
Myersville, Maryland 21773
(301) 293-1110
T*   10

Montbray Wine Cellars, Ltd.
818 Silver Run Valley Road
Westminster, Maryland 21157
(301) 346-7878
T/A/P   10

Provenza Vineyards
805 Greenbridge Road
Brookeville, Maryland 20729
(301) 774-2310/277-2447
(Batojolo)
T/A   10

Whitemarsh Cellars
2810 Hoffman Mill Road
Hampstead, Maryland 21074
(301) 876-1455
T/A/P   10

Ziem Vineyards
Route One (Speilman Road)
Fairplay, Maryland 21733
(301) 223-8352
T*   10

MISSISSIPPI

Almarla Vineyards
Frost Bridge Road
Mathersville, Mississippi 39360
(601) 687-0018
T/A   9

Old South Winery
507 Concord Street
Natchez, Mississippi 39120
(601) 445-9924
T/A   10

Thousand Oaks Vineyard
  & Winery
Route 4, Box 133
Starkville, Mississippi 39759
(601) 323-6657
T*   9

The Winery Rushing
P.O. Drawer F
Merigold, Mississippi 38759
(601) 748-2731
T*   9

NORTH CAROLINA

The Biltmore Estate
One Biltmore Plaza (Box 5375)
Asheville, North Carolina 28803
(704) 274-1776
T/A   10

Duplin Wine Cellars, Inc.
Highway 117 (Box 268)
Rose Hill, North Carolina 28458
(919) 289-3888
(Old North Vineyard, Carolina)
T   8

Germanton Vineyard & Winery
R.F.D. 1, Box 1-6
Germanton, North Carolina
  27019
(919) 969-5745
T   10

LaRocca Wine Company
408 Buie Court
Fayetteville, North Carolina
  28204
(919) 484-8865
T/A   10

Wine Cellars, Inc.
Route 2, Box 27D
Edenton, North Carolina 27932
(919) 482-4295
(Deerfield Vineyards, American
Champ)
T   9

SOUTH CAROLINA

Cardou Winery
P.O. Box 2104 (254 Harrell
  Drive)
Spartanburg, South Carolina
  29304
(803) 579-0675
T/A   10

Carolina Wine Company
(see Tenner Brothers,
  same company)

Foxwood Wine Cellars
Route 3
Woodruff, South Carolina
 29388
(803) 476-3153
(Robert's Ramblin Rose, Dealer's
Choice, AJS)
T/A 6

Tenner Brothers, Inc. (owned by
 Canandaigua Wine Co.
 of New York)
R.F.D. 2, Box 85
Patrick, South Carolina 29584
(803) 634-6621
(Hostess, Richard's Wild Irish)
T/A 5

Truluck Vineyards Winery
Route 3, P.O. Drawer 1265
Lake City, South Carolina 29560
(803) 389-3400/4305
T*/P 10

T E N N E S S E E

Highland Manor Winery
Highway 127 South (Route 3)
Jamestown, Tennessee 38556
(615) 879-9519
T/A 10

Laurel Hill Wines
1370 Madison Avenue
Memphis, Tennessee 38103
(901) 725-0377
T 10

Smokey Mountain Winery
Brookside Village
Gatlinburg, Tennessee 37738
(615) 436-7551
T/A 10

Tiegs Vineyards and
 Cedar Cellars
Route 3, Jackson Bend Road
Lenoir City, Tennessee 37771
(615) 986-9949
T/A 10

W E S T V I R G I N I A

Fisher Ridge Wine Company
Fisher Ridge Road
Liberty, West Virginia 25124
(304) 342-8701
T/A 10

West-Whitehill Winery, Ltd.
200 A Street
Keyser, West Virginia 26726
(304) 788-3066
T/A 10

VIRGINIA

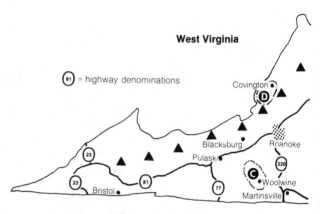

Virginia

West Virginia

(81) = highway denominations

Covington
(D)

Blacksburg
Pulaski
Roanoke

(23)

(23)   (81)
Bristol

(77)

(220)
Woolwine
Martinsville

Tennessee

The state has twenty-four wineries and about 600 acres of vineyard land on a total land mass of about 25,500,000 acres.

Mountain stretches indicated on the map are, from west to east: Appalachians, Blue Ridge, and Piedmont Uplands.

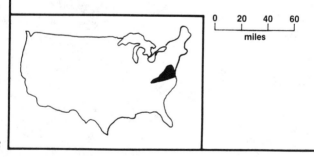

```
0    20   40   60
          miles
```

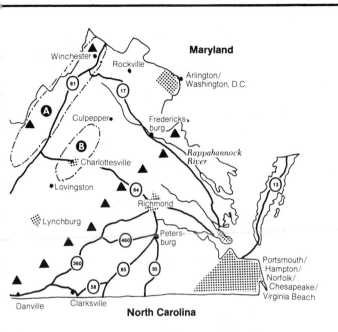

Maryland

Winchester ●

Rockville ●

Arlington/
Washington, D.C.

Ⓐ

Culpepper ●

Fredericks-
burg

*Rappahannock
River*

Ⓑ

Charlottesville

● Lovingston

Richmond

Lynchburg

Peters-
burg

Portsmouth/
Hampton/
Norfolk/
Chesapeake/
Virginia Beach

Danville   Clarksville   **North Carolina**

Viticultural Areas
Ⓐ Shenandoah Valley
Ⓑ Monticello
Ⓒ Rocky Knob
Ⓓ North Fork of the Roanoke

VINEYARDS DOT THE STATE — AS MUCH AS A MERE 600 ACRES CAN — with concentrations in the Blue Ridge, Piedmont, and Allegheny mountains and valleys. For a state one of whose most famous early citizens was a grape grower, Thomas Jefferson, this is not surprising. Nor, I suppose, is the coordinated and unabashed enthusiasm found among Virginia winegrowers, in light of the recent Eastern wine movement. While the words "every year is a vintage year in Rocky Nob" are not yet on everyone's lips, the birthplace of Presidents is alive and vinously well.

But surprises there are. One is the unprecedented high percentage of *vinifera* grapes being planted in a region which many times frustrated Jefferson's efforts to raise those grapes. Estimates from the Virginia Polytechnic Institute and State University are that between 3,000 and 4,000 new acres of *vinifera* alone could be planted and expected to produce good wines in the near future. Most of this acreage would be concentrated on the eastern slopes of the Blue Ridge Mountains. The same source indicates that another 15,000 to 20,000 acres of American, French-American hybrids, and, to a lesser extent, *vinifera* could be planted in the mainly hilly regions in the east and center of the state, while 1,500 acres of Muscadines could succeed in the eastern coastal areas.

In the area known as "Monticello," in homage to the third President, there is much interest — although currently only on a small scale — on the parts of both local and foreign groups. The Americans include Montdomaine Cellars, and Chermont Vineyards, and the Paul Masson winery of California is investing $1 million in a ranch near Charlottesville. The Zonin Company of northern Italy has *vinifera* interests in Barboursville, while a German physician has a few acres of, what else, White Riesling, growing on the Island View Farm (a.k.a. Rapidan) in Culpepper. It is estimated that about 20 percent of the state's acreage is in the Monticello region, considered a viticultural area. A good information source is The Jeffersonian Wine Grape Growers Society, The Boar's Head Inn, Charlottesville, Virginia 22905, which holds the Albemarle County Wine Festival yearly at harvest time.

Other information sources include The Virginia Grape

Growers Association, Route 637, Luray, Virginia 22835 and Vinifera Wine Growers Association, Box 172, The Plains, Virginia 22171. This latter organization, under the direction of R. deTreville Lawrence, publishes a quarterly journal which deals with *vinifera* interests in other non-California states as well.

Lastly, for a booklet, "Guide to the Virginia Estate Wineries and Their Wines," write to the Virginia Department of Agriculture and Consumer Service, P.O. Box 1163, Richmond, Virginia 23209.

V I R G I N I A

La Abra Farm & Winery, Inc.
Route 1, Box 139
Lovingston, Virginia 22949
(804) 263-5392
(Mountain Cove Vineyards)
T* 10

Bacchanal Vineyards
Box 860, Route 2
Afton, Virginia 22920
(804) 272-6937
T/A 10

Barboursville Corporation
P.O. Box F
Barboursville, Virginia 22923
(703) 832-5236/3824
T/A 10

Blenheim Vineyards
Route 6, Box 75
Charlottesville, Virginia 22901
(804) 295-7666
T/A 10

Chateau Natural Vineyard
Rocky Mount, Virginia 24151
(703) 483-0758
T/A 10

Chermont Winery
Route 1, Box 59
Esmont, Virginia 22937
(804) 286-2639
T/A 10

Domaine de Gignoux
Box 48
Ivy, Virginia 22945
(804) 296-4101
T/A 10

Domaine de la Venne
Route 1 (Hwy. 635)
Hume, Virginia 22639
(703) 635-7627/549-9181
(Oasis Vineyard)
T/A 10

Farfelu Vineyard
Route 647
Flint Hill, Virginia 22627
(703) 364-2930
T*   10

Ingleside Plantation Winery
P.O. Box 1038
Oak Grove, Virginia 22443
(804) 224-7111
T/A   10

Island View Winery
Route 4, Box 199
Culpepper, Virginia 22701
(703) 399-1045
(Rapidan Vineyards)
T/A   9

Laird & Company
North Garden, Virginia 22959
(804) 296-6058
(Sly Fox & Ramblin Rose;
   Applejack)
T/A   6

MJC Vineyards
Route 1 (Box 293)
Blacksburg, Virginia 24060
(703) 552-9083
T/A   10

Meredyth Vineyard
   (Stirling Corp.)
Box 347
Middleburg, Virginia 22117
(703) 687-6277/6612
T*   9

Montdomaine Cellars, Inc.
Route 6, Box 168 A
Charlottesville, Virginia 22901
(804) 977-6120
T/A   10

Mountain Cove Vineyards
(see La Abra Farm & Winery,
   Inc.)

Naked Mountain Vineyard
Route 688 (Box 131)
Markham, Virginia 22643
(703) 364-1609
T/A   10

Oakencroft Vineyards
Route 5
Charlottesville, Virginia 22901
(804) 295-9870
T/A   10

Oasis Vineyard
(see Domaine de la Venne)

Piedmont Vineyards & Winery
P.O. Box 286 (Route 626)
Middleburg, Virginia 22117
(703) 687-5134
T*   10

Rapidan Vineyards
(see Island View Winery)

Richard's Wine Cellars, Inc.
120 Pocahontas Street
Petersburg, Virginia 23803
(804) 733-6786
(Mother Vineyard, Old
   Homestead, Imperial Reserve)
T/A   5

The Rose Bower Vineyard &
   Winery
P.O. Box 126, State Route 686
Hampden-Sydney, Virginia
   23943
(703) 223-8209
T/A   **10**

Shenandoah Vineyards
Route 2, Box 208 B
Edinburg, Virginia 22824
(703) 984-8699
T*   **10**

Tri-Mountain Winery
Box 254, Route 1
Middletown, Virginia 22645
(703) 869-3030
T/A   **10**

The Vineyard
State Route 739 (Box 486Y)
Winchester, Virginia 22601
(703) 667-6467
(Virginia Vin Rouge & Blanc)
T/A   **10**

Woolwine Winery
Box 100
(Chateau Morrisette)
Woolwine, Virginia 24185
(703) 745-3318
T/A   **10**

Southeastern State	# of wineries (mid-1982)	grape acreage (mid-1982)	Percent of total acreage			
			Vinifera	French/American	American	Muscadine
1. ALABAMA	1	100*	-	-	20.0	80.0
2. ARKANSAS	8	4,100	3.9	29.3	54.6	12.2
3. DELAWARE	1	50*	NA	NA	NA	NA
4. FLORIDA	3	500	-	-	10.0	90.0
5. GEORGIA	2	800	-	3.1	15.6	81.3
6. KENTUCKY	3	203	1.0	17.2	81.8	-
7. LOUISIANA	0	trace	NA	NA	NA	NA
8. MARYLAND	8	300	18.0	73.7	8.3	-
9. MISSISSIPPI	4	100	1.0	7.0	7.0	85.0
10. NORTH CAROLINA	5	2,500	5.0	5.0	5.0	85.0
11. SOUTH CAROLINA	4	1,700	2.5	2.5	52.4	42.6
12. TENNESSEE	4	200	11.8	61.1	23.3	3.8
13. VIRGINIA	24	600	40.0	40.0	18.0	2.0
14. WEST VIRGINIA	2	100	10.0	45.0	45.0	-
Totals	69**	11,253	5.3	17.4	35.2	42.1

*guesstimates   **73% bonded since 1970.

THE
SOUTHWESTERN
VINEYARD

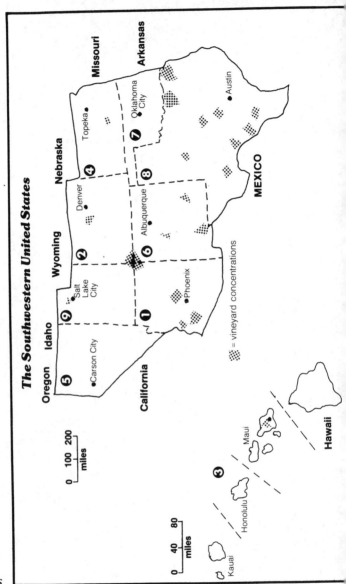

The Southwestern United States

Oregon

⑤ •Carson City

Idaho

⑨ Salt Lake City

California

① Phoenix•

Wyoming

② Denver•

②

⑥ Albuquerque•

Nebraska

④ •Topeka

⑧

Missouri

Arkansas

⑦ Oklahoma City•

Austin•

MEXICO

⑫ = vineyard concentrations

0 100 200
miles

Honolulu

Maui

③

Hawaii

Kauai

0 40 80
miles

This eight-state region has twenty-three wineries and 5,450 acres of vineyards on a land mass of 348,894,080 acres.

Viticultural Areas
None had been applied for at the time of publication but several concentrations of vineyards exist as per the map's indications. Texas' western and north plains regions, as well as the "Four-Corners" region at the intersection of Arizona, New Mexico, Colorado, and Utah are being carefully studied.

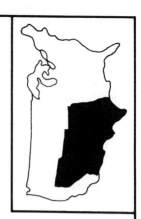

THERE ARE ONLY ABOUT A SCORE OF WINERIES IN THIS NINE-STATE section of the country, fully four-fifths of which have been bonded in the last decade. Aside from the 4,000 acres of *vinifera* table grapes in Arizona, which account for three-quarters of the region's acreage, there are only sparse plantings of grapes for wine use, mainly *vinifera* and French-American hybrids. I suppose that would be par for the course if you accept the traditional Midwestern and Eastern view of the region as a large desert where cacti vie with gila monsters for available moisture.

John Crosby, Jr., president of the Texas Grape Growers Association, will set your views straight: "We know we're in the early stages of development here, but there is so much enthusiasm — and a lot of sound agricultural evidence behind our work — that we are truly confident."

Texas is divided into four sections for viticultural purposes. French-American hybrids are expected to do best in the central and northern sections of the state. American hybrids (chance crosses of the native American species and those brought from Europe) share this area and also extend into the southern-central part of Texas. Muscadines thrive in the eastern fringes of the state south of the northern panhandle. And *vinifera* tend to be successful in the high plains and plateau regions of the western panhandle.

Famed viticulturist T.V. Munson worked with early American varieties — Herbemont, Lenoir, etc. — to arrive at crossbred plants suited to various conditions in and outside of Texas. A memorial stands to his memory: acreage at the Grayson City College near Denison complete with 300 Munson hybrids.

The more commonly recognized French-American hybrids planted in the state are the Baco noir, Chelois, Seyval, Seibel, Foch, and Seyve-Villard varieties. What few Muscadines are planted — Carlos, Magnolia, Jumbo, Hunt, Cowart, and Higgins — tend to flourish in the coastal alkaline strip and serve largely as decorations in the form of arbors when they are not eaten.

The "real action" seems to be in the western sections of the state with the *vinifera* and, to a lesser degree, the French-American hybrids found there. Surprisingly, winter chill — and not attacks by snakes or scorpions, as many a Chicago boy would have guessed — seems to be the main enemy of the vine here. White varieties such as Chenin blanc, French Colombard, and Emerald Riesling grow best, but some vintners claim successes with light bodied Cabernets. Contact the Texas Grape Growers Association, P.O. Box 5557, Midland, Texas 79701.

Utah, Colorado, New Mexico, and Arizona meet head-on in a sub-region of the area known as the "Four Corners." Some educated guessers say that the area could be home to over 200,000 acres of grapeland in the near future, if early trials prove successful. The area has cooler temperatures and higher elevations than most California grapeland, and the *vinifera* varieties can be planted on their own roots. The 4 Corners Regional Commission has had to develop a new system for measuring the needs of grapes within differing microclimates, the Winkler-Amerine system having proved relatively useless outside California, and has begun measuring soil temperatures instead of air temperatures.

Further south, in the Babocomari region of Arizona, more *vinifera* is being planted with the encouragement and know-how of Sardinian vineyardists. Table grapes, as well as wine varieties — Cabernet, Chenin blanc, Sauvignon blanc, and White Riesling — have been planted on a small scale with hopes for one or two thousand more acres if the results prove positive. Arizona's first modern winery, the R.W. Webb Winery, is located in Tucson. It has the notable distinction of being able to process three separate vintages in its small winery. The Mexican harvest comes in during May and June; Webb's own Chenin blanc, Petit Sirah, Cabernet-Sauvignon, and French Colombard are crushed in July and August; and California varieties are trucked in for vinification in September and October. "Texas rot," a grape disease, has given Arizona growers the most problems. Contact the Arizona Wine Growers' Association, P.O. Box 15265, Phoenix, Arizona 85060.

New Mexico's viticultural experience goes back to the 17th century when Spanish colonists made sacramental wine. Until the last part of the 19th century, New Mexico was the fifth largest wine producer in the country. Most of the subsequent harvests were marked by frantic ups and downs. In the last five years, things have begun to change, however. Five wineries have been bonded and the potential for increased acreage is high, especially in the following areas: the Four Corners region already mentioned; the Mesilla Valley area, in the south; the Las Cruces area, also in the south; and near Rosewell, in the east.

The grape growing season is warm and dry with cool nights — a wine-grower's dream — but fluctuating, unpredictable temperatures might bring on disease problems. *Phylloxera* seem not to be a factor. Many *vinifera* seem to thrive, though it is said that French-American hybrids would stand the cool areas of the north and center of New Mexico better.

Most of Colorado's few acres of grapeland are located in the Mesa County area in the east-central part of the state. But the state's only winery, Jim Seewold's Colorado Mountain Vineyards, is in Palisade, near Denver. The winery is, at present, using *vinifera,* including White Riesling, Cabernet, and Chardonnay, and a hybrid, called Cascade, from plantings near Penrose.

"Kansas will always be a wheat state," says one-time grape grower William Rexroad. The growing season is long and there is no frost damage; but summer winds have wreaked havoc on young shoots.

As for Oklahoma, the three wineries in the state use out-of-state grapes, although some maintain that, except for the panhandle, all of the state could support vineyards. They say that American and French-American varieties would do best.

Considering the hierarchical nature of Utah's leading religion, elderberry wine would seem a natural for the state. However, Utah's lone winery, Summum, a 24,000 gallon a year operation located in Salt Lake City, is producing a Chardonnay-Zinfandel blended rosé called "Summon Nectar." Although the grapes used in the rosé are from California, the owners of Summum say that they are planning to plant 100 acres of Cabernet-Sauvignon and Zinfandel in a spot just outside the city.

Slightly farther afield, in Hawaii, Emil Tedeschi, an ex-resident of Napa Valley, is farming twenty sloped areas of *vinifera* varieties, primarily the hybrid Carnelian. His 2,000-foot-high vineyard is just beginning to put its roots into the rich soil of the Haleakala volcano. While he waits for the vines to mature, he is paying the bills with a delicious pineapple wine called "Maui Blanc" (add two shots of rum for a "Maui Wowee?").

ARIZONA

Peter Beope Vineyards
Patagonia, Arizona 85624
(Patagonia Winery)
T/A   10

Brookside Winery
1131 West Broadway
Tempe, Arizona 85281
(602) 967-9836
(tasting/retail outlet only)

Brookside Winery
10240 North 27th Avenue
Phoenix, Arizona 85021
(602) 943-0972
(tasting/retail outlet only)

R. W. Webb Winery, Inc.
4352 East Speedway
Tucson, Arizona 85712
(602) 887-1537
T/A   10

COLORADO

Colorado Mountain Vineyards,
   Inc.
3553-A E. Road
Palisade, Colorado 81526
(303) 464-7948
(Aspen Cellars, Cripple Creek
Cellars, Mesa, Phantom Canyon
   Cellars)
T/A   10

HAWAII

Tedeschi Vineyard, Ltd.
P.O. Box 953
Ulupalakua, Maui, Hawaii 96790
(808) 878-6058
(Maui Blanc, Brut, etc.)
T   10

NEW MEXICO

Corrales Bonded Winery
Box 302B
Corrales, New Mexico 87048
(505) 898-2904
T/A   10

Joe P. Estrada Winery
P.O. Box 202
Mesilla, New Mexico 88046
(505) 526-4017
T/A   10

Rico's Winery
6406 North 4th Street, N.W.
Albuquerque, New Mexico
   87107
(505) 344-2075
T*   10

La Vina
Box 121
Chamberino, New Mexico 88027
(505) 882-2092/533-5273
T/A   10

Vina Madre
P.O. Box 2002
Dexter/Rosewell, New Mexico
   88201
(505) 734-5590
T/A   **10**

O K L A H O M A

Arrowhead Vineyards, Inc.
Route 1
Caney, Oklahoma 74553
(405) 889-6312
T/A   **10**

Pete Schwarz Winery
Box 545
Okarche, Oklahoma 73762
(405) 263-7664
T/A   **10**

T E X A S

La Buena Vida Vineyards
WSR Box 18-3
Springtown, Texas 76082
(817) 523-4366
T*   **10/10**

La Buena Vida Vineyards
Route 2 Box 927
Fort Worth, Texas 76135
(817) 237-WINE
T*   **10/10**

Chateau Montgolfier Vineyards
P.O. Box 12423
Fort Worth, Texas 76116
(817) 448-8479
T/A   **10**

Fall Creek Vineyards
Fall Creek Ranch, Box 68
Tow, Texas 78672
(512) 476-3783
T/A   **10**

Glasscock Vineyards, Inc.
(Box 530)
Fort Davis, Texas 79734
(915) 426-3553
T/A   **10**

Guadalupe Valley Winery
1720 Hunter Road
New Braunfels, Texas 78130
(512) 629-2351
T   **10**

Llano Estacado Winery
P.O. Box 6170,
   Farm Road 1585
Lubbock, Texas 79413
(806) 745-2258
(Cibolo Rojo, Blanco, Staked
   Plains)
T/A   **10**

Moyer Texas Champagne, Inc.
1941 Hwy. 35 East
New Braunfels, Texas 78130
(512) 625-5181
T/A   **10**

Oberhellmann Vineyards
Llano Route, Box 22
Fredericksburg, Texas 78624
(512) 685-3297
T/A   9

Sanchez Creek Vineyards
DSR Box 30-4
Weatherford, Texas 76086
(817) 594-6884
T/A   10

Staked Plains
see Llano Estacado

Val Verde Winery
139 Hudson Drive
Del Rio, Texas 78840
(512) 775-9714
(San Felipe del Rio)
T/A   10

U T A H

Summum Winery
707 Genesee Avenue
Salt Lake City, Utah 84104
(801) 355-0137
T/A   10

Southwestern State	# of wineries (mid-1982)	grape acreage (mid-1982)	Percent of total acreage			
			Vinifera	French-American	American	Muscadine
1. ARIZONA	2	4,160*	100	-	-	-
2. COLORADO	1	25#	NA	NA	NA	NA
3. HAWAII	1	20	100	-	-	-
4. KANSAS	0	60†	NA	NA	NA	NA
5. NEVADA	0	25#	NA	NA	NA	NA
6. NEW MEXICO	5	65	74.2	22.2	2.3	1.2
7. OKLAHOMA	2	25#	NA	NA	NA	NA
8. TEXAS	11	900	45.0	40.0	5.0	10.0
9. UTAH	1	170†	NA	NA	NA	NA
Totals	23**	5,450	90.0	7.3	0.9	1.8

(above percentages arrived at by computing only known breakdowns)

*predominantly table and raisin grapes   #guesstimates   †from 1978 Census of Agriculture   **83% bonded since 1970.

THE
NORTHWESTERN
VINEYARD

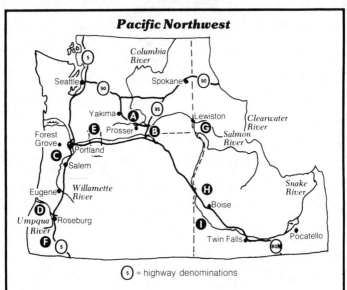

Pacific Northwest

(5) = highway denominations

The three-state area is planted to about 28,700 acres divided as follows:

	Acreage (end of '81)	For wine use*	Wineries (mid 1982)
Idaho	500	100%	3
Oregon	2,100	100%	39
Washington	27,693	27%	26

*other uses include juice, jam or jelly production, or table grape employment.

```
0   50   100
  miles
```

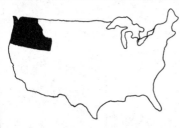

Viticultural Areas
- **A** Yakima Valley
- **B** Columbia River Basin
- **C** Willamette Valley
- **D** Umpqua River Valley
- **E** Hood River Valley
- **F** Medford/Grant's Pass area
- **G** Salmon River area
- **H** Emmett Valley
- **I** Sunny Slope area

"Kahleeförnia Rieslings? No!
Dee only American Riesling I vould recommend
is dot one from Vahsheegtone stet."

SO SAID MY GERMAN-BORN WINE TUTOR, SIG LANGSTADTER, about a decade ago. And where did that Pinot noir-based wine that stunned the Burgundians a while back come from? Oregon, not the Napa Valley. Is the Northwest the only section of this country that can make wines to please a European palate? Is much of this three-state vineyard so much better suited than most places in the Golden State as to produce Rieslings that taste like Rheingauen, or Pinots that resemble Côte de Beaunes or Chablis-like Chardonnays?

Could be, though it might be a good idea not to judge until the area has a few more decades of *vinifera* experience under its collective belt. As it stands now, less than 30 percent of the region's grapes go for wine use, and fully three-quarters are non-*vinifera*.

Washington dominates the area's grape acreage with over 25,000 acres, making it third in the nation, behind California and New York. Seventy percent of this acreage is planted to American varieties, predominantly Concords, whose final identity is grape juice, not grape wine. Still, the Yakima Valley, bordering the Yakima River, and the Columbia River basin are home to the biggest *vinifera* concentrations in the United States outside California. Some 5,000 acres of various northern-climate *vinifera* varieties are planted in Washington, over 90 percent in these two adjacent areas.

Surprisingly, to many who know of the Northwestern climate only from misty Seattleans, these wine regions are desertlike, with hot, sunny days and sandy soils, and they need irrigation. Cool nights, however, moderate these Middle Eastern conditions and also create a moister atmosphere that many consider optimum for the development of beneficial *botrytis cinerea*.

The major problems seem manmade – a propensity for too high yields – as well as God-given – occasional but devastating frigid winter temperatures (the 1978-1979 season was such a case). Local forecasters predict that an additional 20,000 acres each of good wine grapes could be planted in both the Yakima Valley and the Columbia River basin, but that the going is likely to be slow.

Oregon, though dwarfed by its northern neighbor in terms of total grape acreage, has fifty percent more wineries and nearly half as much wine grape acreage. Smaller yields and a greater variation in climate from year to year probably makes this state even more European in nature than Washington.

Most of the vineyards which are located in a strip paralleling the Pacific along the Willamette and Umpqua rivers, are on hillsides that are moderately difficult to work. The grapes in these vineyards are a constant temptation to gourmet critters – not so much insects as birds, especially robins, which must be kept away by netting. Rain during the harvest can also pose problems for the Oregon grower.

On the brighter side, however, there is a dry, clear, and sunny growing season, a fairly frost-free spring, and the possibility of growing vines on their own rootstocks. Northern European *vinifera* varieties such as Rieslings, Gewürztraminer, Müller-Thurgau, Pinots, and Chardonnay seem to have the best chance in central and northern Oregon, while such Bordelais varieties as Cabernet-Sauvignon and Merlot may do better in the southern vineyards around Grant's Pass.

Pioneering efforts in the area of wine legislation were made here. Oregon winegrowers by law, allow themselves to add to a bottle of wine only 10 percent of varieties whose names do not appear on the label (save for Cabernet). They have also banned the use of generic labeling for Oregon wines and require that Oregon wine labels include some sort of appellation of the wine's origin, and the appellation must be 100 percent accurate.

I hitched a train through Idaho about a decade ago and all I could see was grain, not grapes. But, on a very small scale, even Idaho is home to a "wine boom." After an abortive start in the 1960s, when all sorts of wine and table varieties were planted (and later ripped up), the early 1970s saw new energy and new plantings, mostly *vinifera,* along the Snake and Salmon rivers.

Still, this state, like Kansas, is a wheat state, and with that grain comes herbicides such as 2-4-D, which made a mess of efforts to grow wine grapes in Illinois. Such herbicides, and severe winters, will test the tenacity of Idaho's handful of grape growers and winemakers.

For more information on these states' wine happenings, I suggest you write to the following organizations: The Enological Society of the Pacific Northwest, 200 Second Avenue, North, Seattle, Washington 98109 (for Washington and Idaho); and Oregon Winegrowers' Association, P.O. Box 367, Roseburg, Oregon 97470.

The other six states in the Northwestern vineyard each have a few acres of American varieties that stubbornly persist. These grapes are used for snacking, but perhaps, through the faith of their growers, they will lead to the eventual proclamation of a Helena, Bismarck, or Lincoln viticultural area. Right now, it's still grain, timber, and (real) cold country.

IDAHO

Facelli Vineyards
2.4 miles west of Highway 5
  and Peckam Road
Wilder, Idaho 83605
(208) 482-7719/454-1789
(Arena Valley Cellars)
T/A   10

Ste. Chapelle Winery, Inc.
Rural Route 4, Box 775
Caldwell, Idaho 83605
(208) 459-7222
T   8

Weston Vineyards & Winery
Route 4, Highway 55
Sunnyslope, Idaho 83605
(208) 466-3570
T*/P   10

OREGON

Adelsheim Vineyard
Route 1, Box 129 D
Newberg, Oregon 97132
(503) 538-3652
T/A   10

Alpine Vineyards
Green Peak Road (Route 2)
Alpine (Monroe), Oregon 97456
(503) 424-5851
T/A   10

Amity Vineyards
Route 1, Box 348 B
Amity, Oregon 97101
(503) 835-2362
T*   10

Arterberry Ltd.
1011 Alpine Avenue
McMinnville, Oregon 97123
(503) 472-1587
(The Arterberry Ciderworks)
T/A   **10**

Big Fir Winery
17835 S.E. Tickle Creek Road
Boring, Oregon 97009
(503) 658-3039
T*   **10**

Bjelland Vineyards
Bjelland Vineyards Lane
Roseburg, Oregon 97470
(503) 679-6950
T*   **10**

Century Home Wine
Route 2, Box 111
Newberg, Oregon 97132
(503) 538-9743
T/A   **10**

Chateau Benoit Winery
Route 1, Box 29 B-1
Carlton, Oregon 97111
(503) 864-3666
T/A   **10**

Chehalem Mountain Winery
Route 1, Box 99 C
Newberg, Oregon 97132
(503) 628-2417
(Mulhausen Vineyards)
T*   **10**

Cote des Colombe Vineyard
Route 2, Box 266
Banks, Oregon 97106
(503) 646-1223/324-0855
T*   **10**

De Martini Wine Company
251 Camino Francisco
Roseburg, Oregon 97470
(503) 673-7901/672-9584
(Oregon Country, Willow Ranch)
T/A   **10**

Elk Cove Vineyards
Route 3, Box 23
Gaston, Oregon 97119
(503) 985-7760
T*   **10**

Ellendale Vineyards
300 Reuben Boise Road
Dallas, Oregon 97338
(503) 623-5617
T   **10**

Henry Endress Winery
13300 South Clackamas River
  Drive
Oregon City, Oregon 97045
(503) 656-7239
(Henry's)
T*   **10**

The Eyrie Vineyards
939 East 10th Street (Box 204)
Dundee, Oregon 97115
(503) 864-2410/472-6315
(Oregon Spring Wine)
T/A   **10**

Forgeron Vineyard
89697 Sheffler Road
Elmira, Oregon 97437
(503) 935-3530
T/A 10

Glen Creek Winery
6057 Orchard Heights Road
  N.W.
Salem, Oregon 97304
(503) 581-7510
T/P 10

Henry's Winery
Hubbard Creek Road (Box 26)
Umpqua, Oregon 97486
(503) 459-5120
(Henry Estate)
T 10

Hidden Springs Winery
2400 Cottage Street, S.E.
Salem, Oregon 97302
(503) 581-2627
T/A 10

Hillcrest Vineyard
240 Vineyard Lane, Box 3095
Roseburg, Oregon 97470
(503) 673-3709
T 9

Hinman Vineyards
27012 Briggs Hill Road
Eugene, Oregon 97406
(503) 345-1945
T/A 10

The Honey House Winery
26202 Fawver Road
Veneta, Oregon 97487
(503) 935-2008
(Willamette Valley Homestead)
T/A 10

Honeywood Fruit Winery
501 14th, SE (Box 669)
Salem, Oregon 97309
(503) 362-4111
T* 7

Hood River Vineyards
4693 Westwood Drive
Hood River, Oregon 97031
(503) 386-3772
T/A 10

Humbug Winery
300 Hidden Valley Lane
Roseburg, Oregon 97470
(503) 672-3556
T*/A 10

Jonicole Vineyards
Route 1, Box 1118
Roseburg, Oregon 97470
(503) 679-5771
T* 10

Knudsen-Erath Winery
Worden Hill Road
Dundee, Oregon 97115
(503) 538-3318
(Willamette Cellars)
T 8

Mount Hood Winery
4655 Woodworth Drive (Box 65)
Mount Hood, Oregon 97041
(503) 352-6465
T/A   10

Nehalem Bay Wine Company
34965 Highway 53 (Box 440)
Nehalem, Oregon 97131
(503) 368-3500
(Tillamook)
T*   10

Oak Knoll Winery, Inc.
Route 6, Box 184
Hillsboro, Oregon 97123
(503) 648-8198
(Chateau Du Chene)
T*   8

Ponzi Vineyards
Route 1, Box 842
Beaverton, Oregon 97005
(503) 628-1227
(Oregon Harvest)
T*   10

Serendipity Cellars Winery
15275 Dunn Forest Road
Monmouth, Oregon 97361
(503) 838-4284
T/A   10

Shafer Vineyard Cellars
Highway 8, 1.8 miles east of
    P.O. Star Route Box 269
Forest Grove/Gales Creek,
    Oregon 97117
(503) 357-6604
T/A   10

Shallon Winery
1598 Duane Street
Astoria, Oregon 97103
(503) 325-5978
T/A   10

Siskiyou Vineyards
6220 Cave Highway
Cave Junction, Oregon 97253
(503) 592-3727
T/A   10

Sokol Blosser Winery
Blanchard Lane, Box 199
Dundee, Oregon 97115
(503) 864-3342
T   7

Tualatin Vineyards, Inc.
Route 1, Box 339
Forest Grove, Oregon 97116
(503) 357-5005
T*   9

Valley View Vineyard
1352 Applegate Road
Jacksonville, Oregon 97530
(503) 899-8468
(Jefferson State Board)
T*   9

Wasson Brothers Winery
19925 South Leland Road
Oregon City, Oregon 97405
(503) 655-3301
NT   10

WASHINGTON

Associated Vintners, Inc.
4368 150th Avenue, NE
Redmond, Washington 98052
(206) 883-1146
T/A   9

Bingen Wine Cellars, Inc.
315 West Steuben
Bingen, Washington 98605
(509) 493-3001
(Mount Elise Vineyards)
T*   10

Chateau Ste. Michelle
14111 N.E. 145th (Box 1976)
Woodinville, Washington 98072
(206) 488-1133
(Nawico, Hadassim,
Pommerelle, Farron Ridge)
T   7/5

Chateau Ste. Michelle
205 West 5th Street
Grandview, Washington 98930
(509) 882-3928
NT   7/5

Chateau St. Michelle
Paterson, Washington 99345
(no tours until mid-1983)
          6/5

Daquila Wines
1434 Western Avenue
Seattle, Washington 98101
(206) 784-8700
T/A   10

E.B. Foote Winery
3836 34th Avenue, SW
Seattle, Washington 98126
(206) 932-4354
T   10

Haviland Vintners
19029, 36 West (Suite "F")
Lynnwood, Washington 98036
(206) 771-6933
("foret du mer")
T/A   10

Hinzerling Vineyards, Inc.
1520 Sheridan Avenue
Prosser, Washington 99350
(509) 786-2163
T/A   10

Hoodsport Winery, Inc.
Star Route 1 (Box 5)
Hoodsport, Washington 98548
(206) 877-9760
T   10

Kiona Vineyards Winery
211 South 46th
West Richland, Washington
  99352
(509) 967-3212
T/A   10

Franz Wilhelm Langguth Winery
Road F½ and Road 23½, SW
Mattawa, Washington 99344
(509) 932-4990
(Weinbau Vineyard)
T/A   7

Leonetti Cellars
1321 School Avenue
Walla Walla, Washington 99362
(509) 525-1428
T* 10

Lost Mountain Winery
730 Lost Mountain Road
Sequim, Washington 98382
(206) 683-5229
T/A 10

Lowden Schoolhouse Winery
P.O. Box 2275
Walla Walla, Washington 99362
(509) 525-0940
T/A 10

Mt. Rainier Vintners, Inc.
121 23rd Street, SE
Puyallup, Washington 98371
(206) 848-4573
(Rainer Valley, Tahoma Valley
Cellars)
T 8

Neuharth Winery, Inc.
Still Road, (Box 1457)
Sequim, Washington 98382
(206) 683-9652/3706
(Olympic)
T* 10

Preston Wine Cellars
Star Route 1 (Box 1234)
Pasco, Washington 99301
(509) 545-1990
(Columbia River Cellars)
T 7

Puyallup Valley Winery
(see Mt. Rainier Vintners)

Quail Run Winery
P.O. Box 169, four miles north
of Zillah off #80
Yakima, Washington 98907
(509) 457-5115
T/A 10

Quilceda Creek Vinters
5226 Snohomish-Machias Road
Snohomish, Washington 98290
(206) 568-2389
T/A 10

Snohomish Valley Winery, Inc.
1211 2nd Street
Marysville, Washington 98270
(206) 659-9858
(Mountain Valley)
T* 10

Paul Thomas Wines
1717 136th Place, NE
Bellevue, Washington 98005
(206) 747-1008
T 10

Tucker Cellars
Route 1, Box 1696
Sunnyside, Washington 98944
(509) 837-8701
T*/P 10

Manfred J. Vierthaler Winery
17136 Highway 410, East
Sumner, Washington 98390
(206) 863-1633
T   **10**

Woodward Canyon Winery
Route 1, Box 387
Lowden, Washington 99360
(509) 525-2262/4129
T/A   **10**

Worden's Washington Winery
7217 West 45th
Spokane, Washington 99204
(509) 466-8269
T/A   **10**

Yakima River Winery
North River Road (Route 1,
   Box 1657)
Prosser, Washington 99350
(509) 786-2805
T/A   **10**

Northwestern State	# of wineries (mid-1982)	For wine use** (percent)	grape acreage (mid-1982)	Percent of total acreage			
				Vinifera	French-American	American	Muscadine
1. ALASKA	0		trace	NA	NA	NA	NA
2. IDAHO	3	100	500	100	-	-	-
3. MONTANA	0		trace	NA	NA	NA	NA
4. NEBRASKA	0		trace	NA	NA	NA	NA
5. NORTH DAKOTA	0		trace	NA	NA	NA	NA
6. OREGON	39	100	2,100	90.4	4.8	4.8	-
7. SOUTH DAKOTA	0		trace	NA	NA	NA	NA
8. WASHINGTON	27	30	27,693	23.1	negligible	76.8	-
9. WYOMING	0		trace	NA	NA	NA	NA
Totals	69*		30,293	28.3	0.4	71.3	-

trace = less than 25 acres, if any at all.

*88% bonded since 1970

**other uses include juice, jam and jelly production, or table grapes.

The nine-state (only three with wineries) region has a total land mass of 820,687,360 acres (445,205,760 acres without Alaska).

The Wine-Lover's Vocabulary

Acetic: an acid that combines with ethyl acetate to give the vinegary smell that a spoiled wine emits. It is not to be confused with...

Acidic: or tart, sour. All wines contain some acids, predominantly tartaric. Raw, young wines are generally more acidic than older ones. Improperly balanced wines may taste sour because of an abnormally high acid content.

Apples: some Mosel Rieslings, some Chardonnays, and some Chenin blanc wines smell and/or taste of apples as part of their varietal character. Often, an oxidized (q.v.) wine will smell of apples.

Apricots: Sémillons, Muscats (Moscatos), and some sweet Rieslings recall apricots; wines affected by *botrytis cinerea* (q.v.), or noble rot, may often recall apricots or peaches.

Aroma: that portion of the smell of a wine derived specifically from an aromatic grape variety, such as Cabernet-Sauvignon or Chardonnay, as opposed to that portion of the smell derived from other sources (see Bouquet). Grape varieties such as Alicante Bouschet or Palomino, the Sherry grape, are not considered distinctly aromatic varieties, technically speaking.

Asparagus: Sauvignon blanc based wines, especially Pouilly-Fumés or very dry examples from California, will recall asparagus.

Austere: the more prestigious châteaux wines of Pauillac and St. Julien are sometimes referred to thus. It implies a sensation of pleasant bitterness from tannins (q.v.). Think of crisp lemonade as opposed to cola, or country well water as opposed to soft tap water. Beaujolais, Liebfraumilch, or most American jug wines would not be considered austere.

Balance: a balanced wine is one whose constituents — sugars, acids, tannins, alcohols, etc. — are evident but do not mask one another. A young red wine — tannic and acidic — is not considered balanced because these two characteristics mask the other flavor elements of the wine, which, given time, will display themselves.

Bananas: very young white wines – tank samples or freshly bottled wines – will often smell like bananas. The component responsible for this is amyl acetate, which diminishes with age. I have noticed it in many wines (Italian, especially) that are made in a modern stainless-steel equipped winery.

Berries: "berry-like" is a nebulous, fruity characteristic of young red wines, notably Zinfandels or Bacos.

Big: a wine of more flavor, alcohol, etc., than others. A Barolo, Châteauneuf-du-Pape, late harvest Zinfandel, or the like is considered a big wine.

Bitter: one of the four basic taste sensations. A young, red Bordeaux or Cabernet-Sauvignon will taste bitter because of its relatively high tannin content. Tannin is a bitter element in wines.

Black currant: Bordeaux wines with a high percentage of Cabernet-Sauvignon and similarly based California wines may recall black currant flavor.

Body: English wine authority, Michael Broadbent, puts it well in his *Wine Tasting:* ". . . the weight of the wine in the mouth due to its alcoholic content and to its other physical components. These in turn are due to the quality of the wine, to the vintage, its geographical origin, and general style. Wines from hotter climates tend to have more body than those from the north (compare the Rhône with the Mosel, for example)."

Bottle stink: ever open a bottle of wine which, at first, smells wretched, but with decantation (q.v.) or a moment's aeration, loses the odors? Bottle stink, folks.

Botrytis cinerea: Latin name for a mold which attacks grapes on the vine. Under the proper conditions and at the proper time, such a mold will often have a beneficial affect upon the resulting wine's quality. Grapes affected beneficially by the mold, called noble rot, may smell more or less like peaches or apricots, the intensity of the smell being dependent upon the degree of infection of the mold.

Bouquet: as opposed to "aroma" (q.v.), bouquet is more encompassing. It is the odor a wine has which derives from the fermentation process, from the aging-in-wood and bottle process and other changes independent of the grape variety used. Use "bouquet" to describe all the non-varietal smells a wine has.

Breed: according to Michael Broadbent, English wine authority, "a distinctive and distinguished quality stemming from the combination of fine site soil, *cépage* [grape type] and the skill of the *vigneron.*"

Brilliant: perfectly clear, without haziness. Brilliant wines often have higher than normal acidities.

Brix: a measure of grape solids in a juice sample, usually at picking time. The great majority of these solids are sugars which are fermentable into alcohol. By measuring the Brix of grape juice at picking, it is possible to calculate/estimate the final alcoholic content of the wine. So when a wine writer asks a winemaker "what was the Brix at picking" he is not just trying to be cute.

Brut: what Joe Namath used to push; also, the name for the driest type of sparkling wine in a company's line. It connotes a very dry wine.

Bulk (process): a method of producing sparkling wines that is both inexpensive and quick; it involves causing a secondary fermentation in a large tank as opposed to the more classic method of secondary fermentation within the original small bottle. American wines made by this method must state this on the label.

Bunch: term used to describe any non-Muscadine (see "American Grapes" section) grape; most often employed by non-California winegrowers.

Candy: the odor and flavor of young *Blanc de noirs* wines often have candy-like character.

Casky: the odor or, less often, the flavor of a wine stemming from its having rested too long in a wooden tank or barrel. A dank, humid-wood smell.

Carbonic maceration: a method of fermentation, invented by the Rhône-French in the 1930s involving an intra-cellular transformation within whole berries, as opposed to allowing the berries' juice to be expressed and fermented normally. Wines — usually red, but some characters have tried it with whites — fermented this way are referred to as "nouveau" or "primeur."

Character: a wine of good character is one which doesn't just slip down the throat and say "bye-bye"; it says "stop a while, friend. You have just come upon an above-average liquid. Think on it."

Chewy: a fuller-bodied, high-but-balanced acid wine with a greater than average tannin content is considered chewy. Some Bordeaux reds, especially St. Estèphes, or some California coastal mountain Cabernets, are so described.

Citrus: burnt orange or, simply nebulous citrusy flavors are often evident in many Chiantis, Barolos, or California Barberas.

Clean: having no off-odors or off-tastes.

Clone: an asexually propogated vine so produced to better adapt to climatic or geologic conditions. You will often hear of "the Romanée-Conti clone of Pinot noir" as opposed to the Volnay clone.

Cloudy: an aspect of the appearance of the wine which is obvious. Often, there is a protein problem which causes this cloudiness; often, it comes from natural sediment in the wine visible when the wine has been shaken up.

Cold: the meaning is obvious. Too often, wines are served so cold that their odors and flavors are stunted, unable to show themselves.

Cold fermentation: a method of fermenting grape juice into wine which involves keeping the liquid at lowered (circa 55 degrees Farenheit) temperatures in order to conserve as much fruit/varietal character as possible. Stainless steel tanks of huge sizes are often "belted" by freon to arrive at these low temperatures.

Complex: a complex wine is many-faceted. It contains not only the acids, alcohols, tannins, etc., but more. Each sip brings another flavor, reveals another nuance.

Cooked: a smell, hot or burnt, found in "chaptalized" French red Burgundies and Beaujolais. Chaptalization is the addition of "foreign" sugars to a must in order to raise the final alcoholic content of the wine.

Cork(y):   said of a wine that smells more of cork than it does of wine. Such an odor will usually not dissipate, and, if noticed to excess in a wine, provides sufficient reason for returning it to the retailer or restauranteur.

Cork-tease: someone who always talks about the wine he will open but never does.

Cross: a breeding of one variety of grape with another to obtain a more desirable offspring. The "noble" Cabernet-Sauvignon was "crossed" with the "common" Carignane to arrive at the Ruby Cabernet grape, a cross intended to produce a variety capable of surviving the hot climes of the Central Valley well enough to produce a decent wine.

Crush: in wine lingo, the time of year when the grapes are ready for picking. Grapes are not literally and dramatically crushed, but are broken open to allow their juice to run out.

Decant: unlike "recant"; a wine is decanted either to separate the clear liquid from the solids an old wine might have accumulated, or to aerate a wine, to oxygenate it. It usually involves candles and steady hands as well as a good eye.

Dry: a dry wine is a wine without noticeable sweetness; a medium-dry wine is one with a moderate amount of sweetness, and so on. Technically, a dry wine retains little or no sugar after fermentation stops.

Dumb: usually refers to the odor, or lack thereof, in a wine of some future. Many of the younger clarets or Cabernet-Sauvignons are considered dumb.

Earthy: not actually referring to a dirty or soil-like smell or taste, but to a characteristic of the wine derived from its special soil and place of origin. The iodine-like quality that many relate to red Graves wines, or the rubbery character many associate with Mayacamas Mountain Cabernets is called earthy, or possessing "gout de terroir" (taste of the ecosystem, if you will).

Estate-bottled: an overworked term which, classically means that the grapes for the wine in the bottle were grown by the fellow that bottled the wine (and raised, tended, and picked the grapes, as well). Corporate entities make for a dilution of the term insofar as America is concerned.

Fat: generally referring to a wine of higher than average glycerin and/or alcohol content.

Feminine: this term is often used to describe a wine of more delicacy than most: a Margaux as opposed to a Pauillac or a Parducci Cabernet as opposed to a Ridge; so hit me.

Figs: wines from the Sémillon grape variety are often redolent of figs.

Filter: to strain out wine solids by mechanical means, large or small.

Fine: to reduce the solids content of wines after fermentation. In traditional operations, egg whites are used; more often, a Wyoming clay called "bentonite" is used. It does not enter into the finished wine.

Finish: the sensual impression − long or short, strong or weak − that lingers after you have swallowed a wine; a.k.a. "aftertaste."

Flat: usually connoting a wine without acid tang; oxidized (q.v.).

Flor: Spanish word for "flower." You will see this word on some American Sherry labels. It is meant to recall that characteristic of Spanish (authentic) Sherries which is pleasantly yeasty.

Flowery: a nebulous term referring to an indeterminate fragrance akin to flowers in general. Mosel wines are flowery, as are some Chenin blancs, Seyval blancs, and Aurores.

Fortified: wines having had grape spirit added to them are considered fortified; Sherries, Ports, Madeiras, and others fit the bill.

Foxy: the odors and tastes of wines made from the American species of grape (i.e., *vitis labruscana*). A flavor substance called methyl anthranilate is partially responsible for this characteristic. A foxy wine smells and tastes like Concord grape juice. The term refers to the native American Fox grape which grows wild in much of the Northeast.

Free run: wine that is allowed to flow by gravity or wont from the fermenter into proper receptacles. It is considered lighter and less rich than press wine (q.v.) but is often blended with it to arrive at a balanced product.

Fresh: applied generally to younger whites or lighter reds to denote a pleasant, youthful sensation. Beaujolais, for instance, are fresh when consumed young, as are many Zinfandels, Maréchal Fochs, and Bacos.

Fruity: a pleasant fragrance from healthy ripe grapes made into wine; a berry-like quality not necessarily akin to any one fruit but to fruits in general.

Full: see Big, a full-bodied wine.

Generic: a wine that has taken its name from a district — usually European — that has garnered some fame. American "Chablis" are meant to recall the true French product but usually don't. The original intent of such rip-offs was pure and natural: to sell that which is recognizable (to an immigrant population that was familiar with the terms). Nowadays, such names are giving way to more accurate, if less colorful, appellations: Robert Mondavi White, for instance.

Grapey: similar to Fresh (q.v.), also applied to wines which smell and taste almost like fresh-picked grapes, such as Asti Spumante wines.

Grassy: Sauvignon blanc based wines remind many tasters of grass. So who am I to say it isn't so?

Green: usually said of younger, rawish, acidic white or red wine; a rough aspect that usually softens with age.

Green bell peppers: Cabernets (franc and Sauvignon), Sauvignon blancs, and other varieties are said to produce a green bell pepper character (not to excess, one hopes, unles you love pizzas), especially when the grapes are grown in cooler climates.

Green olives: I have had very few wines that smelled of green olives, but those few have been Cabernets.

Hard: akin to Green (q.v.), but indicative more of a high tannin level.

Harsh: A "hard" or "green" wine will generally soften with age; a harsh wine, because of its excessive astringency, probably will not. 1957 Château Latour comes to mind.

Herbaceous: smelling or tasting of soil-covered herbs.

Hot: a wine that reminds you more of alcohol than anything else is considered hot.

Hybrid: grape varieties produced by viticulturists, *usually* involving more than one species as parents, are called hybrids. The great Midwestern and Eastern sections of this country are planted to the so-called "French-American" hybrids, vines that are part *vinifera* and part native American species (*aestivalis, labruscana,* etc.). They were produced in an effort to arrive at vine plants better-suited to particular climates than simple *vinifera.*

Hydrogen sulfide: the smell of rotten eggs or like substances often found in wines whose lees were not aerated before bottling; may dissipate with aeration.

Kraut: perceived in many wines from the Merlot variety.

Labrusca: species of grape whose descendants are widely distributed in America's Midwest and Northeast; often referred to in less-than-noble terms as the "foxy" grape.

Late Harvest: a term seen on (mainly California) wine labels to indicate that the grapes for the wine were left on the vine to ripen, often raisin, for longer than normal. Usually a so-labeled wine will be higher in residual sugar and/or alcohol.

Licorice: some of the Nebbiolo-based wines of the Piedmont region of Italy, such as Barolo, remind many of licorice.

Light: not a pejorative term; somewhat akin to Feminine (q.v.) and the opposite of Big or Full.

Luscious: a rich wine, high in glycerin and, often, in sugar, is some-times referred to as "luscious"; Sauternes, Portos, and Ports and some sweet white wines affected by *botrytis cinerea* fill the bill.

Maderized: a term derived from "Madeira"; a type of fortified wine from Portugal, produced by a combinaton of aging and heating. The color of a maderized wine is yellow-brown to golden-brown, and it smells and tastes oxidized.

Malolactic fermentation: a conversion of malic acid in wine to lac-tic acid which results in a lowering of the overall acidity, and, hence, tartness of the wine. The conversion occurs mainly in wines from cooler climates where there is an excess of acidity in the grapes and wine and usually happens after the alcoholic fermentation. Modern methods, however, allow for simultaneous alcoholic/malolactic conversions brought about by the addition of malolactic inducing cultures.

Masculine: akin to Big and Full.

Matchstick: burnt matchstick odor is that derived from an excess of sulfur dioxide which is added to a wine; with time it will usually dissipate. Many contend that the flavor of wooden matchsticks is a tell-tale signal that a wine contains Pinot noir.

Mellow: a soft, smooth, often sweet-edged wine; a "jug-red" and a well-aged Cabernet-Sauvignon or Zinfandel may both be mellow.

Méthode Champenoise: literally, "(made by the) Champagne method;" the classic, expensive and time consuming way to pro-duce Champagne and many other sparkling wines. It involves a secondary fermentation within a small (twelve ounces to one gallon or so) bottle. The yeasts causing this fermentation are then expell-ed from the bottle which is, after further aging and packaging, sold to the public.

Mint: a term used to express the flavors of wood aging, specifically French oak aging, in red wines. Sometimes a wine aged in oak will display minty overtones.

Mushrooms: older (more than twenty years) red Bordeaux, and a few Cabernets and Zinfandels from California, sometimes smell of fresh-picked, dirt-laden mushrooms.

Must: the term for the mixture of grape juice, skins, seeds, and pulp in a red wine fermentation or just the juice in a white fermentation.

Musty: somewhat similar to Bottle stink (q.v.) but not so definite; it is often indicative of poor wood aging or faulty handling, and seldom dissipates.

Nouveau: term used to indicate a wine that has been made to capture the ultimate in freshness and fruit character but which seldom has any aging potential. Nouveaux are usually made by the carbonic maceration; but its expense makes sped-up normal fermentations for Nouveaux more common.

Numb: akin to Dumb but without connoting that the wine has promise or future; an overly chilled white wine will be numb or odorless.

Nuts: Amontillado Sherries, *vins jaunes* of the Jura area of France, and even some oak-aged Chardonnays display various nutlike overtones. Also, General McAuliffe's reply to the Germans at Bastogne.

Oaky: term used to describe the smell and/or taste of wines that have been aged (usually excessively) in small wood barrels. Some prefer to drink such wines while others prefer to carve them.

Off-smell/off-taste: an offensive aspect of a wine, such as a rotten egg (hydrogen sulfide) odor, or an atypical aspect of a wine, such as a Cabernet-Sauvignon wine smelling or tasting more like a Pinot noir wine; i.e., not true to type.

Oxidized: all wines are oxidized to a degree because of the presence of oxygen in or near them. A high degree of oxidation is not desired in most table wines, while in fortified wines, especially Sherries, a greater oxidation is attained and desired. A table wine smelling more like a sherry and tasting generally lifeless is said to be more or less oxidized.

pH: a measure of the hydrogen ions in grape juice and wine. Recent indications are that the pH is a better measure for the reading of acid balance in a juice than is a reading for the total acidity in a juice. You'll see the term used in writings about wine, but it is better left in the lab.

Peaches: sometimes sensed in Rieslings, Gewürztraminers, or other sweet, late-picked varieties affected by *botrytis* (q.v.), or in many Muscat flavored wines.

Peppermint: sometimes sensed in 100 percent, well-made Pinot noirs.

Phylloxera (vastatrix):   Latin name for a vine louse which nearly destroyed the European vineyards in the late 1800s. Nowadays, most new vineplants are grafted onto a *phylloxera*-resistant rootstock to ensure proper vine health and adequate bearing. *Phylloxera* remains a problem.

Plums: sometimes found in Late Harvest (q.v.) wines of higher than average sugar-at-picking or alcohol contents; also noticed in some Zinfandels, Petite Sirahs (Durifs), Cabernet-Sauvignons, and older Port(o)s.

Pomace: residue – usually grape skins, unused pulp, and seeds – after a fermentation is completed. Pomace is sometimes plowed back into a field for fertilizer but is often dumped for fear of contaminating a vineyard with parasites or other vine problems.

Press wine: that portion of the wine that is pressed from the skins, pulp, etc., after draining off the Free run wine (q.v.). It is usually richer in extract, tannins, and other flavoring materials and is blended back, in varying degrees, with the Free run.

Prickly: a taste sensation derived from small amounts of residual carbon dioxide in wines. Often a "prickly" character will be noticed in white wines fermented cold (the lowering of the temperature tends to integrate more carbon dioxide than usual); its appreciation is relative to the individual taster. A.k.a. "spritzy."

Processed: a term used to describe many California wines, especially the jugs. It connotes, in both smell and taste, a wine that has been put through so many machines, has had so many things added to and/or taken away from it, and has been so manufactured as to appeal to the great American bland palate that it is utterly without redeeming social value or character. "Cheese food" is processed; Stilton isn't. However, such wines are far from expensive to most, except for the cost accountant. Also referred to in hair styles.

Proprietary: one of the three ways Americans label their wines (see also Generic and Varietal) is called "Proprietary labeling." Usually the bottling or producing winery owns the name so that competing wineries are barred from its use. Gallo's "Paisano" is an example.

Prunes: sometimes sensed in old Portos and American Ports of any class.

Quince (apple): some northern white Rhônes (from Marsanne, Roussanne, and Viognier grapes) recall this flavor; however, it has been noticed in such widely divergent wines as Napa Sauvignon blancs and Italian Pinot grigios.

Rack: the process of draining wine from a holding tank so as to separate it from the sediment that has collected at the bottom of the tank. This also serves to aerate the wine if this is desired.

Raisiny: the flavor one senses in wines made from grapes that have more or less dried (shriveled and/or raisined) on the vine; often encountered in hot climate wine.

Raspberries: sensed in many red wines including Zinfandels, Petit Sirah/Durifs, and Gamays.

Residual sugar: a measure of sugar – and a key to sweetness – left in a wine after the alcoholic fermentation is completed. More and more wineries are listing this on their back or front labels as an aid to the consumer.

Resin: the smell, predominating in Greek (and often California) Retsinas, caused by the addition of small amounts of resin to the fermentation. While not actually having had resin added to them, Tavel rosés and American Grenache-based rosés display resinous odors to a greater or lesser degree.

Restrained: see Dumb.

Robust: see Big.

Rotten eggs: the odor a wine rich in hydrogen sulfide will emit; it may dissipate with aeration, but more often it will not dissipate in time for you to enjoy the wine.

Salty: often this term applies to the general mineral content of wines. There seems to be a slight salty/minerally taste to the wines of many countries of the Southern Hemisphere, including Chile, Argentina, and Australia; also noticed in some Mexican wines and in the Sherry wines from Manzanilla, Spain.

Small: akin to Light (q.v.), but connoting more a wine of no special qualities, such as your average jug wine, or low-end varietal (q.v.).

Soft: see Mellow.

Solera: technically, a method of "fractional blending" wherein older wines are blended with younger wines to arrive at a consistent, similar-tasting product. Authentic Sherries and many other fortified wines are produced using a solera.

Sour: see Acidic.

Spicy: many wines will display distinct or nebulous ("what *is* that flavor?") spice-y flavors such as dill, basil, or the like. Often, any tangy character in a wine, such as that in fairly dry Gewürztraminers, will be described as spicy.

Spritzy: see Prickly.

Stemmy: a term applying either to wines actually having been fermented in contact with their stems, or to wines which, owing to an unusually brutal crushing or pressing, contain the bitter tannins of the stem to excess.

Sulfur dioxide: a chemical which is added to most wines of the world and which is necessary for the stability of any commercial wine. Wines with an excess of SO_2 will smell and/or taste like fresh-struck matches.

Sweet: a basic taste sensation dependent mainly upon sugars, but also upon glycerin and alcohols. A sweet (as opposed to a dry) wine is one which usually retains some sugar after fermentation has ended.

Tannin: a natural constituent of most wines, especially reds. It is a bitter-tasting material which is partially responsible for preserving wines during their sometimes long aging periods. Bite a grape seed to experience the flavor of tannin, or have a cup of tea, neat (with a little rye on the side!).

Teinturier: generic name for any grape whose natural juice is red-colored or pink-colored (as opposed to most varieties whose juice is colorless).

Thin: lacking in Body, alcohol; a watery wine.

Tomatoes: not a sought-after taste or odor, it generally arises from faulty fermentation or bottling practices.

Topping up: the practice of refilling (to the top, or bung hole) casks or tanks with wine to assure that there is no air space in the container. Recent discoveries indicate that in a clean, air-tight barrel a vacuum, (and not air) exists, making topping up unnecessary. Topping up is fun after a wined-out night before, though.

Transfer process: a short cut to the méthode champenoise which involves a secondary fermentation in the bottle. The transfer process also involves this secondary fermentation in a small bottle, but the clearing/separation of the yeasts is handled in a batch method rather than individually. The end result is that there is usually less of a yeasty character in Transfer process sparkling wines than in méthode champenoise versions (usually because the yeasts are left in contact longer in the case of the latter than the former), and wines made by the Transfer process are usually less expensive.

Varietal: term used to describe wines made totally or primarily from a single variety of grape.

Vegetables: when a wine smells or tastes of something you have had in a salad, and you cannot pin that something down, it's okay to call it "vegetal."

Velvety: akin to Mellow (q.v.), but more so, without the connotation of sweetness. Someone once said that a velvety wine is "one that coats your tongue like a robe" (ideally one without a zipper).

Vinegar: a no-no for wines; see Acetic.

Vinous: see Winey.

Volatile: most of the flavor components of wines are volatile, or easily perceivable by the nose. Volatile acidity refers to the acetic acid and ethyl acetate content of wines, their vinegary aspect.

Weedy: see Herbaceous; often used to refer to oak-aged Cabernets or Zinfandels.

Winey: ever smell a cheap red wine from the Central Valley in California, the Midi in France, La Mancha in Spain, etc.? No matter how hard you sniff and gurgle that thing, the only comment you end up making is, "Well, it's wine, I guess." Characteristic of many Grenache and Carignane-based wines.

Wood(y):   many wines are aged or treated in wood containers ranging in size from fifty to one million gallons. In well-made, well-aged wines, this wood lends a characteristic smell and taste, depending upon the type and size of wood used, which is just another facet of the wine. Old wood, contaminated wood, or excessive wood aging will result in an overly woody, sometimes astringent, smell and taste.

Yeast(y):   a wine deriving some of its flavor from yeast cells, either during or after its fermentation, is said to smell and/or taste "yeasty." Champagnes of France and many *fino* Sherries are examples, as are types of Grandma's bread.

List of Place-Names
Including Viticultural Areas
(Approved or Unapproved)

PLACE-NAME:
CITY, COUNTY, LAKE,
MOUNT, VITICULTURAL AREA, ETC.
(ABBREVIATION OF MAP)

Code for Abbreviations of Maps

CCC = Central Coastal Counties
CCV = Central Valley
M/L = Mendocino and Lake Counties
M/SB = Monterey and San Benito Counties
NCC = North Coast Counties
N   = Napa County
S   = Sonoma County
SC   = Southern California
S/FH = Sacramento Valley/Foothills Counties

Part One: California

A. Acampo (CV)
   Alameda (CCC)
   Alexander Valley (M/L)
   Amador (S/FH)
   American R. (S/FH)

   Anderson Valley (M/L)
   Angwin (N)
   Arroyo Seco (M/SB)
   Asti (S)
   Atlas Peak (N)

Auburn (S/FH)

B. Bakersfield (CV)
Bennett Valley (S)
Berryessa, Lake (N)
Bodega Bay (S)
Boonville (M/L)
Butte (S/FH)

C. Calaveras (S/FH)
Calistoga (NCC and N)
Calpella (M/L)
Camanche Reservoir (S/FH)
Carmel (CCC and M/SB)
Carneros (N)
Castroville (M/SB)
Cazadero (S)
Ceres (CV)
Chalk Hill (S)
Chalone (M/SB)
Chiles Valley (N)
Cienega (M/SB)
Clarksburg (S/FH)
Clear Lake (NCC and M/L)
Cloverdale (NCC and S)
Clovis (CV)
Coachella Valley (SC)
Coarsegold (CV)
Coloma (S/FH)
Colusa (S/FH)
Contra Costa (CCC)
Conn Creek (N)
Cosumnes R. (S/FH)
Cucamonga (SC)

D. Davis (S/FH)
Deer Park (N)
Delano (CV)
Delta Region (S/FH)
Diablo Range (M/SB)
Diamond Creek (S/FH)
Diamond Mountain (N)
DiGiorgio (CV)
Dry Creek (S)

E. Edna Valley (CCC)
El Dorado (S/FH)
Elk Grove (S/FH)
El Nido (CV)
Escalon (CV)
Escondido (SC)

F. Fairfield (NCC)
Fiddletown (S/FH)
Folsom Lake (S/FH)
Forestville (S)
Foss Valley (N)
Fresno (CV)

G. Gabilan Range (M/SB)
Garcia River (M/L)
Geyserville (S)
Gilroy (CCC)
Glen Ellen (S)
Glenn (S/FH)
Gonzales (CCC and M/SB)
Greenfield (CCC and M/SB)
Green Valley (NCC)
Guenoc Valley (M/L)
Guerneville (S)

H. Hanford (CV)
    Healdsburg (NCC and S)
    Hennessy, Lake (NCC and N)
    Hollister (CCC and M/SB)
    Hopland (M/L)

I. Ione (S/FH)

J. Jackson (S/FH)

K. Kelseyville (M/L)
    Kenwood (S)
    Kerman (CV)
    King City (CCC and M/SB)
    Kingsburg (CV)
    Knight's Valley (S)
    Konocti, Mount (M/L)

L. Lake (county) (NCC and M/L)
    Lakeport (NCC and M/L)
    Lime Kiln Valley (M/SB)
    Livermore (CCC)
    Livingston (CV)
    Lodi (S/FH and CV)
    Lompoc (CCC)
    Los Alamos (CCC)
    Los Angeles (SC)
    Los Gatos (CCC)
    Los Olivos (CCC)
    Lower Lake (M/L)
    Lytton Springs (S)

M. Madera (CV)
    Manteca (CV)
    Marin (NCC)
    Mariposa (CV)
    Mayacamas (N and S)
    McDowell Valley (M/L)
    McFarland (CV)
    Mendocino (NCC and M/L)
    Mendota (CV)
    Merced (CV)
    Middletown (M/L)
    Modesto (CV)
    Monterey (CCC and M/SB)
    Mount Aukum (S/FH)

N. Napa (NCC and N)
    Navarro (M/L)
    Nevada (S/FH)
    North Coast Counties (NCC)

O. Oakville (N)
    Occidental (S)
    Orange (SC)

P. Paicines (CCC and M/SB)
    Palmdale (SC)
    Palm Springs (SC)
    Parlier (CV)
    Paso Robles (CCC)
    Philo (M/L)
    Pinnacles (M/SB) (old name for "Chalone")
    Placer (S/FH)
    Placerville (S/FH)

Plymouth (S/FH)
Pope Valley (N)
Potter Valley (M/L)
Prunedale (M/SB)

R. Redwood Valley (M/L)
Reedley (CV)
Ripon (CV)
Riverside (SC)
Rutherford (N)
Russian River (NCC and N and S)

S. Sacramento (S/FH)
Saint Helena (NCC and N)
Salinas (CCC and M/SB)
Salton Sea (SC)
San Benito (CCC and M/SB)
San Bernardino (SC)
San Diego (SC)
San Francisco (NCC and CCC)
San Jose (CCC)
San Lucas (CCC and M/SB)
San Joaquin (CV)
San Luis Obispo (CCC)
San Mateo (CCC)
San Pablo Bay (N)
San Pasqual Valley (SC)
Santa Ana (SC)
Santa Barbara (CCC)
Santa Clara (CCC)
Santa Cruz (CCC)
Santa Lucia Range (M/SB)

Santa Maria Valley (CCC)
Santa Rosa (NCC and S)
Santa Ynez Valley (CCC)
Saratoga (CCC)
Schellville (S)
Sebastopol (S)
Selma (CV)
Shandon (CCC)
Shasta (S/FH)
Shenandoah Valley (S/FH) – see also Virginia (Va)
Silverado Trail (N)
Solano (NCC)
Soledad (CCC and M/SB)
Sonoma (NCC and S)
Spring Mountain (N)
Stag's Leap (N)
Stanislaus (CV)
Stockton (CV)
Suisun Valley (NCC)
Sutter (S/FH)

T. Talmadge (M/L)
Tehama (S/FH)
Temecula (SC)
Templeton (CCC)
Tulare (CV)
Tuolumne (CV)

U. Ukiah (NCC and M/L)

V. Veeder, Mount (N)
Ventura (SC)
Visalia (CV)

W. Windsor (S)
   Wooden Valley (N)
   Woodland (S/FH)

Y. Yolo (S/FH)
   Yountville (N)
   Yuba (S/FH)

Part Two: States Other Than California

   Code for Abbreviations of Maps

E/Ch	= Lake Erie-Chautauqua area
FL	= Finger Lakes
Mi	= Michigan
Mo	= Missouri
NE/MW	= Northeastern-Midwestern states
NY	= New York
O	= Ohio
Pa	= Pennsylvania
PN	= Pacific Northwest
SE	= Southeastern States
SW	= Southwestern States
Va	= Virginia

A. Alabama (SE)
   Allegheny Mountains
     (Pa)
   Appalachian Mountains
     (Pa and Va)
   Arizona (SW)
   Arkansas (SE)
   Ashtabula (O and E/Ch)
   Augusta (Mo)

B. Batavia (NY)
   Blue Ridge Mountains
     (Va)
   Buchanan (Mi)
   Buffalo (NY and E/Ch)

C. Canandaigua, Lake (FL)

   Catoctin Valley (SE)
   Cayuga, Lake (FL)
   Central Delaware Valley
     (NE/MW and Pa)
   Chautauqua-Erie (NY
     and E/Ch)
   Colorado (SW)
   Columbia River (PN)
   Conneaut (O and E/Ch)
   Connecticut (NE/MW)
   Cutchogue (NY)

D. Delaware (SE)
   Delaware Valley, Cen-
     tral (NE/MW and Pa)
   Dundee (FL)
   Dunkirk (NY and E/Ch)

E. Elmira (NY)
   Emmett Valley (PN)
   Erie (NY and O and Pa)

F. Fennville (Mi)
   Finger Lakes (NY and
      FL)
   Florida (SE)
   4-Corners (SW)
   Fredonia (NY and E/Ch)

G. Geneva (NY and FL)
   Georgia (SE)
   Grant's Pass (PN)

H. Hammondsport (NY and
      FL)
   Hawaii (SW)
   Hector (FL)
   Holland (Mi)
   Hood River (PN)
   Hudson Valley (NY)

I. Idaho (PN)
   Illinois (NE/MW)
   Indiana (NE/MW)
   Iowa (NE/MW)
   Isle St. George (O)
   Ithaca (NY and FL)

K. Kansas (SW)
   Kelley Island (O)
   Kentucky (SE)
   Keuka, Lake (FL)

L. Lake Erie-Chautauqua
      (O and E/Ch)
   Lake Erie Islands (O
      and E/Ch)

Lancaster Valley (Pa)
Leelanau (Mi)
Lodi (FL)(see also
   California:CV)
Long Island (NY)

M. Maine (NE/MW)
   Martha's Vineyard
      (NE/MW)
   Maryland (SE)
   Massachusetts (NE/MW)
   Medford (PN)
   Michigan (NE/MW and
      Mi)
   Middle Bass Island (O)
   Minnesota (NE/MW)
   Mississippi (SE)
   Missouri (NE/MW and
      Mo)
   Monticello (SE and Va)

N. Naples (NY and FL)
   Nevada (SW)
   New Hampshire
      (NE/MW)
   New Jersey (NE/MW)
   New Mexico (SW)
   Newport (NE/MW)
   New York (NE/MW and
      NY)
   Niagara (NY)
   North Bass Island (O)
   North Carolina (SE)
   Northeast (E/Ch)
   North Fork of the
      Roanoke (VA)
   North Plains (SW)

O. Ohio (NE/MW and O)

Ohio River Valley (O
and SE)
Oklahoma (SW)
Oregon (PN)

P. Patchogue (NY)
Paw Paw (Mi)
Pennsylvania (NE/MW
and E/Ch and Pa)
Penn Yan (FL)
Piedmont Range (Va)

R. Rappahannock River
(Va)
Rhode Island (NE/MW)
Rochester (NY)
Rocky Knob (SE and Va)
Rolla (Mo)

S. Saint James (Mo)
Salmon River (PN)
Seneca (FL)
Shenandoah Valley (SE
and Va
see also California:
S/FH)

Snake River (PN)
South Bass Island (O)
South Carolina (SE)
South Haven (Mi)
Sunny Slope (PN)
Susquehanna River (Pa)

T. Tennessee (SE)
Texas (SW)
Traverse City (Mi)

U. Umpqua River Valley
(PN)
Utah (SW)

V. Vermont (SE/MW)
Virginia (SE and Va)

W. Watkin's Glen (FL)
Westfield (NY and
E/Ch)
West Virginia (SE)
Willamette River (PN)
Wisconsin (NE/MW)

Y. Yakima Valley (PN)

Opinions of a
Single Wine-Lover

THE FOLLOWING THOUGHTS DEAL WITH WINE IN GENERAL AND NOT necessarily with American wines only. They deal with practices and attitudes, those of the winemakers as well as those of we winedrinkers. I hope you find them interesting; if you do not, you probably don't like Lake County Zinfandels either, wines I adore.

ON THE "BEST" WINES:

You hear it all the time: "this wine is better than that one," or "this is the best Chardonnay in the world." You read it in wine newsletters: "Of thirty Cabernets, Joe Mugwump's 1975 was the finest." Some people take these proclamations quite seriously; that is, they go out and buy the recommended wines. They buy them because someone else—someone they most likely have never met, someone whose taste may be wholly different from their own—has advised them to do so. Unfortunately, there is a great deal of fuss about this "better" and "best" business when there is very little justification for it.

Quite simply, no wines are "better" than others in the sense of intrinsic flavor because there is no real standard for flavor. Nor is there any single, all-knowing perfect arbiter of wine quality. If there were, you can be sure that by now he or she would have been hired by a wine company to do television advertisements. What some individuals find pleasant in certain wines can be totally unpleasant, or at least less pleasant, to others.

True, some people have tasted more wines and have experienced more and varied taste sensations than most. These people deserve to be listened to or read with more than passing interest. But they still use their own palates—not yours—to judge wines. So their judgments are only guides. The more experienced and impartial the judgment, the more reliable the guide, to be sure. But any guidance in wines is far from foolproof.

So, one well-made wine is intrinsically just as good as another, only different, and suited to different palates.

"You mean there is no real standard of quality in wines?" I can hear you ask. "There is nothing upon which to judge merit? Are you saying that Gallo Hearty Burgundy, and Heitz' Martha's Vineyard, are of equal quality?" Well, yes and no. Yes in the sense that each will eminently, even equally, please a particular palate conditioned to the style and flavor of each. No, if you consider the "complexity" factor.

Scientists at the University of California at Davis, a college whose viticulture and enology staff is world famous, have staged many blind tastings over the past several decades. Their purpose was, among other things, to quantify some reactions to flavors and colors, or hues. They wanted to determine such things as the average threshold levels for sweetness and tartness, and which colors are pleasing to people. Tastings were also staged to determine consumer preferences. Here, complexity played a role.

What is complexity? See "The Wine-Lover's Vocabulary." But for the moment, let's define it as the character in a wine that causes one to say more about a wine than "it's good." If the wine tasted is balanced—with alcohol, acids, water, tannins, and other components all in equilibrium—and the only comment is that "it's dry" or "it's red," the wine is basic, or simple.

But if the color is brilliant, not just clear; if the aroma and bouquet recall several scents, not just one; and if the wine lingers in the mouth, showing many flavors and revealing layers and nuance, that wine is said to be complex. And that wine will probably do very well at a serious tasting. Is is "better?" No. Is it more interesting? Probably. And it will doubtless be considered a fine wine by many people.

So I think we can say that wine quality is a very personal thing.

And no one can justifiably dictate what anyone else should like or dislike, curled lip, nose in the air, or condescending snarl notwithstanding. But if you are looking for a handle on what many would consider quality in wines, you do have one, from Maynard Amerine and Edward Roessler's book, *Wines: Their Sensory Evaluation:*

> "A great wine should have so many facets of quality that we are continually finding new ones. It is this complexity that enables us to savor such a wine without our losing interest in it. For a great wine we cannot find enough words to describe the complexity of sensory qualities. For a simple, ordinary wine the words that come to mind seem to suffice."

If you must rely on someone to help you pick reliable wines, be reassured to know that you are in the same boat as many other people. Americans are still comparative novices when it comes to wines; we have not had the exposure to them that Europeans have had, and, as a result, we tend to approach the topic with insecurity or high seriousness, or both.

Far better to relax, visit a local wine shop or read the writings of a wine commentator and compare his or her statements with what your palate tells you. If he or she has recommended ten wines and you wind up liking seven of them, the chances are that his palate is built along the same lines as your own. You can then depend upon what he or she says or writes to a greater degree than if he or she had scored three or four out of ten. If you approach the subject with a little enthusiasm (and no fears about being "wrong") and apply yourself to it, sooner or later you will not need the advice of wine merchants *or* wine writers.

A COROLLARY TO THE ABOVE:

Using this reasoning, then, it is easy to see the problems involved with two other wine absolutes: breathing and aging.

To let a wine "breathe" is to render it open to greater oxygenation than would occur if the wine bottle were left unopened or if it were opened and simply left to stand. If you look at most bottles' openings, you will straight-away see that it would be a long time before much oxygenation would take place, the opening being so small.

Therefore, substantial aeration and oxygenation will occur if the wine is decanted into another container, thereby exposing all the wine to a great deal of oxygen. What aeration does to the taste of the wine is not completely known. But we do know that an aerated wine, a wine that "breathed" a lot, is usually less fruity than a non-aerated one. It may also be slightly more mellow. There is no arguing that aeration/breathing does change most wines' flavors to some degree (we speak here of non-jug wines, many of which have been so processed as to taste the same no matter what is done to them, be it breathing or strangling).

It would follow, then, that to breathe or not to breathe is a matter of personal taste. After sufficient experimentation with aeration or non-aeration, the wine drinker should be able to come to a conclusion whether or not his palate is pleased by all this breath. It seems ludicrous, at least to this observer, to follow blindly those rules which mandate an hour or two of aeration of that old Bordeaux (or classic Cabernet) unless you *like it* that way.

The same goes for aging, which also changes the wine's character from fresh, fruity, and, in many cases, aggressively varietally true to mellow, subtle, and developed. Try some reds that have been aged for a decade or more and see if you enjoy that rounded-out flavor and enhanced bottle bouquet. You might find instead that you prefer your reds with a bit of tannin and bite left and ought not to age them for so long. It's all in your taste buds, none of which, by the way, were ever cloned from any one expert's tongue.

So relax in your approach to wines, and don't put great stock in what others have to say about the subject of wine quality. And the next time someone says that he has just had the "best Chardonnay in California," ask him what he means by that. Chances are he will not be able to tell you.

ON WOOD AGING:

The abuse of, or the ignorance of, the use of wood aging is, fortunately, on the decline in American wineries. But I thought a few paragraphs might help to speed up the trend.

Two or three decades ago, American winemakers discovered that a part of the flavor of French wines – mainly white and red Burgundies and Bordeaux, but others as well – was derived from the type of oak barrel in which the wines were aged or even fermented. In an effort to approximate that French flavor (at the time, even Californians thought that French wines were "better"), many American winemakers decided to use the barrels for their own wines. With little knowledge of *how* to use these containers, winemakers threw their lovely Chardonnays and such into them and expected some great Montrachet to emerge. It did not, of course, for there is more to Montrachet and any other good wine than where it happens to hibernate. Often what did emerge resembled more a vanilla-flavored alcoholic drink than it did wine.

These winemakers failed to realize several things. One was that the French had decades of experience with such aging. They knew that the conditions of one season made three months in the cask sufficient while those of another demanded that the wine remain therein for six months or longer. They, the French, also had had many harvests to learn when or if they should use brand new oak barrels – much stronger in their oaky flavor – or older barrels. Indeed, most had no choice but to use older barrels as they could not afford the new ones every year.

In addition, American winemakers did not consider what affect the temperature of the aging room – and, hence, of the wine in the barrel – would have on the rate of flavor leaching. Since physical and chemical interactions proceed more rapidly the higher the temperature, more and different wood flavors would be imparted to the wine in barrels at sixty degrees Fahrenheit than to wine kept at fifty degrees or cooler. I have worked in Burgundian *caves* as well as in Californian "cellars;" I used two sweaters in the former and one in the latter.

Knowledge of these and other factors involved in oak aging is slowly being deposited into the collective understanding of our winemakers. But some still persist in turning out bourbonized Zinfandels – the result of too long a stay in American oak that has been charred – or in calling those vanilla-spicy Chardonnays and Sauvignon blancs "varietally true" when the only recognizable variety involved is Limousin oak. Because new enologists are being loosed on the wine world daily, men and women whose barrel aging experience is limited, to put it politely, you can expect more of the same in the future. But when American consumers recognize a wine with excessive wood flavor for what it is and decline to purchase it – especially at the crazy prices many are fetching nowadays – these men and women will get the point.

ON WINE LAWS
AND REACTIONS TO THEM:

I very briefly described some of the laws that American winemakers in the introduction to the California section of the book. But even that superficial coverage should make the average reader conclude that our federal wine legislation – much of it written with significant industry input – is extremely confusing.

Look at our varietal minimum laws: some wines must have 51 percent of their volume derived from the named variety, while for others, the figure will soon be 75 percent or higher. Or notice the spread of percentages between our various place-of-origin laws: they vary from 75 percent to 100 percent.

How about one more? Did you ever look at the bottom of a label of American-made wine? By law, there must be an indication of responsibility for what is in the bottle. The wine producer has two options in terms of the language he may use. One is "Made and Bottled by Winery X." Legal equivalents to this are: "Cellared and Bottled By," "Perfected and Bottled By," and "Vinted (?) and Bottled By." The second option is the phrase "Produced and Bottled By Winery X."

Now, I know that "made" and "produced" do not mean *exactly* the same thing; but even a federal bureaucrat might use the terms interchangeably. Yet the law states that if the first option is used, none (or, by administrative agreement, as little as 10 percent) of the wine in the bottle need have been made – fermented from grapes into wine – by the named winery. The named firm could have contracted to purchase a fresh-made, rough batch from a local bulk-producer and then aged, treated, filtered, and otherwise prepared the batch at the named firm's own facilities. If the second option is used, at least 75 percent of the wine in the bottle must have been produced – fermented from grapes into wine – and all of the wine must have been bottled by the named firm.

These and like regulations can be found in the *Code of Federal Regulations* which anyone is free to stumble through. And, if you are truly interested in translating an American wine label, you can buy and carry this three-inch thick volume around with you when you shop.

Simply put, these and like rules permit real dishonesty and open the door to fraudulent labeling. If a label states "Sonoma County Chardonnay," shouldn't the wine in the bottle be 100 percent from Chardonnay grapes grown in Sonoma County vineyards? And if not, should not the consumer at least be given a clue about what else is in the bottle?

There is nothing wrong with a winemaker touching up (some say "blending" others say "stretching," while still others say "creating a well-balanced melange of flavors") his Cabernet with a little Merlot, Zinfandel, Ruby Cabernet, or even Grenache. Nothing's wrong! Let us leave our winemakers free to make wine in whatever way, with whatever grapes, from whatever vineyards they choose. If the winemaker is proud enough of what he has made – or produced – he will not mind being honest about it on the label.

But let's throw honesty to the side, "best policy" or not. Let's deal only with the simplicity aspect. If we made laws that demanded truthful labeling – and there is no such thing as 75 percent, or 85 percent or 51 percent truthful – then our three-inch book could be a pamphlet.

I would like to suggest a course of action for the winemakers – who helped to write the laws – and for the federal government, which enforces them. Let's simplify things: make every statement on the label conform to reality; i.e., if all a label says is "1981, Finger Lakes, Seyval blanc," then the wine therein must be Seyval blanc and nothing else. If a federal inspection of records reveals that all is in order, terrific. If it is discovered that the wine in the bottle is not pure Seyval, or not entirely from the Finger Lakes, or not entirely from the harvest of 1981 (allowing a reasonable – not more than 5 percent – tolerance level), then the government should have the options of either hanging the scoundrel winemaker, taking his license away, or forcing him to make only Rhubarb wine.

There are some things in wines that are not mentioned on the label. There are many ingredients which winemakers may legally add to grapes, juice, or wine that help to stabilize, clarify, clean, or otherwise treat the product. Most are substances filtered out of wine before it is bottled. Bentonite, for example, is a powdered clay added to the wine to help clarify it. The great majority of this ingredient is filtered out prior to bottling.

Some added substances such as sulfur dioxide, or SO_2, remain in the wine. Sulfur dioxide is added in a variety of forms to help prevent oxidation, to prevent browning in whites, and the like. If it is used to excess, it can make the wine smell of fresh-struck matches. Sulfur dioxide and other substances are added to most wines in extremely small amounts, yet a few wine drinkers complain of allergic or other negative reactions after having consumed them.

The issue of "ingredient labeling" is one that has bounced all around the field since the early 1970s when a consumer group demanded that the government force producers of alcoholic beverages to list all ingredients in wines, added or inherent. After many skirmishes and internecine bureaucratic warfare, the government made its decision. In 1981, the Reagan Administration made it plain that such labeling would not be required. The issue seems to be a dead one; but it has been resurrected in the past and may well be again.

I do not know whether the government should force ingredient labeling on alcoholic beverage producers. The benefits to those very few people the law would help would seem to be far outweighed by the cost to the average consumer of implementing the law. Also, there are peculiarites in the wine industry that would make compliance with a strict ingredient labeling regulation a nightmare. Perhaps some sort of statement to the effect that "this wine like most others carries one or more of the following ingredients," might be a solution.

What bothers me more, actually, is the petulant and inconsistent attitude of many industry spokemen, on this and other issues, who denounce any interference from the federal government or from consumer groups with which they disagree. They pout when the government puts high taxes on wines, or when the federals insist upon certain regulations which the industry feels are discriminatory: "If the government viewed wine as the food it is, healthful and beneficial instead of addictive and sinister, it would reverse its entire regulatory concept," they say. Yes, and if the government *did* consider wine as a food, the winemaker would be constrained by food laws to list the ingredients in his wines.

I can understand the industry's problems with wine legislation, some of which—especially at the state level—is absurd or anachronistic, even counter-productive. And I can understand the suspicions of some individuals in the industry, growers who have developed a distrust for government interference; the last time the Feds came down on them was Prohibition, when they made most winemakers' jobs illegal or useless.

But I hope this suspicion does not cause the industry to counter blindly any and every attempt at regulation. For the wine industry, like the soap, farm, or car industry, needs regulation. Its members are as honest or dishonest as those of any other industry, even though winemakers' products are more interesting. Relax, winemakers, the wine boom has not even started. Ten years from now, when our per capita annual consumption is at the five gallon level, you'll sit back and laugh at today's situation. Good luck.

Bibliography

GENERAL

The Wines of America, Second Edition, Revised. Leon D. Adams. McGraw-Hill Book Co. New York: 1978.

Grapes into Wine. Philip M. Wagner. Alfred A. Knopf. New York: 1976.

Wine Tasting. J. Michael Broadbent. Wine & Spirit Publications Ltd. London: 1971.

The Great Wine Blight. George Ordish. Charles Scribner's Sons. New York: 1972.

Grossman's Guide to Wines, Beers and Spirits, Sixth Revised Edition. Harold J. Grossman. (Revised by Harriet Lembeck). Charles Scribner's Sons. New York: 1977.

Table Wines: The Technology of their Production, Second Edition. Maynard A. Amerine and Maynard A. Joslyn. University of California Press. Berkeley, California: 1973.

Wines: Their Sensory Evaluation. Maynard A. Amerine and Edward B. Roessler. W.H. Freeman and Company. San Francisco: 1973.

Initiation into the Art of Wine Tasting. Jacques Puisais and R.L. Chabanon. Translated by James A. Vaccaro. Interpublish, Inc. Madison, Wisconsin: 1974.

Grape Growing. Robert J. Weaver. John Wiley & Sons. New York: 1976.

A Practical Ampelography. Pierre Galet. Translated and adapted by Lucie T. Morton. Cornell University Press. Ithaca, New York: 1979.

Register of New Fruit and Nut Varieties, Second Edition. Reid M. Brooks and Harold P. Olmo. University of California Press. Berkeley, California: 1972.

The Great Wine Grapes. Bern C. Ramey. Great Wine Grapes, Inc. San Francisco: 1977.

The Vineyard Almanac and Wine Gazetteer, 1981. Gene Tartt. Los Altos, California: 1980.

CALIFORNIA

The Connoisseur's Handbook of California Wine. Charles Olken, Earl Singer, and Norman Roby. Alfred A. Knopf. New York: 1980.

Guide to California's Wine Country. Bob Thompson text. Lane Publishing Co. By the editors of Sunset Books and Sunset Magazine (Menlo Park, California: 1980).

OTHER STATES

The Wines of the East: Vinifera, 1979, The Hybrids, 1978, Native American Grapes, 1980, 3 volumes, paperback. Hudson Cattell and H. Lee Stauffer. *Lancaster, Pennsylvania: L. & H. Photojournalism.*

The Wines of New England. Robert F. Valchuis and Diane L. Henault. Wine Institute of New England, Inc. Boston: 1980.

Winery Trails. Tom Stockley. Mercer Island, Washington: The Writing Works, Inc. Mercer Island, Washington: 1977.

Northwest Wines. Ted Meredith. Kirkland, Washington: 1980 Nexus Press.

MAGAZINES, PAMPHLETS, ETC.

Wines and Vines Magazine. San Rafael: The Hiaring Company.

Wines and Vines Directory, 1981 and 1982. San Rafael: The Hiaring Company.

Wine East. Lancaster, Pennsylvania: L. & H. Photojournalism.

Redwood Rancher/The 1981 California Winery Tour, Maps and Directory, San Francisco: Sally Taylor and Friends.

Eastern Grape Grower and Winery News. Watkins Glen, New York: Eastern Grape Growers' Magazine, Inc.

A Guide to American and French-American Hybrid Grape Varieties.
Robert L. Gloor, Foster Nursery Co., Inc., Fredonia, New
York: 1980

Wine Tour Guide. Watkins Glen, New York: 1981 and 1980.

A Catalog of New and Noteworthy Fruits 1977-1978. (Grape Section] R. M. Pool and J. Einset, New York State Fruit Testing
Cooperative Association, Geneva, New York.

Acknowledgments

MANY PEOPLE ASK ME ABOUT THE WINE-WORLD, HOW I WAS AT-
tracted to it in the first place, how it is in terms of daily routine,
and why do I stay involved and not do something "grown up"
and serious like normal people? Wine, of course, is the answer:
the romance, the complexity, the travel, the unpredictability,
the absolute certainty that whatever we know now will probably
be disproved later, the drinking, the tasting, the sharing with
friends, and the contacts are all wonderfully positive aspects of
what I do for a living. The "contacts", the people I get involved
with in my travels *and* daily routine, have to rank up there at
the top. This wine world, excluding the very few pedants, snobs
and contentious wine experts, is full of sharing, caring, smil-
ing, fun-loving people who know how to live. This book would
have been absolutely impossible to put together without selfless
and non-compensated help of hundreds of people whose names
most never see but whose work behind the scenes makes gather-
ing research for such books almost a pleasure. Thank you one
and all, especially Leon D. Adams, who rekindled my nearly
burnt-out fire after I reacted to some of the more negative aspects
of my world: "You are helping to civilize a country; it's a long
and slow road, but wine and those who write and talk about
it will civilize this country."

*Acknowledgments follow on a regional basis, following the format
of the book.*

California, general: the folks at *The Wine Institute* in San Francisco; R.A. McGregor, Aubrey R. Davis, Swede Severson, Max
Cain and Richard E. Rominger of the *California Crop and*
310 *Livestock Reporting Service;* Fredrik L. Jensen, of the *Cooperative*

Extension University of California; and Professor Harold P. Olmo and Professor Lloyd Lider of the *University of California at Davis.*

California, individual counties: "North Coast" – *Napa:*the late Aldo Delfino of the *Napa County Department of Agriculture* and Mike Dwyer of *The Napa Valley Grape Growers Association; Sonoma:* Millie Howie of the Sonoma County Wine Growers Association; Robert L. Sisson, Sonoma County Farm Advisor and Harry Mc-Cracken, *Agricultural Commissioner of Sonoma County; Mendocino:* Jackie Tidwell, *Parson's Creek Winery* and Nancy Lynn Gray.

California, "Central Coast": Alameda: Joe J. Coony, Director of the *County Cooperative Extension; Monterey:* Rudy Neja, Farm Advisor and *The Monterey Winegrowers' Council; San Benito:* William Coates, Farm Advisor and John H. Edmondson, *Agricultural Commissioner; San Luis Obispo:* Earl R. Kalar, *Agricultural Commissioner; San Mateo:* Laurence R. Costello and R.H. Sciaroni. Farm advisors; *Santa Cruz:* Ronald H. Tyler, Farm advisor, *Santa Clara:* C.O. Howe, *Agricultural Commissioner.*

California, "Sacramento Valley/Foothills Area": Amador: Robert E. Plaister, Farm Advisor; *El Dorado:* Edio Delfino, *Agricultural Commissioner* and Dick Bethell, Farm Advisor; *Sacramento:* Dorothy F. McCandless, *Department of Agriculture; Shasta:* Richard B. Price, Department of Agriculture; *Tehama:* Joseph W. Osgood, Farm Advisor; *Yolo:* Carl Schoner, Farm Advisor.

California, "Southern California": Los Angeles: Charles A. Salverson, Farm Advisor; *Riverside:* Chloe Beitler, Director, *County Cooperative Extension; San Bernardino:* Richard G. Maire, Farm Advisor and Roger L. Birdsall, *Agricultural Commissioner; San Diego:* James R. Breece and Vincent Lazaneo, Farm advisors.

California, "Central Valley":Fresno: Peter Christensen, Farm Advisor; *Kern:* Donald A. Luvisi, Farm Advisor; *Kings:* Robert H. Breede, Farm Advisor; *Madera:* the Board of Supervisors; *Merced:* Rex Lyndall, *Agricultural Commissioner; San Joaquin:* E. B. Eby, *Agricultural Commissioner; Tuolumne:* Roswell D. Roberts, Farm Advisor.

Northeastern U.S.: Connecticut: Jim Bobbitt, U. of Conn; Peter

Kerensky, *St. Hilary's Winery;* and Shorn Mills and Beth Brooks of *Haight Vineyard: Illinois:* Daniel Meador, University of Illinois/Urbana, Willy and Linda Enders, *Terra Vineyard and Winecellar,* Domenico Di Iulio and Irene and Jim Huffman, *Mississippi Valley Wine Society: Indiana:* Richard A. Hayden and Allen Boger, Purdue University; Ben Sparks, *Possum Trot Vineyards; Iowa:* Ed and Valerie Schmidt, *Vitis Vineyard and Nursery; Massachusetts:* Dominic Marini, Fruit and Vegetable Specialist, U. of Massachusetts; George Mathiesen, *Chicama Vineyards: Michigan:* Gordon S. Howell, Jr., Michigan State University; Don J. Fedewa, Michigan Agricultural Reporting Service; Doug Welsch, *Fenn Valley Vineyards and Winecellar; Minnesota:* Carolyn Barrett, *Minnesota Grape Growers Association;* David A. Bailly, *Alexis Bailly Vineyard, Inc.; Missouri:* Bruce Zoecklein and Larry Lockshin, University of Missouri; *Missouri Division of Tourism;* and Lois Grohe, *Heinrichshaus vineyards and Winery: New Hampshire:* John J. Canepa, *White Mountain Vineyards; New Jersey:* James R. Williams, *Hunterdon Co. Wine Growers;* Ernest G. Christ, Rutgers University; and Phillip Alampi, Department of Agriculture; *New York:* Drs. Bruce Reisch and Robert Pool, Geneva Experimental Station; Bill Moffett and Richard Figiel, *Eastern Grape Grower and Winery News;* Stafford H. Krause, *Finger Lakes Wine Growers Association;* Glenn W. Suter, New York Crop Reporting Service; Howard H. Kimball, *Wine Grape Growers, Inc.;* William T. Merritt, *Merritt Estate Winery;* Trenholm Jordan and Thomas Zabadal, Grape Specialists. *Ohio:* Prof. Garth A. Cahoon, Department of Agriculture; Donniella Winchell., *Ohio Wine Producers Association;* and Dean H. Conklin, Div. of Markets, Agriculture Dept. and Thomas Oburn, *Erie Co, Coop. Extension Assn.; Pennsylvania:* Wallace, *Pennsylvania Crop Reporting Service; Rhode Island:* Robert E. Gough, University of Rhode Island; Jim and Lolly Mitchell, *Sakonnet Vineyards; Wisconsin:* Al Jindra and Robert Pronish, *Wisconsin Department of Agriculture;* Bob Wollersheim, *Wollersheim Winery.*

Southeastern U.S.: Alabama: James C. Eddins, *Perdido Vineyards; Arkansas:* Justin R. Morris, University of Arkansas; *Florida:* T. E. Crocker, *Florida Cooperative Extension Service;* Prof. Loren

Stover, *Midulla Vineyards; Georgia:* Maurice E. Ferree, *Cooperative Extension Service,* University of Georgia; *Kentucky:* Gerald Brown, *Cooperative Extension Service,* University of Kentucky; *Maryland:* Roger Wolf; Bruce West, *Maryland-Delaware Crop Reporting Service;* C. P. Hegwood, Jr. and Richard Vine, *Mississippi State University;* Samuel H. Rushing, *The Winery Rushing; North Carolina:* David Fussell, *Duplin Wine Cellars;* Jerry B. Pegram, *Piedmont Grape Growers Association;* E. B. Poling, North Carolina State University, *Agricultural Extension Service;* Tim Thielke, *The Biltmore Company; South Carolina:* John D. Ridley, Clemson University, *Cooperative Extension Service;* Eugene Charles; *Tennessee:* Edward Irwin and Clay E. Easterly, *Tennessee Viticultural and Oenological Society;* Alan McKay, *McKay's Tire Center; Virginia:* Lynn Bowles, *Montdomaine Cellars;* Walter Luchsinger, *Piedmont Vineyards;* E. L. Phillips, Virginia Polytechnic Institute, *Cooperative Extension Service;* Felicia W. Rogan, *Albemarle Harvest Wine Festival;* Archie M. Smith, Jr., *Meredyth Vineyards:* Lou Ann Whitton, *Commonwealth of Virginia,* Dept. of Agriculture; *West Virginia:* N. Carl Hardin, West Virginia University; Robert F. Pliska, *West Virginia Grape Growers Association.*

Southwestern U.S.: Arizona: Peter Beope, *Peter Beope Vineyard;* R. G. Fowler, University of Arizona; Eugene A. Mileke, Ph.D. University of Arizona, *Cooperative Extension Service;* Adrian Bosman, *Arizona Wine Growers' Association.* R. W. Webb, R. W. Webb Winery; *Colorado:* Anthony H. Hatch, Colorado State University, *Agricultural Extension Station; Hawaii:* Haiyu Kumanawanalaya, Fruit Specialist; Emil P. Tedeschi, *Tedeschi Vineyard and Winery; Kansas:* William D. Rexroad; *New Mexico:* Darrell T. Sullivan, New Mexico State University; *Oklahoma:* Herman A. Hinrichs, Oklahoma State University; *Texas:* John Crosby, *Texas Grape Growers' Association:* George Ray McEachern, Texas A & M University, *Agricultural Extension Service.*

Northwestern U.S.: Idaho: Walter J. Kochan, University of Idaho; *Oregon:* Warren W. Aney, Jr.; Bill Blosser, *Sokol Blosser Winery;* Scott Henry, *Oregon Winegrowers' Association;* Jeffrey L. Lamy, *Business Economics, Inc.* Portland; Bill Malkmus, *Tualatin*

Vineyards; Washington: M. Ahmedullah, Washington State University, *Irrigated Agricultural Research and Extension Center:* Alec Bayless, *Grape Growers Coop.,* Mercers Island; Raymond J. Folwell, *Washington State University;* Ted Meredith, *Nexus Press,* Kirkland; Mike Wallace, *Yakima Valley Appellation Committee;* Jack Watson, Horticulturist.